TEXAS TORNADOES COLLECTION 1

Three Christian Football Romances

LORANA HOOPES

I

DEFENDING MY HEART

I originally wrote this book as part of a series with other authors. It was originally title Her Second Chance Forever Groom.

In March 2020, I got the rights back and had to change a few things. This new edition is dedicated to Diana who lost her battle to cancer on March 30, 2020. She was a friend, a wife, a mother, and the most amazing woman I have ever met.

Due to the quarantine of the Coronavirus, none of us even got to say goodbye. Nor will we get to attend her funeral. This dedication is just a small way to tell her how much she meant to all of us, how sad we are she's gone, and how we wished we could have been there at the end.

Life is short. Never go to bed angry and hold your loved ones close because you never know when God will call them home.

NOTE FROM THE AUTHOR

I really enjoyed getting to write a football book. I've been a football fan for years. I grew up watching the Dallas Cowboys in the 90s when they were a powerhouse team. To that end, you might notice my main character's name is Emmitt.

Emmitt Smith was always my favorite player. Not only was he an amazing running back, but he didn't rely just on his football career. He finished his college degree and that's what I found truly inspiring about him.

So, this book is dedicated to the amazing athletes who inspire us with your work ethic, with your drive, and with your never quit attitude.

Emmitt Brown tossed in his bed, sending his sheets tangling around his feet. Figured. At least now they matched his feelings. He stared up at the white ceiling, wishing his mind could be as blank as the canvas above him. The conversation from a few hours earlier replayed in his mind like a broken record. An accusing broken record.

"You know what I've decided?" *Matt Johnson, the defensive line leader asked as he lifted his glass.*

Around the table, the men shook their heads. It had been a long day after attending the funeral for their owner's wife, who'd almost been like a surrogate mother to them all. She always invited new recruits over for dinner and often brought cookies to practices. She was a ray of light for the team of mostly men who often let practice and games wear them down.

Two months ago, she had been fine. Then she'd announced that she had a rare form of cancer. She'd told them all with a smile on her face and a confidence in her voice that made them believe she would beat it. But it had taken her instead.

Something in the chemo treatment had set off an infection in her body, and within hours, Leo, the owner, was taking her off life support and saying goodbye. The rest of the team didn't even get to make it to the hospital before it was all over.

"I've decided life is too short to live with regret. Diana always lived life to the fullest and though she was taken too soon, maybe we can all have the second chance she didn't get. I know I've got things in my past I wish I had handled differently, and I bet you all do too. So, I'm going to spend the time off making those things right. Who's with me?"

Emmitt glanced around at his fellow teammates. He too had things in his past that he wasn't proud of, but he wasn't sure if he was ready to face his greatest regret.

Matt held his fist over the center of the table, like he always did before they exited a huddle and ran out onto the field. "What do you guys say? How about we spend this time before Christmas making things right? Making Diana proud of us?"

Jordan White, middle linebacker, nodded and placed his hand on top of Matt's. "I'm in."

Andrew Markum, always the hesitant one, leaned back and ran his hand across his chin. "Matt, I don't know. Sometimes it's better if stuff in the past stays in the past."

Emmitt could understand that viewpoint. The stuff in his past was more than he was sure he could face again, much less in just seven days.

Sid Lawson, strong side-back and the epitome of the strong, silent type, grunted in his usual manner but put his fist in too. "Fine."

That meant it was Emmitt's turn. He couldn't say no. It would raise too many questions, but how could he respond without having to face his shameful past? Deflection. It worked wonders on the field. Maybe it would work with the guys too. "We always have things we can ask forgiveness for."

Andrew sighed but placed his hand in as well. "You know we're always in this together." He punctuated his words with a friendly eye roll.

Matt smiled at them as he looked from one man to the other. "We make amends. For Diana."

"For Diana," the men echoed, and for a moment Emmitt was bolstered by their camaraderie. *Maybe he could do this.*

So, Matt had regrets, but didn't they all? Still, why did he have to recommend they go home and face them? And why had Emmitt agreed? He had spent the last few years running from his regrets, and he wasn't sure he was ready to go back yet. Had he changed enough?

He'd been working hard on becoming a better man. In fact, it was what had driven him to God, and he knew that part of making that transition completely was apologizing to those he had hurt. Still, every time he thought about it, he chickened out. Mantras of *what he'd done was too awful, he hadn't changed enough,* or *apologizing wouldn't change anything* blazed in his head. Though Emmitt knew none of those were true, the words played over and over, crippling him. His kryptonite.

With a sigh, he reached for his Bible. When the demons reared up in his head like this, the only way to quiet them was to immerse himself in God's word. His fingers traced the seam around the Bible and caressed the leather. Most people at his church never brought Bibles anymore, they just whipped out their phones or tablets, but Emmitt enjoyed the feel of the physical book. The weight, the smell, and the peace it brought when he held it in his hands, when he cracked it open, and when he quieted his heart enough to let God speak to him through it. That would be hard tonight with his thoughts careening all over the place like pinballs in an arcade machine, but he would try.

Before he opened the book, he closed his eyes and took a moment to reach out to God. Emmitt wasn't even sure the prayer had words as much as a desire for God to show him what he needed. Though he didn't often, tonight he let the book fall open, and wouldn't you know it, he landed in Ephesians chapter four. He read over the words, and when he got to verse twenty-five, he knew these were the words from God.

"What this adds up to, then, is this: no more lies, no more pretense. Tell your neighbor the truth. In Christ's body, we are all connected to each other, after all. When you lie to others, you end up lying to yourself."

Oh, how fitting those words were. He was lying to himself. His teammates called him "The Reverend" or "Rev" for short because he was always praying or using scripture, but he was lying to them the same way he was lying to himself. The same way he had lied to Mia over five years ago.

Emmitt knew he had to go back. He had to make amends though he didn't even know where to begin, but that knowledge didn't tame the twisting flame in his stomach. He would just have to trust that God would open Mia's heart. At least long enough for Emmitt to apologize.

He replaced the Bible on the nightstand and turned off the light. It was going to be a long night, and an even longer tomorrow.

"CARTER, IT'S TIME FOR BED," MIA CALLED AS SHE TURNED OFF the sink and dried her hands. There hadn't been many dishes tonight as she tried to cook the dinner in one pot, but still she missed the dishwasher. Washing by hand every night was killing her skin, and it gave her too much quiet time to think.

"But Mom, I'm not tired." His whiny protest was punctuated perfectly with a large yawn as he looked up from his tablet. Mia was glad she and Marcus had purchased it for his Christmas gift last year. She would never have had the money to get it for him this year, and while she didn't give him much screen time, it was her saving grace when he was extremely needy. And he'd been extremely needy a lot since Marcus's death. Not that she blamed him, but she was already stressed trying to be both the mom and the dad as well as the sole breadwinner. She just had no patience left to deal with neediness.

"Uh huh, I see that, but it's still bedtime. Let's go, sport." As she ushered him down the hall of their tiny one-bedroom apartment, she wondered if life would always be like this. Five and a half years ago when she'd married Marcus, they'd had big dreams. He was going to open his own business and become a wealthy entrepreneur, but after his third business idea failed, he had given up and taken a job at the local high school. It hadn't been the fame and fortune he had hoped for, but they'd been content. At least until a drunk driver took his life.

After Marcus's death, Mia had been forced to sell their modest house and move Carter into this tiny apartment. She'd taken a job at the restaurant down the street because the tips generally paid better than a traditional minimum wage job, but she was working overtime just to keep a roof over their heads. And she missed spending time with her son. Time, she knew, was the one commodity you never got back.

She helped Carter change into his pajamas, sighing as she realized he was outgrowing these as well. He only had two pairs and both were now well above his ankles. She'd have to stop at the Goodwill soon and see if they had any a size up.

"Momma, when will Daddy be back?" he asked as he climbed into the bed and snuggled his bear. It was a question he asked at least once a week, and while Mia knew his nearly five-year old brain just wasn't capable of processing her response, she was tiring of giving it.

She brushed his hair back from his forehead and flashed a small smile. "Carter, baby, Daddy's not coming back. He had to go live with God."

"Forever?" His sad eyes pulled on her heartstrings.

"Forever, buddy, but you and me? We will be just fine." At least as long as nothing happened to her job. Or her car. Or the apartment. Or herself. That was a lot of things hinging on those last five words.

He yawned again and his eyes shut for a moment before pulling open again. "Do you think God will ever send me a new daddy?'

This was another question he asked often. "I don't know, bud. We'll have to wait and see." His eyes closed again, and she placed a soft kiss on his forehead before pulling the blanket up to his chin and tiptoeing out of the room.

Would God send another man her way? She didn't know. For the first few months after Marcus died, she couldn't imagine ever marrying again, but now, almost a year later, the thought had popped in her mind once in a while. She still wasn't sure she could marry for love, but if he was a good man, a believer, she could consider marrying to have someone by her side. A friend to share the evenings with and someone who could help her provide a better life for Carter than the one she could by herself.

She sank down on the couch, not bothering to change her own clothes, and grabbed her Bible from the nightstand. Mia knew a lot of people in her situation would have turned from God, claiming He didn't exist or didn't hear her prayers since it appeared her life wasn't improving, but He was all she had and she refused to turn her back on Him. Still, she did wish He would reveal His plan for her. She didn't think she could keep going this direction much longer.

2

Emmitt sighed as he passed the small sign welcoming him to Kempton, Texas. He'd thought when he left this town that he wouldn't be back. He'd even flown his parents to San Antonio the first few Christmases after he'd left to avoid returning to this dinky town. Then he had helped them move out of Kempton and retire in Florida. It wasn't the town's fault, and it hadn't been awful growing up here, but once he'd betrayed Mia, the guilt had kept him away, gnawed at his insides, and convinced him that nothing remained for him here.

In fact, he wasn't even sure Mia still lived here or that she hadn't married. Maybe she had been whisked away by some wealthy businessman or maybe she had decided to move elsewhere and was now working a dream job and making millions, but Emmitt knew that probably wasn't the case. That was a fantasy he had spun the last several years to make himself feel better about what he'd done. People rarely left Kempton. He had been the exception and not the rule.

The town had changed little, and he pulled into the one gas station to fill up and ask around about Mia. If she was still here, the attendant working inside would probably know her. Kempton was so small that everyone knew everyone else—where they lived, who their parents were, what secrets they tried to hide. Emmitt both missed and hated that part of the small-town vibe. Having people really know you wasn't something he had experienced since joining the San Antonio Saints and he missed that. But it was his own fault. He had only shared what he wanted the other men to know, keeping most of him and his shameful secret locked away. And San Antonio was a large town. He didn't even know his neighbors' names, nor did they know his. It was easier to keep his secret in a town where people passed each other without a word.

The bell above the door jingled as he pushed it open and a young clerk looked up at him. Good, this kid looked too young to remember him, but he might be too young to know Mia as well.

"You getting gas?" the kid asked.

"Yeah, forty dollars please." Emmitt pulled out his wallet and tried to sound as if he didn't need the answer when he posed the next question. "Do you know Mia Baker?"

"Mia Baker?" The kid scratched his head as his forehead wrinkled in thought. "There's a Mia who works at Manny's, but I don't know her last name. Sorry."

A waitress? Mia had always had plans of becoming an interior designer. Why would she give that up to become a waitress? "Is she about my age with strawberry blonde hair and blue eyes?"

"Uh, I think she has reddish hair. Never paid much attention to her eyes. She's too old for me, you know?" The kid shrugged as he picked up the money and placed it in the register. "Do you need a receipt?"

"No, thank you," Emmitt said and exited the gas station. If he was about to see Mia again, what he needed was a large helping of courage.

Mia groaned as she checked her watch. She was going to be late again. Her boss was going to kill her. "Carter, let's go." She hated the angry tone in her voice, but if she lost this job, they would be kicked out of their tiny apartment and forced to move back in with her parents.

"I can't find my shoe, Mom."

Mia clenched her teeth to keep from emitting an agitated growl. This was a daily occurrence. No matter how many times she told Carter to put his shoes by the door, he never did. Instead, he kicked them off wherever he felt like it, and they were forced to go on this hunt every morning. What made it worse was that Carter was in that stage where his shoes could literally be a foot in front of him on the floor and he still wouldn't see them. And forget looking under anything. If they were under a blanket or a shirt, they might as well not exist in his world.

She began walking toward the bedroom, checking all the regular places she found his shoes as she went. Under the couch? Nope. In the hall closet? Not there either, but she struck gold in the bathroom. "I found one," she called out as she grabbed it from the floor. Why his shoe was in the bathroom was beyond her, but hopefully he had the other one.

She found him in the bedroom, sitting on the bed. Just sitting. *Don't yell. Keep your cool.* "Were you even looking?"

"Yeah, but my leg started hurting, and I needed to sit down for a minute."

This was another issue they faced nearly daily—these weird phantom pains of Carter's. She hoped they were just growing pains, but she worried they were more. Unfortunately, she didn't have the money to get them checked out, so she would just have to keep praying they were nothing.

"Okay, well, here's one shoe. Let's find the other." She handed the shoe she had found to him and then proceeded to pick up the clothes littering the floor until she found the other. After helping him get that one on as well, she grabbed his bag and ushered him to the door.

"Do I have to go to Grandma's again today?" Carter asked with a sigh as he climbed into his booster seat.

"Yes, buddy. Mommy has to go to work, and you are too young to stay at home by yourself." Mia was just thankful that her parents lived in the same town. She didn't know how they would survive if she had to pay for childcare as well. Her parents were older, but still in good enough shape to keep up with a rambunctious five-year-old most days. Still, Mia felt badly. Her parents were supposed to be enjoying their golden years and instead, they were having to help raise her son.

"All right, but tomorrow can we go see a movie?"

Mia wanted to say yes. She wished she could take him to the movies once a month as a treat, but the money just wasn't there. "How about we go to the park tomorrow morning before my shift?" At least the park was free, and on a good day, he would find a few other kids to play with and keep himself entertained for a while. Since she didn't work until the afternoon, they'd have a few hours in the morning to play.

"Okay, I guess."

She hated the resignation in his voice. This was not the childhood she had planned for him. She'd planned to stay home with him until he started school, take him to the park and on long walks. Then, once he was in kindergarten, Mia had hoped Marcus would be able to spend off time with him and that she could either return to school to finish her interior design degree or at least work a job where she could set her hours to have more time at home. Sadly, that just wasn't the hand they had been dealt.

A moment later, she pulled into the driveway of her parent's home. "Come on, buddy, let's go. I'm running late already." She chanced a glance at her watch, and her heart sank further. Fifteen minutes? She had never been this late before.

"Hey Mom," she said as her mother opened the door. "Sorry, I have to drop and run, but I'm late. Again." Mia turned to Carter and squatted down to his level. "Be good and have fun. I'll be back to get you after my shift."

He nodded, but Mia did not miss the sadness in his eyes. She sent a prayer heavenward as she climbed back into the car. "Please Lord, please help us."

3

E mmitt pulled into the parking lot of the only family restaurant in town. There were a few other eateries in the small town, but he remembered Manny's as being the best and, according to the gas station clerk, it was possible Mia worked here. He had no idea if he would even still recognize her or if she would recognize him, but there couldn't be too many women the right age who worked here. He pulled on a ball cap and tugged it low to his eyes. It didn't always keep people from recognizing him, but it helped.

"Just one?"

Emmitt glanced up at the pretty blonde hostess decked out in white and red and nodded. Just one. He was starting to tire of hearing those words, but practice and games kept him busy. Plus, the few women he had met since joining the team were more like groupies than women he could see spending a lifetime with. The cleat chasers would appear at team parties and throw themselves at the players. A lot of the other players engaged in one or two-night stands, but that had never been appealing to Emmitt. No, he'd made the mistake of being intimate before marriage once, and he wasn't going to do it again.

"Is the counter okay?"

"Sure." Counters didn't generally have the most comfortable seats, but he could understand why they would want to sit a single customer there instead of a booth or a table that could hold more people. Plus, the place was already busy and most of the tables in the restaurant were occupied.

She led him to the chair at the end and placed a menu in front of him. A string of Christmas lights hung down from the ceiling, though they were off currently, and silver tinsel lined the back wall in a decorative pattern. "Someone should be with you shortly." Her eyes glanced around and her face took on a worried expression. "I think Mia is running late again."

Emmitt had no idea if the Mia who worked here was the Mia he had dated, but he supposed he would find out soon enough. He picked up the menu and perused the items. Though nothing sounded appealing, he decided on a burger and fries as it was typically hard to mess them up, and he was not a fan of breakfast for lunch.

"Can I get some service around here?" a man down the bar asked. Agitation covered his face and permeated the air around him.

"Yes, sorry I'm late." He recognized her voice before he even saw her enter. Her reddish hair was pulled back in a ponytail and mostly covered with a Santa hat that sat askew on her head. She was still adjusting her apron as she exited the kitchen as if she had just arrived, and she wore a harried expression on her face. Though he wasn't used to seeing her flustered, she hadn't changed a bit. Still slender and lithe, her uniform flattered her figure, and though he couldn't see her eyes at the moment, he knew they would be the deepest blue he had ever seen.

"Where's your manager?" the man growled. "I've been waiting for someone to take my order for ten minutes."

A blush bloomed across Mia's face. "I'm sorry, sir. I'll take your order right now. There's no need to contact the manager."

"Oh, I think there is," the man said snidely as he looked around the room, as if hoping to garner support from the other patrons.

"Hey, man, she said she's sorry. How about you let her take your order and I'll buy your lunch?" Emmitt spoke up. It was not the way he had wanted to tell Mia he was here, and from the angry glare she shot him, she was not pleased to see him, but he couldn't let this brute walk all over her.

The man turned fierce eyes on him, and his face pinched together as if he wanted to start a fight, but then a greedy gleam glistened in his gaze. "You'll buy whatever I want?"

"Whatever you want," Emmitt said.

"Fine," the man returned his attention to Mia. "I'll have the chicken Alfredo bowl, a side salad, and a slice of cheesecake for dessert." He glanced back at Emmitt. "And a large coke to drink."

The man sounded pleased with himself, and Emmitt kept himself from rolling his eyes. The man's meal would probably add up to less than thirty dollars, and that was well worth the price to Emmitt to have the man quiet down.

"What are you doing here?" Mia hissed as she stopped in front of him. She kept her voice low so as not to draw attention, but he could hear the strain of emotion in it.

"I came to see you." Where were his eloquent words? Not that he'd practiced on the drive here or anything, but he usually wasn't lacking in articulation. However, with her blue eyes shooting icy daggers into him, he felt at a loss for words. What was he doing here? Did he really think she would just forgive him and want to be friends?

But that wasn't what this was about. This was about having no regrets. Whether she forgave him or not was her choice, but he would apologize and return to the team with no regrets. Well, that wasn't entirely true. If he had truly lost his chance with Mia, he would return with the regret that he had ruined it, but he wouldn't regret trying to reconnect with her.

Her eyes flicked to the sides as if checking to see if anyone was watching them. "You saw me. Now you can leave."

"Not without eating first." Emmitt had no place to be. He'd planned to be here for a few days, apologizing and hopefully making up with Mia.

She shot him another hate-filled glare. "Fine. Let me put this man's order in and I'll be right back to take yours."

As she whirled away, the sweet scent of strawberries and vanilla wafted on the air. She was still using the same shampoo. He had always loved that scent, had loved sniffing her hair as she curled into his arms or laid her head against his chest. And he'd been haunted by that smell, which had lingered on his pillow for weeks after their one night together. Their beautiful, terrible, guilt-inducing night together.

Mia returned a moment later but though she held a notepad to take his order, her eyes did not meet his. "What can I get for you?"

"I'll take the hamburger and fries and an iced tea."

Mia issued a curt nod before turning back to the kitchen window to place his order as well. Then, without another word or glance his direction, she bustled off to take care of her other customers.

Emmitt sighed. This was going to be harder than he'd thought.

MIA TRIED TO KEEP HER COMPOSURE AS THE LUNCH CROWD RAN her ragged, but it was so hard with him sitting there watching her. What was he doing here? Not only had she had to deal with the angry customer, but then he'd swooped in like some knight in shining armor to diffuse the situation. He probably thought the gesture alone would sweep her off her feet and she would fall head over heels for him again and forgive him. Well, he was wrong; she was not that girl anymore. She was no longer the naïve twenty-year-old who had fallen for the hometown hero and hung on his every word. No, that girl had died the day Emmitt left town for good. Without a word, without an explanation, without an apology. She'd heard nothing from him for over five years, so what was he doing back in town? And why did he want to see her?

She placed his bill down in front of him, but he made no move to pay it. He didn't seem to be in any hurry.

"How about a slice of pie?" he asked instead.

"Sorry, we're all out," she spat back at him.

"No, you're not. I can see half a pie sitting in the display case over there."

Gritting her teeth, she snatched up his bill and shoved it in her pocket to fix. Then she grabbed a slice of apple pie from the display case and set the plate and a fork in front of him.

He picked up the fork, but made no move to eat the pie. "What time are you off today?"

She crossed her arms and leaned away from him. "For you? Never."

His lips cracked a small smile as he chuckled. "I deserve that, but I flew all the way from San Antonio to see you, and I'm not leaving until you let me talk to you."

"You said enough when you said nothing at all," she said as she moved on to another customer, but his words snagged in her mind. He'd flown all the way here to talk to her. Why? What could he possibly have to say after five and a half years? It didn't matter. She'd worked hard to build up her walls after he'd left. Even Marcus hadn't been able to completely tear them down, but he'd understood, and he'd married her anyway. And though she'd been happy, she'd never completely forgotten Emmitt. No, you never forgot your first love.

As Mia ducked into the kitchen area to adjust Emmitt's bill, Heather, her best friend and the hostess, appeared at her side. "Who is that man out there?"

"The behemoth with the wide shoulders?" Mia asked as she added the pie to the bill.

"Yes, he certainly seems to be content to stay awhile."

"Yes, he does." Mia blew out a frustrated breath.

"You know him?" Heather asked. Her eyes grew to saucers, and her hand flew to her mouth. "Is he…?"

"Yes, he is, and we're not going to discuss it." Heather was the one person who knew the truth, but Mia had sworn her to secrecy years ago.

"What does he want?"

"He wants to talk. Says he came all the way here to talk to me."

"Are you going to talk to him?"

Mia snatched the adjusted bill and whirled on her friend. "I don't know. I can't imagine it would be a good idea, but I have the feeling he won't leave town unless I say yes."

"I think you should at least hear him out," Heather said as she followed Mia back to the dining area.

"We'll see," Mia whispered before slapping the adjusted bill down on the counter in front of Emmitt again. "I can't talk tonight. I have plans when I get off." She didn't. Unless she counted picking up her son and making him dinner as plans. But Emmitt didn't need to know that.

"I only need a few minutes," he said as he picked up the bill and perused the total.

"I don't have a few minutes. Not anymore." Mia moved on to the next customer before Emmitt could say anything more. Though she was curious what he had to say, she felt it would be better if she simply sent him packing. At least then, she would not be swayed by him again.

She heard Emmitt sigh behind her, but it was not until she heard the squeaking of his barstool against the floor, signifying his departure, that she turned back his direction. Her eyes widened at the sight of Ben Franklin on the bill. "You've overpaid me," she called out to Emmitt's back.

He turned and offered a small smile. "No, I haven't." Then he walked out of the restaurant.

4

"Mom, can we go to the park now?" Carter stood in front of her, dressed and ready. It never ceased to amaze her how he could get ready so quickly when it meant going to the park but dragged his feet when it meant going to her parents' house.

She checked her watch. It was only nine am, and she didn't have to be at work until two. If they left now, he would have plenty of time to play and wear himself out. "Okay, let's go."

As the park was just down the street, she didn't bother with driving, but she did grab her sunglasses and house keys. Though December and early in the day, the air was warm from the sun's bright rays. It had been unusually warm the last few days. Mia considered ducking back in the house for sunscreen, but Carter was already running ahead of her. With a sigh, she pushed the thought from her mind. Surely, he would be okay for a few hours, and they would leave before the worst time of day. Her mother had always told her that burning time was between eleven and two, and they would leave the park by eleven to give her time to get ready and drop him off before work.

Her feet slowed as she approached the park. A man was sitting on her favorite park bench—the one that allowed her to see all parts of the playground. Normally, she wouldn't care. She'd either join the man or sit on another bench, but a quick scan of the park showed Carter was the only kid here so far. Her protective mother instincts kicked in. He was probably just someone out for a walk who had decided to take a break, but there'd been too many stories of predators on the news lately. She wasn't about to take that chance and ignore him.

She approached the stranger, but stopped before giving him a piece of her mind. It was Emmitt, but it was too late to turn back. Carter was already on the playground. "What are you doing here?"

He looked up and smiled at her. "I was thinking about how to get you to talk to me."

"How did you know I lived around here? Did you follow me home?" Her shield was up, and even though she knew he had left the restaurant before she did the previous day, she couldn't imagine how he could have found her unless he was following her.

"No, this was one of my favorite parks growing up. I thought coming here would help me think of a way to reach you."

She sighed and plunked down next to him on the bench. She still didn't really want to hear what he had to say, but perhaps listening to him would ease his conscience and allow him to leave. "Fine, Emmitt, what did you want to say to me?"

He looked at her with those deep soulful eyes that had always sent her heart careening in her chest. Even now, she felt it start to beat faster, and as the moment drew out, she pursed her lips together to keep from urging him to get on with it.

"I wanted to say I was sorry," he finally said.

"Sorry? You're sorry? For what? For wasting three years of my life? For telling me you loved me when you obviously didn't? For leaving without a word?"

His face appeared to fold in on itself, and for just a moment, she felt badly, but it was only a moment. He'd left her, not the other way around. She'd been the one left wondering what had happened, what she had done to make him run without an explanation.

"For all of that and more," he said.

That was his idea of an apology? She should have known. He'd never been one to open up about his feelings, but she'd hoped that was only age and that maturing would change that side of him. Evidently, it hadn't. "Fine, you said your apology. Now you can go." She forced a smile and waved to Carter, who had climbed up the large slide and was now hollering and waving his arms at her proudly.

Emmitt turned to look at Carter. His eyes widened as he seemed to realize who the boy was for the first time. "He's your son?"

"Yeah, he is. Carter." Mia bit her lip to keep from spilling more. She'd decided on her story over five years ago, and there was no reason to change it now. "After you left, I was a mess, but thankfully Marcus came along and helped me rebuild my life."

"And where is Marcus now?" Emmitt asked looking around the playground.

"Dead," Mia said in a matter-of-fact tone. "He was killed by a drunk driver a year ago."

Emmitt turned to her and reached out a hand. "Mia, I'm so sorry."

"Don't," she said, shying away from his touch. "You don't get to feel badly for me, and you definitely don't get to console me. You lost that privilege when you left without a word after the draft." Unbidden, the image of their last night together flashed into her mind.

"This is so exciting, Emmitt," she said as they watched the teams on the TV announce who they were choosing.

"It's nerve-wracking," he said as he squeezed her hand. "What if it's New York or California that takes me? I'll be so far away."

"That won't happen." His mother set down a bowl of popcorn

on the table in front of them. "I've prayed that God will keep you close."

"Our next team is the San Antonio Saints. They've been watching quite a few players including weak linebacker Emmitt Brown and safety Jordan Granger," one of the announcers said.

"They could definitely use either of those positions, so let's see who they choose," the other announcer said.

The view on the screen shifted to the owners of the San Antonio Saints and the coach stood. "Our pick is Emmitt Brown from Texas Tech University."

"That's you," Mia squealed and pulled Emmitt in for a hug. "San Antonio isn't that far."

"Yeah," he said, but his voice didn't hold the emotion she expected.

"I didn't know how it would be," he said, "and when I got there, it wasn't the life I wanted for you. I wanted you to be able to finish school and go into design, not be my shadow."

"You shouldn't have chosen for me. You never even gave me the option."

"I know. I should have." His gaze dropped to his lap and he ran his thumbs over his forefingers.

"I've thought about that day a lot since I left—"

"But not enough to come back," she said, interrupting him. "You never came home after that. Not even for your family. And I heard they moved a few years ago. Did you do that too? Move them away, so you'd have even less reason to return home and possibly see me?"

He shook his head, but she could see that he knew she was right. It was written all over the expression on his face. "I was selfish then, but I've changed. I became a Christ follower—"

She held up a hand, interrupting him again. "You were already a Christian."

His eyes slowly met hers again, and the sadness in them pulled at her heart. "No, I thought I was, but if I had been, if I'd truly been listening to God, I wouldn't have let that night happen. I took something from you that I shouldn't have—that wasn't mine."

So now he was going to try and be noble? Where had that nobility been for the last five and a half years? "You didn't take it from me. I gave it to you. It takes two, remember?"

"Yes, but had I been the man of God I claimed to be, I wouldn't have let you."

"So, because of that, you thought it would just be better to leave? To never explain yourself? To leave me wondering?" She'd worked so hard to build up her emotional wall, to put him securely behind it at a distance where he could never hurt her again. Yet, sitting here with him, she could feel him chipping away at the wall, and she worked harder to keep it intact.

He opened his mouth to speak, but before he could, a sharp scream followed by loud cries filled the air. Mia bolted toward the playground, screaming Carter's name as she did.

EMMITT WATCHED MIA RUN TOWARD HER SON FOR JUST A MOMENT before adrenaline kicked in and he followed. A young boy lay on the ground, tears streaming from his face, and his ankle twisted in a painful position.

"It's okay, honey," Mia said, though Emmitt could hear the fear in her voice.

"It hurts Mommy."

"May I?" Emmitt stepped forward and before Mia could object, he lifted the small child in his arms. He looked down at the boy's face and was surprised to see not the blue of Mia's eyes, but dark brown like his. The boy had the same shape to his face as Mia did, and his nose appeared similar, but that's where it ended. The rest of the boy's face must be his father's. Emmitt forced his face to remain stoic as thoughts of a child with Mia surfaced in his mind.

"What are you doing?" Mia asked, following behind him.

"Taking him to the hospital. My car is parked right over there. Did you drive?"

"No, but…"

He could see the hesitation in her face, hear it in her voice. She didn't trust him, which made sense after how he had hurt her, but he was not going to just let this kid keep crying in pain. "Look, I get it. You don't trust me anymore, but I'm here, I have a car, and I can get him there faster than an ambulance could get here. Cheaper too." It was a cheap shot, and he knew it. He could tell money was on her mind more often than it should be, but it worked. Her mouth folded into a tight line, and she nodded.

When they got to his car, he debated his next course of action. His keys were in his pocket, but he would need to set the boy down to get them.

"Where are your keys?" she asked, as if reading his mind.

"In my right front pocket." He indicated with his head and watched as indecision crossed her face. "I can put him down."

"No, I want to move him as little as possible. I'll get them." She took a step closer and then reached into his pocket. Her eyes caught his and a pink flush crawled up her neck. So, he could still affect her. He found that thought satisfying as she certainly still affected him. "Got them," she said and broke their gaze. She unlocked the door and opened it, and Emmitt leaned down and loaded the kid as gently into the backseat as he could.

He moved to shut the door, but she stepped forward. "I'll sit in the back with him."

With a nod, he moved to the driver's side, fired up the car, and pulled out as soon as she was situated.

5

Mia chewed on her thumbnail as she paced the hospital restlessly. They had taken Carter for x-rays, but that was nearly an hour ago. Why wasn't he back yet?

"Can I get you anything? A coffee? Food?"

She looked over at Emmitt, who was still waiting with her. She wasn't sure why he hadn't left, but for the moment she was grateful for the company. "No, my stomach is too knotted for anything. What's taking them so long?"

Emmitt shrugged. "I don't know. I'll go ask at the desk."

As he sauntered toward the nurse's station, she resumed her pacing. Suddenly, the doctor who had whisked her son away appeared in the hallway. His grim expression turned her heart to ice. Was it worse than a break?

"Mrs. Conrad, I have some news. Would you like to wait for your husband to return first?" He nodded toward Emmitt who was returning their direction.

"No, he's not my husband. Just a...a friend." Actually, she didn't know what Emmitt was at the moment, but having driven her here, she supposed he counted as a friend for now.

"All right. Well, Carter did sustain a fracture of his ankle. We got the bone set and the cast on. He'll be groggy for a few hours, but you should be able to take him home tomorrow."

Relief flooded Mia and her shoulders relaxed. "Thank you," she said and then his words registered. "Tomorrow? Is that normal for a break?"

The doctor's lips pursed, and his gaze shifted to the floor before returning to her eyes. "No, it isn't. Unfortunately, we did find something troubling on the x-ray."

"What?" Mia felt as if someone had punched her gut. All the air flew out of her lungs. Her knees buckled and she grabbed for the wall to keep herself from falling.

"There are some markers that indicate osteosarcoma. We'd like to run further tests."

"What is osteosarcoma?" Emmitt asked, coming up beside her. He placed a hand on her shoulder, offering strength. Only a hand, but it was something.

The doctor looked to Mia for consent before answering the question. She hesitated only a moment. If it was something serious, she would have to tell him eventually. "It's fine. He can hear. What is osteosarcoma?"

"It's a cancer of the bone. Has Carter ever complained of his legs hurting before?"

It was Mia's worst nightmare come true, and a weight pressed on her chest, causing her voice to come out small and weak. "Yes, but I thought it was just growing pains." She covered her mouth with her hand. She was an awful mother.

The doctor nodded. "Yes, that's common with this cancer. This type of cancer is usually only found when someone comes in for another type of treatment like Carter's break, and it's rather rare for someone so young, so it's possible it's something else entirely. However, we'd like to be sure, so we'll do a biopsy to determine if it's cancer, and *if* it is, we'll run an MRI to make sure the cancer hasn't spread. Once we know what we're dealing with, we can determine treatment options."

Mia wrung her hands together. Cancer. Was this her fault? Had she passed this to him? Had his father? "Is there something I could have done? If I brought him in sooner?"

"Not necessarily. We won't know exactly what we're dealing with until we run the tests."

Mia nodded, but it didn't ease the guilt that covered her like a second skin. Her voice was barely more than a whisper when she spoke again. "Of course I'll do whatever it takes, but that sounds expensive." The words came out slowly and she hated that instead of just focusing on her son, she was having to think about how she would pay for tests and treatment.

The doctor's face folded in sympathy. "It can get expensive. Do you have insurance?"

Mia shook her head and tried not to feel like a total failure. "My husband died last year, and I've been working at a restaurant. They don't offer insurance."

Pity—that dreaded expression that Mia hated—crossed the doctor's face. "We can work out a payment plan, but we can't move forward until we know what's going on, so not performing the biopsy really isn't an option."

"Of course, I'll figure something out." She didn't know what, as she had no money. Even a payment plan wouldn't help unless they would take twenty dollars a month. She could move out of the apartment, but then where would they live? Back with her parents was possibly an option. One she hated, but what choice did she have? "Can I see Carter?"

"Sure, I'll take you back." The doctor paused and shifted his gaze to Emmitt as if asking silently if he was coming too.

"Go ahead," Emmitt said. "I'll wait for you here and drive you home when you're done."

"You don't have to do that," Mia said. She didn't really want him to stay, but she couldn't just tell him to leave. Not after he'd driven them here and offered to wait around and drive her back. Whatever he had done in the past, he was offering to be her rock right now. And she needed a rock. She hated that she did, but she did.

"I have nothing else to do, remember? I only came here to see you. You go be with your son for as long as you need. I'll be here when you need me."

Mia smiled gratefully and then sighed. Work. She still had to go to work today, but how could she go? Carter needed to stay overnight, and he was too young to stay in the hospital by himself. But, if she didn't go, she would no doubt be fired, and Heaven knew she couldn't afford to take the day off. Especially now. She'd been late too often recently, and her boss would likely not see this as a viable excuse. She'd have to call her mother and see if she could come up to sit with him while she was at work. "Thank you. I won't be long. Unfortunately, I have to be at work in a few hours."

EMMITT WATCHED MIA WALK DOWN THE HALLWAY AND disappear into a room before he returned to the nurses' station. There was no way he was going to let the hospital bills drain Mia financially. The pain and uncertainty had been written all over her face, and her admission that she had no insurance only drove the knife in deeper. If Emmitt had taken Mia with him, if he had married her, she would have insurance.

"Excuse me," he said to the woman at the station, "who do I talk to about paying someone's medical costs?"

The woman smiled at him, but questions swam in her eyes. "I'm sorry? You want to do what?"

"I want to pay for Carter..." He trailed off. He didn't even know Mia's last name. "That woman I was with. Her name is Mia. Her son is young, four or five. He broke his ankle, and I want to pay for his treatment. All of it. His mother doesn't have insurance.

Nor does she have the means to pay his bills. I do. So, how do I set that up?"

The woman blinked at him, seemingly incapable of speaking for a minute. "Um, I'll send you to billing. I think they can help you with that, but you'll need his last name."

"Can you help me with that? Please? I don't want to bother his mother while she sits with him, and I'd really like to get this taken care of before she finds out."

The woman bit her lip. "I'm not supposed to."

He was going to have to try a different tactic. He leaned forward and stared directly into her eyes. "What's your name?"

"Betty," she said.

"Well, Betty, do you like football?"

A small smile pulled at the corners of her lips. "This is Texas, sir, it's pretty hard not to like football."

He returned the smile, flashing the most charming one he could. "Okay, well, I play for the San Antonio Saints. I'll send tickets for you and your family back here if you'll help me out."

Her eyes widened as recognition dawned on her face. "You're Emmitt Brown?"

"Yes, I am, and I could use a favor."

She nodded, still apparently awestruck, but her eyes glanced down to the computer screen and her fingers tapped the buttons. "Conrad. His name is Carter Conrad."

"Thank you, Betty." He tapped the counter and then followed her directions down the hall to the billing department where he received the same shocked expression from the woman there.

"Why would you want to pay someone's medical bills?" the woman asked as she pushed dark-rimmed glasses up her nose.

"Because she can't. Because he's a kid." Because it's my fault, he added silently, but this woman didn't need to know that.

"Okay, well, we certainly don't get requests like this every day, but yes, it's possible. I'll have all bills go to your address. I just need you to fill out this form." She slid a paper across the counter to him and Emmitt began filling it out.

"Can you do one more thing?" he asked when he was finished. "Can you make it anonymous?"

"You don't want her to know?"

"Not yet. I'll tell her when it's time."

The woman blinked at him. Clearly this was not normal behavior. "Okay, I'll notate the account."

With that done, Emmitt returned to the waiting area and sat down in one of the chairs. He closed his eyes and placed his chin on his clasped hands. *Lord, I know that doesn't make up for what I've done, but please… If it's Your will, save this boy.*

❧ 6 ❧

Mia tried to keep her emotions in check as she entered Carter's room. How could she leave him here to go to work? He looked even smaller than his almost five years in the large bed, especially with the cast dwarfing his ankle. "Hey bud, how are you feeling?"

"Okay," he said with a shrug. "It doesn't hurt so bad anymore and they have TV. Can I stay here for a little bit?"

Mia bit back the tears that threatened to overflow. She should be here with her child all day, but there was little money as it was. That detail was punctuated by the fact that he wanted to stay in a hospital for the TV. What kid wanted to stay in a hospital? Hers, it appeared. Cable had been one of the first things she had dropped after Marcus's death. She had no time to watch it, and the hundred dollars a month was definitely spent better elsewhere. Unfortunately, that meant Carter was reduced to the few DVDs they had purchased over the years if he wanted to watch TV, and Mia knew he was tired of watching the same movies over and over again. Not even the local channels came through their older model television. "Yeah bud. You actually get to spend the night. They want to run some tests on your leg."

"Does that mean I won't have to go to Grandma's?"

"It does, but I still have to go to work, so Grandma will come here. At least until I get off. Then I can come stay with you."

Carter's face scrunched for a moment as if considering this option. "Okay, I think that will be fine. I'm sure I can find some cartoons until Grandma gets here."

Oh, to be a child again and simply worry about cartoons instead of payment plans and treatment options. "That's good, buddy," Mia said as she brushed his bangs back on his forehead. If only it were that simple. She tried not to worry about the future as she looked at him, but it was impossible. How was she ever going to get the money to pay for this stay? Let alone any future tests and treatments he might require? She swallowed the lump forming in her throat and tried to keep her voice even. "I'm going to call Grandma and then I have to get to work, bud, but I'll see you as soon as I get off."

"Okay, bye Mom."

She kissed his forehead and tried to not think about how many more times she would get to do this. What if the cancer was bad? What if he never made it out of this hospital? No, she couldn't think like that. She'd already lost Marcus. She couldn't lose Carter too. That would be too cruel.

As she started back toward the waiting area, the tears built up behind her eyes, blurring her vision, and she sank to the floor. They spilled, one by one, like droplets from a leaky sink down her cheeks, and she pressed her hand to her mouth to keep from crying out. How could this be happening?

"Are you okay?"

Mia looked up to see Emmitt standing over her, concern etched in his handsome features. As he looked down at her, the dam broke. She didn't want his pity, and she lashed out at him.

"No, I'm not okay. My son might have cancer, I have no money to pay for his treatment, and I have to get to work and leave him in the hospital alone. I feel like the worst mother in the world, and you showing up unannounced isn't helping." Her hand flew to her mouth as his face fell. "I'm sorry, that was uncalled for. I know you're just trying to help."

He held out a hand and helped her stand. "It's okay. That's a lot for anyone to deal with, but I'd like to help. Please, tell me what I can do."

Mia blew out a breath that landed somewhere between a chuckle and a sigh and ran her hand through her hair. "Can you cure cancer? Buy me a winning lottery ticket to afford the treatments?" She shook her head and sighed. "I'm sorry, you don't need to be dragged into this. If you can just take me home, you can get back to your life. I'll figure something out."

"How about this? I take you home and then I come back here and hang out with Carter?"

"No, it's fine. I'll call my mother. She usually watches him during the day, so I'm sure she can come in and sit with him."

"Fine, then at least let me buy you dinner tonight."

She started to shake her head again, but he cut her off. "You have to eat, and I'm sure whatever I bring will taste better than hospital food."

"I can just bring something from Manny's," she said. While having company sounded appealing, it was Emmitt. Emmitt, who had always sent her heart fluttering and held a power over her. Emmitt, who had left her with a broken heart. The last thing she needed was to be around Emmitt, especially when she was vulnerable like this.

"I'm not taking no for an answer. I've haven't been the best friend, but friends help each other out."

At the mention of the word friend, she folded. They weren't friends now, but they had been once and though she didn't like asking for help, she didn't have a ton of close friends who could take the time off to sit with her like he could. "Fine, thank you, but I don't get off till nine."

"You're welcome, and that's fine. Now, let's get you home before you're late for another shift."

EMMITT STARED AT THE OPEN BIBLE IN FRONT OF HIM. HE HAD returned to the hotel room hoping to do his devotional after dropping Mia off at her house, but all he could think about was Carter. Nobody should get cancer, least of all a child with his whole future ahead of him, but Emmitt knew it happened all the time. It had just never happened to someone he knew, and though he didn't have children himself, he couldn't even imagine how Mia must be feeling. He had lifted the financial burden from her shoulders, but he wanted to do more. He just wasn't sure what.

Beside him, his cell phone rang, and he picked it up without even checking the caller ID. "Hello?"

"Rev? It's Tucker Jackson. I need some advice." Tucker was one of the younger players on the team. Picked up in the final round of drafts, he had yet to play a game this season and Emmitt knew he was frustrated by that.

"Sure, Tucker, what can I do for you?" His mind was not really in the right place to be doling out advice, but it was one of the consequences for the character he had created. The men thought because of his faith that he was a good sounding board and they often brought their problems to him. Sometimes he felt more like a Catholic priest than a linebacker.

"I just got word they want to trade me. I don't know what to do, man."

Emmitt's heart hurt for the younger man. It was hard to get on a team, think you were a part of their family, and then realize you didn't mean as much to them as you thought. But being traded also wasn't the worst thing in the world. Yes, he would have to start over on a new team, make new friends, but perhaps he would get to play instead of warming the bench.

"Tucker, I'm sorry. Where do they want to send you, do you know?"

"The Texas Tornadoes. They're a good team, but I feel like I just haven't gotten the chance to show the Saints what I have."

"I know it's hard, but trades are a part of the game. When is the trade happening?"

"As soon as the season is over. The Tornadoes are out of the championship running this season, so they agreed to let me finish the season with the Saints."

Emmitt nodded even though he knew Tucker couldn't see it. Trades were common this time of year. As soon as teams realized they were out of the playoffs, they started looking at how to improve their team for the next year before the draft. Drafts were a crap shoot—owners never really knew what they were getting because college ball was different than pro football. A lot of amazing college players froze when they got out under the cameras. Trades, however, worked more in the owner's favor. They could generally see the player in action in at least one game. Plus, they could put the players through a few extra trainings before the season ended. Emmitt would be sad to see Tucker go, but he couldn't help wondering if they were trading him for a replacement for Matt Johnson. He'd said more than once this was his last year, and the defensive line would crumble without a decent replacement.

"My suggestion is to look at this like an opportunity. You have the chance to show this new team what you have, to show them you belong on the field and not on the bench. I know it's hard to start over, but sometimes it's for the best. And I'll still be here for you. Whatever you need, you can always call on me."

"Thanks, Rev. I think you're what I'm going to miss most. You always made me feel included. Thanks for listening, and I'll see you at practice in a few days."

As Emmitt hung up the phone, Tucker's words raced around in his head. He might have made Tucker feel included, but he'd excluded Mia when it really mattered. He'd left without a word. Embarrassed and ashamed, he hadn't known how to apologize to her, so he'd put it off and thrown himself into playing. And somehow, the days had turned into months and the months into years. And now she was here. Working a dead-end job with little money. And her son was growing up without a father and might have cancer. How costly one choice could be.

Emmitt didn't know what the solution was, but he was determined to make it up to Mia and Carter. Maybe he could become like a surrogate father—one who took the kid to ball games and threw the football around with him. At least that way, he would have a man in his life. Emmitt might have made some huge mistakes in his past, but he was determined to be a good example for the kid. And for Mia. He had to prove to her he had changed.

Mia did her best to focus on work, but her mind continued to wander to Carter. Was he okay? Lonely? Missing her? She knew her mother was at the hospital with him, but it didn't ease her worry. She should be with him. She should be holding him and spending every second with him. Especially if his seconds were now limited.

"Mia, I need to talk to you," Daryl said, bringing her crashing back to reality.

Her heart sank as she looked at him. His face was long and his bottom lip folded in as if he'd rather be doing anything other than talking to her. And she knew this was it. He was going to fire her. She'd known it would be coming. It wasn't like she could hide her tardiness forever, but she needed this job. Especially now. How would she pay bills if she had no income coming in?

With a heavy heart and an invisible weight pressing down on her shoulders, she followed him to his small office at the back of the restaurant. He shut the door and cleared his throat. "There's no easy way to say this, so I'm just going to come right out with it." His gaze flicked around the room—the dingy walls, the worn carpet, anywhere but her face. "I hear you were late again yesterday."

She wondered how he found out. Had that customer complained after all? It didn't matter, really. What mattered now was owning up and convincing him she would try harder. "I was, and I'm sorry. I wish I could say it won't happen again, but Carter...he's having a hard time."

Daryl held up his hand. "I understand that. Truly, I do..."

Mia hated it when people said that. Especially people like Daryl. Daryl was twenty-two years old, fresh out of college, and his parents owned the restaurant. He had no idea what it was to lose a spouse or raise a child alone and she doubted he lived paycheck to paycheck.

"But I need someone I can count on," he continued. "Someone who isn't going to keep the customers waiting."

"I understand sir, but Carter broke his ankle this morning and is in the hospital. I didn't even stay with him today. I came in even though I wanted to be with him because I need the job." Mia hated begging, especially to someone younger than she was, but she saw no other option.

"I'm sorry to hear that, but I still have to let you go. You can come in tomorrow to pick up your final paycheck, but today is your last shift."

For the second time that day, tears stung her eyes, but Mia was determined not to cry. Not at work and not in front of Daryl. She would figure something out. She didn't know what, but she trusted that God was faithful and He would provide something.

"Understood. Thank you." She left Daryl's office before the tears could start and hurried into the bathroom. Squeezing her eyes shut, she willed the tears away and then splashed water on her face. She would make it through the rest of this day and be the best waitress possible. Maybe Daryl would see and reconsider but even if he didn't, Mia would know that she had done her best and she could leave with her head high. It might not be much of a victory, but pride was about all she had left at the moment, and she would take it.

When her shift ended that evening, she handed in her name tag and apron to Daryl and walked out without another word. Her tears stayed at bay until she shut her car door, and then they streamed down her cheeks in shiny rivulets faster than she could wipe them away. She didn't try to stop them but let them flow. Better to get them out now than cry at the hospital in front of Carter. He would blame himself if he saw her, and she didn't need that.

He was asleep in the bed when she entered the room, and Mia swallowed her disappointment. Even though it was after nine, she'd hoped he would be awake when she arrived, but the biopsy must have worn him out. She motioned her mother to step into the hallway. She needed to talk to her mother, but the conversation wasn't for little ears who would worry too much, and Carter could be a light sleeper.

"How was he today?" Mia asked as she gathered her courage for the harder topic.

"He was fine. Watched entirely too much television, but what else can a boy do when he's confined to a bed. Do you want to tell me how he broke his ankle?"

Mia could hear the blame in her mother's voice and see it in her scolding gaze. Her mother probably thought she hadn't been watching Carter close enough and maybe she hadn't—what with being distracted by Emmitt. It was certainly a lecture Mia had heard more than once, but she couldn't blame her mother. Like Mia, her mother only wanted what was best for Carter, and Mia wished she could provide for him as her parents had provided for her. But she was only one person trying to do the job of two people.

"He fell at the playground today, but there was nothing I could have done. However, his ankle is the least of my worries."

Her mother folded her arms across her chest. "What do you

mean? I'd say a broken ankle on a five-year-old is a pretty big deal."

Mia bit the inside of her lip. She did not want to cry in front of her mother. Not because she didn't think her mother would support her but because she was afraid once she started crying, she might not be able to stop. "Not compared to osteosarcoma which the doctor thinks he might have."

As expected, her mother's eyes widened and her hand flew to her mouth. "Cancer? Is that why they took him for tests today?"

Mia swallowed the massive lump in her throat and blinked against the tears that burned in her eyes. "Yeah, and I was fired today for being late yesterday, so on top of dealing with cancer, I have no idea how I'm supposed to pay for any of this."

Compassion flooded her mother's face. "We'll figure this out somehow. You can move back in with us. We can continue to watch Carter while you find a new job. Goodness knows your father is driving me crazy now that he's retired. Having Carter around all day would be good for us."

A tear sneaked out of her eye and trailed down her cheek. Mia swiped it away. "Where am I going to find a new job, Mom? This is Kempton. We only have, like, one job a year open up, and that's usually only when someone goes off to college or dies. It's December, so college is out of the question and I'm not sure I have time to wait for someone to die."

"Then you'll have to look outside of town. It will make your commute longer, but if you're staying with us, it won't matter because we can put Carter to bed if necessary."

Though that was an option, it was not one Mia enjoyed, as it would mean even less time with Carter than she had now. "Yeah, maybe. I'm not going to start looking tomorrow though. I'm going to stay home with my son and decide what to do. Thank you for sitting with him today."

"Of course. He is my only grandson, and you know I'd do anything for him. However, if you'd only—"

"Mom, stop it." Mia tried not to grimace at her mother's words. While they sounded innocent enough, disappointment threaded them. Disappointment that Mia hadn't had more children before Marcus died. Disappointment in the fact she had married Marcus in the first place and not someone wealthier. But lack of income hadn't been what killed Marcus.

"I'll call you tomorrow, Mom." Mia gave her mother a hug and watched her walk away before re-entering Carter's room. As he still lay sleeping, she pulled up a chair and sat beside him. Relishing the silence, she closed her eyes and opened her heart to God. She needed a miracle and He was the only one who could supply one.

EMMITT GRABBED THE BAG OF CHINESE FOOD FROM THE PASSENGER seat of his car. He hoped Mia still liked Chinese. He had forgotten to ask, but he'd ordered her sweet and sour chicken and broccoli beef, dishes that she'd loved when they'd been together.

A stop at the visitor's desk yielded him a name tag and clearance to continue down the hall, but he stopped short as he entered Carter's room. The boy was asleep in the bed and beside him, Mia sat in a chair with her eyes closed. Should he wake her or just leave the food and go? It was late, but he didn't want her food to spoil. Before he could decide, her body jerked and her eyes flicked open.

"Emmitt? How long have you been there?" She rubbed her eyes as she sat up straighter.

"I just arrived." He held up the bags. "With dinner."

"Thank you." An audible rumble filled the air, and Mia dropped her eyes in embarrassment. "I guess I am hungry."

Emmitt set the bags on the nearby table and pulled a chair over. He handed her one Styrofoam container and then set the other in front of his place. "How are you doing today?" he asked her as he opened the lid. The sweet, salty smell of chicken and rice floated out to him.

"Don't ask," she said with a shake of her head. "My son is sick and in the hospital, and I got fired."

"What?"

"Yeah. It's been a day to say the least." The sarcasm was clear in her voice and Emmitt's heart went out to her. He may have covered her medical bills, but she would never make it without a job. "Sorry, I'm not great company. Would you be willing to pray for the food?"

"Your company is fine," he assured her. "And I don't mind at all."

She nodded, and Emmitt said grace over their dinner. "So why were you working at a restaurant instead of interior design like you studied in college?" he asked after saying Amen. He speared a piece of steak and pepper and shoved it in his mouth. Mia might have preferred milder Chinese dishes, but he enjoyed a little heat in his.

She moved her rice around with her fork as if deciding what she wanted to say. "Well, after you left, I took some time off college to clear my head. Then I met and married Marcus and then Carter was born. I stayed home with him the first few years, but when Marcus died, I had to get a job, and one that paid. As I'd never finished my design degree, no one would hire me, so I turned to waitressing. The work wasn't hard and the tips paid well, but it's been a challenge trying to deal with Carter. He misses his father, and I've been late more times than I'd like to admit. Today, my boss decided he'd had enough and he fired me."

Emmitt swallowed his food and regarded Mia across the table. "What are you going to do?"

"I have no idea. My mother suggested moving in with her and my dad, but not only do I not want to do that, but I don't think it will really save much money, as I'll have to find a job out of town. However, with no job, I don't really have a lot of options."

Before he had thought the idea all the way through, Emmitt blurted out, "Why don't you come work for me?"

"Doing what?" Mia asked with a raised eyebrow. "You're a pro-football player. I don't think I have any skills that would help you."

"Actually, you do. I've been meaning to redecorate my house, but I've been so busy I haven't hired a designer. If you did it, not only could you get publicity that would land you jobs in the future, but you could stay on-site with Carter. I have a guest house in the back."

"Emmitt, I don't think that's a very good idea."

"It's a perfect idea. He could stay in the house with you while you work. I've got a few more days off before I have to be back for practice. I could keep him entertained when you needed quiet time. Plus, we have a great cancer hospital there. *If* it's cancer, they'll probably refer you there anyway."

He could see the hesitation in her eyes, but he also knew he'd hit a nerve with the hospital. Kempton was not known for its hospital care, and she would want the best care for Carter. "You really have a job for me? This isn't just some ruse to get me to your house, so you can break my heart again, is it?"

Her words pierced his heart, but he knew he deserved them. "I really have a job for you. I know I screwed up badly in the past, but let me do this for you."

Mia bit her bottom lip—a trait he had found endearing when they dated and one that always meant she didn't know what to do. Her eyes flicked from him to her son lying in the bed. With a giant sigh, she nodded. "Okay. *If* it's cancer and they refer me to San Antonio's hospital, then I'll do it."

❦ 8 ❧

"You're taking my grandson six hours away from here?" The anger and disbelief was evident both in her mother's voice and the stiff posture of her hands jammed onto her hips.

"Hear her out, Maggie," her father said from the kitchen. He had offered to entertain Carter in the other room while the women talked but apparently he was still listening.

"He's offering me a job, Mother. One that pays well and allows me to spend the days with Carter. Plus, the hospital there is top notch. I met with the doctor earlier and the biopsy confirmed it's osteosarcoma. He's referring us to Methodist Hospital anyway for treatment."

"But six hours away? And right before Christmas?"

Mia shrugged. "Faster if you fly, and we can't wait, Mom. They want to start treatments right away, and we were lucky enough to get an appointment with one of the doctors there tomorrow."

"And who is this mysterious benefactor anyway who swooped in at just the right moment to offer this job?"

Mia bit the inside of her lip. She didn't really want to tell her mother because even though she'd been a fan of Emmitt's in the beginning, she had turned on him when he left Mia, but she would not lie to her either. "It's Emmitt."

As expected, her mother's eyes widened, and her eyebrow arched in that way Mia had always hated as a child—that way that said she was in trouble. "Emmitt Brown? Mia, what are you thinking?"

"I'm thinking that he has money and that he offered me a job. I'm thinking that Carter is going to need to be at a good hospital to get the treatment he needs, and I'm thinking that this offer will allow me to spend time with him both day and night just in case..." Mia didn't finish the thought, but she didn't have to. The expression on her mother's face showed it was heavy on her mind as well.

"He is going to be fine. Do you hear me?"

Mia sniffed back the tears crowding her throat. "He will because he's going to get amazing treatment in San Antonio. I know you will miss him, but this is what he needs right now. This is what I need right now." Though she wished it had been anyone besides Emmitt who had offered her the job, she would not say no to this gift horse. Not only would the job be enough to help pay his medical bills, but Emmitt was well known. If she did a good job, this opportunity could launch her interior design business, and with Carter starting school next year, she wanted a job that she could do during the day to spend time with him at night.

Her mother tilted her chin up and sniffed. "You're right. Go get our boy the best care he can get. Just be careful with your heart, Mia. I don't want to see it get broken again."

"I will, Mom." Though they didn't hug often, Mia pulled her mother in for one now. She had no idea when she might see her again. No idea how long this job would take and no idea how much treatment Carter would need. She was taking a leap of faith, and while she had no problems trusting God, she still had reservations about trusting Emmitt.

"Hey, bud, give Grandma and Grandpa a hug and a kiss, and then we better hit the road." Emmitt had not only offered to forgo his plane tickets and drive with them back to San Antonio, but he had paid for a moving company to box up their things and ship them there. While Mia had no intention of staying forever, she knew Carter would appreciate having his things there—few as they were—and the doctor had said the treatments could take three or four months.

"Bye Grandma," he said as he hobbled over to where they stood. The doctor had placed a walking cast on his foot because crutches were too unwieldy for most children. Still, the sight of him limping tore at Mia's heartstrings, but she knew there was much worse in his future. She prayed he wouldn't lose his smile or his sweet personality on the arduous road ahead.

With the goodbyes said, she helped Carter into her car and then drove to the hotel where Emmitt was staying. As he had flown in initially, they would be dropping his rental car off in town and then heading to San Antonio in her car. She hoped it would make it. Her car was over ten years old and had some quirks.

The air conditioner only worked sixty percent of the time, not favorable when one lived in the hot, dry belt of Texas. Even in December, the temperature often sat in the mid-sixties and the last few days, it had even hit seventy-five a few days. The radio station seemed to only pick up country music even though there was a pop station in town that should have come in clear. And the gas gauge wasn't always reliable. More than once, she had run out of gas on the road and had to walk to the lone gas station and borrow a can to fill up.

"Did you get everything taken care of?" Emmitt asked as he approached the car.

"I think so. Carter's all set back there with some coloring books, his tablet, and a pillow. The moving company is coming this evening to pack everything up and my mother will supervise.

Nothing bad will happen on her watch. I grabbed a few snacks for the trip, but I don't have money for gas."

Emmitt waved his hand. "I'll cover the cost of gas. Consider it part of your moving expense, and we'll talk about the rest of the budget when we get there."

Mia took a deep breath and blew it out. "Okay, then I guess we're ready."

Emmitt planned out the drive back in his head as they drove to the rental car company. He still had so much he wanted to tell Mia, but he doubted she would want to talk about the past with Carter in the back seat. Hopefully, he would find some time alone with her after the boy went to sleep. Getting her to take this job had been a miracle, but he kept praying God would give him more opportunities to show her how he'd changed.

After dropping off the keys and transferring his bags to Mia's car, they were on the road again. "Do you remember when we drove back here one Christmas break and I fell asleep at the wheel?" he asked when the silence pressed in on him and he could take it no longer.

It had been a scary trip to say the least. He'd had a late practice, so he'd asked her to take the first shift of driving so he could sleep, but somehow their wires had gotten crossed as she'd had to stay up late for a final. Emmitt had thought he was in better shape than she was, but two hours outside of Lubbock, he'd been woken by the shaking of the car as it swerved over the rumble strips. His eyes had snapped open and his foot had slammed on the brakes as the car fishtailed off the road and into the ditch. Thankfully, the car hadn't been damaged and they'd gotten back on the road ten minutes later. It had taken a lot longer for his heart to slow down.

"Let's not talk about the past," Mia said. "Tell me about football. What's it like?"

Emmitt swallowed his disappointment at her subject change, but he humored her. "It's a lot of work. Four-hour long practices nearly every day except for the days we play or the days we travel. Then there's a lot of soaking sore muscles after and being stretched by the trainer. And don't get me started on ice baths."

"What's an ice bath?" Carter spoke up from the back seat.

Emmitt turned in the seat to look at Carter. The kid was sprawled across the back seat with his foot propped up on a pillow behind Emmitt and his head and back propped against the door behind Mia. His tablet was in his lap, but he was also surrounded by a dozen stuffed animals ranging from dinosaurs to bears, and a stack of books. Did kids always travel with this much stuff?

"An ice bath is just what it sounds like. They fill up a tub with water and ice cubes and then you soak in it. Supposedly it helps fight tears in muscle fibers and lessens muscle soreness. Some even say it leads to a faster recovery, which I guess I can agree with because I always feel fully recovered after about ten minutes in one of those baths."

Carter grinned at him. "That sounds fun. Do you think it would work for my foot?"

"Ah, I wish, but breaks are a different ball game altogether. Those just take time, my man."

Carter's grin faltered, and his eyes fell to his foot. "Have you ever broken anything, Mr. Brown?"

The kid didn't even know what a loaded question he had asked. Emmitt supposed he had broken Mia's heart and his own for that matter, but as for broken bones... "Just my knuckle when I was young. Before I started playing football, I thought I might like baseball. My first day at tryouts they put me at second base. The ball took a wicked bounce as it reached me, and instead of bouncing into my glove, it hit my ring finger on the other hand. Chipped my knuckle. I kept playing but by the end of the practice, I knew something was wrong because my knuckle had swelled up and was purple."

"I never heard that story," Mia said as she shot him a sideways glance.

Emmitt shrugged. "You never asked about broken bones." In fact, Mia had never asked about his past much at all. He wasn't sure if it was because she genuinely didn't care or because she had worried about him getting injured and hadn't wanted to know.

"Anyway, that's most of my time during the season anyway. Of course, game days are a little different. All the lights and TV crews make it feel surreal, and a lot of times, I'll get done with a game and not even remember what happened. It's like adrenaline kicks in and takes over. I'll watch the game on TV later and it will feel like a whole new game."

"Do you have any off time?" Mia asked.

"Not much during the season. We're on a short break right now so we can celebrate Christmas with our families early. We play on Christmas Eve this year."

She took her eyes off the road long enough to shoot him a wide-eyed gape. "You play on Christmas Eve?"

"Not every year, but this one, yeah, and the rest of this season will be a little tougher because our owner's wife died last week."

Mia shot him another expression that bordered between sympathy and a warning. He realized too late she probably didn't want him talking about death in front of Carter.

"How did she die?" Carter asked from the backseat.

"Old age," Emmitt lied. Though he prided himself on not lying, he thought God would forgive him this one.

"Oh, my dad is in Heaven too. Maybe he'll see your owner's wife."

"Maybe so, kid. Maybe so." Emmitt sat back against the seat. He'd thought the silence was bad, but having to think about what he said so as not to affect Carter was a lot harder. How did Mia seem to do it so effortlessly?

He sneaked a glance at her from the corner of his eye. Her jaw was tight and her hands clenched the steering wheel, but he'd seen her softer side, and he marveled at how easily she could shift between them. Was that something she'd always been able to do or was that a trait she'd gained with motherhood? He realized he didn't know, and the weight settled on him again. He had been so selfish. How much else had he not noticed about Mia back then?

❦ 9 ❦

"This is where you live?" Carter asked in an awed voice as they pulled into the driveway of Emmitt's expansive home.

"It is." He said it matter-of-factly and Mia sensed no bragging or pride in his voice even though the house was clearly worth bragging about. At two stories, it appeared to span half a city block and had to have over three thousand square feet.

"Whoa, and we get to stay here?"

"Well, you can hang out with me during the day while your mom works, but I have a guest house out back that you'll sleep in."

"Why do we have to sleep out back? This place must have like one hundred rooms."

Mia exchanged a quick glance with Emmitt before answering. He was clearly leaving this up to her to explain. "It just wouldn't be proper for me to stay in a house with Emmitt since we aren't married. It might give people the wrong idea."

"That's stupid," Carter said crossing his arms. "People should mind their own business. Isn't that what you always say, Mom?"

Mia shook her head. Of all the things she said, *that* he decided to listen to. "They should, Carter, but Emmitt is a pro football player and unfortunately that means he is in the public eye more than most people. It's just better this way, and I'm sure the guest house is lovely."

"I think you'll find it suitable," Emmitt said with a laugh. "Shall we head inside and I'll give you the tour?"

Mia agreed, and after helping Carter out of the car, she followed Emmitt up the walkway. Colorful cobbled stones and not concrete made up the path, creating a piece of art work that accented the beautiful shrubbery and flowers along the sides. He must have a gardener and spend a fortune on water because Texas wasn't known for its life-giving rains. Not even in San Antonio.

The expansive front door opened into a large atrium, and her eyes widened as Carter's mouth dropped and "holy cow" slipped out.

"Are you wanting the whole house redesigned?" Mia asked softly. From what she could see, it didn't need it. The house appeared elegantly designed as it was.

"Oh no, not the whole house. Just my bedroom and the family room. The rest of the house was done before I bought it, but I finished the family room after, and I never liked the way the master bedroom was done. The carpet is green, for goodness sake. Who has green carpet?"

Mia had seen several houses with green carpet when she was studying design, but it wasn't her favorite either, and it had to be done with just the right touches or it did look odd.

"Shall I give you the tour and then show you to the guest house?"

Mia and Carter nodded, but neither of them could manage much more than that. His atrium was nearly larger than their whole apartment back in Kempton.

"Okay, well over here is the kitchen."

Kitchen was an understatement. A large island sat in the middle of the room, the gold that threaded the marble gleaming under the bright lights. The double fridge took up half of one wall, and the four ovens took up the rest. There was a large closet-sized pantry and another counter that ran around the rest of the room and under an impressive window. Mia wasn't much of a cook, mainly because she didn't have time, but she thought she might enjoy cooking in a place like this.

The dining room came next, a formal affair with wainscoting and a table that could easily seat twelve. Mia wondered if there was a less formal room to eat in because she could see Carter making a mess of this one.

Emmitt led them to the living room next and Mia nearly echoed the "wow" that came out of Carter's mouth. The far wall not only held a giant big screen television but at least four different gaming devices and a shelving unit full of books, movies, and games.

"Do you know how to play all those?" Carter asked.

Emmitt smiled. "I do, and if it's okay with your mom, we'll play some while she works."

"Please Mom, can we?" Carter turned his puppy dog eyes on Mia, and she sighed. How could she deny him? With his broken foot, it wasn't like he was super mobile anyway, and the time spent here would be something he could remember forever.

"Yes, in moderation. I will not have you playing video games all day."

"Scouts honor," Emmitt said as he held up three fingers. "We'll read and play outside as well."

"Hard to play outside with a cast," Carter grumbled.

"Don't worry, I have ideas."

As Emmitt shot Carter a wink, Mia felt a chink enter her carefully constructed wall. She'd always thought Emmitt would make a wonderful father, and she was getting to see that side of him now. Even more importantly, she was seeing a genuine smile on Carter's face for the first time in a long time. She hoped this hadn't been a terrible idea. She didn't need Carter getting attached to Emmitt. He had made it clear that football meant more to him than anything else.

Finally, they reached the family room. Though built well, Mia could see the tiny clues that it had been added after, and Emmitt hadn't done much with it. The walls were a blank slate, as was the bland furniture.

"What do you want done in here?"

Emmitt shrugged. "I don't really know. I want it to be inviting, a place where people could gather to talk or play games. No TV in here though."

"That sounds lovely," Mia said, but she wondered who the people were. Teammates? A girlfriend? He hadn't mentioned one, but he was too handsome not to have one.

"Yeah, I've always loved the thought of a place where you could unplug from technology and hang out with the people you care most about." His eyes fixed on hers and Mia felt her breath catch. Yes, this had definitely been a terrible idea. Too many more days of him talking like that and looking at her like that and she just might find herself falling for him again. And that would be bad. Very, very bad. Because she was only here for her son. Here to do a job to pay for his bills and here to get him the best care she could. Right?

EMMITT ENJOYED WATCHING THE PINK TINT COLOR MIA'S FACE AND her eyes flick away from his. It meant he still affected her, and if he still affected her then maybe he could have a second chance with her. He hadn't even known he wanted one when he'd made the trip initially to Kempton, but he felt different when he was around her—happier, freer, more content. Emotions he hadn't realized he'd been missing the last few years. Until now.

Plus there was Carter. Though he'd always hoped to have his own children, Carter appeared to be a cool kid. He reminded

Emmitt a lot of himself when he was young, and he wondered what it would be like to have a family sitting up in the box watching him play instead of having no one. His parents had come to a few games, but most of Emmitt's tickets were given out to random fans, and while that was nice, it wasn't the same as having family there.

"I'll show you the bedroom later because it's upstairs, but how about I take you to the guest house now and you two can get settled?"

"That sounds great," Mia said.

Emmitt led the way back to the kitchen and opened the sliding glass door. A large patio with a pool, a grill, and several deck chairs separated the main house from the guest house.

"You have a pool?" Carter asked.

"I do, but I'm afraid swimming is out of the question until you get out of that cast, buddy."

"Aw man."

"That's your guest house?" Mia asked, her view going to the large house beyond the pool.

"Yep. It's a three bedroom, two bath house complete with its own kitchen and laundry room."

"Why do you need two houses?" Carter asked as they made their way around the pool.

"I don't usually, but the guest house came with the main house, and I guess it works out for times like these."

"Why do you need such a big house for just you?"

At that Emmitt had to pause. Why had he bought the large estate? Because he'd hoped to fill it with family one day? He'd like to say that was the reason and it was certainly the one he had used to convince himself to plunk down the money required, but if he were honest, it had probably been more for the image. All the players had nice houses and fancy cars, and Emmitt had succumbed to the trap of vanity as well.

He shook his head. Here he thought he'd become so virtuous,

reading his Bible every night and going to church and letting the guys call him Rev, but he had just traded one sin for another. "You know what, bud? I really don't, but the house is paid for, so I guess I'll stay here for a while."

Carter shrugged but said nothing more, and Emmitt opened the door to the guest house. "Luckily, this place is a single story," he said as he ushered them in, "so it should be a little easier for you to get around."

The inside of the guest house was much more modest but still decorated tastefully. The front door opened to a large open concept living room, dining room, and kitchen. To the left, a hallway led to the bedrooms and the hall bathroom.

"This is where we get to stay?" Carter asked.

"Is it okay?" Emmitt had seen the one-bedroom apartment they had been living in back in Kempton, and he'd thought the guest house would still feel like a vacation home compared to it.

"It's awesome. Can I pick my room, Mom?"

"Sure, go ahead," Mia said.

He hobbled down the hallway and then turned. "Mom, you'll get to have your own room too. You won't have to sleep on the couch anymore."

Emmitt dropped his eyes as he saw the blush rise up Mia's neck. He'd suspected she was sleeping on the couch when he'd realized their apartment was only one-bedroom, but hearing it confirmed spurred his guilt once again. Here he had this grandiose house—two of them—and she was sleeping on the couch in her living room.

"Mia, I'm…"

"Don't," she said, cutting him off and shaking her head. Her voice was heavy with emotion. "You made your choice a long time ago, and I made mine. Just because I didn't end up where I'd hoped doesn't mean I want you feeling sorry for me."

No, she never had wanted anyone feeling sorry for her. She had always been one to see the glass half full, and she had always believed she would do something great with her life. Those were just some of the things he had loved about Mia, so why had he left her? Had he been so scared she wouldn't fit in with his new life? Had he been ashamed of what the other players might think? Mia wasn't classically beautiful, especially with her face full of freckles. She was more girl next door than runway model, but she had always been beautiful to him.

Or had he really just been running from their night together? Even though they'd planned to wait until marriage, he had slipped the night of the draft pick. He'd been so excited and he'd wanted to share that excitement with her. He'd wanted to share everything with her, and it had been an amazing night. Until the reality of it crept in. Until he began to worry about the disappointment both their families would feel if they found out. Until the thought of running away to escape the shame convinced him to leave the one thing that had truly made him happy. Until the guilt had taken ahold of him, tied a noose around his neck, and told him he was no longer good enough for her.

"Why don't you go check out the master suite while I go get the luggage?" he said, changing the subject. The guilt lay heavy in the air tonight, and he could feel Satan trying to grab control of him, trying to whisper how awful he had been to leave Mia without a word, and how he deserved the single life he had chosen.

He stepped outside and let the cool air wash over him. He'd fought those feelings for so long, and he'd made peace with God, but making peace with Mia was a whole new thing. It was harder, especially with everything life had thrown at her. He touched the small gold cross that hung around his neck as a reminder and turned his face toward the sky. "Lord, help me to show her I've changed and help me help her."

Mia awoke with a start and looked around the unfamiliar room a moment before reality came crashing back in on her. She was in Emmitt's guest house. She was going to decorate two rooms in his house. Her son had cancer. Those last four words were sobering enough to wake her completely and urge her to tiptoe in to check on Carter.

He had chosen the room next to hers, and she was glad. She'd always been protective of him, but now she felt the need to watch him constantly, which was irrational. The doctor had been optimistic when he told her the tumor was in Carter's bone and would require chemo and surgery, but he felt the prognosis was good. And it wasn't like Carter had succumbed to brittle bone disease all of a sudden. He wasn't more likely to break any more bones than he would have been a year ago, but knowing that didn't stop the fear from creeping up her throat.

She pushed open his door. Just to make sure he didn't need anything, she told herself, but it was really to verify that his chest still rose and fell. That oxygen still filled his lungs. That he hadn't passed away in the night. It was morbid, she knew, but that's what the word cancer did. It left black clouds of questions and doubts and fears hanging in the air. Clouds that followed her wherever she went.

Carter lay in the large bed, his dinosaur pajama-clad arms peeking out from under the covers. She held her breath and watched, but yes, the blanket rose and fell with his rhythmic breathing. Relief flooded her. She could relax a little, long enough to take a shower at least. And maybe have some breakfast.

She had just sat down with her Bible and a cup of coffee when the soft thumps of Carter's walking cast carried down the hall.

"Hey bud, how did you sleep?" she asked when he reached the kitchen.

"Mostly good. I miss the rest of my stuffies, but they'll be here soon, right?"

A smile pulled at the corners of Mia's lips. Even with everything going on with him, all he could think about was his stuffed animals. "Yes, bud. The movers should arrive today and then all your stuff will be here."

"Cool. What's for breakfast?"

Mia nearly laughed out loud at the sudden shift in topic. Carter had always been like that. Once he got the answer to his question, there was no need to discuss it any further. He was ready to move on. "I don't know. Let me look."

She hadn't taken the time last night to peruse the kitchen offerings so she hoped that something lay in the cupboards. They could always walk over to the main house, but that might mean eating with Emmitt, and Mia wanted to avoid that as much as possible. It was hard enough to fight old feelings just being near him and in his guest house, but she knew it would get infinitely harder if she began doing routine things with him like eating meals and watching TV. No, she needed to keep those boundaries up as much as she could. To protect herself. And to protect Carter.

"Let's see. I spy some cereal. If we have milk, are you up for that?"

His face scrunched as he climbed into one of the chairs at the table. "Is there Cinnamon Toast Crunch or something chocolaty?"

"Um..." Mia perused the offerings. Raisin Bran, Cheerios, and... "I think you might be in luck. This looks like Cinnamon Toast Crunch."

"Yes, I'll take it."

Another few minutes of searching yielded a bowl, a spoon, and some fresh milk. As Mia poured Carter's cereal, she wondered if Emmitt kept this place stocked all the time or if he had called ahead and had someone do that for him. He certainly hadn't had time to stock it himself, but if he did keep it stocked, who usually stayed here? Friends? Family? Women?

She shook her head to clear that thought. There was no need to picture the parade of women that must march through Emmitt's life as a professional athlete. Was that why he had left her? Had he been ashamed of her? Or had he just wanted to be free to date whoever might throw themselves at him? Nope, she didn't need to think about that either. The past was the past, and it needed to stay there. And his present was...well, she didn't know what it was, but what happened in his life now was none of her concern.

Her stomach rumbled, reminding her that she hadn't eaten either, and after the refrigerator yielded fresh eggs and bacon, she fried some up and joined Carter at the table. It would be a long day today. She planned to draw up some designs for Emmitt's family room and bedroom, then she and Carter had a meeting with the cancer treatment team at the Methodist Children's Hospital. Her doctor in Kempton had told her to be ready for chemo treatments anywhere from a month to ten weeks before surgery and then for several treatments after surgery. Mia had no idea if the job for Emmitt would take that long, and she wondered where they would stay if she finished early.

EMMITT WOKE WITH A SMILE ON HIS FACE. HE'D ENJOYED SHOWING Mia and Carter around his place yesterday, and he was looking forward to spending the day with them. Maybe he would even take them shopping with him. Christmas was only a few days away and his place had no spirit, but for the first time in years, he wanted it to.

After a quick shower, he headed downstairs to see what Anton, his cook and personal assistant, was whipping up for breakfast. Anton was a nutritionist who specialized in athletic fitness. Emmitt had been fortunate enough to find him through one of the coach's referrals, and he'd agreed to take on the role of preparing Emmitt's food and watching the house while he was gone. Anton had quickly become a close friend as well.

The smell of bacon and eggs greeted him as he walked into the kitchen. Anton stood by the stove, a spatula in hand. "You're back early. I wasn't expecting you for a few more days."

Emmitt nodded. "Yes, I was expecting to stay there longer, but it turned out not to be necessary. Did you get the guest house stocked as I asked?" He hoped Anton had picked up the groceries he'd asked him to. It would be awful if Mia woke up to empty cupboards.

"I did. Do you want to tell me who is staying at the guest house?"

"A friend who needed a job and a place to stay close to Methodist Hospital."

Anton's brow shot up as he turned the burner off and filled a plate for Emmitt and one for himself. "Uh huh, and does this friend have a name?" He flashed Emmitt an inquisitive expression as he set the plate in front of him.

"Mia," Emmitt said.

"As in ex-girlfriend Mia?" Anton's eyes widened as he sat down across from Emmitt. He didn't always eat meals with Emmitt but he would when he had time.

"Yes, that's the one. After Diana's death, Matt decided we

should live without regrets, so he asked us all to take care of whatever we regretted. The way I left Mia when I joined the Saints is my biggest regret."

"And is she sick?"

"No, her son is. Osteosarcoma."

"Whew." Anton let out a low whistle. "That's heavy. You sure you want to get involved in that?"

Emmitt sighed. "I have to. It's my fault that she didn't become a designer. When I left without an explanation, she took time off college and never returned. I can't make up for the past, but I can help her future. So, I hired her to redo the family room and my bedroom."

Anton looked as if he wanted to say more, but before he could, the sliding glass door opened, and Mia and Carter stepped in.

"Oh, I'm sorry," Mia said when her eyes landed on Anton. "I hope we aren't interrupting anything."

"No, you're fine. Mia, this is my friend and personal assistant, Anton. Anton, this is Mia and her son, Carter." A feeling of sadness swept across Emmitt as he took in the dark circles under Mia's eyes. He had hoped offering her a job would ease some of her worry, but he should have known better. Cancer was enough to worry anyone, and he couldn't imagine it affecting a child.

Anton swallowed his bite and then stood and held out a hand. "Pleased to meet you, Mia, Carter. I also cook Emmitt's meals, so feel free to join him if you'd like."

"Oh, we're fine. It seems someone stocked the guest house for us. I assume that was you."

"Yes, ma'am," Anton said with a nod. "And if you need anything else, just leave a list on the counter here, and I'll happily pick it up for you."

"Thank you, but I'm sure whatever you bought will be fine." Mia turned her gaze to Emmitt. "When you're done, do you think you could show me the bedroom? I'd like to start working on plans this morning before Carter's appointment."

Right, Carter's appointment. He had forgotten that was today. Well, that might change Emmitt's plans, but perhaps he could drive them and then they could all go shopping after. "Of course." He shoveled the last bite of egg into his mouth and picked up the last strip of bacon. "I'm ready now," he said when he finished chewing.

Mia nodded, but her gaze slipped to Carter.

"I could get Carter set up with a video game if that's all right with you," Anton said.

"Please Mom?" Carter begged.

Mia hesitated a moment before nodding. "Sure, that would be fine. Thank you."

"Yay, what all does he have? Not that it matters. I don't have a game system, so I haven't played much anyway."

Emmitt bit back a smile as Anton led Carter from the room. Then he turned to Mia. "Shall we?"

"Yeah, sure," Mia said, though her gaze remained on the empty doorway her son had passed through.

Emmitt led the way up the stairs and down the short hallway to the master bedroom. As he pushed open the door, he scanned the area quickly. He was rather certain he had put everything away, but it never hurt to double check.

"Ah, I see what you mean," Mia said, stepping into the room. Her eyes scanned the room, and he tried to look at it from a designer's point of view. The furniture was probably fine, but he had done nothing to bring any sort of theme into the room. And it was a large open space with only his bed, nightstand, and dresser filling any of the room.

"Do you have any thoughts for how you want the room to look?"

Emmitt shook his head. Design was definitely not his thing. "Uh, inviting? I want it to be a relaxing space where I can unwind. The only thing I know for sure is no more green carpet. Maybe a beige or tan carpet?"

Mia chuckled and shook her head. "You never were much for the intricacies, were you?"

"I'm not even sure I know what the inter…intra…whatever you said are," he said with a laugh.

"Okay, well I have some ideas. You have a great space here that you could do a lot with. What if we went with neutral tones and added a chest to the foot of the bed to store blankets and things in? Then we could add a chair and a reading lamp to the window. Once it has new curtains, it would be the perfect reading spot. A few landscape pictures would bring the room to life as well. Are you okay if I change your bedding?"

Emmitt smiled as Mia rattled off everything she wanted to do. He didn't know what half of it meant, and he wasn't sure he'd ever use a reading corner, but he could see her curled up there, reading at night while he watched TV. "I'm okay with whatever you want to do. I hired you for your creative eye and mind."

"All right. Well, I'll draw up a few plans to show you and then we can discuss the budget. Sound good?"

"Sounds perfect," Emmitt said with a smile.

With a sigh, Mia shut off the alarm on her phone and set her pencil down. She hadn't gotten as much done on the designs as she wanted to, but it was time to head to the hospital for Carter's appointment.

She wandered out of the dining room, where she had been working, into the living room. Carter sat on a footstool while Emmitt sat in a chair next to him. Some racing video game was on the screen, but that wasn't what caught her eye. No, what caught her eye was the smile on Carter's face, the light emanating from his eyes that she hadn't seen in a long time, and the matching expression on Emmitt's face. He was like a big kid himself. Always had been.

She'd met him in high school when her family moved to Kempton. Her dad had thought it would be a nice sleepy town to retire in. Mia had thought it was just sleepy, but then she'd met Emmitt, star defensive player for the Kempton Kings, and he had stolen her heart. Well, first he'd stolen her notebook. Then he'd stolen her heart.

Mia had always been a sketcher, and she took her notebook with her everywhere. Emmitt had tried to get her attention, but she'd been too angry at moving to the small town to care about anything, including boys. Then one day her notebook had disappeared. When he returned it later, he had drawn a horrible picture of the two of them with the words 'Will you go out with me?' underneath. Annoyed and flattered at the same time, Mia had agreed, and they'd quickly become inseparable. They'd even attended college together, though Mia had been a year behind him, but when he got drafted everything had changed.

And she would do well to remember that. He might look different now and say the right words, but she was sure he was the same selfish person inside. The person who had spent a night with her and then left without a word. The person who had shattered her heart into a million pieces.

"Carter, buddy, we have to go."

"Aw, Mom, do we have to?"

"Yes, we have to. We have an appointment in an hour and I have no idea how bad the traffic might be." In fact, she didn't even know exactly where she was going. She would be relying on her map app to lead the way. It was usually correct, although once or twice it had led her into a neighborhood when she was looking for a restaurant or vice versa.

Emmitt looked up at her. "How about you let me drive?"

Mia shook her head. "No, that's not necessary. I'm sure I can find it."

"I'm sure you can as well, but I was hoping we could do some Christmas shopping afterwards. This place could use some seasonal cheer."

A smile stretched across Carter's face. "Yeah, Mom, can we? We haven't decorated for Christmas yet and it's only a week away. How will Santa find us if we don't decorate?"

Mia sucked in her breath and bit her lip. She didn't need to spend any more time with Emmitt, but how did she say no to Carter? The answer clearly was that she didn't. Not with everything that was happening to him. "Fine, but only if he isn't too tired afterwards."

"Yay," Carter hollered and the two high-fived. Mia shook her head. She loved seeing her son happy, but she didn't need him getting attached to Emmitt, because eventually they would be going home and he would be staying here. And he'd already broken her heart—she didn't need him breaking her son's as well.

The ride to the hospital wasn't quiet—Emmitt and Carter continued to jabber on about some video game—but Mia was absorbed in her own thoughts. This would be the first time meeting with Carter's new team and she had no idea what to expect.

"Would you like me to come in with you?"

Mia jumped at Emmitt's words and his hand on her arm. She had planned to say no—she'd lived without him the last five years and she could continue to do so—but going in alone now that they were here felt daunting. "Please." It was only one word, but it was all she could muster. Fear clawed at her throat and pressed against her windpipe.

"Of course." He turned off the car and opened the door for Mia before helping Carter out of the back seat.

As they walked into the hospital, the urge to grab his hand swept over Mia. She wanted the comfort of his touch, but she couldn't do it. Wouldn't do it. Not after the way he'd left.

"I'm Mia Conrad. We have an appointment for Carter Conrad," Mia said when they approached the check-in desk.

The woman smiled at them and then looked up their appointment. "Yes, you're all checked in. Dr. Goodwin will be with you soon."

"Is this going to hurt, Mommy?" Carter asked as they sat down. Mia's heart broke at the fear in his voice, and though she could lie to him, she wasn't going to.

"I don't know, honey, but what I do know is that this will make the pain you've been feeling in your leg stop. That's good, right?"

"Yeah, I guess." But his eyes dropped to the floor.

"Hey, after this, how about you pick out the tree from the lot?" Emmitt asked. "Any tree you want."

Carter glanced up at him. "And decorations?"

"You bet. We have to deck the place out good."

Though Carter perked up a little at that, Mia could still sense the cloud of fear hanging around him, see the weight of it pressing in on his small shoulders. When would they catch a break?

EMMITT COULDN'T IMAGINE THE ANXIETY COURSING THROUGH Mia, though he could see it on her guarded expression as she stared out the window. Carter wasn't even his kid and he was worried. The doctor had suggested ten weeks of chemotherapy before the surgery to remove the tumor and then another five weeks of chemo after. Plus, there would be the side effects of chemo to deal with— nausea, vomiting, mouth sores. None of it sounded fun to Emmitt, but he was determined to cheer them both up.

He pulled into The Christmas Store, which was a store that specialized in Christmas offerings year-round. Emmitt had no idea how they stayed in business the other ten months of the year, but he was glad they existed today.

"Let's go get a tree," he announced, forcing cheer into his voice. Perhaps if he could fake it enough, it would rub off on all of them.

The somber mood lasted until they stepped inside the building. Then Carter's eyes lit up and the corners of his mouth twitched. "Wow, I've never seen anything like this."

Even Mia appeared speechless as she gazed in wonder at the store. The front was filled with artificial trees of all kinds. Along the walls were rows and rows of ornaments, and upstairs was filled with trains and miniature villages, stockings, and cards. "This is..."

"Magical, right?" Emmitt smiled at her, remembering their last

Christmas together. He'd been so close to buying her a ring that year, but his so-called friends—the other players on his college team—had told him to wait. They had warned him that pro football was different, that he might have to move across the country, that a long-distance relationship would never last, that he didn't want to settle until he knew what was really out there. And he had listened to them. He had let their stupid words fester in his brain until they felt true, and he hadn't bought the ring. Instead he'd bought her a leather-bound sketch book—still something she enjoyed but not the gift he should have given her.

She caught his eye and smiled. It was still guarded, but he wondered if she were remembering past Christmases. Ones when it actually snowed and they chased each other around his yard and built giant snowmen. Others where it was cold but the snow refused to fall and they would sit by his fireplace and stare out the large bay window sipping hot chocolate. He hadn't had a Christmas like that since he left. Now, his Christmases were either a quick trip to Florida where his parents lived or games. He didn't even think he'd put up a tree in the last five years.

"Let's pick a tree first," Carter said, eyeing the forest before them. He might have had a cast on, but he was still quick when he wanted to be, and he took off down the right side of trees. "I want a giant one," he shouted back to them.

"Thank you for doing this," Mia said as they followed in his wake.

"You're welcome. I only wish I could do more." And then he realized he could. He turned to her and grabbed her hands before he thought about it. "Mia, the guest house is yours for as long as you need it. Even if you finish the job earlier, feel free to stay as long as you need to."

Her eyes caught his and then fell to their clasped hands. "Emmitt, I..."

"No, I'm serious. No one uses the guest house, so it's yours, and it would be cheaper than flying back and forth for treatment."

"Mom, Emmitt, come see this one," Carter called to them, and just like that, the spell was broken.

Mia pulled her hands out of his grip and headed toward Carter. "Thank you, Emmitt. We'll see."

He hated the expression on her face, the distrust she still held for him, though he couldn't blame her. Even more, he hated that he had made her that way, and he wondered if he would ever be able to redeem his actions of five years ago.

12

Mia watched Emmitt struggle with the enormous tree. She should probably offer to help, but it was much more entertaining watching him wrestle the monstrous beast Carter had picked out. It had to be nearly eight feet tall and at least three feet around. It was a good thing it was an artificial tree because Mia couldn't imagine the cleanup from all those needles had it been a real tree.

"No one help me here," Emmitt teased. "I've got this all under control."

Across the room, Carter giggled from his perch on the couch. Bags of ornaments surrounded him, and he pulled them out one by one and snipped off the tags. "It looks like the tree ate you."

"I hope not," Emmitt said as he pushed the tree into the final position and stepped back. "I don't think I'd taste very good." He plugged in the cord and the lights on the tree came to life.

"It's so pretty," Carter said. "Can we hang the ornaments now?"

"We can, but let's move them a little closer so you don't have to walk so far." Emmitt gathered the bags and placed them closer to the tree and then fished out the package of hooks. "Want to help us, Mia?"

A million reasons as to why she shouldn't flooded her mind. How many times had she done this with Emmitt and imagined their future together? Imagined the sound of Christmas music filling the air and the two of them dancing around the tree in their socks and pajamas. Imagined him lifting their son or daughter up to place the angel on top of the tree. Too many times for sure, but those were different times. Tonight was about making Carter happy, so she agreed.

There was no music playing, but Mia could almost forget about Carter's cancer as she watched him hobble to the tree and hang his ornaments. He had always loved Christmas and loved decorating their much smaller tree at home, but his favorite thing had always been opening gifts. She wondered what she would get him this year as she had no money. Would it be awful if she asked Emmitt for an advance to buy Carter a few gifts? Surely, he would understand the reason for it. She would ask him tonight once Carter was asleep.

It took them nearly an hour but finally the tree was fully decorated, and while it wasn't beautiful in the traditional sense—Carter had a tendency to place a lot of ornaments in the same spot, leaving other large patches bare—it was beautiful to her.

"Want to put the angel on top?" Emmitt asked Carter.

Carter nodded and grabbed the golden angel. "Be careful," Mia said as Emmitt bent to lift him. Though she knew from his well-defined shoulders and biceps that he was probably strong enough, fears of Carter falling and breaking another bone rushed through her mind.

"I'll be careful. I promise," Emmitt said. With ease, he scooped Carter up and held him in place until the angel was situated. Then he returned him to the ground just as softly. It was the perfect picture Mia had always imagined it would be, and it pulled at her heartstrings.

"Okay, buddy, let's get you to bed," Mia said. It wasn't that far past his bedtime, but she needed to break up this family picture before she said something she might regret later.

"Aw, Mom, do I have to?"

"Yes, you have to. I need you to get some good sleep tonight before your first treatment tomorrow."

"Okay," he said with a sigh. "Night, Mr. Emmitt."

"Night, buddy. We'll hang out again tomorrow before your appointment." He ruffled Carter's hair and the boy turned adoring eyes up at him.

Oh, dear. Mia had been hoping not to see this bond develop. Yes, she wanted a man in Carter's life, but she wanted someone he could look up to. Someone who would be around while he was growing up. And that someone was definitely not Emmitt. She should have thought this through better. She should have known that Emmitt, with his charming smile and house of toys, would have been like candy to a kid such as Carter who had none.

"I'm going to put him to bed, but then can we talk for a minute?" Mia asked Emmitt.

"Sure. I'll be in the living room. Join me whenever you're ready."

Mia nodded and escorted Carter out of the main house.

"Mr. Emmitt is awful nice, isn't he, Mom?" Carter asked as they entered his room.

Mia pursed her lips together as she thought about how to answer him. "He is, buddy, but Emmitt's job keeps him busy a lot of the time. In fact, he'll probably have a game coming up soon, so don't be surprised if he isn't around as much when that happens."

The movers had arrived earlier, but they hadn't unpacked the boxes and in all the commotion, Mia had forgotten to do it as well. She opened the boxes and began searching for a pair of jammies for Carter.

"Can we watch him play some time?" Carter asked, stifling a yawn.

"Maybe, but we're not really here to watch Emmitt. We're here for me to work and you to get better." Nope, this one was more stuffed animals. He would want those tomorrow, but she wouldn't mention them now or he would have a fit searching for every stuffed animal until he found them all.

"But can't we do both?" He sat on the bed and Mia saw the dark circles under his eyes. He needed sleep. She opened the next box. Bingo.

Thankfully, the movers had packed the clothes nicely instead of just throwing them in a box—Mia wondered how much extra Emmitt had paid for that service—and a pair of matching jammies lay right on top. "We'll see, bud," she said as she helped him out of his clothes and into the pajamas.

"I think it would be cool if Mr. Emmitt were my new dad," he said as his head hit the pillow. "Do you think you might ever marry him?"

What did she say to that? Did she tell Carter she had planned to marry Emmitt? That she had thought out their wedding down to the type of cake and the first song they would dance to? That she had imagined herself at every game of his, cheering him on? Of course she didn't. That would be too much for his four-year-old brain to handle. Heck, it was too much for her twenty-five-year-old brain sometimes.

"I think I could marry someone like him," she said instead. "If God sends the right man to me."

Carter's eyes closed and his hand curled under his pillow. Mia watched him for a moment. In this bed, he didn't look sick. He looked content and happy. If only she could keep him like this forever. His eyes popped open and focused on her. "Maybe He already has," he said sleepily and then his eyes shut again.

Mia waited for him to say more, but the rhythmic rise and fall of his chest told her he had drifted off to dreamland. Was Carter right? Was God giving her and Emmitt another chance? No, this was business and nothing more. She needed to remember that. He was her boss, not her boyfriend, and she was about to ask him for an advance.

EMMITT SAT IN THE LIVING ROOM WAITING FOR MIA TO RETURN. What did she want to talk to him about? Was it possible that she was walking down memory lane like he was? Had she felt the electricity between them earlier as he had? The soft pad of a footfall grabbed his attention, and he looked up to see her in the doorway.

Her face held a conflicted expression, and he wondered what was going on in her head. "Hey, come on in. Do you want anything to drink?"

"No, I'm good," she said, shaking her head. "This won't take long." She crossed the room to the chair across from him and sat down. She folded her hands in her lap and stared down at them a moment. "I need to ask you something."

"Sure, anything." He scooted toward the edge of the chair to lean closer to her.

"Well, I know I haven't started yet, but Christmas is less than a week away, and I really want to get Carter something. However, as you know, I have no money. Do you think I could get a small advance? Just enough to buy him a gift?"

Emmitt had not been expecting those words. Nor had he thought about the fact that Mia might not have enough money to buy presents for Carter. It was sobering to say the least. "Yes, of course, and I'd be happy to purchase a few gifts as well." He was already making a list of everything he would love to get the boy.

Mia held up her hand and shook her head. "No, that won't be necessary. Today was great, but I can't let you spoil him. It would make it even worse when we go home and he has to go back to our little house without all of this." She waved her hand around the room.

"What if you don't?" Emmitt asked.

"What if I don't what?" Her eyes locked on his, and Emmitt felt his courage wane. Was this what he wanted? He should be sure before he offered. It wouldn't be fair to do this to her again.

But he was sure. He'd been almost positive when he'd seen her for the first time back in Kempton, and today had solidified that feeling. He wanted Mia back in his life. And Carter too. He wanted a family. "What if you don't go back?"

He grabbed her hands and stood, pulling her up beside him. "What if you stay? What if we try again? I was wrong to leave last time, Mia. I was weak and confused and I let others' opinions sway my own. But, I've been on my own for the last few years, and I've hated it. Being with you these last few days has made me realize how much I want this. You. Carter. A family. What if God brought us back together so we could have a second chance?"

Something flickered in her eyes. Surprise? Confusion? Joy? He couldn't tell. "Emmitt, I…"

He needed to show her—to convince her that he'd changed. He pulled her closer and lowered his face to kiss her, but before he could, she placed a finger on his lips.

"I don't think it's a good idea, Emmitt. You're my boss right now, and I should focus on that."

Right. Boss. He had thought she was feeling something too, but she was just doing her job. He'd lost his chance with her. He dropped her hands and took a step back. "You're right, of course. I'll be happy to give you an advance of whatever you need."

"Thank you," Mia said. "I'll list what we need to purchase tomorrow so I can get started for you."

Emmitt nodded and watched her walk toward the doorway. "Mia?" She turned and looked at him. "Will you and Carter at least come to my game on Christmas Eve? I have box seats and no one to ever use them. It would mean a lot if you would watch me play."

A small smile pulled at her lips. "We'll see." And then she was gone.

Emmitt sank down into the chair and dropped his head into his hands. Right now, he hated Matt for pushing them to do this 'no regrets' pact. True, he had apologized for his regret, but now he was seeing what he could have had—what he threw away—and realizing that he would never get that. At least not with Mia. And Emmitt thought that realization might be worse than any regret he might have had. Because this regret would never change.

13

A sigh escaped Mia's lips as she stared at the list she had created. She needed to unpack their things, purchase the supplies she would need to do the rooms for Emmitt, and take Carter to his appointment that afternoon. It felt like more than she could do in a week, much less a day.

"Can I have cereal again, Mom?"

Mia smiled at Carter, who had hobbled into the kitchen and stood staring at her in his too small train pajamas. Clothes. She needed to buy him clothes as well. "Of course, bud." She took a bowl down from the cupboard and filled it with cereal. "Do you think you could unpack some of your boxes today while I'm working?" she asked as she grabbed the milk from the fridge and filled the bowl.

"By myself?" Carter asked.

"Yes, by yourself. I need to get some work done for Emmitt today, and I won't have time."

"Maybe Mr. Emmitt would help me unpack," Carter said excitedly. "Then we could get done quicker and play games."

"I don't think Mr. Emmitt has time to do that. He has a game he needs to start preparing for." She set the bowl down in front of him and then filled her mug with coffee before sitting down.

"We could at least ask," Carter grumbled as he shoved the spoon into the bowl.

Mia opened her mouth to respond, but before she could, a knock sounded at the door. Emmitt? It had to be as she knew no one else here.

She opened the door to find not only Emmitt but Anton and a pretty brunette.

"Oh, good, I was hoping we wouldn't wake you," Emmitt said. "Can we come in?"

"Um, sure." Mia held the door open and stepped back. What were they doing here and who was the woman? She was glad she had gotten dressed before making her coffee this morning.

"Mr. Emmitt, do you want to help me unpack this morning?" Carter asked.

"Carter," Mia began, but Emmitt cut her off.

"That would be great. How about Mr. Anton and I help you guys get settled here and Kris here can help your mom with decorating?"

"Hi, I'm Kris with a K. It's short for Kristina," the woman said, stepping forward and holding out her hand. "Also known as Anton's better half."

"Hah, you wish, woman," Anton said with an affectionate smile. It was clear these two were dating.

"Um, nice to meet you," Mia said, returning the shake. "I appreciate the offer, Emmitt, but I should probably unpack myself."

"Nonsense, Mia. You have a lot on your plate already. Let us help you. It's what friends are for."

Mia barely knew Anton and she had just met Kris, but she couldn't deny the help would ease her over-full schedule. "Okay," she agreed with a sigh, "but you can leave the boxes in my room alone. I'll take care of those."

"Deal," Emmitt said.

"And I'd love to offer my help with whatever you need. I'm not a designer, but I've watched a lot of shows on TV and would love to see the action in person," Kris said. "Plus, I know my way around the city if we need to purchase anything."

"We definitely do," Mia said with a small smile before turning her eyes to Emmitt and Anton. "Okay, if you're sure."

"We're sure. We'll have this place all unpacked and set up for you guys before Carter's appointment today."

Mia still wasn't sure this was the best idea. Having Carter spend more time with Emmitt without her would probably just deepen his desire to have the man as a father, but it did appear to be the best option for her to get everything done.

"All right," she said with a sigh and walked back to the table to grab her list. "Kris, do you want to come with me and we'll see what we still need to purchase?"

"You bet. Whatever you need."

Mia turned to Carter. "You be on your best behavior for Mr. Emmitt and Mr. Anton, do you hear?"

"Aw, Mom, I'm not a little kid," he mumbled as pink spread out along his cheeks. But that's exactly what he was. A little kid. Her kid. Hers and Emmitt's.

She glanced up at Emmitt, wondering if he had figured it out yet. Had he processed the timeline? She'd been careful to be vague, and strangely, Carter didn't look much like Emmitt. Not yet anyway, but she could see more of his features appearing in the boy's face every day. His eyes were beginning to take on the same shape as Emmitt's, and a dimple had appeared in his cheek a few months ago. A dimple that looked very much like the one Mia used to tease Emmitt about even though she had always loved it.

She would have to tell Emmitt—but not yet. Not until she was sure. Sure that he wouldn't disappear again and leave them in a lurch like he had last time. True, he hadn't known about the baby and perhaps he would have come back for her if he had, but Mia hadn't wanted that kind of relationship. She wanted to know he *wanted* to be with her, not that he was with her because he felt he had to be. She wanted love and not just a sense of duty.

She shook her head to clear the thoughts. There was no time to think about that now. "Just remember your manners," she said to Carter and then led the way out of the guesthouse.

EMMITT WATCHED MIA EXIT WITH KRIS BEFORE TURNING TO Anton. "You sure it was a good idea to get Kris involved?" He didn't know Kris well, as Anton usually didn't bring her over, but she'd seemed pleasant enough the few times he had met her. Still, he didn't want to overwhelm Mia.

"She wanted to, man. She loves to help. Besides, you want Mia to stay, right?"

Emmitt nodded. More than anything he wanted Mia and Carter to stay.

"Then she needs a friend here. If there's one thing I've learned about women, it's that they need someone to vent to. Kris is great at listening."

"Are we staying?" Carter asked. "Like forever?"

Anton blanched as Emmitt turned to Carter. He hadn't thought the boy had been listening. "Would you like that?"

The smile that lit up Carter's face stretched from ear to ear. "I'd love that," he shouted. "I told Momma last night that you should be my new dad."

Emmitt blinked, shocked at the kid's honesty. "Oh, and what did your mom say to that?"

"She said she'd marry someone like you. If God sent her the right man, but I think He already has."

Anton chuckled and slapped Emmitt on the shoulder. "I'd forgotten how kids have no filter, but I can't argue with him. Now we just have to convince her."

Yes, but Emmitt knew that would be the hard part. Mia had always been stubborn, and he'd given her good cause to distrust him. He'd thought they'd been reforging a connection yesterday but then she had pulled away again. What would it take to convince her that he'd changed for good?

✻ 14 ✻

"So, how long have you and Anton been together?" Mia asked as they drove back to Emmitt's house. She had wanted to paint before they did anything else, so after moving the furniture to the middle of the room, they had driven to a local hardware store to pick up paint and supplies.

"Almost a year," Kris said as she pulled into the driveway. "He was the instructor in a nutrition class I took. It was love at first sight. For me at least."

"And for him?"

Kris shrugged as she placed the car in park. "I think it took him a little longer. He thought he wanted to play the field and keep his options open."

"What changed his mind?" Mia asked.

Kris turned off the engine and faced Mia. "Emmitt did, actually. Evidently, he told Anton about how he'd lost the woman he loved when he'd listened to his teammates' advice to remain single. I can only assume he was talking about you."

"What do you mean?" Mia asked.

"Girl, are you crazy? I may not know you, but every girl in the world wishes they had a man who looked at them the way Emmitt looks at you. That man is clearly still in love with you."

"That man left me after he got drafted without a word. No goodbye, no closure, nothing. That's not how a man who loves a woman acts."

"Agreed," Kris said with a nod, "but it might be how a man who was influenced by friends might act."

Mia had never thought about the powerful influence of friends. She'd never been on a team, but she'd known enough people who had and they had often spoken about the family feel of being on a team. "But why wouldn't he reach out when he realized he was wrong?"

"Fear," Kris said. "Maybe he didn't know what to say. Maybe he felt guilty about the way he left. All I know is that I can guarantee you that Emmitt isn't that man anymore."

Mia wished she could be as certain as Kris, but she wasn't sure her heart could take rejection again. "Maybe you're right, but I'm not the same woman anymore either. Anyway, let's take the stuff inside. Perhaps we'll have a little time to paint before I have to take Carter to the hospital."

Kris said nothing more as she helped Mia unload the supplies and carry them in, but Mia could see the unspoken words on her face.

"Okay, bud, not a word to Mom about our plan. Do you think you can do that?" Emmitt asked as they finished unpacking the last box.

"Momma said it isn't good to keep secrets from her," Carter said, squeezing his dinosaur.

"He's got you there," Anton said with a laugh. He broke down the box and folded it flat.

Emmitt shot his friend a look before turning to Carter. "Your mom is right. You shouldn't keep secrets from her, but secrets are things you never tell. This is merely a surprise. We will tell her, but not until Christmas. Do you think you can keep from telling her until then?"

Carter puffed out his little chest. "Of course I can. I'm good at surprises."

"All right then. It's about time to head out for your appointment, so why don't we go grab your mom and if you feel up to it, we can get ice cream on the way home."

"Yes, ice cream. Will you come with us, Mr. Anton?"

"No, I've got some other things to do," Anton said as he picked up the stack of flattened boxes, "but I'll come see you tomorrow, and I'll be at the game Christmas Eve, okay, bud?"

"Sounds good," Carter said. "Maybe we can play more video games?"

"You bet." Anton turned to Emmitt. "I'm going to grab Kris too, but we'll both be by tomorrow before you head to practice. Let me know if you need anything else."

"Thank you," Emmitt said, "for everything."

Anton smiled and waved as he exited, and Emmitt turned to Carter. "Let's go get your mom."

They found Mia in the family room sealing up a can of paint. Tan splotches that matched the one painted wall dotted her hands and cheek. "Oh good, I was just about to come get you. Just let me wash up and we'll head out."

She dashed out of the room and Emmitt heard the sound of running water from the kitchen.

"Okay, I'm ready," she said when she reemerged.

Emmitt smiled and stepped closer to her. "Well, almost ready."

"What do you mean?" she asked. "Did I forget something?"

"You did. A little paint right here." Before she could move away, Emmitt reached up and brushed at the paint on her cheek. It didn't come off though, having dried to her cheek. "Well, that didn't go as I planned," he said with a chuckle.

Her eyes held his gaze, and he wanted to lean down and place his lips against hers, but Carter was watching. Mia broke contact and stepped back. "I'll be right back."

This time when she returned, the smear was gone, replaced with a red mark from scrubbing. "Okay, let's go."

Forty-five minutes later, they were following the doctor down the hall to the chemotherapy treatment room. Emmitt could sense the tension in Mia's shoulders, and he grabbed her hand. She glanced down at it and then back at him, but she didn't pull away.

"All right, big guy," Dr. Goodwin said when they reached the room. "Why don't you pick a chair and we'll get you all set up?"

Emmitt glanced around the room. It appeared to be divided by age with half of the room decorated with animals on the walls for the younger kids and the other half with superheroes for the older kids. There were recliners set about the room covered in colorful blankets and each one held a stuffed animal.

Carter hobbled over to a recliner that held a stuffed T-Rex. "I'll take this one."

"Good choice. Now, this is going to sting a little while we get your port in, but we have headphones with music you can listen to if you want."

"Okay, but can Momma hold my hand?"

Dr. Goodwin smiled and helped Carter into the chair. "You bet, and your parents can stay with you the whole time."

As Mia didn't correct Dr. Goodwin, Emmitt didn't either. Instead, he squeezed her hand and offered a supportive smile.

"Okay, big guy, we just need to verify some information before we begin. Can you tell me your name?" Dr. Goodwin asked as Mia sat down beside Carter and grabbed his hand.

Carter giggled. "It's Carter Conrad."

"And how old are you?"

"I'm four." He held up his hand with his thumb folded down across his palm.

Dr. Goodwin smiled. "Okay, one more question. Do you know your birthday?"

"Yep, it's February eighth," he said proudly.

"Very good," she said.

Emmitt watched helplessly as a nurse joined Dr. Goodwin, and, after giving Carter a shot of anesthesia, they made an incision in his upper chest and inserted the port. The boy only grimaced once or twice, but Mia squeezed Emmitt's hand harder with each step. He was glad to be her support, but the whole procedure made his stomach turn. Emmitt didn't know how Mia could watch at all.

Once the port was in, the treatment began and Dr. Goodwin pulled over an additional chair for Emmitt. He sat there the entire hour watching Mia watch her son. What must that kind of love feel like? He knew he loved Mia, but loving her was different than loving a child. With every grimace on Carter's face, Mia would bite her lip and squeeze her eyes shut. Emmitt knew she must be holding back tears, and he wished he could do more for her.

Mia's heart broke as she put Carter to bed that evening. Dr. Goodwin had told her he might be tired, but he never went to sleep before nine. Here it was barely eight o'clock and he was already sound asleep in his bed.

Mia supposed she should be glad. At least asleep he felt no pain, and it allowed his body to heal. He hadn't talked about the procedure much on the way home, but she'd felt the pain with every grimace of his face. And even though she didn't want to lead him on, Mia had been grateful for Emmitt's presence. He'd said nothing the entire hour. Simply held her hand and watched in stoic silence. She was glad he didn't know Carter was his son right now because the pain of watching your child go through chemotherapy was excruciating, and while she knew she needed to tell him, she didn't want to ruin his last two games. No, it could wait until the season was over.

Satisfied that Carter probably wouldn't wake up again tonight, Mia left his room and wandered over to the main house. She wasn't even sure why. She had already thanked Emmitt at dinner, but the need to not be alone weighed heavy on her.

"Everything okay?" he asked when she found him in the living room. An open Bible filled his lap and reminded her that she hadn't spent nearly as much time in the Word as she should have recently.

"Yeah, I just didn't feel like being alone. Carter is asleep, and the silence was getting to me."

He patted the open couch next to him. "Want to join me in my devotional? Ironically, I'm in the book of Luke, chapter twelve."

"Why is that ironic?" she asked as she sat next to him. Her scripture memorization was obviously a little rusty.

He smiled at her. "Because it's all about trusting the Lord with our fear."

"Then I think I could definitely stand to hear it. Please read."

As Emmitt read the chapter aloud, Mia thought back to when they had dated. Though both had claimed to be Christians at the time, she couldn't remember a time they had read the Bible together. She wondered if their relationship might have been stronger if they had. She certainly felt stronger after listening to his deep voice read.

"Why did we never do this when we were dating?" she asked when he finished the chapter.

He sighed and closed the Bible before turning to her. "Because I wasn't the man of God I should have been. I told you before that I thought I was a believer, and maybe I was, but I wasn't strong in my faith. I let the world influence my decisions too much— including the night with you. Had I been stronger, had we been doing this then, I would have made sure we waited until we were married.

"We would have done it right. I don't know about you, but while I will never say I didn't enjoy that night, I certainly didn't enjoy the guilt that consumed me after. It was what kept me away. I knew I had taken something from you that didn't belong to me, and I didn't know how to apologize. So I turned to God, and I grew in my faith. I didn't want to see you again until I was sure I could be the man you needed."

She should tell him. Right now. He had opened the door, and she should do the same. Apologize for not telling him about Carter, but she couldn't. Instead, she did the only thing she could think to do. She wound her arms around his neck and kissed him.

His body tensed momentarily, probably in surprise, and then he was kissing her back. Mia felt everything in that kiss—his hurt, his sorrow, his need for forgiveness—and she gave back what she could. She had no idea where this would leave them, but she knew that at this moment nothing felt more right than being in his arms.

"Come to my game Christmas Eve," he whispered into her ear as the kiss ended. "I want you there with me. You and Carter both."

As he pushed her hair behind her ears and stared into her eyes, Mia knew that was what she wanted too. She wanted to be there to support him. She wanted to be his family. "If Carter feels up to it, then I promise we'll go."

February eighth. Emmitt sat up in bed with wide eyes. *Could it be?* He tried to think back to high school health class. A pregnancy lasted nine months, right? *No, it was longer, but how much longer?* He needed his phone. His memory wasn't that good, and it was too early in the morning. He grabbed the phone from the nightstand and pressed the button to turn it on. Google would know. Clicking quickly to the app, he typed in *how long is a pregnancy?*

Forty weeks? So that was almost ten months. February was the second month so ten months back from that would be... He counted backward in his head. *April?*

April. The same month as the draft. The same month he and Mia had their one and only night together which meant that either she was with another man right before or right after Emmitt... Carter was his son.

His son. Why hadn't she told him? Well, he knew the answer to that. He'd left without a word and never called her again. She probably thought he wouldn't care, but he did. The question now was did he tell her he knew? No, she must not want him to know yet. She probably wanted to be sure he would stick around this time, and he couldn't blame her. He could wait for her to tell him, but he had no idea if he'd be able to keep the smile off his face. He had a son.

"Well, you look like you had a nice break, Rev," Tucker Jackson said as Emmitt entered the locker room a few hours later.

"It didn't start out that way, but it is looking better." Emmitt smiled as he took off his tennis shoes and pulled out his cleats. "Has your break gotten any better?"

Tucker shrugged and tugged on his shoulder pads. "I'm still not excited about the trade, but at least I get to stay in Texas and I get to finish the season with the Saints. I'm trying to stay optimistic."

"That's good. Optimism is undervalued. Sometimes looking for the bright things in life will bring them to you." Emmitt pulled out his pads from the locker and donned them.

"Oh yeah? What got brought to you? Because you seem happier than normal. Not that you aren't normally happy, but you know what I mean."

Emmitt chuckled as he shrugged into his jersey. "I do know what you mean. God gave me a second chance with a woman I loved. I was young and stupid when I left her, and I've regretted it since. However, Matt made us promise to take care of our regrets over the break and those words gave me the courage to find her again. Now she's here and coming to the game tomorrow night." He didn't tell Tucker about his son though the words danced on the tip of his tongue. He wanted to shout the good news from the rooftop, but not until Mia confirmed it. Though he was ninety-nine percent positive, there was always the slim chance he was wrong.

"That's good, man. No regrets. Maybe I'll have to think about that. Anyway, see you out there."

"Yes, see you out there." Emmitt gave his body a final once over to make sure he was geared up and in regulations. Then he sat down on the bench to pray. It was something he did before every practice and every game. Though injuries were rare, when they did happen, they were usually series-ending and sometimes worse. So, he always prayed for safety for everyone on the team, and now, knowing he had a son, his safety was more important than ever before.

When he finished his prayer, he headed out onto the field for practice. There was a special peace that filled him when he was out on the field. Maybe it was the bigness of the stadium. Maybe it was the lights. Maybe it was the camaraderie with his teammates. Whatever it was, he enjoyed the time.

MIA SMILED AT KRIS AS THEY FINISHED PAINTING THE FAMILY room. Kris and Anton had arrived before Emmitt left for practice, and because Carter was still sleeping, Anton had offered to stay with him while Mia got to work.

"It's looking really good," Mia said as she surveyed the walls. So far, all they had done was paint, but the room already looked better, more complete. "I'd like to purchase some pillows and wall art. Do you think Anton will be okay with Carter for a little longer?"

"He will be fine," Kris said with a laugh. "This is like his dream—getting to play video games with a kid all day. I never play video games with him, but maybe I should."

"Do you think marriage is in your future?" Mia asked.

"I hope so. Seeing your son just makes me want kids even more." Kris pulled on her jacket and grabbed her keys.

Mia grabbed her jacket and purse from the table and followed Kris to the car. "Kids are amazing. Trying sometimes but amazing nonetheless. Even with everything going on, I wouldn't trade him for the world. Speaking of which, can we stop by a toy store as well? I'd like to pick up a few gifts for him."

"Of course," Kris said. "I bet Christmas is even more fun with kids."

Mia didn't tell her that the fun depended on your financial situation. Not that she needed to be wealthy, but it broke her heart when she couldn't even afford new clothes for Carter for Christmas, much less a toy that he might like. This year though, she was determined to get him something special with the advance Emmitt had given her. It would make it that much harder to pay the medical bills, but it would be worth it to see a smile on his face.

Carter was awake and playing games with Anton when Mia and Kris returned a few hours later.

"How are you feeling, buddy?" Mia asked as she set down her bags to give him a hug.

"Much better, Momma. I slept a lot, huh?" Though his voice was chipper, dark circles still ringed his eyes.

"You did, but Dr. Goodwin warned us you might. Did you get some food?" He had barely eaten anything after the treatment yesterday, and she worried he would get too skinny if he didn't eat more.

"Yeah, Anton made me the best mac n cheese before we started playing. You should have him teach you how."

Mia chuckled as she ruffled his hair. "I'll get right on that, dude. After I finish wrapping your Christmas gift. Unless you'd rather me spend the time learning how to make mac n cheese."

Carter's eyes lit up. "Is Christmas tomorrow?"

"No, tomorrow is Christmas Eve, but if you feel up to it, Mr. Emmitt has invited us to his game tomorrow night, and then we can open presents the next day."

"Yeah, I want to watch Mr. Emmitt play." He turned to Anton. "Will you be there too?"

Anton looked back to Kris, who nodded. "Yeah, buddy. Kris and I will be there too."

"All right, it's settled then," Mia said with a laugh. It felt good to laugh and see her son smile.

Mia's jaw dropped as Emmitt led them into the luxury box. She'd always thought it was just seats behind a pane of glass in the middle of the field, but she'd been so wrong. There were chairs that sat near the glass, but there was also a wall of big screen TVs, couches and other plush chairs, a fully stocked bar, and a private bathroom.

"Wow, I understand the name now," Mia said as her eyes scanned the room.

"I'm glad you were able to come," Emmitt said, squeezing her hand. "I've often thought about having you watch the game from up here."

Mia flashed a teasing smile his direction. "Oh, you have, have you?"

"We get to watch the game from here?" Carter asked, interrupting the moment.

"You do, bud. I have to get down to the field to warm up soon, but Anton and Kris should be here shortly. Plus, there's a catering crew that works the game. You just let them know if you need anything."

Carter's eyes grew wide. "Anything?"

Emmitt chuckled. "Well, anything food or drink wise. They aren't Santa Claus, but he'll be coming tonight." He flashed a wink at Carter before turning to Mia again.

She could see that he wanted to kiss her, but she hadn't told Carter about them yet. Mia was fairly certain he wouldn't mind, but it was still something she wanted to discuss with him before he saw them kiss. So, she pulled him in for a hug instead and whispered in his ear, "I'll have a kiss for you after you win."

"You better," he returned, tickling her ear with his breath. "I'll see you guys after the game."

And then he was gone, and Mia and Carter were alone, but not for long. Soon, other people started filling the room. Mia felt completely out of her element as women dressed much nicer than her entered the room. She had worn her best skirt and shirt ensemble, but some of these women appeared more ready for a theater performance than a football game. Some appeared to know each other, but others shared her nervous expression. She wondered if they were other players' girlfriends or wives. Perhaps one day, she would get to know them, but for now she hoped Kris arrived soon so that she would at least have a friend to talk to.

"Mom, let's sit up here by the glass so we can see Mr. Emmitt," Carter called as he hobbled toward the chairs closest to the glass. He climbed up in one chair and Mia took the one next to him. Kris and Anton slid in next to her just before the game began.

"Sorry, we hit traffic," Kris whispered. "Did we miss the kickoff?"

Mia shook her head. She didn't think so, but she hadn't really watched football since Emmitt left.

"Which one is Mr. Emmitt?" Carter asked, squirming in his chair.

"He's number seventy-eight," Anton answered, "but I don't see him yet. Oh, wait, there he is."

Mia followed Anton's finger and after a moment, she was able to pick out number seventy-eight. She smiled with pride as she watched him tackle an opposing player. He really did look powerful and at home out on the field.

The game progressed quickly after that, and by halftime, the Saints were ahead but not by much, and anxiety coursed through Mia. Emmitt had told her they needed to win this game in order to make it to the championship game.

"I'm going to get something from the caterers. Can you stay here with Kris and Anton?" she asked Carter.

"Sure, this is fun." He had barely looked away from the field the whole first half. Mia had the sneaking suspicion that if he recovered from the osteosarcoma that she would have a football player on her hands in the next few years.

She made her way over to the bar and snagged one of the menus. As she scanned the offerings, the conversation from two women a few feet away carried over to her.

"They're playing much better," one woman said.

"They sure are. I bet it's because of their pact."

"Pact? What pact?"

"Andrew said the defensive linemen made a 'no-regrets' pact before the break. They were all to go make amends for their biggest regret. Maybe it cleared their heads and helped them to focus."

Mia looked over at the two women. One was blonde, the other brunette. They didn't appear upset by this so-called pact, but anger coursed through her. Was that the only reason Emmitt had come to Kempton? Was it not to apologize and seek forgiveness but to clear his head so he could play better? Was she simply a box to check off so they could win this game?

"Did you need something?" one of the caterers asked as he approached her.

"No, I don't think I'm hungry any longer," Mia said. She returned the menu to the counter and walked back to the chairs, but she suddenly had no desire to watch the rest of the game.

"What's wrong?" Kris asked, as if sensing her mood.

Mia shook her head. She couldn't believe she had fallen for Emmitt's act again, but she didn't trust herself to speak. At least, not yet.

EMMITT COULDN'T CONTAIN HIS SMILE AS HE HEADED UP TO THE box to get Mia and Carter. Having them there had spurred him to play his best game ever, and he couldn't wait to hear what they thought.

"You did it, Mr. Emmitt," Carter said as soon as he saw him. "I watched the whole game."

Emmitt held his hand up for a high five from the boy—his son. Now that he knew, he could see his features in Carter's face—his eyes for sure. He wondered how he didn't see them at first. "You did? That's awesome. I think I played better because you were watching."

"Hmph," Mia said as Carter smacked his hand.

Emmitt turned to her, prepared to flash a smile, but it died on his face. Mia's expression was grim, and he wondered what had happened. Had someone been rude to her? He didn't know all the people who used the luxury box, but he thought most of them were nice.

"Is everything okay?" he asked her and reached for her hand.

"Fine. Let's just go home." Her words were short and she moved her hand out of his reach. Something had definitely happened, but the question was what?

"Okay, let me just say goodbye to Anton and Kris." He looked around for them but neither were in sight. Had something happened between them then?

"They've already gone. Said they had something they had to do tonight."

Right. It was eight o'clock on Christmas Eve. They had probably had plans with his parents. Emmitt was pretty sure Anton's folks celebrated Christmas Eve instead of Christmas Day. "All right then. I'm ready."

Mia nodded and walked past him. The ice she left in her wake chilled him to the bone. Trying not to worry, he took Carter's hand and helped him hobble back out to the car. Though Carter prattled on most of the ride home, the mood in the front remained tense. Emmitt knew he would have to get Mia alone to pry the answer out of her. And he would need to do it soon or the gift he had bought to give her tomorrow would have zero meaning.

"Can I help you put Carter to bed?" Emmitt asked when they arrived back at the guesthouse.

"I think we'll be fine," she said, stepping out of the vehicle before he could open the door for her.

"I want Mr. Emmitt to read to me tonight," Carter said from the back seat.

"Fine. I'll get you ready and he can read to you."

Emmitt felt like a third wheel as he watched Mia get Carter ready for bed. It was clear she wanted nothing to do with him, but he had no idea why. When Carter was in his pajamas, Mia kissed him and then sailed out of the room without even a side glance at Emmitt.

"Okay, buddy, what do you want to read?" Emmitt asked as he looked around at the few books. He would have to get Carter more books. He wanted his son to be the reader he never was.

"The Cat in the Hat," Carter said with a yawn.

Emmitt opened the book and began reading the famous story. Before he was halfway through, Carter's eyes were closed and his chest rose and fell. Though Emmitt could have watched him sleep all night, he knew he had to find out what was bothering Mia first. He laid the book on the floor and then walked softly out of the room.

"Do you want to tell me what's going on?" Emmitt asked as he approached Mia.

Anger flashed in her eyes as she folded her arms across her chest. "Were you going to tell me about the pact?"

"Pact?" For a moment he was confused.

"Yeah, the pact. The 'no regrets pact' you guys made so you could clear your heads and win your last two games?" She made angry air quotes with her fingers as she said the words "no regrets."

"That wasn't what it was about," Emmitt said.

"Oh really? Why don't you tell me what it was about then?" She leaned against the counter and fixed him with an icy stare.

"It was about Diana. When she died, it affected all of us—perhaps Matt the most. Diana had always lived life to the fullest, so Matt wanted to do something in honor of her. He decided he would go home and fix the biggest regret of his past, and he challenged us to do the same."

"So I was a challenge? I can't believe I fell for you again."

Emmitt let out a frustrated breath. She had this all wrong, but he was afraid he wasn't explaining it well at all. "You weren't the challenge. The challenge was simply the push I needed to make the trip. I'd wanted to apologize to you for years, but I had no idea how."

"So what you're saying is that if it hadn't been for the pact, you still wouldn't have had the courage to apologize to me."

"I don't..." Emmitt fumbled over his words. He didn't under-stand why she was so angry. "Why does it matter what brought us back together?"

"It matters because I needed it to be me. I needed to know you were with me because you wanted to be and not because the guys convinced you to apologize to me."

"Is that why you didn't tell me Carter was my son?" The words came out before Emmitt could stop them. He had said he would wait for her to tell him, but it was too late now. "Because you wanted to make sure I was with you for you and not because I felt cornered?"

Her eyes widened. "When did you…?"

"Yesterday morning. When the doctor asked him his birthdate at the hospital, it stuck with me, but I couldn't figure out why. Then yesterday I woke up with this crazy idea that a February birthday might make conception really close to April. I googled it to be sure and figured he was either my child or you were with Marcus right after we were together. I couldn't fathom that possibility, and the more I looked at Carter, the more I realized. He has my eyes and my dimple."

Suddenly the fire left Mia and she sagged against the counter. "I'm sorry. I should have told you sooner. It all happened so quickly. You left without a word and then I found out I was pregnant. I met Marcus shortly after that, and though he knew I still loved you and was pregnant with your child, he offered to marry me and raise Carter as his own. I couldn't say no."

Emmitt crossed the space between them and pulled her into his arms. "Mia, you did what you thought was right. I don't blame you. We both made mistakes back then, but we don't have to keep making them now." He pushed a strand of hair behind her ear and cupped her chin so her eyes were locked on his. "Should I have come to apologize sooner? Yes, but I'm glad the pact spurred me to find you. Should you have told me five years ago you were pregnant? Yes, but I understand why you didn't."

"You're not angry?" she asked in a small voice.

"I am a little angry but not at you. I'm angry at myself. Angry that I left the way I did and that I didn't reach out to you sooner, but even more than that, I'm sad. Sad that I missed the first four years of Carter's life. I don't want to miss any more. I don't want to spend one more day without the two of you in my life. Please, tell me you can forgive me."

Tears spilled down Mia's face and she nodded. That was all the confirmation Emmitt needed. He pulled Mia to him and placed his lips on hers. That kiss said more than words ever could anyway. It asked forgiveness, it accepted apologies, and it healed the last five years.

When they pulled back, he looked down at her. "What do you say we wrap some presents for our son?" he asked as he wiped the wet sheen from Mia's cheek. She smiled and nodded, and Emmitt knew this would be his best Christmas ever.

17

Christmas morning dawned early for Mia, but she didn't mind. For the first time in months, she was actually looking forward to Christmas. She and Emmitt had wrapped the gifts for Carter the night before and though it was more than he usually received, Mia was thankful Emmitt hadn't gone crazy. She didn't want Carter equating money with gifts.

"Momma, let's go open presents," Carter said again from the side of her bed. This time he added an arm shake.

"Okay, buddy, just give me a second to get my eyes open." She yawned and blinked a few times, but finally she was able to keep her eyes on him.

"Let's go, Momma."

With a laugh, Mia pushed back the cover and stepped out of bed. She hoped her hair wasn't too much of a mess because she didn't think Carter was going to give her time to brush it or her teeth for that matter. Grabbing her robe as they left her room, she shrugged into it as they walked down the hallway.

The crisp morning air greeted them as they opened the front door, but thankfully, there was no snow on the ground. Not that it snowed often on Christmas Day in Texas, but it had happened in the past.

"Look, Momma, smoke," Carter said as he blew out a cloud.

"Yep, that means it's cold. Let's get inside before you freeze."

Mia hoped the sliding glass door would be open. She had forgotten to warn Emmitt how early kids got up on Christmas, but the door slid open.

"Emmitt might not be up yet, bud," she warned Carter as they walked toward the living room.

"Does that mean we'll have to wait to open presents?" he asked.

"It does, but I'll bet you'll have a stocking to check out." In fact, they had filled the stocking with books, small toys, and candy. Hopefully it would entertain him until Emmitt woke.

However, as they entered the living room, Mia stopped in surprise. Emmitt was not only awake but appeared to be waiting for them. A Santa hat sat atop his head and he wore a red and white sweatshirt over red sweats. "Merry Christmas you two."

"Merry Christmas, Mr. Emmitt," Carter said as he hobbled forward to hug Emmitt. Mia flashed a smile at Emmitt. They had agreed to wait until Carter was a little older to tell him that Emmitt was his birth father, but she knew it must be hard on him all the same.

"Merry Christmas, bud. You ready to open some presents?"

"Yeah!" Carter hollered and pumped his fist in the air.

"Good. Why don't you and your mom sit on the couch, and I'll bring the presents to you?"

Carter nodded and crawled up on the couch. Mia sat beside him and flashed another warm grin at Emmitt. He had really gone all out this morning. He brought over the first gift and Mia enjoyed watching Carter tear into the stack of books.

"Will you read these to me later, Mr. Emmitt?" he asked.

Emmitt laughed—a deep, rich laugh as Mia poked Carter in the shoulder. "And what am I? Chopped liver?"

"You can read too, Mom."

His next present was a stack of the newest kid-friendly movies. "To add to our collection," Mia said.

"Thank you, Mom."

Then came the clothes. Having always been tight on money, Mia was a big proponent of the four gifts for Christmas—something they want, something they need, something to wear, something to read. True, movies weren't something he needed, but it had been such a hard year that she had relented and allowed two wants. Besides, the one thing he needed—a cancer-free bill of health—she couldn't supply him anyway.

Finally, came his final present—a new game for him to play. His eyes lit up as he pulled back the paper. "Wow, thank you Mom, but I don't have a gaming system. What happens when we have to go home?"

"Actually, can you hold that question for just a second, buddy?" Emmitt asked. He returned to the tree and grabbed a small box from underneath it. Then he returned and held it out to Mia.

"For me?" She hadn't had the money to get Emmitt anything, and she certainly hadn't expected anything in return.

He nodded. "Open it."

Mia tore off the wrapping paper and sucked in her breath when the black velvet was revealed. Her eyes shot to Emmitt's, but he said nothing—merely smiled and urged her to continue. With trembling fingers, she pulled back the lid and her hand flew to her mouth.

Emmitt dropped to his knees and took the box from her. He held the ring out to her. "Mia, I am so glad you came back into my life, and I can't imagine continuing without you and Carter. Will you marry me?"

"Momma, say yes. Then my Christmas will be perfect," Carter said, tugging on her arm.

Mia smiled as a chuckle escaped her lips. "Yes. I will marry you."

EMMITT COULDN'T STOP SMILING AS HE PLACED THE RING ON Mia's finger. He had never imagined when Matt asked them to deal with their old regrets that he would not only reunite with Mia but find out he was a father as well.

"I know it's Christmas, but I'd love to get married before the championship game. I want to introduce you to everyone as my wife, so if you are amenable, Anton could marry us in the next few days, and we could have a traditional wedding later when we have more time to plan."

Mia blinked at him, obviously in shock. "You want to get married in the next few days?"

He took both of her hands in his. "I do. We've lost five years. Let's not lose any more." He hoped she said yes, because he and Anton had already made plans. Anton had filled out the paperwork for his justice of the peace credentials online.

"I have nothing to wear. No bouquet. No ring for you."

"I'll take care of all of that. We can go pick out a dress in a few days and a bouquet. All you have to say is yes."

"Come on, Mom. Please say yes."

Mia looked over at her son, who stuck out his lip for good measure, and Emmitt had to bite his lips together to keep from laughing. "Okay, yes, let's do it," Mia said.

Emmitt couldn't fight the emotions running through his body. He pulled Mia up to his chest, wrapped his arms around her waist, and kissed her. Even though it wasn't a married kiss yet, in Emmitt's heart, he knew he had married her five years ago the night he had spent with her. And he knew that having survived what they had already, nothing was going to keep them apart this time.

"I'm afraid I didn't get you anything," Mia said when she pulled back.

"Yes, you did. You said yes. That's the best Christmas gift you could ever give me."

"Ever?" she asked with a teasing glint in her eyes.

He caught her innuendo and pulled her close once again. They would do it right this time, but like her, he wanted more children. And this time, he wanted to be there with her every step of the way.

18

Mia stared at her reflection in the mirror. Odd, how this wasn't her perfect dress - there hadn't been time to find the "perfect" dress - but she still felt this was right. Having already been married once before, her simple ivory dress held no frills, but it hugged her figure in all the right places and fell to the floor in a cascade of satin. The lace detail across the bodice accented her slender shoulders, and the heart-shaped cutout in the back hinted at her smooth back.

The dress was new, and the garter she wore on her left thigh was blue. Her shoes were old, but she was still missing something borrowed.

The dressing room door opened behind her, and her mother's head appeared. Relief flooded Mia. She hadn't been sure her parents would show up - they certainly hadn't been thrilled about the engagement notice or the timeline of the wedding. Her mother had even asked if she was pregnant again, but Mia couldn't fault them. They'd been through this once already, and she knew they were worried not only about her own future but Carter's as well.

"May I come in?" Her mother's voice was soft and held a note of apology.

"Of course. I'm so happy to see you."

Her mother entered, shutting the door behind her. "I may not be sure of this union, but I wouldn't miss it for the world. Now, before I say anything else, are you sure you want to go through with this?"

Mia smiled at her mother's apprehension. She'd had her doubts as well, but Emmitt had distilled every one of them day by day, and her love for him now consumed her, overshadowed only for her love for God and her son. "I'm sure, Mom. Emmitt's changed. He's the man we always thought he could be, and he's Carter's father. Nothing could be better than uniting this family."

Her mother nodded, and her lips split into a wide smile. "I just wanted to be sure." She reached into her purse and withdrew a box. "You look beautiful, but I bet you could use something borrowed, am I right?" She opened the lid to reveal a stunning string of pearls.

Mia gasped and blinked back the tears that stung her eyes. "Mom, it's perfect. Thank you."

"No crying now. If you start, then I'll start, and you know what happens when I start crying."

Mia chuckled and dabbed at her eyes as her mother took the pearls and placed them on her neck. Now, she felt complete. Her mother smiled behind her and squeezed her shoulders.

The door opened again and Kris appeared in the entrance. "Are you ready? Everything else is in place."

Mia turned and hugged her mother before grabbing her bouquet and nodding at Kris. "I'm ready."

Kris was her only bridesmaid, but that was fine with Mia. The two had become close in the last week, and she knew they would be friends for the foreseeable future. Emmitt had asked Anton to be his best man, and while he had invited his teammates, most hadn't been able to attend. Mia had worried that might bother him, but he hadn't seemed to mind.

As they reached the closed door of the small sanctuary, Mia

couldn't help but grin. Carter stood absolutely still in a black suit, his eyes glued to the small white pillow in his hands.

"He hasn't looked away from it yet," Anton said, catching her eye and flashing a wink.

"I have to concentrate real careful, so I don't drop it," Carter said without looking up.

"You're doing great, buddy." Mia didn't have the heart to tell him that the ring on the pillow was just for show and that Anton had the real ring in his pocket.

"Well, I better go find my seat," her mother said, giving her a quick hug before darting inside the door.

"You ready to do this again, Dad?" Mia asked.

Her father smiled at her. "I'll do it as many times as needed to get it right."

"It's right this time, Dad. I know it."

The music changed then and Anton pulled the door open. Mia's eyes caught Emmitt's across the room, and the world around her grew silent. She was about to marry the man she had loved for as long as she could remember, and nothing else mattered.

**

Emmitt looked up as the back doors swung open. His eyes caught Mia's, and his breath stilled. She was a vision in her satin ivory dress. Her hair was piled on her head and accented with flowers, and a few tiny tendrils snaked around her ears. He couldn't wait to touch those tendrils.

Though he wanted nothing more than to keep his eyes on Mia, he forced his gaze to Carter, his son, who was walking down the aisle. Well, inching might have been a better word. The boy was moving slowly, and all his concentration was on the pillow in his hands. Emmitt bit his lips to keep from smiling, and a hushed titter of laughter scattered throughout the room.

When Carter finally reached the stage, he turned and smiled out at the audience, lifting his eyes for the first time. Only then, did Anton and Kris begin their walk.

And then it was Mia's turn. He kept his eyes on her until she was beside him and had handed her bouquet to Kris. Then he took her hands in his. He could feel their heartbeats pulsing in union, and he knew the rest of their life would be the same.

"Dearly beloved, we are gathered here today..."

He barely heard the rest of the preacher's words as Mia consumed his focus. Only when a cough sounded behind him did he turn to see Anton holding out the ring. Right. Vows. They needed to exchange vows before she would be completely his. He took the ring, repeated the preacher's words, and slipped the ring on her finger. She did the same for him, and as the gold band slid onto his finger, he finally felt the weight of his past mistakes ease off his shoulders.

Thank you, God, he thought as he looked up at the ceiling of the sanctuary. *Thank you for taking my mistake and turning it into a masterpiece.*

"I now pronounce you husband and wife. You may kiss the bride."

THE EPILOGUE

E mmitt thought his nerves had been on end before the championship game, but that was nothing compared to the fear, hope, and love coursing through him right now. They had won the game in the final two seconds, and that night had been euphoric. Hoisting Matt on his shoulders for the last time with Jordan, having Mia and Carter meet him on the field, introducing her to everyone as his wife had all been amazing life-changing memories, but this was so much more.

He grasped Mia's hand and squeezed. The eyes she turned on him swam with fear, but she forced a brave smile as she returned his squeeze. Today was the day they would find out the results of Carter's latest scan.

After ten weeks of treatment and countless nights with no sleep as one of them sat up with him or both of them prayed over him, he had undergone surgery to remove the tumor from his bone. Not the way he had wanted to celebrate his birthday, but the doctors had insisted they got it all. They even added that it had been a relatively small piece of his bone, which meant that while he would never play professional football like Emmitt, he might be able to walk without a limp, maybe even run.

But then there had been four more weeks of treatment. Those had been even harder because not only was Carter's body tired of the toxic chemicals coursing through him, but his young brain couldn't process the why. To him, the tumor had been removed, so why did he have to keep doing the thing that made him sick? Getting him to the hospital had been a constant battle, and nerves in the house had run high.

Dr. Goodwin closed the file and folded her hands together. She took a deep breath and then lifted her eyes to meet theirs. "Mr. and Mrs. Brown—"

Emmitt felt the invisible cord around his heart squeeze. He didn't think Mia and Carter could handle it if the news was bad, and not having a solution for them would tax him as well.

"I'm pleased to say that Carter's scans came back negative."

Negative? Did she say negative? Emmitt glanced over at Mia. Tears ran down her face and her shoulders bowed forward as if bearing a heavy burden. Was she happy? Sad?

"We will want to monitor him and re-scan every six months, but for now I can say that Carter's cancer is in remission."

"Remission." The word felt like honey on his tongue. "He's cancer-free?"

Dr. Goodwin smiled and nodded. "He is."

"Praise God!"

"So no more treatments? No more chemo?" Mia's voice was quiet and small next to him.

"Not for now, and as long as his scans come back clean, he won't have to undergo them again."

"Thank you, Dr. Goodwin."

"You're very welcome. These appointments are my favorite by far. I'll give you a few minutes to process your emotions and then I'll be back with Carter."

As she left the room, an enormous sob escaped Mia's lips. Emmitt pulled her to his chest. He knew the emotions were of joy and not sadness, but he also knew she needed to let the tears fall.

He held her until the tears ceased, and then he wiped the traces from her cheek. "Are you ready to give Carter a hug?"

"Almost," she sniffed. "I just have to tell you one thing first."

Emmitt held his breath as the cord around his heart squeezed again. Did she have her own bad news? Had he misread her tears? "What is it?"

"We're pregnant."

With a cheerful laugh, Emmitt pulled her to her feet. Yes, winning the championship game had been amazing, but this day definitely took the cake.

"Momma, Daddy, I'm cancer free," Carter said as the door opened and he limped across the room to them.

"We know, buddy," Emmitt said, lifting him into the air. "What a glorious day!"

"It's the best day ever!" Carter said with a wide smile, and Emmitt couldn't agree more.

The End!

If you loved Emmitt and Mia's story, would you be willing to leave a review? Reviews help other readers find books they will enjoy.

And don't forget to turn the page for a sneak peek at Run with My Heart

AUTHOR'S NOTE

First off, let me say how glad I am that you read this book. I so enjoyed writing this series. So much so that I have three more football books planned. I hope you'll continue the journey by following Tucker Jackson to the Texas Tornados.

I've been a football fan since the age of four. I'm from Texas so football is king down there. I used to watch every Sunday with my father, and when I was in college, I actually got to attend a game at the old Cowboy stadium. I haven't made it to the new one yet, but it's on my bucket list.

I grew up watching football when the Dallas Cowboys were a powerhouse – Troy Aikman, Michael Irving, and of course my favorite Emmitt Smith. As I said in the note at the beginning, I loved Emmitt's drive and the fact that he earned a degree and didn't just rely on his football talent. Turns out he's not a bad dancer either if you watched him win Dancing With the Stars.

So, if you've enjoyed reading this author's note so far (and really, how could you not?) I am offering, for today only, a page where you can sign up for my weekly newsletter for the low, low price of absolutely nothing.

Included in this weekly newsletter is many wonderful things

like pictures of my adorable children, chances to win awesome prizes, new releases and sales I might be holding, great books from other authors, and anything else that strikes my fancy and that I think you would enjoy.

Even better, I solemnly swear to only send out one newsletter a week (usually on Tuesday unless life gets in the way which with three kids it often does). I will not spam you, sell your email address to solicitors or anyone else, or any of those other terrible things.

Join me here and receive the free short story as my thank-you gift for choosing to hang out with me. It's fun and entertaining. I promise.

Prayers and blessings,

Lorana

II

RUN WITH MY HEART

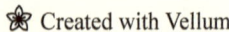

To Robin Bolton who did a fantastic job editing this book.
To my wonderful readers who inspire me to write everyday.
To my father who got me into watching football when I was young.
To Emmitt Smith who was my favorite ball player of all time. He had so much class, and I loved how he finished his degree as well. Such an inspiration!

19

Tucker Jackson's blood boiled as he watched the seconds on the clock run out. The buzz of the clock felt like a nail straight to his heart as did the cheers from the other team's fans. Three points. Just three measly points. How could they have gotten so close? They had tasted the victory and then lost it.

An urge to hit something surged within him, and he curled his hand into a fist to keep it at bay. He thought he'd quelled the angry beast that lived inside of him with his boxing classes. Boxing classes that his friend and former teammate, Emmitt Brown, had recommended when his anger had surfaced because of the trade. And they'd been helping. Five days a week of pounding a bag was generally enough to appease the hunger. So, anger wasn't usually his go-to emotion anymore, but *this* was ridiculous.

This was their second loss in a row, and both were by fewer than ten points. Sure, this was the toughest part of the team's schedule. The teams they were playing now had good records, but the Tornadoes did too. At least they had. If they continued playing like this, they would lose their spot in the playoffs. With this loss, they were now sitting in the wild card position. Which meant that instead of a week off to recover, they had to play in the wild card game and win to move to the quarterfinals. One more loss, and they would be out. Their season would be over. They had to win the next game.

And the next game was on Christmas Day just ten days away. Not the best day to play a football game. Morale was always worse when they had to play on a holiday because everyone wanted to be at home with their families, especially the ones with kids. Tucker didn't have any kids, and he wasn't that close to his family anymore, but he didn't enjoy playing on Christmas Day either. Christmas Day was for watching silly holiday movies and eating too much.

He took off his helmet, clenching it in his left hand, as he joined the line of his teammates. It was tradition after every game to slap hands with the opposing team members. It was supposed to encourage camaraderie and discourage fighting, but Tucker wasn't sure how effective it was. Maybe it had been back in high school, when their jobs and paychecks hadn't been on the line, but this was pro-football. How much money the team paid you depended on individual playing time during the games and team performance throughout the season, so every play mattered. Every game mattered. And slapping hands with the men who had just lowered your paycheck often felt unnatural and forced.

Tucker kept his eyes down as he made his way through the line. "Good game. Good game." The rote words rolled off his tongue without a conscious thought as his mind wandered back to the trade that had landed him here. Last year at this time, he had been on the Rebels. Sure, he hadn't gotten to play as much, but the Rebels had won the Championship game. He even had the ring to prove it, although it meant less than it might have because he'd known even then he was getting traded to the Texas Tornadoes.

Trades happened in football. All the time. But why did it have to happen to him? He'd always been one of the best — in high school and in college, but he hadn't even gotten the chance to show the Rebels what he could do. And yes, the Tornadoes were letting him run more, but what good was that if they didn't win? Perhaps, if the Rebels saw how good he was, they might trade for him back, but even that was a shot in the dark. Had a team ever done that? He didn't know.

With the obligatory congratulatory line finished, Tucker headed toward the locker room. Blaine Hollis, quarterback, captain, and longest team member stood at the door smiling and patting the guys' shoulders as they entered. Blaine was the definition of good sportsmanship. In fact, Tucker was fairly certain his face would be next to the word in the dictionary. Win or lose, the man always had a smile and an encouraging word. Most days Tucker found it refreshing — it reminded him of his former teammate, Emmitt, who everyone had called "Rev" — but not today. Not after losing a game they should have won.

"Good game." Blaine nodded and clapped Tucker on the shoulder. "We'll get them next time." Hollis was a good guy, but he was always spouting platitudes like these. Platitudes that felt empty when the loss column rose in number instead of the win column. Tucker was tired of his optimism. Optimism and platitudes didn't win championships.

"Will we?" Tucker asked. The condescension in his voice surprised him. He wasn't normally so pessimistic, but he hadn't adjusted to Southlake the way he thought he would have by now. People had flocked to him in the past, but he was beginning to wonder if that had been more because of his family's money than who he really was.

His father was a prominent attorney in San Antonio, and he had donated a lot of money to buildings and charities to get his name on things — a dormitory hall, a high school stadium, a hospital wing. The fame benefited Tucker, and he had never lacked for anything in his life — except maybe a father who was physically there. However, he was not experiencing the same thing here. Not that the people weren't nice, it was just that they were also like him. He didn't stand out. Not like he used to. "If we lose the next game, we're out for the rest of the season. If you had just let me run that last play…"

Blaine shook his head and fixed his steely eyes on Tucker. His voice dropped to his serious captain's tone — the one that declared he was in charge, and he would not allow backtalk. "I made a call. They were all over your running game today. Maybe it would have played out differently if you had run but maybe not. We can't win every game, Tucker, and if you only focus on the ones we lose, you will never find the joy of playing the game."

The joy of playing the game? This wasn't some neighborhood tackle game. This was his livelihood Blaine was being so blasé about. "Is that what you guys told yourselves when you lost last year?"

Tucker stared defiantly at Blaine. He knew Blaine wasn't to blame for the Tornadoes' losses last year; he was a good quarterback. In the top five of the league to be exact. The problem was that there were thirty-two teams and only two made it all the way to the championship game, so sometimes being good wasn't good enough. Still, he couldn't seem to tame the anger coursing through his veins.

"Shower and get out of here," Blaine said with a nod toward the locker room behind him. "You need some time off." Though his words were forceful, and his level gaze backed them up, he didn't raise his voice or yell. Tucker might have felt better if he had. The quiet, even tone reminded him of his mother's scolding when he'd been in trouble growing up; and just like then, it quelled Tucker's anger and made him realize his mistake.

"Blaine, I'm sorry, man. I'm just frustrated." Tucker knew he had stepped over the line, and if he didn't get back in Blaine's good graces, he'd be riding the bench and probably facing another trade. In fact, if he didn't watch it, he'd wind up with a label on his back that would make every team in the league shy away from him. And then where would he be?

"We all are, but I wasn't kidding. Go clear your head and decide if this is still *where* you want to be, *what* you want to be doing. IF it is, I'll see you at practice at noon tomorrow."

Tucker knew better than to argue. Like a scolded puppy, he hung his head and shuffled past Blaine, barely managing a "Yes, sir." He berated himself as he walked to his locker. His temper was getting the better of him. Again. And he needed to get it under control. This was a struggle he thought he had won but apparently he hadn't.

Around him, the banter from his teammates created a soft buzz. A few words bypassed the static and reached his ears — favorite plays of the game, mistakes they'd made. How did they all appear in better spirits than Tucker? Why did he let his frustration get the better of him? Why did he always focus on the worst-case scenario?

SHELBY DOLL SIGHED AS SHE WATCHED QUINN ATTEMPT TO dribble a basketball and give up when the ball refused to bounce. She had already put air in the ball twice this week, but it seemed to deflate as soon as she filled it. Just another thing she needed to replace if she only had the money.

"Uh oh, I know that sigh," her friend Kenzi said beside her. "What's wrong?"

"What's always wrong?" Shelby didn't know why Kenzi even asked. It was always the same answer. "Money. The rent is due on this place by the end of the month, and we don't have it. Attendance has dropped since that trampoline park opened up down the street."

She didn't want to wish ill on any business, but that place was the bane of her existence. They'd come in a few months ago with flashy signs, a new sparkling building, and more money to spend on advertising and specials than she'd make in a year. The town of Southlake was rather affluent, and most families had been using the community center because it was the only option. When the trampoline park opened, those that had the money to spend had pulled their kids, leaving the few other kids who were already scraping by as the only customers.

"That place is just a fad," Kenzi said with a wave of her hand. The sparkly pink of her nails caught the light and sent tiny rainbows of colors dancing across the nearby wall. Kenzi always had her nails painted, and it changed with her mood or her outfit. Shelby, on the other hand, rarely painted her nails, and when she did, it was never a frivolous red or a fluffy pink color. A clear polish was much more functional.

"It won't last," Kenzi continued, "and when kids tire of it, they'll come back here because you are amazing." She flashed her famous cheerleader smile — the one that had made her one of the most popular girls in college — as she squeezed Shelby's shoulder.

Shelby didn't know about that. When she had taken over managing the center a year ago, she had felt amazing, but now she felt... behind the times. "What if they don't? Those kids out there need us." Her eyes found Darby, the young girl with glasses bigger than her face whose father had just been killed in the line of duty. Her mother needed this place for Darby, but she was strapped financially now that she was a single mother. And then there was Quinn. Tall and skinny, kids often picked on him at school because he spent more time reading than playing sports or the newest video game. But here he was just one of the gang. His mother was battling cancer, so there was no extra money there. And there was Benji. She still wasn't sure exactly how he had become paralyzed as he never talked about it, but his father had left when he was young and his mother worked long hours.

There were other kids, but these three always stood out to her because they seemed to need the center the most. She scanned the gymnasium again. Once, they had watched nearly every school age kid in town for at least a few hours after school. Basketballs would echo across the floor as teams played. Others had staked out one corner of the gym for reading and playing cards. Still another part had been the creative hangout for students who enjoyed theater and role play. But then the trampoline park had opened and offered its flashy new entertainment for kids, and most of them had left.

Now, there were only a handful. A few basketballs still thudded against the floor, but even they sounded sad as if the kids couldn't muster the emotion of delight that had previously lived there. Now, most of the kids read or worked on homework, and the muted atmosphere broke Shelby's heart. Quinn placed the ball back into the rack and didn't even try another. He shuffled to the bleachers and sat down next to Darby.

"What if they don't?" she asked again. "What if, come the new year, we can't pay the rent, and we have to close the doors forever?" They had always run on a tight budget, but the drop in enrollment had quickly drained what little reserve they had kept. If anything unexpected happened that would need repairs, there wouldn't be any money to do so. Plus, Christmas was right around the corner, but there would be little cheer at the center this year. There was no money for decorations, no money for a party, and no money for gifts. Shelby pushed her wire-framed glasses up her freckled nose and sighed.

Kenzi flashed a sympathetic smile as she wrapped an arm around Shelby's shoulders. "We'll just have to pray that doesn't happen."

Prayer. Shelby knew how important that was; but while she would never stop praying, she couldn't stop the tiny voice that often whispered in her ear that she wasn't seeing her prayers answered yet. Was God even listening to her? Did He even care? Couldn't He send the money if He really wanted to? Drop a winning lottery ticket on the front doorstep? Or have a wealthy family leave a donation?

"I think we may need more than just prayers for help," Shelby said with a final glance at the gym. "We might need to pray for a miracle."

20

He shouldn't be here. He knew it, but he seemed incapable of keeping his feet from crossing the threshold into the dimly lit bar. No one even looked up as Tucker pulled the door open, even with the gust of cold air that ushered him in.

Snow would hit their town soon. He could smell it when the wind blew — that cold, crisp scent that made plants curl up their roots and sink lower in the soil. The sharp bite in the air that seemed to gnaw through even the thickest jackets and sweaters to chill the bones. Snow didn't come often to Texas — especially not central Texas where the town of Southlake nestled between Keller and Grapevine — but the weather had been different this year. Colder, wetter, more extreme, and he felt that it would happen.

The acrid scent of cigarette smoke floated in the cloudy air as Tucker crossed the dingy floor to an empty barstool. An old country song crackled softly through overhead speakers that had seen better days. In fact, most of the interior of this place appeared to have seen better days. He wondered if the employees even noticed it anymore, but he doubted it. The one man he saw behind the bar wore an expression of boredom and acceptance as if this was good enough.

Tucker pulled out the barstool, unsurprised to see a rip in the upholstery. It fit his mood and mirrored the dilapidated feeling the rest of the place exuded, but for a reason he couldn't really explain, the cushion also held comfort. He abhorred finding comfort here, but he seemed incapable of changing it.

All he had ever wanted was a relationship with his father. But because of his job, his father only seemed interested in two things — working and drinking. He wasn't an alcoholic by any means; but after working long hours, he would disappear to his study and nurse a beer. At least that was what he would do on the evenings he came home. Some nights, he hadn't even come home before Tucker and his sister had been asleep. So, Tucker had associated drinking with being close to his father. He only ever drank one; but while the frosty glass sat in front of him, he could pretend it was something they had in common — something they could bond over.

Things hadn't always been this way. Tucker could remember a time when his father came home before dinner in the evenings, when he would scoop up Tucker and his younger sister and carry them around the living room under his arms like an airplane, when he would circle his arms around his wife's waist and kiss her neck as she tried to cook dinner, and she would playfully shoo him off. There was a time when laughter filled the house and a cheery glow surrounded the rooms, but all of that changed when his mother died.

Tucker had been in junior high then, worrying stupidly about acne and girls while a deadly tumor sprouted inside his mother's head. A tumor that grew tentacles and stealthily curled itself around different areas of her brain. A tumor none of them knew about until she died in her sleep one night. Tucker hadn't been the one to find her, for which he had been grateful, but his father had.

And it had changed him. Within a week, he'd stopped coming home for dinners, and he'd hired a cook to take care of the meals for Tucker and his sister, Whitley. Occasionally, he would arrive home before they retired to bed, but more often than not, Tucker had been the one to make sure they both had done their homework and gone to bed at a decent hour. In one week, he had basically lost both his parents and been forced to grow up faster than any teenage boy ought to. When other boys his age were worrying about home-work and girls and the latest gaming system, he had been forced to worry about dishes and laundry and the well-being of his sister.

His father had poured money on them after that, as if money could make up for the loss of their mother. Or maybe, he had done it in an effort to assuage his guilt for being gone so often. Either way, Tucker had hated that money. That money had replaced the one thing he really needed at the time — a parent. His anger had started about that time. Anger at the loss of his mother, anger at his father, and anger at the money his father had doled out instead of time.

Yes, the money had been the main target of his anger. Until it started opening doors for him. He had talent, but he was pretty sure it was his father's sizable donation that had earned him a role on the varsity football team as a freshman. Perhaps, he had attained the title of captain of the team in his junior year (a title normally reserved for seniors and, most often, quarterbacks and not running backs) on his own, but it could have also been the new sports equipment his father had provided even though he never attended a game. Then, there was the full ride scholarship to a prestigious university that might have been based upon his talent or the amount of money his father had thrown to the program.

Either way, Tucker had enjoyed the benefits and the title of star running back for four years until he'd been picked up in the draft. His father's money had certainly paved the way for a cushy ride that may or may not have existed without it, and so Tucker had swallowed his angry feelings not realizing he was fostering their growth with his denial. It was only once he was on the Rebels' roster that things had begun to change.

Being chosen in the draft had been a dream — one that he'd been pretty sure would happen — but a dream nonetheless. However, when he'd arrived in the Rebels' locker room the first day, he'd realized it wasn't the dream he had thought it would be. His father's money meant nothing here. Almost all of the players had come from money just like he had. Some even more, and some were legacy football players. Their fathers and grandfathers had played the game, so regardless of talent, they had found their way in.

That had been the hardest pill to swallow. He hadn't been signed as the main running back or even the backup running back. Instead, as a backup to the backup running back, he rarely got the chance to play in games, but he'd been sure once they saw his talent that would change. Except the Rebels had traded him before he could prove himself, and now he was playing for a team who just couldn't seem to get their act together. And it was frustrating.

"Hey, you're Tucker Jackson, aren't you?"

Tucker glanced up at the man who belonged to the voice. He sat a barstool over and looked out of place in his expensive suit. Clearly a man who normally appeared well put together, he had obviously been served one too many as his voice held the slur of inebriation and red splotches dotted his face.

"No, man. You've got the wrong guy." Normally he enjoyed being recognized, even signing autographs for fans though some players hated it. But today he just wanted to nurse his wounded ego and dwell in the past.

"Yeah, you are." The man stood, swayed on his feet momentarily, and then grabbed the bar to steady himself. His dress shirt hung out of his pants on one side and held the stain of whatever he'd eaten most recently. Still, he looked like a man who had money or wanted people to think he did. "You cost me a grand today."

Oh great. *This* he definitely didn't need. He knew people bet on sporting events even though it was illegal, but he'd never met anyone who actually did. Tucker imagined this man would be buying his beer had they won the game, but since they hadn't.... well, the man might be unsteady on his feet, but he looked solid and like an angry bull about to charge. Even as inebriated as he was, he might still be able to do some damage to Tucker. Damage that could keep him from playing in the next game.

"Look, man, I'm sorry you lost money, but betting on football is illegal." Tucker kept his voice neutral as he spoke and then returned his gaze to his drink. He hoped the man would take the hint and leave him alone. Unfortunately, either the man was stubborn, or his good sense was clouded by liquor. Perhaps it was a combination of both.

An angry snort came out of the man's mouth, and he shoved a pudgy finger in Tucker's face. "It wouldn't be an issue if you hadn't lost the game. Who taught you how to carry the ball anyway, your sister?"

Tucker tried to remain calm, but he'd never liked fingers shoved in his face; and he certainly didn't allow anyone to talk badly about his sister. He'd had to defend her all through school when her reaction to their mother's death had been to misbehave. Rumors had often circulated about her, and Tucker had squelched them one by one, usually through a nice payoff but occasionally with his fists when the perpetrator refused to let up. Fighting had been frowned upon in high school, but it was even more taboo in pro-football. A public fight could get you fined or suspended if anyone got hurt. Not to mention jail time if assault charges were filed.

"My sister is actually a pretty impressive running back," Tucker said in a last-ditch effort to diffuse the man. Maybe he would take the joke and let it go.

"Then maybe they should hire her and let you go," the man said as he pushed Tucker's shoulder.

That touch broke the tenuous thread Tucker held on his anger. He slapped the man's hand away and jumped up from his barstool so quickly that it fell to the floor behind him. The loud bang of metal on the hard floor halted the conversation around them, and Tucker felt the eyes of the strangers on him. His hand shook as he forced it to his side. He couldn't punch the man now. Not here and certainly not with all these people watching. "I said let it go, man."

Having already paid for his beer, Tucker turned to leave. Regret that he hadn't been able to finish the drink in peace circled him like a cloud, but it paled in comparison to the regret he would face if he got suspended. His body still burned with anger, and he hoped the cool outside air would calm him down, but he never got the chance to see. Before he was halfway to the door, the force of something, or someone, knocked into him from behind and sent him careening into a table before forcing him to the floor. His breath rushed out in one gust as his ribs collided first with the sharp edge of the table and then with the hard floor. Then, he felt the pain as punches landed on his sides.

He rolled over, unsurprised to see the drunk man bending over him, but determined not to let the man beat him to a pulp. When his fist came close again, Tucker grabbed it and pulled. The sudden shift sent the man collapsing to the floor beside him, and Tucker let his own fists fly. He only meant to incapacitate the man long enough to get out of the bar, but once the first punch landed, he couldn't seem to stop the next one. Or the next.

It was only the presence of an arm grabbing his, and the pressure of a knee in his back forcing him to the floor that cleared his hazy red fog. "That's enough."

The voice was deep and unfamiliar, and Tucker twisted his head to see who it belonged to. The lone bartender stared back at him. He hadn't appeared threatening, but Tucker could feel the man's strength as he pinned Tucker's arms behind his back.

"It wasn't my fault. I tried to leave," Tucker said.

"I know. I saw it happen. Still had to call the police though. Have to report all fights that happen and file a report for the damages."

Tucker scanned the area and saw a broken chair and an upended table. "I can cover the damages."

"Sorry, it's the owner's rule, but I'll make sure they know you didn't start it."

Tucker wasn't sure that would matter to the team. It might keep him from getting officially charged, but he doubted the coach would just let this slide. Especially after his outburst at Blaine earlier.

Defeated, Tucker relaxed and waited for the cops to arrive, but when the cold metal snapped around his wrist, he knew his worst fears had come true.

As Shelby watched a kid on a bicycle ride by outside the window, her thoughts turned again to the center. What could she do to raise money and awareness? The annual Christmas party often helped, but it wasn't enough, and it certainly wouldn't help this year if they couldn't find the money to host it. Could they do a fundraiser? Possibly, but what kind? It couldn't be anything that would cost the families of the kids though. They were the ones struggling already. It would have to be something to reach the other members of the community — either the ones who had stopped coming or perhaps those who didn't even have kids but could see the value of the place. The question was what would that be?

"Shelby, can you come set the table?"

The voice of her mother calling from the kitchen pulled her away from her plotting. With a sigh, she rose from the couch and walked to the kitchen to grab plates and silverware.

"Mom, do you know of any kind of fundraiser that would get the community involved in donating to the center?" Shelby asked as she pulled out the solid black plates they used for everyday occasions. Her mother owned China, beautiful china that she had been willed when Shelby's grandmother died, but she only pulled it out at Thanksgiving and Christmas. That gene of practicality had trickled into Shelby as well, although it had morphed. She saw no use for the china even at holiday dinners. Why have a set of plates you only used once or twice a year? In her modest apartment, she had only one set of plates and silverware, and they had been purchased on sale at Walmart. Of course, she also had no current need for china. Not with being a single woman who ate most dinners at her parents' house.

"Is money still an issue?"

Shelby chuffed out a breath. "When isn't it? The trampoline park stole most of our clients, and the ones we have left can't afford a rate increase. I haven't even heard from the normal donors about the Christmas party yet, and at this point, I'm not even sure we'll have the money to have one."

"Hmm." Her mother wasn't a businesswoman. She was a nurse, but she was still the smartest woman Shelby knew and she often had ideas that no one else thought of. "I assume you're thinking larger than a bake sale."

Shelby managed a slight chuckle as she pulled the silverware from the drawer and laid it on the top plate. "Yeah, I don't think baked goods are going to pull the kind of money we need."

"What about a celebrity? Someone who would draw in a different crowd." Her mother crossed to the island and retrieved a potholder from the drawer.

"That's a great idea, but I don't know any celebrities. Kenzi might though. She's much more outgoing, and maybe she has some connections. I could ask her tomorrow. What kind of celebrity are you thinking?"

Her mother shrugged. "I'm not sure it matters, but isn't there a pro-sports team housed around here somewhere?"

Shelby didn't watch sports, but it was her job to know the local businesses when she was canvassing for donations; and she knew there was a football team housed in Southlake. "There is a pro-football team. The Tornadoes I think, but what would a football player do at the center?"

Her mother picked up one of the pots and led the way to the dining room. "Well, he could talk to the kids about football, maybe teach them a few plays. Think of it like a learning clinic maybe or a gym class. People could pay to workout with him and possibly get an autographed ball or something."

Shelby's mother knew as much about football as Shelby did, but what she was saying made sense. The wheels began turning in her head. "Yeah, that's a good idea. Even just having one of the players signing merchandise for a small fee would bring in some money. I'll call tomorrow and see if any of them would like to come out and help. Hopefully, at least one of them has a good heart and some time because I have nothing to offer them in return."

Her mother set the pot on a heating pad in the middle of the table and turned to Shelby. "You have your amazing smile and a heart for those kids. Any man should find that enough."

Shelby knew her mother was just being an encouraging mother, but the words reminded her instead of how she was still single. She knew it was just that she hadn't found the right man yet, but that didn't make her heartache any less real, especially when it seemed like someone from her high school was getting engaged every week. "Thanks, Mom. We'll see if you're right."

"I'm always right. Didn't you know that?" her mother said with a teasing smile. "Now, while I get the rest of the table ready, why don't you find everyone else and tell them dinner is ready?"

"Sure thing."

Dinner had always been family time in the Doll household.

While other families around them appeared to be drifting further apart, doing their own things, lost in their tablets and smartphones, Shelby's parents had been determined to keep their family together. Because of that, dinner had always been a sit-down family affair when the family lived together, even if they had often been passing each other at breakfast and eating lunch at different places altogether.

After Sam and Scott and finally Shelby moved out, the family still tried to eat dinner together as often as possible. And when Sam had married Iris, she had joined them as well. They couldn't come every night since they lived about an hour away, but they came as often as they could and always at least once a week.

Shelby enjoyed the nights they came over. Not just because she loved seeing Sam, but she and Iris had formed a bond. Neither had a sister growing up; and like kindred spirits do, they had sensed that longing in each other and become fast friends.

Scott, like Shelby, was still single, but he would occasionally bring his flavor of the month over to meet the family. Their mother said he was just picky and that's why he dated so many different women, but Shelby was pretty sure Scott liked being single. Unlike herself.

She couldn't wait to start a family of her own, but being the quiet introvert that she was, meeting men was hard and carrying on a conversation even harder. Forget asking a man out on a date; she'd rather have a root canal. So, she continued to pray about it, and every time she did, she felt God telling her to wait — that He had someone for her. She just wondered when her mystery man might show up.

Shelby found her father, brothers, and Iris in the main living room. The boys were arguing about some game on the TV, and Iris was working a crossword puzzle. "Dinner's ready, guys. Mom made chicken alfredo."

Shelby wasn't sure they had Italian anywhere in their family, but somehow Italian dishes had always been the family's favorites and chicken alfredo topped that list. Especially when her mother made the alfredo sauce from scratch.

"Mmm, I do love Mom's chicken alfredo," Scott said as he and Sam rose from the couch. Iris stuck a pencil in her book, closed it, and set it on the table before joining them.

The savory smell of parmesan, cream, and chicken was strong as they entered the dining room. Shelby inhaled deeply and let the scent fill her nose and comfort her. There was something about Italian food that always made her feel... safe? She wasn't sure "safe" was the right way to describe how she felt, but it was as close as she could get.

For some reason, Italian food reminded her of simpler times. Times when her biggest worry was finding time to finish reading the new novel she had started or studying for the science test she hated, instead of how to fund a community center and worrying about what would happen to the kids who needed the center if she couldn't get the money.

"Does anyone have anything we should pray over?" her father asked as he took his seat. His eyes travelled from one adult to the next.

"Shelby does. Go ahead and share, baby girl."

With a smile, Shelby squeezed her mother's hand. Though she was twenty-four and no longer a little girl, she didn't mind the nickname. Her mother had called her that for as long as she could remember.

"I could use prayer for the center. We're struggling financially right now, and I really need a miracle to keep the doors open."

"One miracle coming up." Her father's words held a teasing note, but Shelby knew he was serious. He had always believed in the power of prayer and always held on to the notion that God still provided miracles. When Shelby had asked one time why her prayer didn't get answered, he'd told her it had — just not in the way she'd expected. Shelby knew that if God didn't provide the funding for the center that her father would tell her perhaps God had something different planned for her. While she would accept that, she hoped that wasn't going to happen because the center wasn't just about her. It was about all those kids who needed a place to stay as well.

She closed her eyes and listened to her father's prayer, but even though she said "amen" it didn't lessen the worry in her heart.

"Tucker Jackson?"

Tucker lifted his head at the sound of his name. The guard, a lithe man with a shaved head and more than a few tattoos who went by the name Mike, stood at the door of the jail cell. He looked much fiercer than he'd turned out to be. He'd checked on Tucker every half hour for the first few hours — but Tucker would still be glad when he was released and able to return home.

Sitting in a holding cell with three other men, one who reeked of alcohol and snored louder than a freight train, was not his idea of a good way to spend the night. Thankfully, the other two men hadn't seemed to know who he was and had left him alone. Even better, the man from the bar had been placed in a different holding cell, but Tucker was still very relieved to hear his name.

He stood, stretching his stiff legs, and crossed to the open door. "Thanks, Mike, my dad finally show up?" Tucker hadn't wanted to get his father involved, but better him than anyone on the team. So he'd used his one call to phone his father. Perhaps with his money, he could make the whole thing go away before anyone found out.

He'd been working, of course, but had promised to do what he could.

The guard dodged his stare and shifted from one foot to the other. "Something like that." He blinked and Tucker noticed the back of his eyelids were tattooed as well. He couldn't imagine how painful that had been; and he wondered if Mike was just a sadist, or if he had been using the pain from the needle to cover up some larger pain in his life.

Mike locked the cell door after letting Tucker out and then led the way out to the processing area. However, as the door opened and Tucker caught a glimpse of the figure waiting for him, his heart sank. It was not the stocky figure of his father, but the lean physique of Blaine Hollis waiting for him. How in the world had Blaine found out? And why was he here?

Tucker gathered his personal items, taking an extra moment to compose himself as he shoved his keys and wallet in his pocket, before turning to face Blaine.

"He all set?" Blaine asked Mike as if Tucker wasn't standing right next to him.

Mike glanced quickly at Tucker before dropping his gaze back to the counter. "Yes, sir, he's good to go."

"Good. Let's go, Jackson." Blaine headed for the exit without giving Tucker a chance to say anything. Tucker's stubborn streak wanted to refuse, to demand to know where his father was and why Blaine was here, but he could tell from the stiff set of the quarterback's shoulders that this was not the time nor the place. What could he say anyway?

The tense silence filled the space between them like some invisible third party as Tucker followed Blaine to his Ford Mustang. Red, yellow, and orange streaked the sky in a beautiful artistic pattern as the sun rose, but Tucker couldn't enjoy it. He was too worried about his future. Blaine unlocked the doors and motioned Tucker into the passenger seat, but he said nothing until they were both inside and the doors were closed.

"What were you thinking, Jackson?" Blaine's voice was low, but Tucker did not miss the anger that threaded it. "This isn't what I meant when I told you to think about your job."

"I wasn't trying to start the fight, Blaine." Tucker hated that he was having to defend himself to Blaine of all people. "I was trying to enjoy one beer. One. But then the man poked me and spouted off about my sister, so I got up to leave. He tackled me from behind, man. What was I supposed to do?"

"You're supposed to keep your cool," Blaine said in a tight voice. "We are in the public eye, Jackson, so everything we do is scrutinized. On top of that, our record isn't where our fans or the owners would like it to be. You may not like it or agree with it, but that puts added pressure on us. We can't afford any negative publicity right now. Not that it matters, but what was the fight about?"

Tucker shrugged, knowing his explanation changed nothing. "The guy was drunk and evidently he bet a grand we would win the game yesterday. Needless to say, he wasn't too happy when we lost."

Blaine's sigh shook his broad shoulders, and he gazed out the windshield as if trying to think of what to say. Tucker took the opportunity to ask the question burning in his throat.

"Why are you here, Blaine? I called my father, not anyone from the team."

For just a moment, Blaine's jaw tightened, the muscles rippling beneath his skin. "Your father was buried in a case, Jackson. He couldn't make it, so he called Coach and Coach called me."

Disappointment blanketed Tucker's shoulders. His dad couldn't even find time to help out his son when he was in jail? He shouldn't be surprised; he couldn't remember the last time his father had been there when he needed him. "So, what's the verdict? Am I suspended?"

"No, not suspended. Your father may not have been able to be here, but he is still influential. Your charge was only going to be disorderly conduct anyway; but he got it dropped completely, so you wouldn't face suspension. However, you will have a hefty fine to pay, and we're going to have to find some way to improve your image in case this gets out. Some sort of community service."

"Community service?" Tucker exploded. "I was defending myself."

Blaine shot him a silencing look. "Community service is not negotiable. You have a chip on your shoulder, Jackson. It's affecting your game play, and now it's affecting the whole team. I don't know what your story is, but I think it's time you took a look at how the less fortunate live. Maybe that will give you some perspective."

Perspective. Blaine knew nothing about perspective. His father was probably in his life, and he probably attended every game Blaine had ever played. Tucker clenched his jaw to keep from saying the words rising in his throat. It would do no good to argue with Blaine right now. "What kind of community service and for how long?"

"I'm not sure yet. Coach and the public relations guy are going to look at some options. The judge didn't officially assign any, so that means they don't have to align it with the incident at the bar. This is more a requirement from the team. I'm sure it will be low key, but I would keep your evenings free. At least for the foreseeable future."

"What about practice? What about the next game?" This couldn't be happening. He hadn't started the fight. He'd tried to leave. Yes, he might have punched the guy one too many times, but he was only defending himself. Who could blame him?

"You'll still attend every practice and every game. The service will be done in your off time, and if you don't fulfill the time, then you will be suspended without pay for the remainder of the season. Should we happen to lose before the championship game, you will fulfill that suspension at the beginning of next season. Am I clear?"

"Crystal." Tucker said as he slumped against the seat. He

should be grateful. It was better than being suspended, but giving up his evenings to do charity work was certainly not how he had planned to fill his time.

SHELBY STARED AT THE PHONE AS SHE THOUGHT OF WHAT TO SAY. How could she persuade the football team to send one of the players to help her out? She had nothing to offer in return besides the good karmic feelings of helping others out.

"You can't make the sell if you don't at least try," Kenzi said from behind her.

"I know, but what if they say no? Our usual donors have been so quiet this year. What if it stays like this? What if people are too busy or too focused on themselves to care about others? What if we're seeing the end of charitable donations?"

Kenzi's right eyebrow lifted as she chuckled. "Wow! Doomsday much? Seriously, you were made for this. Call them, tell them the amazing things you do, and ask them for a player to hold a clinic or a signing or whatever. I'll bet you'll be surprised by humanity's response. I don't think we've completely fallen into the abyss yet."

"You're right," Shelby said with a shake of her head. She wasn't usually this dramatic, but it had just seemed the last few months that people cared less about the other people around them and more about their electronics. She'd seen more and more people scrolling their phones as they walked or during meals while others sat across from them, and their last fundraiser — a carwash in the summer — had been an absolute flop. People had said they were too busy to stop or that they'd come by later. Except they never had. The kids had been so disappointed. Shelby just didn't want to have to disappoint them again.

She took a deep breath and picked up the phone. She'd Googled the information for the team when she'd first arrived at the center and had found the public relation manager's number. As her fingers pressed the buttons, she sent up a silent prayer for the right words to say.

The phone rang once, twice, three times in her ear. Disappointment pressed down on her shoulders, but just as she was about to hang up the phone, a voice answered.

"Hello? This is Blaine Hollis. How can I help you?"

Blaine Hollis? She didn't think that was the name she'd seen on the website. Had she dialed the wrong number? Her fingers hadn't been shaking that badly, had they?

"Oh, hello, I thought I was about to get a voicemail." Shelby's words spilled out in a frantic ramble. She took a calming breath and tried again. "My name is Shelby Doll. I'm the director of the Southlake Community Center. Perhaps you know that we serve the community as a low-cost alternative for after school and summer care for children." Ugh, she sounded like a bad saleswoman, the kind who didn't know what to say and therefore just rattled off all the details.

"I'm calling because we are looking for donations to keep our doors open. I don't know if your organization does this sort of thing, but I wondered if there might be any players on your team who would be willing to host a clinic that we could charge for or an autograph signing or something." Shelby shook her head as she paused. She really should have scripted her speech better. Practiced it on Kenzi or something.

"You want a football player to come and host a clinic at the community center?"

The man on the other end said the words slowly and thoughtfully, but Shelby wasn't sure if he was mocking her or just chewing the idea over.

"Yes, sir. It would be great community service, and I imagine it would be a great outreach for the team as well. Meet the community, sign some autographs, I'm sure your fans would eat it up." Finally, she sounded like someone who knew what she was talking about. She waited as the silence drew out. What was he thinking?

"What did you say your name was again?"

"Shelby. Shelby Doll."

"Well, Shelby Doll, I think I know of just the player for you."

She could hear the smile in his voice and her heart sped up. Could she really be about to get her miracle? "You do?"

"I do. His name is Tucker Jackson. I'll send him over this afternoon, and you can work out the details."

Shelby felt like jumping from her chair and dancing around the room. "Thank you. Thank you so much."

"No, thank you, Shelby."

She found his wording odd as she hung up the phone. Why did he sound as if she had just given him the miracle instead of the other way around?

"They have someone?" Kenzi asked.

She had been so quiet that Shelby had forgotten she was still in the room. "Yeah, a Tucker Jackson."

Kenzi's eyes grew to the size of quarters as her head dropped forward, sending her brown hair swishing across her thin shoulders. "Tucker Jackson? The running back?"

"Uh, maybe?" Shelby wasn't even sure what a running back was, much less if Tucker Jackson was one. "I didn't ask. The guy said Mr. Jackson will be here this afternoon."

"Oh my gosh! This is huge. Can I take a slightly longer lunch to go home and change?"

"Change?" Shelby's eyes roamed over Kenzi's outfit. Tight stretchy pants that accentuated her figure and a flowy blouse was her outfit of choice today. Not exactly what Shelby would classify as professional attire, but Kenzi generally worked with the kids where her full outfit was rarely seen by parents, and no one had complained yet. "Why? You look fine."

"Yes, but fine is what you wear when the cute UPS guy is stopping by with a package. It is not what you wear when Tucker Jackson, star running back for the Texas Tornadoes, is stopping by." Kenzi flashed her best puppy dog face and clasped her hands together under her chin. "Please?"

"Fine." Shelby rolled her eyes. She certainly hoped Kenzi didn't lose herself over this guy. It wouldn't be the first time, but she needed her friend's head in the game if they were going to save the center.

"Jackson, Tony, I have the perfect solution."

Tucker looked up as Blaine re-entered the room, a giant smile on his face. He had been manning Tony's phone while Tony gave Tucker an earful about public image. As if he didn't understand the importance of public image. His father had never attended a game, but he'd made sure Tucker and Whitley were by his side every time he made some big donation to the school or a local charity. "Public image," his father had told him once when he asked why they had to be there. "If the people love you, business is always better." Somehow, his father had lost sight of the fact that your children loving you was just as important.

"What solution, Blaine?" Tony's voice held a note of irritation. No doubt he'd had at least another ten minutes of brimstone he'd wanted to rail down on Tucker's head. The man was great at his job, slick and professional without being slimy; but Tucker believed he was as good as he was because he loved the sound of his own voice. He would talk your ear off any chance he got.

"I just took a call from the community center. They are looking for a way to increase revenue, and they want a football player to host a clinic and sign some autographs."

"A clinic? What would I do at a clinic?" Tucker asked. He'd heard of clinics but not usually by active players. They were normally put on by retired players looking to stay active in the limelight, either to help with endorsements or because they just couldn't handle no longer being in the public eye.

Blaine shrugged. "Who cares? Teach them how to hold the ball, how to run routes, bore them with football stories, whatever you want."

"I don't think that's a good idea—"

But Tucker didn't get to finish because Tony held up his hand to interrupt him. "Now, hold on, Tucker. Blaine might be onto something. If we do this correctly, we could show you doing a good deed for the community. Build morale for both you and the team."

"But I've never held a clinic before. I wouldn't even know what to do."

"Nonsense, how hard can it be to teach a few kids how to hold the ball and run a play?" Tony asked.

Tucker shook his head. Tony had never played football, so he didn't understand the complexity behind the game. And he didn't seem like the type to hang around kids, much less teach them, but Tucker knew he wasn't going to win this argument. Besides, as far as community service, he could probably have been assigned worse. Picking up trash on the side of the road or helping out in a nursing home definitely sounded like more work than teaching kids about football.

"Will the clinic satisfy all my required hours?"

"Probably not. The team wants you to fulfill twenty hours. The clinic itself would only be a few hours, but I bet the center could use some help during the week, especially with kids being out of school for Christmas break. They are out next week, aren't they?"

Tucker shrugged. He didn't have kids, so keeping up with a school schedule was not something he did.

"Well, you can find out for sure from Shelby. If you helped out before and after practice all next week, then it might satisfy the hours. Right, Tony?" Blaine turned his attention to the PR director who was nodding thoughtfully.

"Yes, I think that could work. Try to get the clinic scheduled in the evening so parents can come. That way it benefits the kids and helps build our fan base."

"Exactly. Plus, it would show your good will and all," Blaine said.

Though he phrased it as a suggestion, Tucker knew it wasn't one. Blaine expected him to spend the next week at the center as if it were a job. "Fine, I'll report there Monday morning."

"Actually, the director is expecting you this afternoon to hash out the details of the clinic. She'll need time to organize and promote it, so you should head over there now."

Tucker sighed as he nodded. There was no use arguing with Blaine once he grabbed hold of an idea. And how hard could it be, really?

SHELBY TAPPED HER WATCH AGAIN AND SIGHED. KENZI HAD BEEN gone over an hour, and their doors would open for kids in less than forty minutes. There was no way she could run the center and watch the kids by herself.

"Excuse me, I'm looking for Shelby Doll. Do you know where I can find her?"

Shelby glanced up at the masculine voice she did not recognize and blinked. A dark-haired man stood before her. His hands were shoved in the pockets of his leather jacket, and his chocolate brown eyes looked as if he'd rather be anywhere else. Normally, she might take offense to that, but at this moment, she'd rather be somewhere else too. Somewhere where she wasn't in charge, where kids weren't counting on her, and where she wouldn't have to stare at disappointed faces all day.

"I'm Shelby Doll. What can I do for you?"

"I'm Tucker Jackson. I'm the football player who will be running the clinic and whatever else you need next week."

So this was Tucker Jackson. He was definitely not what she'd expected. She'd expected someone with a friendly attitude or a smile at the very least. This man before her looked as if just being here pained him, and she wondered if he'd been assigned to do this for some reason instead of volunteering out of the goodness of his heart. She supposed she shouldn't care. Though she had no idea who he was, it was clear Kenzi did, which meant other football fans probably would as well. And she was desperate, so as long as he could be nice and bring in a crowd, he would do in her book.

She stood and extended a hand, plastering a big smile on her face in hopes it would prompt him to do the same. "Of course, Tucker. Nice to meet you. Have you ever put on a clinic before?"

"Afraid not," he said with a shake of his head and a nonchalant shrug, "but how hard can it be, right?"

Shelby swallowed her sigh. She had been hoping he would come with ideas at least, something she could work with, but it appeared she'd have to be helping him with the whole thing as well as dealing with his surly attitude. "Okay, well, why don't you come around here and join me? We can hammer out some details." She motioned for him to proceed through the main door and then met him in the hallway.

A clean, masculine scent flooded her nose as he sat across from her, and Shelby forced herself not to focus on how handsome he was. His dark eyes were even more alluring up close as there appeared to be swirls of gold and green in them, and his jawline could have been chiseled from stone it was so perfect. If only she could wipe the expression that resembled a grimace from his face.

"So, tell me how these clinic things usually work," he said.

"Well, we open for kids at two in the afternoon during school. They are out next week for break, so we'll be open all day, but I would suggest we shoot for something around five or six as I'm sure some parents will want to get autographs from you as well. We could start a sign up today and get the word out to the local TV and radio stations. Do you think Wednesday evening would give you enough time to prepare?"

Tucker paused as if running through his schedule in his head. "I have practice every afternoon next week. It usually ends by four though, so yeah, Wednesday should be fine."

She wished he sounded more excited about it. It would do her no good to have a celebrity if the celebrity acted like he'd rather be watching paint dry. "I'm sorry. I asked for someone who might draw in a crowd, and no offense, but you seem like you might push them away right now. Why exactly did they send you?"

His jaw tightened, and a tiny vein bulged in his neck. She'd obviously hit a nerve with her question. "To be honest, they sent me because I need to fulfill some community service hours. Don't worry though, I'm a good actor, and I'll put on my best performance during the clinic."

"Right." His words did nothing to reassure her, but what other option did she have? He was who they had sent, and she had no time to try and find someone else. The end of the month was quickly approaching as was Christmas, so if she wanted to pay the rent and possibly provide a party for the kids, she would just have to do her best with him. "Let's do the clinic at six then, so people have time to get off work. We can offer some food for sale here so they have no excuse of missing dinner, and then you can sign autographs after. That way people have to register for the clinic to get the autographs."

"What's the money for anyway?" Tucker asked.

Shelby couldn't imagine that he really cared, but she humored him and answered the question anyway. Perhaps if he knew how important this clinic was, he could find a positive attitude.

"Keeping the center open. We have a flat fee for facility use each month and a fee for the after-school program. We lost a lot of our kids when the trampoline park opened down the street, so money is tight right now, and we usually have a Christmas party for the kids. Some of our families can't afford much in the way of gifts, so we try to have something small to hand out to each of the kids."

Tucker nodded as if he understood though Shelby wondered if he'd ever spent a Christmas poor. Had he ever celebrated without a tree because his family couldn't afford one? Or given coupons as gifts because there was no money to purchase anything? She doubted it, but even as the thoughts circled in her head, God convicted her. She didn't know him, didn't know his story. Maybe he had known hard times. Maybe his gruff expression had more to do with him not knowing how to run a clinic than with him not wanting to be here.

"Oh, I see our guest has arrived," Kenzi said appearing behind Tucker and mouthing, "oh my goodness, he's dreamy" at Shelby. She had changed out of her flowy blouse and into something slightly more low-cut than Shelby preferred she wear at the center. She would have to have a talk with Kenzi about image and how her first priority had to be the kids and not Tucker.

"Hi, I'm Kenzi Lanham, Shelby's assistant." She stuck out her hand, shifting into her fake pageant queen, cheerleader persona. It was one she had perfected, one that got her almost anything she wanted, and one that drove Shelby crazy. Shelby rolled her eyes. Kenzi didn't look as though she'd spent an hour on her face even though Shelby knew full well that she had, and while she was glad to see her arrive before the kids did, she certainly didn't need her distracting Tucker while they tried to plan.

"Uh, Tucker Jackson, nice to meet you."

Shelby didn't miss how his eyes brightened a little when he touched Kenzi's hand. He certainly hadn't had that light in his eyes when he had shaken her hand, but Shelby was used to this. Kenzi had always been the outgoing one, and with her dark hair and green eyes — she was beautiful. It was no mystery that men were drawn to her. The only surprising thing was that she was still single.

Actually, that part wasn't a surprise either. Kenzi had always been a little flighty. She'd dropped out of college because she hadn't known what she wanted to do with her life, and she jumped from one man to another because she had no idea what she wanted in a man. However, she'd made it her mission to date as many as possible until she figured it out.

"Kenzi, Tucker and I need to plan the clinic for next week. Do you think you could make sure everything is ready for the kids who will be arriving soon?" Shelby made sure to emphasize the words so that Kenzi would realize they were not a question.

Kenzi's lips pursed in a slight pout as if she were going to argue, but Shelby shot her a warning glance. She was still in charge here.

"Yes, of course. Tucker, if you need anything, you can holler for me. It was great meeting you, and I'm sure I'll see you around."

Sugar dripped from Kenzi's voice accompanied with just the right amount of eye batting. Were those false lashes? Shelby rolled her eyes. Kenzi could teach a class in flirting.

"I'm sure you will," Tucker said with a smile. "Does she work here every day?" he asked when Kenzi was out of sight. He might have been talking to Shelby, but his gaze remained at the doorway as if willing Kenzi to reappear.

"Yep, every day," Shelby said through clenched teeth. She resisted the urge to smack him to bring him back to the discussion at hand. If she had any other option, she would kick this guy to the curb. But she didn't. It was him or nothing, and nothing wasn't really an option. Not if she wanted to keep the lights on and the doors open. "I think we're almost finished here, but do you need anything else for the clinic? Any supplies?"

"What?" He blinked and then returned his gaze to her.

"Supplies. For the clinic." Perhaps if she said the words slowly and deliberately, they would register in his neanderthal head. "Do you need anything?"

"Uh, footballs, I guess, and maybe cones to set up boundaries." His face muscles twitched, and she could tell he was trying not to cave in to the desire to check the doorway again. Kenzi was pretty. Okay, more than pretty, but why did every man have to go gaga when they saw her?

"I know we have cones, and I think we have about ten footballs." She'd have to air them up the night before to make sure they weren't flat, but that wasn't a huge deal. "Will that be enough?"

"It should be fine, yeah."

"Okay, well, then I think we're good."

"Right. Uh, what about next week? What time do you want me here?"

Shelby stared at him. He hadn't even wanted to be here, but suddenly with the appearance of Kenzi, he seemed to find that appealing. She leaned back and crossed her arms. She needed him for the clinic, but she had no use for him for the rest of the week. Well, actually she did. Volunteers were hard to come by, and with the school kids out for the next two weeks, she could use another adult around. Tucker, however, seemed like he would be more interested in ogling Kenzi than helping out with the kids.

"Look," he said with a sigh, "I'm sorry. I'm no good at this. This whole situation wasn't my fault, and I guess I'm a little irritated that it feels like I'm being punished for it."

She had no idea what situation he was even talking about. The clinic? Or whatever he had done that had resulted in him being volunteered to run the clinic?

"My team wants me to fulfill twenty hours of community service, and they expect me to serve it here. Helping out. So, what can I do?"

Shelby regarded him a moment longer. She wanted to tell him

no, that she didn't need his scowling face around the center, but her conscience told her that maybe he had been given a raw deal. Being punished for something she hadn't done would probably make her angry, and perhaps she would have a similar reaction if she were thrown into unknown territory like he clearly was. Besides, it was Christmas, and she could use the help.

"Fine. We aren't open on the weekend, but next week, we're open all day because there's no school. If you can be here at eight am, I can put you to work."

He blanched slightly and blinked at her as if shocked by the time. For a moment, Shelby thought he was going to retract his offer, but then he squared his broad shoulders and nodded. "I'll have to leave in the middle of the day for practice, but I can come by before and return after if you need as well."

"Sounds good. The kids will be here soon. You're welcome to stay and meet them if you'd like, and if you want a tour of the center, I'm sure Kenzi would be glad to show you around." She didn't know why she was offering, but maybe she was hoping he would get Kenzi out of his system before next week.

"I might just do that," he said, "Thanks." And before she could say another word, he had ducked out of the room.

"You're welcome," she said sarcastically to the now-empty chair. Shelby knew it wasn't Kenzi's fault, and she had no desire to date someone like Tucker Jackson; but she did wonder why she couldn't get him out of her head. He was not her type, nor did he seem to want to be here; but still she found his face popping into her mind. His dark eyes, his strong jaw, his broad shoulders. Why? With a sigh, she shook her head. That worry could wait for another day. She had much more important things to worry about right now, like the fact that the kids would be arriving at any moment; and she needed to be prepared.

23

Tucker crossed the big gym and glanced around for Kenzi. He didn't see her in the main room, but there were a few doorways leading out of the room. Perhaps she was down one of them. As he headed toward the first doorway, his gaze travelled the faded white walls. The building could definitely use a little TLC. Not only did faded paint cover the walls, but scratches marred the floor. More than that though was the ambiance. The place felt sad, like happiness had packed up its bags and left. Tucker shivered and wondered why kids came here at all. Was there really no other place they could afford?

He couldn't imagine having to spend time in a place like this; but then again, he'd never had to. Before his mother had died, he'd had her to go home to; and after that, his father's money had paid for sports teams and leagues to keep him busy after school. What did these kids have going for them? Well, they had Shelby and Kenzi. They both seemed nice enough. Maybe they brightened the place up.

Tucker found Kenzi hauling a rack of sports equipment out of a supply closet. She was certainly a perk he hadn't expected. When Blaine had said a woman ran the center, Tucker had hoped perhaps she might be easy on the eyes; but while Shelby was pretty, she was also the epitome of uptight. Her hair had been meticulously sprayed into place in a tight bun — all but one tendril that had somehow snuck loose — and she dressed more like an old time librarian than a manager in her pencil skirt and button-down shirt. There was something about her though, something that sparked when they shook hands. Kenzi, on the other hand, was bright and cheery and definitely more concerned with her appearance than her boss.

"Can I help with that?" He flashed his most disarming smile at her and was pleased when she returned it in kind.

"Sure, thanks. Did you get everything settled with Shelby?"

"I think so. I'll have to spend some time this weekend figuring out exactly what I'm teaching these kids, but it should be fine."

She tilted her head coyly at him. "Somehow, I don't think you'll have any problem coming up with something."

"Thanks." He stared at her for a moment before asking the question that had been burning on his mind since the moment he saw her. "I have to ask. What are you doing working in a place like this? It doesn't really seem to suit your," he paused, trying to think of the appropriate word, "style, at least not like it does Shelby's."

"No, I'm definitely not like Shelby," Kenzi said with a laugh. Her gaze traveled to the reception area, "but she's my best friend and she has a heart of gold. When she needed someone to help out at the center, I stepped up, partly to see her in action and partly because I think I'm hoping some of her rubs off on me."

She wanted to be more like Shelby? "Why?" Tucker hadn't meant to say the question aloud, but it had slipped out.

Kenzi focused her green eyes on him. "Because she's the best person I know. I grew up with money and had anything I wanted, but Shelby?" She shook her head. "Shelby worked for everything she has. She began volunteering in this center when she was in high school because she felt called to. Then she worked here part time while she attended college. She could be managing any place she wanted, she's that amazing; but she chose to come back here. To give back to her community. I only hope that one day I'm as selfless as she is."

Tucker looked back toward the reception area with new eyes. Perhaps he'd been too hard on Shelby. What was it Blaine had said? That he needed to see how the less fortunate lived? Maybe Blaine hadn't been as privileged as Tucker thought. Maybe he was someone like Shelby, who'd known hard times and come out better on the other side because of them. Guilt the size of Texas settled on Tucker's shoulders. He'd been throwing himself a grand pity party over having to do a little community service while Shelby willingly gave of herself to help those around her.

"You sure were talking to Tucker for quite a while." Shelby flashed Kenzi a look out of the corner of her eye as she shut down the computer for the night. Tucker had stayed for an hour talking with Kenzi after he finished with Shelby, but at least he had been nice to the kids. Or she figured he had because no one had complained.

Kenzi shrugged. "I guess. We mainly talked about you though."

"Me?" Shelby nearly choked on the word. "Why would you talk about me? What did you say?"

Kenzi rolled her eyes. "Relax. I simply told him how amazing you were and how you give your all for these kids."

Kenzi never ceased to amaze Shelby. One minute, she was leaving Shelby hanging by taking an extended lunch break to doll up for some guy, and the next, she was singing her praises to the very same man. "Well, thanks, but I doubt he cares about stuff like that. He said he was here because the team assigned him community service. I think he'd rather be anywhere else, and if I had any other way to bring money in, I might just let him go." She grabbed her coat and purse and flicked off the lights.

"Don't be too hard on him," Kenzi said. "I get the feeling he's a good guy underneath. He just hasn't figured out how to show it yet."

"Hmph. I hope he figures it out by Monday, or his surly attitude might send the last few clients we have running for the hills."

Kenzi linked her arm through Shelby's as they walked toward the front door. "First of all, he was great with the kids — I saw no surly attitude. Second, what is it you always tell me about worrying?"

"That you don't do it enough?" Shelby asked.

"No. That you can't change tomorrow by worrying about it. God's got this. Right?"

Shelby paused and stared at her friend. She had always said that. At least until she became the manager, and her worry load had tripled. Perhaps it was time to take her own advice and turn those worries over to God. Heaven knew she hadn't been doing a great job trying to take care of things on her own. Perhaps, this was God's way of showing her that. "You're right. God's got this, and He will provide one way or another."

Kenzi's face broke into a wide smile. "That's my girl. Now, how about we grab dinner out somewhere? It's so late that I'm sure you've missed the family dinner."

Shelby glanced at her watch. Kenzi was right. Her mother always served dinner promptly at seven, so no one could use the excuse that they didn't know what time it might be. Normally, Shelby was closed up by six forty-five and, thanks to the close proximity of the center to her parent's house, managed to pull into the driveway ten minutes later. Tonight, closing had run long. It was already past seven-thirty, and her stomach groaned in protest at the extra wait time.

"Okay, what do you have in mind?"

"Just a little Thai place I've been meaning to try for ages. We'll

take my car, and I'll bring you back here for yours later. Deal?"
Kenzi wiggled her eyebrows the way she had in college when
she'd wanted to get Shelby to lighten up and give up studying for
the night. It was a comical effect on her flawless face but one that
always managed to elicit a smile from Shelby.

Shelby rolled her eyes; but just like in college, she couldn't
keep her mouth from twitching into a smile. She locked the front
door and then faced Kenzi. "Fine."

"Yes. We're going to have so much fun."

Shelby wasn't sure about that, but as she followed Kenzi to her
car, she couldn't deny that she felt a little lighter. Like maybe
everything would turn out all right.

24

Tucker groaned as the blaring beeping blasted away his peaceful slumber. He hated alarm clocks. It was just one of the many reasons he enjoyed the football lifestyle. Since practices rarely started before noon, he almost never had to wake up to the harsh sound of the alarm. Instead, he could lie in bed and wake up leisurely with the sun. At least, normally he could. Today, he had to be out of the house in an hour. He'd told Shelby he would be there when the center opened, and that was less than two hours from now.

He dragged himself out of bed and plodded toward the shower. It was still dark outside and cold, so cold. Perhaps he should look into those heated floors after all. Most of the house was carpeted, but the bathroom had cold marble flooring. Easy to clean but like an ice box when it was cold.

Tucker stepped into the shower and turned the water to hot. He'd always enjoyed the steam, but it was even more invigorating today. It pushed the last bit of sleep from his eyes, but it also had the unfortunate effect of clearing the fog from his head which allowed his mind to think about the day ahead. What in the world would he do with kids all day? They had seemed nice Friday evening, but he had only spent an hour there. Most of that had been introducing himself and then talking with Kenzi while they kept an eye on the kids. Today would be longer, and he wasn't much of a kid person. Maybe that was because he'd had to grow up so quickly. Maybe it was the reminder of his own past before his mother died. Whatever the reason, he'd never been great with kids. Sure, he would sign their footballs and shirts and pose for pictures, but he was always more comfortable when there were no kids in the crowd.

With a sigh, he turned the water off and stepped out of the shower. He would just have to make the best of the situation. After all, it was only for a week. One week, and then his community service obligation would be over. He could concentrate on the game and return to sleeping in.

SHELBY GLANCED UP FROM THE FLYER SHE WAS MAKING AS THE door opened. Tucker Jackson strode through right on time. She'd had her doubts that he would show up again, but she supposed she was glad. Her high school volunteer who normally helped out during Christmas Break had texted her last night stating she didn't feel well and probably wouldn't make it in for the day, which would have left Kenzi and Shelby in quite a pickle if Tucker hadn't shown up. Though their count was low enough that two people could watch the kids, it would have meant no break for either of them all day, and that made for a long day. Hopefully, Jennifer's illness was temporary and not typical high school flaking. She had seemed responsible, but Shelby had noticed a shift in some of the younger generation.

"Perfect timing," she said as he signed in on the log. "Can you come around here? I need to have you fill out a volunteer form, and I'd like to see what you think of this flyer for your clinic." She'd mentioned the event to the parents when they picked up their kids on Friday, but she wanted flyers to give the kids to take home as a reminder and to hand out to anyone new. Plus, she hoped to find some time to post a few around the town today.

"Uh, sure." He might have been speaking to her, but she thought that his eyes were definitely looking for Kenzi. Shelby tried not to let it bother her. After all, she was used to being in Kenzi's shadow, but she couldn't deny that a part of her wanted to step out and be noticed for once.

He appeared in the doorway a moment later, and she waved him into the room. She slid the volunteer form she had pulled out earlier across the table to him.

"What's this?" he asked as he picked up the paper.

"The volunteer form. Every volunteer has to fill one out. I should have had you do it the last time you were here, but I forgot. It's straightforward information — name, address, phone number, blood type."

His eyes shot up. "Blood type?"

Shelby bit back her smile; she hadn't thought he would be this easy to tease. She put on her best serious face and tried to keep her voice neutral. "Of course, just in case you fall or the kids attack you and we need to rush you to the hospital."

He cocked his head at her and narrowed his eyes. "You're joking with me, aren't you?"

"Yes, I am." Shelby forced her face to remain deadpan though she could feel the giggle building inside her. "We haven't had anyone fall around here in a very long time."

He shook his head and began filling out the form, and Shelby counted the seconds in her head. How long would it take him to realize…?

His head shot up. "Wait, the kids don't really attack people, do they?"

The giggle escaped her lips at the slight panic in his eyes. He was way too gullible. "No, I'm kidding. It's really just so we can get ahold of you if necessary, and we have to keep a record in case anything ever happens that needs to be investigated. Don't worry, though, it never has."

"I didn't take you for having such a sense of humor," Tucker said as a small smile pulled at his own lips.

Sense of humor. Yep. That's what she had. Kenzi had the magnetic smile, personality, and figure; and Shelby had... Humor. "There's a lot you don't know about me," she said softly under her breath. She didn't think she'd said it loud enough for him to hear, but when he paused and glanced at her from the corner of his eye, she had to wonder. Thankfully, he said nothing though and just continued filling out the form.

"Okay, all done." He clicked the back of the pen before laying it on the paper and sliding both her direction.

"Thanks." She picked up the form and rolled back to the desk, placing it in a manila file folder next to her computer.

"There's already a file on me?" he asked.

"What?" She chuckled and shook her head as he grinned at her. So, he had a sense of humor too. "Yeah, the team sent over your rap sheet. I had no idea." She'd meant the words as a joke, but as his jaw tightened, she could tell that something had hit a nerve. *Did* he have a rap sheet? Was that why he had been assigned community service? He hadn't actually told her what he'd done. Had he done something worth being punished for? He'd said it hadn't been his fault, but had he been lying? She wanted to know more, but she could tell he wasn't going to open up about it. Surely, it couldn't be anything that bad. They wouldn't send someone violent to a center to work with kids, would they? No, of course they wouldn't; she was just being paranoid. Still, perhaps she could call later and get more information.

"Um, well anyway, here's the flyer I've been working on for the clinic. Can you tell me what you think?" He crossed the small room to stand beside her, and the scent of his woodsy cologne filled her nose. He wasn't as tall as her brothers, but there was something solid and masculine about his presence. A tremor raced down her back, and she forced herself not to shiver.

"It looks good," he said, "but you might want to include the price. People won't like it if they think it's free and then we charge them when they show up. How much are you charging anyway?"

"I'm not sure. I know you haven't done this before, but what do you think is a good rate? Fifty dollars? More? Less?" She'd crunched a few numbers over the weekend and knew they needed to charge as much as people would be willing to pay, but she wanted to hear his thoughts too.

He ran his hand across his jaw. The soft scratch of skin against stubble filled the silence. "I think fifty is too low. Plus, you're trying to increase enrollment, right?"

Shelby nodded. "That is the ultimate goal. I need to pay January's rent first and foremost, but getting more kids back in the program is the only way we'll succeed long term."

He pursed his lips as if thinking again. "I know you want all your kids to be able to attend, but what if we have a sliding scale? The price is one hundred per kid, fifty for those who are current members, and seventy-five for anyone who signs up for the next month and pays in advance. Plus, you could offer a discount for families who have more than one kid."

Shelby blinked, blindsided by his logic. She hadn't known many athletes in high school, preferring to hang around students who read or debated instead; but she'd had a generalization in her head about them. Stereotypical jocks who only thought about how to bulk up, win, and get girls. Tucker was proving that wrong. "That's a great idea. How do you seem to know so much about charging rates? I thought you said you'd never done this before."

His smile faltered, and a small sigh proceeded his words. "My father is a prolific donor. I'm pretty sure he could turn it into an

Olympic event if he wanted. Needless to say, I've heard all the spiels, read all the flyers, and deciphered all the doublespeak."

She nodded and began typing in the corrections. There was obviously a story here between him and his father, but again Shelby didn't pry. She was great at listening, but he didn't know her well enough to open up to her; and whatever was going on between him and his father had affected him greatly. It probably still was.

"Better?" she asked when she finished.

He leaned over her shoulder again and nodded. "Yeah, now it looks great."

"Good, thank you. Did you think of anything else you might need?" She turned to look at him and nearly jumped out of her skin at how close his face was. Her heart thundered in her chest.

"No, I think I'm good." His eyes held hers a moment before he leaned back. "What would you like me to do today?"

"Um." Shelby was still trying to get her heart under control. Why was she reacting like this around him? He wasn't interested in her; he'd made it abundantly clear that he preferred Kenzi. So, why did she feel like a giddy schoolgirl? "The kids will be arriving soon. Do you want to air up the balls and make sure they're ready to go?"

"I'd be happy to. Where do I find them?"

Shelby grabbed the supply room key from the rack and then handed it to him. She walked to the doorway and pointed to the far side of the large gym wall. "Straight over there. You can't miss it."

He tossed her a lopsided smile as he walked away, and Shelby took a deep breath. She needed to get herself under control. Tucker was volunteering. Nothing more. And she would do well to remember that.

TUCKER FORCED HIMSELF NOT TO GLANCE BACK AT SHELBY AS HE walked toward the supply closet. What had happened in there? Yes, it had been nice to see her sense of humor, but she was so not his type. So, what had that moment been about? That moment where they locked eyes and he felt like she was glimpsing his soul? It must just be the situation. He was out of his element here. His guard had just been down. That was all. Right?

He opened the supply closet and flicked the light on. The room was tiny, barely larger than a single stall bathroom. One silver rack filled with basketballs, footballs, and volleyballs took up most of the space. Though the rack was full, all of the balls appeared to be low on air. He wondered if they had ever been filled up before, but as he inspected them closer, he realized that wasn't the issue. These balls were old and worn. He looked around for an air pump and spied an older handheld model in the back corner. It too appeared to have seen better days. He surveyed the rest of the supplies with fresh eyes and realized that everything in the center could stand to be replaced. It was a wonder Shelby was keeping this place open at all.

He grabbed the air pump in one hand and the silver rack in the other and wheeled it out to the main area. The basketballs were on top, so he started with them. He had just inserted the needle when he heard high-heeled steps behind him.

"Hey, Tucker, Shelby said you were airing up the balls. Would you like some help?"

Kenzi wore tight jeans that showed off her toned legs and an oversized sweater today. Her smile was just as bright as it had been on Friday, and he felt himself mirroring her expression. "I'd love that, but there appears to only be one pump." Her face fell in disappointment, and he hurriedly continued, "But, you could hold the needle in while I pump, and it might go faster."

"Sure, I can do that." She picked up the ball and cradled it in one arm while holding the needle in place with her other hand. Not the way he would have done it, but he supposed it worked.

"So, I know you said you started working here to help Shelby out, but how long has it been?" he asked as he began pumping the handle.

"Only for the past year since Shelby became the director. I went to college for a time, but I didn't really know what I wanted to do. So, I'm taking time off while I decide. I volunteered a few times with Shelby before she took over and enjoyed it; so when she offered me a full-time position, it seemed like a good job until I figure out where I want to go."

He took the ball from her and squeezed. It felt full enough, so he removed the needle and bounced it. Satisfied, he placed it back in the rack and handed her the next one. "So, you still don't know what you want to do?"

She shrugged. "Not really. I like talking to people and I'd love anything where I could be in the public eye, like a reporter or something. But, I don't want to jump into anything until I'm really sure. So, for now, I work with Shelby. It pays the bills and allows me to meet people."

Tucker couldn't imagine not knowing what he wanted to do with his life at this age. From the time he'd started playing football his freshman year of high school, he'd known that it was what he wanted to do. But he supposed it happened. He'd attended college with several people who had floated from one major to the next because they couldn't decide what career path they wanted.

Still, it was odd how different Shelby and Kenzi were. He'd thought it was just the outside appearance, but evidently it ran deeper. Shelby not only appeared more professional in her attire, but she also seemed to know what she wanted out of life. Whereas Kenzi screamed fun with her tighter, brighter clothing, but he wondered how long the fun would last. Tucker wasn't sure he was ready to settle down; but when he was, he wanted someone who knew where they were going.

"Have you always played football?"

Kenzi's voice shook him back to the present. She had shelved the second ball and was inserting the needle into the third. "Um, since high school. I began playing my freshman year, and not only did it turn out I was pretty good at it, but it was an escape for me."

"An escape?" Tiny wrinkles crossed her forehead as she scrunched her brow. "What did you need to escape from?"

Tucker opened his mouth to answer, but he wasn't sure he was ready to talk about his mother's death. Nor was he sure he wanted to tell Kenzi. He didn't know why, but he sensed Shelby would understand his pain more than Kenzi would. "Oh, you know, high school angst and all that," he said instead. "Do you have high school kids who come here?" He couldn't imagine older kids enjoying time in the center. It was too plain, too outdated.

"No, most of our kids are elementary and middle school aged."

"That makes sense. I suppose that once you can drive, you can take care of yourself." Or once your mother dies and your father withdraws, he thought to himself.

"Yeah, it's too bad more don't volunteer though. We have one girl, Jennifer, who helps out during breaks and summers, but we could use more. I think teenagers could be great mentors for the younger students, but I remember high school. The last thing I wanted to do was give up my time after school, especially to hang out with younger kids." She placed the third and last basketball on the shelf and turned to the footballs.

Tucker eyed the faded and worn pigskin with a frown as she inserted the needle. "Are those all the footballs the center has?"

"Yeah, Shelby has been wanting to replace them forever, but she hasn't had the money. Most of what we make pays rent and our salaries. She pays a part-time janitor, but his job is next on the chopping block." She shrugged. "Replacement equipment just keeps dropping lower on the list."

Tucker glanced back at the office where he was sure Shelby sat trying to figure out a way to bring in more money. A sting of something he didn't recognize tugged at his heart. Pity? No, that wasn't quite it. Sorrow? He couldn't even give it a name. All he knew was that he felt for Shelby. She was trying so hard to keep the center open, and she certainly wasn't doing it for money or fame like most people he knew. In fact, the thought convicted him. Maybe he could do something more to help out. More than just the clinic and volunteering this week.

25

Tucker pulled into the stadium parking lot and took a deep breath as he turned off the engine. He couldn't believe how tired he was already. Unsure if it was due to the early morning or the hours spent with the kids, he feared he would be dragging during practice today. And he didn't think he could afford to do that. A frustrated sigh escaped his lips as he grabbed his bag of gear off the passenger seat and headed toward the locker room. He would have to push the exhaustion away and make sure his focus was on practice.

Practices were normally his favorite time of the day, but now? Not only was he tired, but anxiety gnawed at the back of his brain. It was his first practice since the incident last Thursday, and he didn't know what to expect. Had Blaine told everyone else about the assault? Had they found out by some other means? Would they treat him differently? It had already been a struggle trying to fit in on this team after the trade; he certainly didn't need anything else alienating him.

Tucker glanced at his watch again. He was half an hour early, but he'd planned it that way to make sure he was dressed and ready before anyone else. Now that he had a blemish on his record, he would have to toe the line from here on out or start adding some positive checks to his name to clear the stigma. What better way than to be prepared for practice? He'd had to leave the center a little earlier than he'd planned, but he'd promised Shelby he would return after practice.

He pulled open the heavy metal door that squeaked loud enough to wake the dead. Someone should really put some oil on it. Perhaps he should add that to his list as a good deed. As he turned the corner to the locker area, he stopped short. He hadn't expected to see anyone here yet, but there was Blaine, already dressed in his practice jersey and reading a book as he leaned against his locker. Tucker hadn't really pegged Blaine as a big reader.

"You get everything ironed out with the center?" Blaine asked as Tucker dropped his bag on the bench that sat between the two rows of lockers.

"Yeah, the clinic is scheduled for Wednesday night at six, so I may have to leave practice early." Tucker opened his locker and took out his helmet, setting it next to his bag before unzipping the large duffel and pulling his practice gear out.

"That's no problem. We'll probably be done earlier that night anyway. You're going there this evening after practice, right?"

Tucker wasn't sure if Blaine was asking out of curiosity or to check up on him and make sure he was fulfilling his part of the bargain, but he guessed the latter. "Yes, I'm going there tonight, and I was there this morning."

"Good. Don't forget. Every day this week. The director will be keeping track for me. You definitely don't want to miss a day, or you might find yourself missing the next game." He placed a bookmark in his book, closed it, and shoved it in his locker. "I'll see you out on the field."

And then he was gone, and Tucker was alone in the locker room. With a sigh, he peeled off his shirt and changed into his practice one. He hated having to answer to Blaine. The man appeared too perfect, and Tucker wondered if he ever did anything wrong. He would definitely be relieved when this week ended.

SHELBY STARED AT THE LIST OF POSSIBLE DONORS SHE HAD created and sighed. Calling businesses and asking for money was not her strong suit, but it had to be done. Her calculations showed that even if all the current kids and the ones who had left attended the clinic they would have enough for another month of rent, maybe two, but that was it. And that was if all the kids attended which Shelby knew was not a reality. Some would be busy, some wouldn't be able to afford it, and some might not even care about football. That meant she needed to get the word out to the community and quickly. She hoped that by calling the local businesses, she might be able to drop off flyers tonight or tomorrow morning for them to hang up. If she was really lucky, she might be able to secure a few donations in exchange for sponsorship mentions.

Her first call though had to be to the newspaper and radio stations. It was short notice, but she hoped they would be able to run a Public Service Announcement or something. She had tried to call on Friday, but by the time she'd had everything hammered out with Tucker, no one had been answering the phones.

"Woodville Gazette, how may I direct your call?" the woman on the other end said.

"Hello, this is Shelby Doll from the community center. I'm not sure who I need, but I was hoping to speak with someone about running an ad for an event we have coming up on Wednesday."

"That would be Marcia Walker. I'll connect you."

Shelby held her breath as the phone rang and rang and rang. She sighed when the voicemail picked up. She had been hoping to talk to a real person; but as time was of the essence, a voicemail would have to do. Hopefully, Marcia would call back, but if not, she'd try again tomorrow morning. She left a message and then replaced the phone in the cradle.

The next number yielded a voicemail as well. As did the place after that. By the time she finished the list, she had only been able to speak with people at two of the businesses. Both had agreed to let her hang flyers, but only one was considering a donation. "Holiday times are tough," they'd said which had made Shelby nearly laugh out loud. Didn't they know that was the exact reason she was calling?

She wondered when the shift had happened. When exactly had people stopped donating? She'd noticed it over the years, even as a volunteer — fewer and fewer donations coming in, but this year had to be the worst. And it wasn't just the community center. She'd noticed it at church too. People had stopped putting tithes in the offering plate when it was passed. She supposed some people gave online like she did, but her church always posted the amount of money received each week, and she'd noticed it getting lower and lower.

"Hey, last kid is gone, and Tucker and I straightened up," Kenzi said knocking on the doorframe. "You gonna head out of here some time tonight?"

"Yeah, I was just trying to get us some coverage for the clinic on Wednesday, but it's not looking good. I'm going to canvas the businesses tomorrow to see about posting flyers. Did you make sure all the kids got one?"

"We did."

"I might have an idea," Tucker said, appearing behind Kenzi. "I could check with the PR rep for the Tornadoes and see if they would put something on our website."

Shelby's heart soared. "That would be amazing exposure. Do you think he'll do it?"

Tucker shrugged. "I don't see why not unless it's a time thing, but I'll call him as soon as I leave here. Do you have anything else you need me to do?"

"Not for tonight. Thank you though." Shelby shut off the computer and grabbed her purse. "It's time to call it a night anyway." She pulled on her coat and flicked the light off. Maybe things would work out after all. If Tucker could get the clinic posted on the webpage, that would have to draw in some new people. She followed Kenzi and Tucker toward the door, dropping her head to rummage for her keys in her purse.

"Oh my gosh, it's snowing."

"What?" Shelby's head popped up at Kenzi's statement. Sure enough, tiny flakes flitted past the window. Snow? Why was it snowing? They lived in central Texas where it almost never snowed.

"I knew it," Tucker said as he pushed open the door. "I felt it the other night. That chill in the air."

"It can't snow." Shelby locked the front door and then pulled on her gloves. "What if it keeps people from coming to the clinic?"

"Don't worry," Kenzi said, tilting her head back and opening her mouth to catch a snowflake. "It's barely anything. I doubt it even sticks."

But Shelby wasn't so sure. The little voice of doubt in her head had started up again. What if it wasn't just a dusting? What if it turned into something more? What if it snowed enough that they had to cancel the clinic?

Unlocking her car, she climbed inside and turned the key to let the engine warm up. As she did, she watched the flakes of snow glide past her window. "Please stop snowing," she whispered as her eyes scanned the gray clouds. They were dark and heavy, and right now they were teasing her; but she knew at any moment they would open up and dump the snow they were concealing. It would blanket the ground, sending tremors of excitement through all the kids as they prayed for enough snow to build a snowman or go sledding or have a snowball fight. Daggers of disappointment would pierce all the parents as they dreaded having to drive on the icy streets.

Shelby usually loved the snow; she always had. Memories of playing in the snow with her big brothers and building giant snowmen with her dad were some of her favorites from when she was young. Of course, here in Texas, it didn't snow nearly as often as it had in Nebraska where she grew up until her father's company moved them out to Fort Worth; but she'd still always prayed for snow every December.

Her mother had never enjoyed the snow as much as Shelby had. Perhaps she had when she was little, but snow in Nebraska rarely closed businesses, and it almost never closed hospitals. Since her mother was a nurse, it had often meant her getting up for work extra early to drive the snow-covered streets safely. Her shift had been full of helping others who were not so cautious, and finally when her shift ended, generally after running at least an hour later than planned, she would have to make the treacherous drive back home in the dark. Shelby had never fully understood why her mother didn't enjoy the snow. Until now.

Now, as the cold from the outside invaded her car and chilled her insides, she could understand her mother's reaction. Now that she had responsibilities and an upcoming event that dangled precariously already, she could see the snow not for the magical wonderland that it was, but for the havoc-wreaking disaster it might become.

If it snowed too much, the center would have to close, and that would be disastrous with the unpaid rent hanging over her head and the Christmas party still not funded. Plus, delivering flyers and asking for donations would be a lot harder if Shelby had to do it trudging through snow. Even worse, the snow might keep people from attending the clinic. And then where would she get the money?

Though she didn't normally pray for God to influence the weather, she found herself doing it now as she drove to her parent's house. "Lord, please don't let the snow stick. Please let it pass us.

You know how much this center means to the community and the kids. Please."

Shelby groaned as the snow fell heavier, and her windshield wipers worked extra hard keeping her windshield cleared. The rhythmic swishing of their blades sent her heart pounding even faster as the scene outside her window became more like a snow globe freshly shaken.

How she used to love snow globes. They were the one trinket she always bought when her family took a trip somewhere. Sam always bought a shot glass, Scott collected hats, but Shelby had always gravitated to the snow globes. For a time, they had lined her shelves; and some nights, she would take one to bed, shake it, and wish she could live in the tiny house or village that appeared so peacefully nestled in the swirling snow. As she had gotten older, her interest in them had waned. She wasn't even sure where they had ended up after she moved out though, and she hadn't thought of them in ages. They were forefront in her mind now, however, as the snow grew thicker and swirled lazily out the window; and unless Shelby was imagining it, the ground sported a fresh white color in places. It was sticking.

She parked the car in her parent's driveway and rushed inside. The warmth from their heater blanketed her as she shook the white powder from her hair.

"Oh no, is it snowing?" her mother asked as she entered the room.

"It is," Shelby growled as she removed her shoes. "It started off light, but it's definitely getting thicker out there. I'm praying that it stops."

Her mother's brow lifted. "You? Praying it stops? I thought you loved the snow."

"I do, but it's the worst time right now. If it keeps snowing, it might cancel the clinic I have planned on Wednesday. Without that, I don't know how we're going to get the money we need."

"Well, I'm sure God will provide for you. Heaven knows we

need the center to give those kids a safe place after school and during breaks. Try not to worry about it too much right now. Dinner's ready. Are you hungry?"

Shelby spared one more glance out the front window before heaving a resigned sigh, nodding, and following her mother to the dining room.

Scott, Sam, Iris, and her father were already seated around the large table when Shelby and her mother entered. The extra leaf had been put in, but it was still a tight squeeze for the six of them. She wondered what would happen when she and Scott got married. Would her parents purchase a larger table, or would the family dinners fall apart? She certainly hoped it wasn't the latter. Except for Kenzi, who could always get her to talk, these family dinners were the only other place Shelby really felt comfortable, whole, loved.

"Ah, there's my two favorite girls," her father said as they pulled out their chairs. "For a moment, I thought we were going to have to start without you."

"No, sorry, I just had to drive slower due to the snow," Shelby said as she sat in her chair.

"Is it snowing?" Iris craned her head around Sam to see out the dining room window.

"It is and it's getting thicker by the minute. I could use some prayer that it stops before it shuts down the fundraiser I have scheduled for Wednesday," Shelby said. "The center could certainly use the money."

"Well, why don't we add that to the prayer for tonight," her father said as he held out his hand. Around the table everyone grabbed the hand next to them and bowed their heads. "Lord, we thank you for this food that you have provided. We thank you for the time we are able to spend together as a family and for the jobs you have given us all. Please help the community center find funding to stay open. We know there are many in this town who are struggling and need the doors to stay open. In your name, Amen."

"Amen," Shelby echoed as she opened her eyes. She glanced out the window, but the thick snowflakes now looked more like a white curtain than individual crystals. It appeared God was not in the business of granting miracles tonight.

26

Darkness still filled the room when Shelby's alarm went off, but it took her only moments to shake the sleep from her eyes. She had to check the snow. Pushing the plush comforter back, she swung her legs out and into her fluffy leopard print house shoes that she always kept by the side of her bed. Even though her room was carpeted, it was always cold in the morning. The poor old heater just couldn't seem to keep up with the draft that drifted in through the old windows.

A few steps brought her to the window, and she pulled back the curtains. The streetlight gave just enough illumination to see that snow still fell softly to the completely white ground. She let the curtain fall back over the window and padded back to her night-stand where the remote sat.

She punched the button, and the old television hummed to life. It was a flat screen, but not the fancy ones that were so popular today. She had no Apple TV, no Roku device, and definitely no 3D. No, this was a television she had purchased used when her last television had given up the ghost. The screen flickered for a moment before coming into focus, and Shelby curled her feet up under her to watch the news report.

"While we expected snow, we did not predict it would happen this quickly or that we would get this much," the woman on the screen said. Her blonde hair fell in perfect waves to her thin shoulders, and though Shelby had often heard that TV cameras made people look ten pounds heavier, this woman didn't appear to have any extra weight on her. Her hand motioned to the screen behind her, and Shelby marveled at how good she was at making it appear she could see the image on the screen when Shelby knew a green screen was the only thing behind the woman. It was fascinating technology.

"The streets are still slick, and the DOT is recommending that you give yourself an extra half hour of driving time to navigate the icy roads. The good news, for those of us who have to commute to work, is that the sun is expected to come out today; and temperatures are expected to rise to the mid-forties, melting all the snow by late afternoon."

"Yes," Shelby jumped up from the bed and danced an awkward jig over to her closet. She might not have rhythm, but what she lacked in style, she made up for in exuberance. And she knew just who to thank this morning. The snow would be gone by tomorrow which meant the clinic could continue as planned.

She jumped in the shower, whistling as she washed. Maybe they could even take the kids out back to play in the snow if they all brought warm enough coats. She knew they would go stir crazy if they were stuck in the center while the snow taunted them from the ground.

Her joy lasted through breakfast, through brushing her teeth, and bundling up for the cold. It even lasted through the slightly terrifying drive where she almost swerved off the road when she was forced to brake at the bottom of a slight hill, but it died as she pulled into the parking lot of the community center. She had no idea why, but an ominous feeling that something was wrong fell on her shoulders as she parked the car and got out.

Nothing looked out of place. Snow covered the roof, but thankfully, it still appeared to be in one piece. The windows weren't cracked or broken, so what was it?

With careful, deliberate steps, Shelby made her way up the sidewalk. She'd have to get some salt on it quickly before anyone slipped and fell. Hopefully they had some in the supply shed. The supply shed? Had something happened to it? Was that why she felt something was wrong? She quickly veered to the right and toward the shed, but when she rounded the corner, she stopped. The shed looked fine, and the lock still hung securely on the door. So, that wasn't it either.

Shaking her head, she returned to the center and unlocked the front door. The lights flicked on like normal, so it wasn't the loss of electricity that bothered her. Had she left her computer on? The deposit out? She didn't think so. Closing was habit for her, and she did it the same way every night. Shelby opened the reception area door, but there was no light coming from the computer and no deposit bag on the table.

She must be going crazy. It was probably just the fear of not getting the money needed that had her freaking out. Opening the desk drawer, she placed her purse inside and then took off her coat. The chill set in immediately. She needed to get the heater turned on, so the kids wouldn't freeze when they got here and then maybe fix herself some hot tea.

The thermometer was located on the way to the kitchen, and she clicked it on and cranked the dial up a few notches for good measure. Then she turned on the kitchen light and grabbed the kettle from the stove. It still had a little water in it, but figuring she might need more, she took off the lid and placed it under the faucet. She turned the handle, but no water came out of the faucet. Shelby tapped on the handle. Was there a clog somewhere? Had the landlord forgotten to pay the water bill? No, she would have gotten a notice if that was the case, wouldn't she?

"Shelby? Are you here?" Tucker's voice carried through the quiet building.

"In the kitchen," she called back.

"Everything okay?" he asked as he stepped through the door frame.

"Not really. We don't seem to have water." She turned the faucet again to show him, and a frown creased his features.

"Do you know where the water shut off valve is?"

Shelby blinked at him. Water shut-off valve? What was he talking about? She didn't have any water, so why would she need to shut it off? "I don't know. Why?"

"I think your pipes might be frozen, and if we don't get the water shut off before they start thawing, they could burst."

Shelby's eyes widened. Was this what her ominous feeling had been about? "That would be bad, right?"

"That would be very bad. Burst pipes usually cause flooding which could shut the center down for weeks."

"No! No, no, no." She shook her head as she began pacing the floor. "We can't shut down for weeks. If we shut down, we'll lose the last few clients we have, and then I'll have no way to pay the rent." Shelby was babbling, but she couldn't stop. This was her nightmare come true, and she'd thought they were finally going to be able to save the center.

"Shelby." Tucker grabbed her arms and stilled her pacing. "We can fix this, but I need to shut off the water. Is there a basement area?"

Basement? She tried to make her brain work, but not only was it still focused on the problem; it was also now reacting to Tucker's touch. Heat from his hands pulsated through her arms, and she felt mesmerized by his stare. "Basement?" This time she managed to say the word out loud. "Yes, I think there is."

"Okay, can you show me?"

Shelby nodded, blinked, and forced her mind to concentrate. "Yes, yes, of course." She led the way out of the kitchen and down the narrow hallway that led to the basement area.

"Wait here. I'll be right back."

As Tucker disappeared through the doorway, Shelby knotted her hands together and closed her eyes. She needed the peace that praying brought.

TUCKER MADE HIS WAY CAREFULLY DOWN THE NARROW STAIRS. The last thing he needed was to fall and injure himself before the next game. He shivered as the air grew even colder and wondered if the basement was even insulated. No wonder the pipes had frozen.

His foot hit the floor and he glanced around the small room. Actually "room" might have been an overstatement. He could touch every wall from where he stood, but thankfully that made it easy to find the water valve. It creaked and groaned under his grip, but he managed to switch it off. Now, they just had to find a way to thaw the pipes without causing them to burst.

Not being a plumber, he didn't trust himself to know the best way to thaw them. Thankfully, he knew a plumber who owed him a favor. He made his way carefully back up the steps and found Shelby with her hands tightly clasped and her eyes closed. Her lips moved slightly as if praying.

He cleared his throat, not wanting to alarm her, but wanting to let her know he was there. Her eyes snapped open.

"Did you find it?"

"I did, and I got it turned off. However, I'm no expert at this. If we try to thaw them and do it wrong, we could still cause them to burst. I recommend we call a plumber."

Her bottom lip folded under and sadness filled her eyes. Her hands twisted together, and her words tumbled out like an avalanche. "A plumber? But that will cost money. I don't have any money, and the landlord is on vacation until the end of the month. Plus, what if he can't come right away? We can't afford to close the center, but I can't have kids here if there's no water."

He crossed to her and placed his finger under her chin, lifting her eyes to his to get her attention. "Hey, I know a plumber who owes me a favor. Let me call him and see if he can come out. We'll figure out what to do from there."

She nodded, but his heart still went out to her. She looked so stressed, like anything else might send her screaming for the hills, and he wished he had a way to shoulder her worry. "I'll be right back, but trust me, it will be okay."

Tucker hoped he hadn't spoken too soon as he stepped away from her and dialed the number of his contact. It rang in his ear, and he clenched his jaw. "Come on, Teddy, pick up. I need you to pick up." He glanced back over his shoulder to make sure Shelby was still out of hearing range.

"Perfect Plumbing, this is Teddy. How can I help you?"

Tucker breathed a sigh of relief at the sound of Teddy's voice. "Hey, Teddy, it's Tucker Jackson. You remember that favor you owe me?" Tucker had run into Teddy at a fundraiser this past summer. The man had been desperate for tickets to the season opener for his son's birthday; and as Tucker had few friends at the time to invite, he had offered up his box seats in exchange for a favor in the future.

"Tucker Jackson. Of course, I remember. Bummer about the loss the other night, but you guys will pull it out, right?"

"I sure hope so." Tucker hated being reminded of the loss, but he knew Teddy meant nothing by it. It was something all fans said at some point as though they could commiserate with how hard the players trained only to still lose. "Anyway, I have a friend over at the community center. The cold weather froze their pipes, and we need to get them thawed so she can open today. You think you could squeeze in a little time to come check it out?"

"For you, man, I'll make some time. Let me get dressed and grab my tools. I'll be there in under an hour."

"Thanks, Teddy, you're a lifesaver." Tucker punched the end call button and turned back to Shelby.

"Okay, he said he can be here in an hour."

"Thank you." She looked back toward the entrance. "Do you think we can still open? I don't want to turn people away, but I'd hate to let them in if we aren't going to have water."

"I'm sure he'll be able to get the water running again. What else do we need to do to prepare for the kids' arriving?"

Her brow furrowed as she thought. "Salt. We need to lay salt on the sidewalk."

"Okay, that's good. Do you have any here?"

"I think we have some in the supply shed. Let me get the key and we can go check."

Tucker followed her back to the reception area and waited while she grabbed the key. He wondered when his view of her had shifted. When he'd first met her, he'd found her so stiff that he'd wondered if a rod had been jammed into her spine. She had looked as if she didn't know the meaning of the word relax much less how to do it; but over the last two days, he had seen her sense of humor and how much she cared for these kids. Now when he saw her, he didn't see her as stiff and unapproachable. Instead, he saw a strong woman who would do anything for those she cared about. And he found it attractive and appealing.

"Okay, I've got it," Shelby said dangling the key in front of her face. "What?"

"Nothing." Tucker couldn't tell her how he felt. Not yet anyway. He needed to know if she felt anything for him first, and he should probably wait until his time here was finished. It would be way too uncomfortable to continue working with her if he shared his feelings and she didn't reciprocate them, and he still had to fulfill his hours. "Let's go."

Another car had pulled into the parking lot while they were inside, and disappointment flooded Tucker when he realized it was Kenzi. Shelby would probably send Kenzi with him to get the salt instead of going herself now.

"Hey, everything okay?" Kenzi asked as she stepped out of her car.

"The pipes are frozen so there's no water right now, but Tucker called a plumber to come check them out," Shelby returned. "We were just heading to the shed to see if there's any salt."

"I'll go with him to get the salt. You should stay out here and let parents know when they arrive," Kenzi said.

Tucker bit back his disappointment and shivered in his jacket. He'd rather go with Shelby, but right now, he just wished they could get moving. Already, the cold was seeping in through his jacket, and he needed to do something to warm up. He hoped Teddy arrived soon because he would have to leave for practice a little early with the icy roads, and he'd like to be here to discuss the price arrangement.

Shelby glanced at her watch and blew out a breath, sending a white vapor cloud into the air. "You're probably right, although I thought people would be arriving by now. I hope the snow isn't keeping them away." Shelby handed the key to Kenzi and then scanned the parking lot. "Can you see if there's a shovel as well? Maybe if we shovel the parking lot, they will come."

Tucker couldn't help the grin that sprang to his face at her allusion to the old Kevin Costner movie. There was that sense of humor again. Was that part of what was intriguing him now?

"Come on, Tucker. Let's see what we can find." Though she was not dressed for snow in her tight jeans and high heeled boots, Kenzi led the way confidently across the parking lot.

The supply shed appeared to be in decent shape on the outside, but Tucker wondered what they would find inside. He feared everything would be old and worn out like it was inside the center.

"Okay, let's see if there's salt and a shovel in here." Kenzi inserted the key into the lock on the door of the small shed and turned it. Tucker heard the distinctive click and then Kenzi was pulling the door open. The shed was packed from one end to the other, and Tucker wondered how they found anything when they needed it.

"Ugh, he could at least keep it a little neater," Kenzi said as she scanned the contents. Her eyes flicked to the ceiling. "Great, no light either. Well, I guess we'll just have to be super careful. Why don't you take that side, and I'll take this one?"

Without waiting for him to agree, she moved to the left and began scouring the shed. Tucker shook his head as he moved to the right. Visions of him tripping on something or stepping wrong and twisting his ankle flashed through his head. It would not do to get injured here.

"Here." He grabbed the handle of the sole shovel he saw leaning against the wall. It wasn't even a snow shovel which wasn't unusual as this area didn't receive snow that often, but it would make shoveling the snow a long and arduous process. "There's only one though unless you want to use a broom."

"I'm not sure a broom will do much good, but I found the salt. It's too heavy for me to lift, so if you can grab the salt, I'll take the shovel."

Tucker scanned the rest of the shed to see if there was anything else they could use, but while the shed was filled with all sorts of odds and ends, nothing looked as if it could move snow. He handed Kenzi the shovel, muscled the large bag of salt onto his shoulders, and followed her out of the shed.

27

T he first car pulled in a few minutes later. With slumped shoulders, Shelby walked out to greet them.

"Is the center not open today?" the woman asked. Shelby recognized her as one of the more affluent moms who was now using the trampoline park down the street.

Shelby shook her head. "We will open, but unfortunately, our pipes froze. We're waiting on a plumber to thaw them, but we can't open until we have running water."

"So you don't even know if you'll open for sure?" Agitation filled the woman's voice as she glanced at her watch.

"I'm sorry. I know we'll open, but I don't have a specific time. I have no idea how long it takes to thaw pipes, but we can't have the kids here without access to water. I'm sure you understand." Shelby tried to keep her tone friendly though frustration erupted in her at the woman's agitation. Here was a woman who barely used them anymore, yet she was angry that she couldn't drop her son off now when she was being inconvenienced by the snow.

The woman heaved an enormous sigh. "I do understand, and I guess I'll call later to see if you're able to open. Right now, I have to get to work as well." She turned to her son. "Guess it's Grandma's for you today after all."

"Aw, Mom, Grandma's is so boring."

"Maybe it will only be for an hour or so. She can bring you back over here if the place opens..."

Shelby didn't hear the rest of the conversation as the woman rolled up the window and drove away.

"It will be okay," Kenzi said, appearing behind her. She held a spade in her hand that didn't look as if it would do much good in the snow. "I'm sure the plumber is on his way, and Tucker has already started salting the sidewalk."

Shelby followed Kenzi's pointing hand to see Tucker shaking large salt pellets on the icy sidewalk as he stepped carefully toward the door. "Yeah, that's great, but will the plumber make it before other people show up and I have to tell them that I have no idea when we'll open? What happens if they tell the other parents about the closure before we can get it fixed?" She turned as another car entered the parking lot and sighed. "Be right back."

"Hey, Shelby, is the center going to be open today?" This mom she recognized — Diana. Her ginger hair made it nearly impossible to not remember her, and Shelby had been surprised when she had pulled her sons out. She'd thought they really enjoyed the center, especially since both of them were planning to play basketball in high school.

"Morning, Diana." Shelby flashed her brightest smile, hoping it would ease any concerns Diana might have. "We do plan to open as soon as possible. Unfortunately, the cold weather froze our pipes, so we have no water right now. I've got a plumber on the way, and as soon as he thaws the pipes and we have water again, we'll open the center."

Diana's face tightened, and her smile wavered. Shelby knew that face. She'd seen it with every parent who had pulled their child. They'd flashed the patronizing, non-apologetic expression even as their words had tumbled out. "It's not you," they had said, but Shelby knew in a way it was. If she was more exciting, if she had more money, if she only had something to draw them in. . . And then a light went off in her head. She glanced back at Tucker who had evidently finished with the salt, taken the shovel from Kenzi, and now appeared to be attempting to move the snow with the less than ideal tool.

"I'm sorry, Shelby, I need to know they have a solid place to go this afternoon, and I won't have time to call and check."

Diana was a law clerk at the busiest law firm in the city, so not only was she probably late, but Shelby knew she would have a hard time getting away to bring the boys back. More than once, Shelby had been forced to call the backup number on the boys' sheet when she'd needed a quick response.

"Sure, I understand, but it would be a shame for the boys to miss the chance to hang out with Tucker Jackson." Shelby hoped she was hitting the nonchalant tone she was aiming for.

Diana's eyes lit up, and the corners of her mouth lifted again. "Tucker Jackson? From the Texas Tornadoes?" Her hand touched her throat as her eyes scoured the area for the star.

"Yep, he's come to help out at the center. Hoping to give back to the community and all. Have you seen the flyer about the clinic he's putting on tomorrow evening?" She bit her lip to keep from sharing any more excitement. She couldn't believe she had even said that much, especially since she had no idea for sure that the center would even be open tomorrow night. What if the pipes still burst before the plumber arrived?

The two blond boys in the back leaned forward, stretching against their seatbelts. "Mom, we have to come back and meet him. Please?"

Indecision crossed Diana's face, and she turned her slender wrist to check her watch. "Well, I guess I could stay for a little bit to see what the prognosis is. Work will probably make me stay late anyway."

"Yes." The exuberance in the boys' shout matched the feeling in Shelby's heart, and she forced herself not to join in with their cheer.

"Great, why don't you pull in over there." She pointed to the front row of spots that Tucker had somehow managed to clear out. "We should be able to get inside soon and then I can get you a flyer."

"They're staying?" Kenzi asked when Shelby returned to her friend's side.

"Yep." Shelby couldn't tame the smile that graced her lips. "I told them about our local football hero, and they decided to stay to see if the center will get to open. I guess they decided it might be worth the wait to spend the day with him."

❧ 28 ❧

Tucker glanced up as he felt eyes staring at him. Five cars were now parked in the lot waiting for the center to open. He hoped Teddy arrived soon because he would hate for Shelby to have to send the people away.

He tossed another trivial amount of snow to the side — he might as well have been using his hands at this rate — and then paused. Why did it feel as if the passengers in those cars were staring at him? Did they recognize him? He wasn't wearing any official team gear; and his coat, although fitted, was black and not flashy. Underneath, he wore jeans and a loose sweatshirt — definitely not the attire that grabbed attention. Since he couldn't see inside the car windows, he had to assume they couldn't see his face well either. None of that eased the feeling though.

Relief flooded him when the plumbing truck pulled into the lot. Teddy. At last. Now, he could busy himself with helping the guy and escape the uncomfortable feeling. The truck pulled to a stop in front of him, the noise of the engine oddly loud in the otherwise quiet stillness. The engine idled for a moment as if the occupant did not want to step out of the warm embrace the heater offered, but then it too stilled and the silence returned.

The driver's door opened, and Teddy, wearing only a flannel shirt for warmth, stepped out of the cab. He was a large man, but Tucker found it hard to believe he wasn't freezing.

"Thanks for coming so quickly, Teddy," Tucker said, extending a hand.

"You're welcome though I have to tell you, I'm not usually up this early and certainly not when it's this cold outside."

"I hear you," Tucker said with a smile. "If you'll follow me inside, I'll show you the issue. I got the water shut off, but I have no idea how to thaw pipes."

"You shouldn't do it yourself anyway," Teddy said. "I've seen too many well-meaning homeowners flood their house trying to thaw pipes. Let me get my tools, and we'll see what we've got."

As Teddy returned to the truck, Tucker glanced at the parking lot again. There were now seven cars, and one was close enough that he could see the face of a child pressed against the glass. They were definitely here to see him. Well, he could tune them out. Just like during a game.

He'd always been able to do that — tune out the taunts along with the cheers. Probably because, after the first few times of looking, he'd realized his father wasn't in the stands — he was never in the stands — and he'd been the only one who had mattered to Tucker. So, Tucker had just pretended the stands didn't exist. He'd pretended he was just playing with his friends in the park down the street like he had when he was eight and life was still easy. That had gotten him through high school, and it would help him now.

"Okay, lead the way," Teddy said.

Tucker was only too happy to oblige. He turned his back on the peering eyes and led the way to the front door. "How is your son doing?" he asked as he pulled the front door open.

"He's good. Loved getting to watch the game from the luxury box. Thanks again for that."

"You're welcome. Listen, the director here is pretty strapped for money and the landlord is out of town at the moment. If I get you some tickets for next season's opener, do you think you could wait on payment?"

"I don't know, Tucker. It's Christmas and Jack wants some new Xbox game."

"I get that, but listen, I'm hosting a clinic here tomorrow where I'll be teaching the kids some running plays and signing footballs and shirts. Everyone else is paying a hundred dollars to get in, but how about you bring Jack and consider your entrance fee your down payment? I promise you that the landlord is good for it, and you'll get the full amount when he gets back in town." He actually knew nothing about the landlord, but he trusted Shelby. He couldn't see her working for someone underhanded.

"You'll sign whatever we want?" Teddy's eyes narrowed and he stroked his large chin thoughtfully.

"Whatever you want, Teddy."

"All right. You got yourself a deal, Jackson. You better work out your hand tonight though. I don't want it cramping in the middle of all that autographing."

Tucker smiled and clapped Teddy on the shoulder. "I'll do my best. Here's the door to the basement. It's pretty tight down there, but do you think you'll need some help?"

Teddy shook his head. "No way, man. I don't know what I'm going to find down there, and I am not going to be responsible for injuring Tucker Jackson during the playoffs. The mayor would probably yank my license. You know he's a fan."

Tucker nodded. The mayor attended nearly every game. "I do, but Teddy, I promise to be careful."

"No can do, Tucker. My license says that all my guys have to be bonded and insured. I doubt you are either, but I promise I won't be long."

Tucker knew he wasn't going to win this argument. Teddy seemed like a good man, a rule follower, and Tucker wasn't going to push him to do something else. He would just have to return to shoveling and hope Teddy finished quickly.

Shelby turned at the tap on her shoulder.

"What did you tell these people, Shelby?" Tucker asked, motioning to all the cars. "I can feel them staring at me, and it's kind of creepy."

Shelby smiled. "Well, I mentioned to the first lady that you were going to be helping out this afternoon, and she decided to wait in hopes we open. I think she might be hoping to see you, and I'm fairly certain she called the other parents because it's been a steady stream since then."

"They're all waiting for me? Why?"

"I don't know. Maybe they're hoping to shake your hand or something, but this is great publicity for the event tomorrow. If we have this kind of turnout tomorrow, we should raise enough money for rent and the Christmas party, and I have no doubt these people will tell their friends."

Shelby smiled as she realized once again how in control God was. The snow had provided an excuse for Tucker to be seen outside. Not only that, but it had sent some of her previous families, who might not have known about the clinic, their way. But her smile faded as she remembered the pipes. If they weren't able to open tomorrow, all of this publicity would be for naught.

"Of course, all of that hinges on if we can open. Did your friend say anything about the pipes?"

"Not yet, but he just started looking around down there. Give him a few minutes. He knows the situation and that you're in a time crunch."

Shelby nodded, but she couldn't keep the fear from constricting her voice. "Tucker, what am I going to do if he says we can't open? I don't have the money to keep this place open much longer."

Tucker placed a hand on her shoulder. "I don't think you'll have to worry about that. I know the center is old and in need of repair, but I have a feeling the rest of the pipes will be fine. Besides, the snow is letting up. Knowing Texas weather, the sun will be out in ten minutes and all of this will be melted by noon."

Shelby glanced at his hand on her shoulder. It was just a touch, a friendly touch, but her skin was on fire under his hand. She had felt the same heat earlier when he touched her face. Was she falling for him? She couldn't be. He was *not* her type, or more to the point, she was not his type; but the look he was giving her now and the one he had given her this morning? She didn't know what to make of them. But she couldn't think about that right now. She had a center to focus on, and she didn't need to be getting distracted by a romance. Unfortunately, that logic didn't slow her heart rate or even her breathing which suddenly felt restricted.

"Thanks, Tucker."

Her gaze met his, and the squeezing sensation on her lungs tightened. His eyes were so dark. So dark that she felt as if she were falling as she gazed into their depths. She couldn't remember the last time a man had affected her like this. Was he feeling something too?

"Okay, it looks like the pipes are okay." The plumber's voice interrupted the moment, and Tucker's hand dropped from her shoulder as he turned to face the man. Shelby blinked and tried not to focus on the cold spot that now pulsed where his hand had been.

"I've got a machine thawing what I can reach, and I've turned up the heat in the rest of the center to get the ones in the walls. I'd like to take a look around and see how we can insulate them better, so this doesn't happen again; but you can open now. The water pressure will be a little low until all the ice melts, but you do have water."

"Thank you." Shelby checked her watch. It was nearly nine in the morning. She wasn't sure how the parents who had stayed had managed it, but she was certainly thankful.

After a final glance at Tucker, Shelby led the way back into the center. The heater was definitely working overtime and she could feel the warmth caressing her before she made it to the reception area to remove her coat. She fired up the computer and grabbed the stack of flyers that sat neatly next to it.

Then she slid the window open that separated the reception area from the main gym and smiled at the line of people waiting to come in. "Okay, open for business." She handed a flyer to the first mother. "Will you be staying all day?"

"Definitely. Cooper is such a big fan." Evidently, his mother was too because the woman barely glanced at Shelby as she took the paper. Her eyes were locked on Tucker who was shaking hands with the children as they entered.

"Wonderful, well, that flyer has all the information about the clinic we're holding tomorrow night. Cooper could get some training and bring something to be autographed. It's one hundred dollars if you're not a monthly member, but you can save twenty-five if we get you signed up to use the center through January."

"Sure, that sounds great. Will Tucker be working here through that time?"

Shelby paused as she thought of how to answer. Tucker was required to spend twenty hours at the center, and he'd already fulfilled four of those hours. Even with only being able to get three or four hours a day, he'd be done with his obligation by the end of this week or early next week. That would take him through Christmas but definitely not through the entire month of January. While she hoped he would decide to stay after that, they hadn't discussed it.

"I don't know, but I do know he'll be here through Christmas."

"Oh, okay. Can I just pay for the rest of December then?"

Shelby's heart dropped but she forced her smile to remain pleasant. "Of course. I'll get that set up for you."

The next woman's response was nearly identical, as was the woman's after that. By the time, Shelby had handed out the flyers and registered the kids for afternoon care, she had ten more people who said they would continue through the end of the month, but no one who committed to staying longer. While she was grateful for the extra money, it begged the question of what she was going to do after Tucker was gone.

"Hey, I have to get to practice, but I'll see you at four."

She glanced up at Tucker who stood at the reception window. "Yes, of course, thanks for the help this morning."

"No problem." He flashed her a lopsided smile, tapped the counter, and then he was gone.

❧ 29 ❧

Tucker pulled into the parking lot of the stadium, glad to see it only half full. He wasn't late then; he'd been afraid he might be, having to drive slower than he normally would. Though the snow had stopped, the roads were still pretty slushy. Since Texas drivers rarely had to deal with snow, they were extra cautious, making the drive even slower than it had to be. A part of him wondered if they would even have practice today. Because it rarely rained and almost never snowed, the stadium only had a partial roof which meant the field might still be covered in snow. Even if it wasn't, it would probably be a soggy mess.

He grabbed his bag, locked his truck, and headed for the locker room. But as he reached the door, the unease pulled at his heart again. The guys had said nothing yesterday, but would they know today? Would Blaine tell them? A part of him didn't think so. After all, Blaine was the captain, and it was his job to make sure there was unity and harmony on the team. Spreading negative information, even if it was the truth, about a team member certainly wouldn't do that. But what if Blaine was tired of dealing with him? What if he saw this as a way to remove Tucker from the team? Sharing the information about his community service might create enough tension on the team to get him traded again.

Tucker took a deep breath and tried to clear his head. Blaine wasn't like that. He'd done nothing but be supportive to Tucker, so there was no reason to think he would change now. Besides, even if Blaine had told the other guys about the incident, Tucker would own up to it. He had been in the bar, and he could have refused to throw a punch. His actions were his alone, and he needed to stop passing the blame to others.

He opened the door, fully expecting the hum of conversation to hush as he entered, but it didn't. The men who were there gave him a head nod, but no one shot him an accusatory gaze. Tucker threaded his way to his locker and dropped his bag on the bench.

"How did it go at the center last night?" Blaine asked, coming up behind him.

Tucker sighed and glanced around the room. Blaine's voice was low, but he had been hoping to avoid discussing the center. "It was fine. I aired up some balls and entertained the kids for a while."

Blaine nodded. "Good. Glad to hear it. Just keep your head down. No more fights, no more bars. Understand?"

Tucker had no desire to step in a bar again, but agitation stirred in his stomach at Blaine's words. He hated it when Blaine acted like this. He hadn't had a father figure in years, and he definitely didn't need Blaine trying to fill the role. "Yeah, I got it, Blaine."

Blaine stared at him a moment longer before issuing a curt nod. "Good. Suit up and be ready to go in ten. We've got a long practice today, and only a few more days to get prepared for the next game."

After donning his pads and practice jersey, Tucker jogged out onto the field for practice. True to Texas form, the snow had stopped. The temperature had risen, though it was still cold without his heavy jacket on. Most of the snow had melted, leaving soggy ground beneath. Whatever snow had remained on the field had been cleared, but the moisture made the ground slick and spongy beneath his feet just as he'd expected. A perfect recipe for injury if he wasn't careful. He wished he'd left the center sooner because his muscles were cold and tight as well, but there was no additional time to warm up.

Rubbing his arms to get the blood circulating, Tucker jogged over to the huddle where Blaine was giving the directions for the day. "Okay, I want to run an 'up the middle' and an 'off tackle.' The next team we're facing has the number one defense in the league, so our running game is going to be important. That being said, Jackson needs to remain healthy, so no tackles today. Touch only. Is that clear?"

The men nodded and Tucker took his place in the line. At the snap of the ball, he moved toward Blaine, took the ball, pocketed it in his arms, and ran up the middle of the line. He growled as his foot lost traction in the soft ground, and he stumbled before anyone had the chance to touch him.

"All right, let's try that again," Blaine hollered as Tucker stood up. Frustration raged through Tucker as he made his way back to the line of scrimmage. Mud coated the front of his pants and socks, and his shoes squished, making his feet even colder.

"You all right?" Blaine asked.

"Fine, let's just run it again." Tucker handed the ball to Blaine, wiped his hands on the cleanest part of his jersey, and took his place in the line once again.

"Hut," Blaine yelled, and Tucker took off once more. He tucked the ball and pushed through the middle line managing a measly five yards.

"Let's try an 'off tackle' this time," Blaine said as he held out a hand to help Tucker up.

Tucker nodded and took his place once again. This time when the ball snapped, he ran toward the right line after making sure the ball was secure in his arms. He broke through the line and was just about to kick his speed into gear when he felt a shove on his back.

It wasn't that hard, really, but due to the slick grass, it sent him stumbling forward to the ground.

As if fuel had been poured on a flame, anger burned within him, and he jumped up to confront the guy who had pushed him. "What's your problem? Blaine said no tackles."

"I didn't tackle you. It was a touch, man, chill out."

"It was a shove, and you know it." Tucker pulled back his shoulders and moved until he was chest to chest with the other player.

"All right, enough," the coach said, jogging onto the field and interrupting the two men before it could escalate into a fight. "Tucker, take five. We'll run some passing plays while you cool off."

"I don't need to cool off. He needs to learn what a shove is."

"I said enough. Bench. Now."

Tucker narrowed his eyes at his teammate and then stalked off the field. As he sat on the bench watching the next few plays, he tried to slow his heart and calm his breathing. He'd been doing so well the last few days, so why did his temper have to flare up now? Even more importantly, what could he do to stop it?

"WHAT'S WRONG?" SHELBY ASKED AS TUCKER YANKED OPEN THE front door. The scowl on his face reminded her of his first day, but she hadn't seen it since. He'd changed, at least when he was in the center.

"Tough practice," Tucker said, shaking his head. "What do you want me to do?"

"Come here and talk to me first. If you go out there looking like that, you'll scare the kids away, and I'd like them to come back tomorrow." She was teasing, mostly, but she did worry about him being around the kids like this. They had enough worry on their plate without adding whatever was bothering him to it.

Tucker sighed but nodded, and a moment later, he had dropped his bag and plopped down in the chair across from her. "I'm sorry, Shelby. I probably should have told you this earlier, but I have this anger issue. It doesn't come up all the time, and I've been managing it with boxing classes; but after our last loss, I mouthed off to the quarterback. I don't even know why — it wasn't his fault, but sometimes I just can't seem to stop it. Today, it happened again. One of the guys pushed me a little too hard and sent me sprawling to the ground, and I almost lost it." He dropped his head into his hands. "I don't want to be so angry, but I have no idea how to stop it."

Shelby pursed her lips together and placed a hand on his arm. She wondered if his anger issues had played a part in earning him community service. "Tucker, are you a believer?"

"You mean like a Christian?" he asked, raising his head.

"Yes, I mean like a Christian."

He shrugged and ran a hand across the back of his neck. "I don't know. I mean, I guess I believe there's a God, but I can't say I've been close with him. At least not since my mom died. We pretty much stopped going to church then."

Tucker's words hit Shelby like a brick, and she leaned back. No wonder he had anger issues. She'd seen it with the kids in the center who lost a parent or went through a messy divorce. Some retreated, some grew depressed, and some dealt with anger. She tried to think of the right words to say. "I'm sorry. I didn't know about your mom. How old were you when she died?"

His hand moved from his neck to his chin. "Twelve. Much younger than any boy should be when they lose their mother. Plus, my dad withdrew into his work after that, and I pretty much had to raise myself and my sister."

Shelby blinked back the tears stinging her eyes. "Tucker, it's no wonder you're angry then. That is more than any child should have to deal with, but you don't have to deal with it alone. I know it's not the same because you can't see Him or touch Him, but God is your Father too, and He loves you. More importantly though, He can help you tame your anger and find forgiveness."

Tucker's hand stilled and his eyes locked on hers. "Do you really believe that? You really think He can take away my anger?"

She touched his arm again. "I know he can. I've seen Him do it. My mom was just like that when I was growing up. She would get angry over every little thing. So angry that I used to hide under my desk when she would scream and yell. It was the only place that felt safe. And then one day, she just stopped. She stopped being mad all the time, and she turned into this amazing woman. I didn't ask her about it for a long time because I was afraid I might remind her and she would start yelling again; but one day, I got up the courage. She told me that God took her anger away. That she prayed for peace, and He gave it to her. Now, I know your situation might be a little different, but if God could do that for my mother, then I know He can do it for you as well."

Tucker held her gaze a moment longer and then nodded. "I believe you, but I'm not sure I know what to do."

"I could pray for you," Shelby said softly. "If you want."

He took a deep breath, and Shelby forced herself to remain quiet while he thought. Then his hand covered hers, and the corners of his lips turned up. "I'd like that."

Warmth flooded Shelby as she closed her eyes. She hadn't been sure he would be open to it, but she was delighted that he was. "Lord, I want to thank You for being a good Father to us. I know it isn't always easy for us to put our trust in things we cannot see, but I know that You can deliver peace. My friend Tucker needs that peace. Please take away his anger and help him find forgiveness. Also, help him to see You. Amen."

Shelby opened her eyes, unsure of what she would see. Tucker's face appeared softer, less rigid. "Thanks, Shelby. I am sure that I still have a lot to learn, but I do feel better. Now, what can I do to help tonight?"

"Well, I think Kenzi and Jennifer, our high school volunteer, could use some help with the kids. What do you say we go find them?"

"Sounds good."

"Ah, there's the star of the day," Kenzi's voice carried across the gym as Shelby and Tucker approached. "Who wants Tucker to play hide-and-seek with us?"

The kids cheered and the sound warmed Shelby's heart. She sneaked a glance at Tucker and saw that he was smiling as well. He probably didn't even know it, but being around these kids was helping him too. Changing him.

"I haven't played hide-and-seek for years," Tucker said, rubbing his hands together. "I bet I can find some good spots though. You coming, Shelby?"

Shelby shook her head. "You go ahead. At least one of us needs to stay out here and be the adult. Just in case."

"Suit yourself," Tucker called as he headed toward Kenzi and the kids.

For a moment, Shelby envied Kenzi. How was she able to be so carefree and not seem to care about responsibility? It had been this way as long as Shelby could remember. She'd been the focused one in high school, worrying about grades and studying every night. Kenzi had been the one attending parties and cramming the night before tests. In college, Shelby had only joined the studious sororities while Kenzi had joined the ones who partied. Kenzi represented the side that Shelby would never be, and she supposed that was why they worked. They were like yin and yang, like peanut butter and jelly, complete opposites who complemented each other and together made a force to be reckoned with.

Still, that didn't mean Shelby didn't want to have fun now and then. She wished she could let loose and play with the kids too like she used to, but if she didn't stay in control — if she didn't keep a tight eye on the center — she knew it would go up in flames. And that was something she couldn't let happen. It was too important to the kids, especially the kids like herself who hadn't been born into affluent households and couldn't afford the latest gadgets and gimmicks.

With a sigh, Shelby returned to the reception area and pulled out the list of businesses she had canvassed earlier that afternoon. Thankfully, Jennifer had been truly under the weather yesterday, and, feeling better, she had come in this morning shortly after Tucker left. That had allowed Shelby to leave the center for a few hours to pass out flyers and beg for donations. Unfortunately, she hadn't been able to secure any, but the interest for the clinic had been high.

She had saved the center for the day, maybe even through January if everyone showed up tomorrow night, but they still had a long way to go. Plus, there was the Christmas party; she still needed to find a donor to help out with that. Their regular guy had been strangely silent so far this year. Perhaps a reminder call would help.

She had just picked up the phone when the front door opened. Sylvie Sanders from the channel five news floated in looking just as perfect as she did on television. Her blonde hair flowed like golden silk around her shoulders as if some invisible wind kept it aloft, and her figure was the perfect hourglass in her smart, tailored suit. A man holding a large camera entered behind her.

"Can I help you?" Shelby had no idea why Sylvie and her cameraman might be at her center. Had they heard about the clinic? Or about Tucker? It was possible but highly unlikely. It made more sense that they were lost though how people got lost today with maps on their phones was beyond her.

"Yes, we heard that Tucker Jackson was working here and was holding a clinic tomorrow night, is that correct?"

So, they were here because of Tucker. Had the newspaper called them? Or maybe Tucker's PR guy had — she had forgotten to even ask him about that today. Either way, Shelby supposed she shouldn't look a gift horse in the mouth — the center could definitely use the publicity — but it would be nice to have somebody do a story on the center just because it helped out the local kids and not because a pro athlete was around for the week. "He's volunteering here, yes." Shelby hoped the smile on her face didn't look as fake as it felt.

"Wonderful. Could we talk with him? This has feel-good story written all over it." Sylvie's words were as smooth and polished as her appearance, but they were hollow and empty. Shelby wondered if the woman even knew what a feel-good story was.

"Sure. Let me see if I can find him. He's playing hide-and-seek with the kids, so it may take me a moment." Why was she trying to discourage this? This was just the kind of publicity the event needed. But deep down, Shelby knew why. It was because Sylvie was the epitome of perfection. She was blonde, beautiful, and the type of trophy woman that a professional athlete would want to show off on his arm. She even made Kenzi seem average which made Shelby feel even more invisible. So, while she appreciated the news station running the story, she just wished someone other than Sylvie Sanders was covering it.

Sylvie's perfect eyebrows arched on her wrinkle-free forehead, and her lips twisted into a condescending smile. "Hide-and-seek? In this place?" Her nose turned up at the last two words as if she couldn't believe she had to stand in this building. "Why don't you just call him on his cell? Surely that would be faster."

It would be faster, and Shelby had his number; but there was a part of her that wanted to make Sylvie wait. The woman looked as if she never had to wait, as if everything she wanted in life was delivered to her on a silver platter at the snap of her finger. No, not a silver platter, she probably had a golden one. The perfect fourteen carat gold to match the tiny hoops in her ears and the delicate bracelet on her slender wrist. So, yeah, she could wait.

"It might be faster, but we discourage cell phone use at the center. We want the adults to be engaged with the children, and we've found that devices are distracting, so we don't allow cell phones except for emergencies." It wasn't exactly the truth, but it wasn't a flat-out lie either. It was the policy Shelby herself followed, and she had asked Kenzi and Tucker not to have their phones out when the kids were around; but there was no strict policy. She felt a little guilty fibbing to Sylvie, but she pushed it aside.

"I'm sure it won't take me very long to find him." Shelby mirrored Sylvie's condescending smile before exiting the room to begin her search. As she crossed the big gym, she felt very conspicuous in her bargain store pants and blouse. She normally considered herself a smart dresser; she always looked professional even if her clothes were purchased second hand, but next to Sylvie, she could have been the poster child for dowdy.

Tucker wasn't in the kitchen or in the hallway. Where could he be hiding? She felt like time was speeding by and dragging at the same time. If it took too long, would Sylvie leave? Would she do a story about how terrible the manager was? Shelby quickened her pace, determined not to find out.

She pulled open the door to the supply closet and sighed in relief when she saw Tucker inside.

"Shut the door," he said. "You're going to give me away."

"Sylvie Sanders from channel five is here. She wants to interview you."

His eyes lit up. "Sylvie Sanders? The blonde?"

Shelby shrugged. Was Tucker's excitement over the interview or the woman conducting it? She shouldn't care; he hadn't expressed an interest in her. At least not in words. But there'd been moments. Moments where she thought he felt something for her, and imagining him with Sylvie felt wrong. Yes, on the surface, they worked with their good looks and perfect jobs; but there was more to Tucker than the stereotypical athlete who always dated the modelesque women. At least, she had thought there was, but maybe she'd been wrong. "That's the one."

"Lead the way then."

Shelby led Tucker back to Sylvie and tried not to grimace when the blonde batted her eyes at him.

"Tucker Jackson. A little birdie told us you were working here. Do you mind telling us what you're doing in a place like this?"

Shelby bristled at Sylvie's insinuation. Yes, the place needed sprucing up, but it wasn't like it was a landfill or a deathtrap the way Sylvie was making it sound.

Tucker glanced at Shelby before pasting a smile on his face and turning his charm on. "I wanted to give back to the community."

Oh, brother. Shelby rolled her eyes as she made her way back to the reception area. It wasn't like she had expected him to admit he was only here to serve community service hours, but she hadn't thought he would lay it on so thick. Shelby hoped this interview brought some good publicity to the center and didn't backfire on her. The last thing she needed was anything else to go wrong.

30

"So, how did we do?" Kenzi asked as Shelby closed out the register.

"Not bad. Thankfully, the landlord will cover the pipes when he returns, and I think we made enough today to pay January's rent. At least we will if the clinic tomorrow night is a success as well."

"Well, that's good. Thank goodness Tucker Jackson came along when he did, right?" Kenzi had that annoying lilt in her voice — the one she used when she was trying to persuade someone to do what she wanted — but Shelby was immune. She'd become Kenzi's friend because she enjoyed hanging out with her, not because she'd been sucked in by the charms that seemed to make everyone else fall under her spell.

Shelby shrugged. "I guess. I mean he's certainly been helpful, but we'll have to see how tomorrow goes." She placed the money in the deposit bag and zipped it closed.

Kenzi rolled her eyes. "He's been amazing, and you know it. This is about that reporter, isn't it?"

Heat flamed across Shelby's cheeks, and she turned away as if looking for something. She hated that Kenzi knew her so well, hated that she was envious of the reporter. Or maybe not the reporter per se, but the way Tucker had interacted with her. He'd been charming and smiley, almost flirtatious. Maybe it had just been to get a good interview, but she was no longer sure. She'd thought Tucker had connected with her when he'd opened up about his anger and let her pray for him, but apparently she'd been wrong. "It's not about the reporter, though did you see the way he acted? Those two deserve each other. Probably both hung up on their money and good looks."

"Oh. My. Gosh. You like him."

"What?" Shelby turned back to Kenzi to see her wide eyes sparkling.

"You like him. Tucker Jackson. You think he's cute."

"I don't... He's not..." Shelby blew out a frustrated breath. "Okay, fine, I think he's cute, who wouldn't? But it's not like it matters. I am not the type of girl that a guy like Tucker notices. He notices girls like you and Sylvie Sanders."

"I think you're being entirely too hard on yourself. You have a lot to offer a man like Tucker."

Shelby cocked her head at her friend. "Wait, I thought you liked Tucker. Why does it sound like you are trying to convince me to give him a shot?"

Kenzi shrugged. "I like the idea of Tucker, and yes, he is easy on the eyes. But, I think he's looking for something more than I can offer him. I was telling him last night that I didn't know what I wanted to do for a job, and he got this funny expression on his face. And then he looked toward the office. Where you were."

A weird feeling that straddled the fence somewhere between embarrassment and denial erupted in Shelby. "I doubt he was looking at me." Except they'd had that moment yesterday. That moment where he'd lifted her chin, and she'd thought some spark had passed between them. And then more moments earlier today. But then there was Sylvie and the way he had acted with her. Shelby didn't didn't know what to think.

Kenzi's lips twisted into a teasing smile. "I'll take that bet. I think you're wrong about him, and if you'd let me do a little makeover on you, I could get him to notice you the same way he did Sylvie. You're beautiful, Shelby. You just hide it."

Shelby lifted her chin and clutched the money bag tighter. "I don't need a makeover. If a man doesn't like me for who I am, then he isn't the man for me."

"Famous last words of a spinster," Kenzi said with a smile.

Shelby marched over to the door and flicked off the lights. "I will not be a spinster."

"Who's a spinster?"

Shelby jumped at the sound of Tucker's voice behind her and nearly dropped her keys. She hadn't known he was still in the center. "No one. What are you still doing here? I thought you left."

"I needed to see you first. Do you think I could skip coming in the morning tomorrow? The coach moved practice up, and I'd like to spend the few hours before it hammering out what I want to show the kids. I can make up the missed time next week."

"Sure, that would be fine. How did the interview go?" Shelby wasn't sure she wanted to hear his answer, but the question came out anyway.

He cocked his head at her and smiled. "It was fine. Sylvie seems very nice. A little high maintenance but nice. Anyway, I'll see you tomorrow." He grabbed her hand and squeezed it. "Thank you for earlier. I'm going to take your advice."

Shelby watched him walk out of the center and then turned when she heard Kenzi cough behind her.

"See? I told you he likes you."

"No," Shelby shook her head, "that was nothing. He was just thanking me."

Kenzi's brow lifted. She was not convinced. "Uh huh, well he held your hand while he thanked you which wasn't necessary. I would say that there's something there. If he asks, would you go out with him?"

"I — I don't know. I mean we're so different. What if we went out and it didn't work out?"

"What if it did?"

Shelby had no answer to that. She'd only had a few steady boyfriends, and they had all seemed to become bored with her long before they even thought of proposing to her. Could Tucker be different? Was there something to the old saying that opposites attract?

Tucker woke with a start to the light coming in his window. What time was it? He opened his eyes and groaned. Eleven? Shelby had allowed him to take the morning off to prepare for the clinic tonight, and he had planned to work on the plays he wanted to show the kids. However, somehow he had slept through his alarm. He was supposed to be suiting up for practice right now. Why hadn't anyone on the team called him? Frustrated, he punched the home button to wake his phone only to see that Blaine had called him. Twice. He must have been so exhausted from yesterday that he'd slept through the alarm and through the calls.

He punched the number to return the call as he jumped out of bed and began grabbing clothes for a shower. "Blaine? It's Tucker," he said when the quarterback answered.

"Tucker, how nice of you to return my call. You do realize you're supposed to be here getting ready for practice, right?" The tone of his voice rubbed at Tucker's irritation, but he forced himself to remain calm.

"I do. I'm sorry, man, but I am on my way. Just give me half an hour to take a shower and grab some food, and I'll be there."

"I know this work at the center is throwing off your hours, but missing practice could get you benched for the next game."

Tucker pinched his lips together as the frustration bubbled within him. Blaine was infuriating. Yes, it was his fault for being late, but if Blaine only knew how hard he'd worked last night. He'd had no idea that playing with kids would require so much energy, so much mental effort. Blaine probably didn't either. The man most likely didn't even have a family; he was probably some amazing AI unit as perfect as he was. Tucker was about to issue a snide retort when Shelby's words from yesterday flashed in his mind. Though he wasn't sure he was ready to come back to God fully, he was prepared to try. He issued a silent prayer, hoping that God would understand his hesitation, and then took a deep breath. "I understand Blaine. I'll be right there."

He jumped into the shower, wishing he had more time to enjoy the warm pelts of water. For as long as he could remember, he'd enjoyed showers. The heat, the steam, the feel of the water washing away the old. His favorite part was watching the cloud of steam roll out and fog the mirrors when he was done. It made him feel a little like a rockstar. His mother had often teased him that he would be the death of her with his hot water bill.

His mother. Was Shelby right? Was his mother's death still affecting him a decade later? Would he ever stop feeling sadness and anger over her unjust and untimely death? Tucker washed the last of the soap out of his hair and turned off the water. The hot water hadn't even been on long enough to create steam.

He regarded his reflection in the mirror and wondered how different he might be if his mother hadn't died, if his father hadn't thrown himself into his work, if Tucker hadn't had to become the parent for both him and his sister. Would he even be in this situation? Somehow he doubted it. He doubted he would have been as angry, and, therefore, he probably wouldn't have been in the bar. Maybe he wouldn't have even been traded.

But, it was no use living in the past. His mother was gone, and life was what it was. What he needed to do now was to focus on the present. Get to practice. Finish his time at the center. Win the championship. Give his anger to God?

Shelby's words from yesterday floated through his mind again.

Could God really take his anger away? It had seemed to lessen after he prayed, so could there be something to it? Could He help Tucker forgive his father? He supposed it was possible, but he didn't have the time to think more about it right now. Right now, he had to focus on getting to practice before he got benched for the rest of the season.

31

"Excuse me, but when is this clinic going to start?" A woman bouncing a baby in her arms asked from the front row. The scowl on her face matched several others throughout the crowd.

Shelby stared out at the sea of faces filling the gym. She should be happy to see this many people here. And she was. Except there was one face missing. The face that really needed to be here. Tucker's. Where was he?

She'd called him half an hour ago when he missed the set-up time and then again ten minutes ago when the families began arriving, but she'd gotten his voicemail both times. She'd let him have the morning off to prepare, but surely he hadn't forgotten or flaked on her. She'd been under the impression he was at least a man of his word.

"Sorry I'm late." His loud voice quieted the din momentarily, and then the kids went crazy when they realized who it was. He crossed the room to Shelby's side and whispered the apology again in her ear. "I'm so sorry."

A tingle shot down her spine as his breath tickled her ear. "You know, even volunteers are supposed to show up on time." Shelby kept her voice low, but she arched her left eyebrow as she waited for whatever lame excuse he was going to throw at her.

His mouth pinched into a tight line. "Yeah, I know, practice ran long even though it was supposed to end early."

"I get that, Tucker, but these kids depend on us. When we say we are going to do something, we have to follow through."

"I know," he said. "I do, and I brought some new balls to make up for it." He held up a bag. "Now, how do you want me to get this started today?"

She wasn't really done reading him the riot act, but she supposed she should show a little grace since he had brought balls and a ton of new kids into the center. "I'll introduce you, and you can take it from there. Sound good?"

He nodded, and Shelby held out her hand to quiet the room again. "Are you guys excited?" she asked.

"Yes!" The yells of the room nearly pushed her back. They were definitely excited.

"Did you bring something for Tucker to sign? If you did, hold it up."

Around the open area, arms popped up with footballs, t-shirts, and other items clutched in their hands.

"All right, you guys look ready, so I'm going to turn this over to Tucker Jackson of the Texas Tornadoes."

More yelling and clapping raised the decibels another level, and Shelby felt like she was back at the one rock concert she had attended in college. It had been Kenzi's idea. Concerts weren't really Shelby's thing, and, after nearly losing her hearing for a day following the noise fest, she had never attended another one.

She watched for a moment as Tucker introduced himself, hoping he was a decent speaker. Her fears proved unfounded though as he held the room's attention even as he began explaining how the clinic would go. Inch by inch, Shelby backed up until she felt she was far enough back to not be a distraction, and then she turned and walked back to the office.

With a sigh, she sat down at the small desk and pulled out the few cards they had on donors. She didn't like using Tucker's name, but maybe if she mentioned he was here for the rest of the month, they might be more willing to donate.

The first name on the list was Lydia Benson. Lydia had been a local designer before her business took off and she moved to New York. She would probably be too busy — that's the excuse she had used last year and the year before — but Shelby had to try. Maybe reminding the woman of her roots and of the tax break that a donation provided might help.

"Lydia's Designs, how can I help you?"

Shelby didn't recognize the nasally, professional voice on the other end of the phone, but she knew it wasn't Lydia herself. The woman had always had a lilt to her voice that oozed high society even before she joined their ranks. "Yes, is Lydia available? This is Shelby Doll."

"Shelby Doll?" The voice paused as if searching her memory or a computer. "Are you a designer?"

"Uh, no. I run the community center in Southlake, Texas, Lydia's hometown."

"Oh." Immediately, the tone of the voice on the other end shifted. The polite professionalism was replaced with bored impatience. "I'm sorry. She's very busy right now with her new line. You can give me your number, and I'll make sure she gets the message."

"Yeah. Sure." Shelby doubted her number would ever cross Lydia's desk. One down and only three to go. What would she do if she received the same response from the rest of them? She closed her eyes and issued a prayer.

The next name was Dr. Bill Gaines. He probably wouldn't be able to come to the phone either. As the prominent surgeon in Southlake, he was usually either in surgery or golfing. However, he'd grown up in the center, so she knew he had a soft spot for it. She dialed the number on the card and held her breath.

"Surgical Institute of Southlake, how may I direct your call?"

"Hi, this is Shelby Doll with the community center. I was hoping I might speak with Dr. Gaines."

"I'm sorry Dr. Gaines is in surgery. Would you like to leave a message?"

Shelby didn't want to leave a message. Messages could be ignored, avoided, forgotten. She wanted to speak to a live body, to work her persuasive magic, but she was striking out today. "Yes, thank you. I'll leave a message." Perhaps, she could be charming enough on his machine that he would return her call or at least be open to speaking to her when she called again.

Shelby twirled the blonde strand of hair that always escaped her updo as she listened to his voicemail. When she heard the beep, she sat straighter in her chair and smiled brightly. She'd felt silly in college when they'd had to practice smiling on phone calls. No one could even see her, but after listening back to the calls they had recorded, she'd had to agree that a smile came through the phone in the brightness of the tone. And every salesperson knew that a friendly tone was half the battle of getting a sale. Or in her case, a donation.

"Hello, Dr. Gaines, this is Shelby Doll from the Southlake Community Center. I know you are very busy, but I also know this center was a large part of your life growing up. We are looking for donations for our annual Christmas party, and I know the kids would love to see your name on the sign. You are such an inspiration to them, and remember that every donation is tax deductible. Please give me a call at 555-7663 so we can deliver some cheer to the youth of Southlake."

She let her smile fade as she hung up the phone. Just two names left. Could she manage to get one of them on the line, or was she going to have to go out knocking on doors again tomorrow to find new donors?

"Lord, please," she prayed softly as she picked up the next card. "We need a miracle."

Tucker stared at his reflection in the cloudy mirror and sighed. He looked exhausted and he'd only been here a few hours. He was enjoying teaching the kids, but, while he still had the signing to do, he'd needed a break from the noise for a minute. He understood now why people worked with kids. There was something rewarding in their smiles, their energy; but he did not understand how people dealt with the noise. The kids seemed to have never heard of volume control, and they would ask questions on top of each other. Did they really think he couldn't hear them when he was only five feet away? And why didn't their parents intercede? Most of them were in the room, congregating against the wall and on their phones, but in the room.

Perhaps the phones were the problem. He knew some of them were recording their child participating in the clinic, but the others? Some of them never even looked up as their kid caught the ball and ran the routes he had taught them. It made him wonder if the kids were just as invisible at home, and the thought tugged on his heart. That he could definitely relate to.

He splashed cold water on his face and made a mental note to bring Tylenol if they ever did this type of event again. The pounding in his head didn't appear to be subsiding any time soon. He grabbed a paper towel from the dispenser and sighed when he realized it was the last one. He'd have to ask Shelby to replace it. Or maybe Kenzi. She'd been helping him out with wrangling the kids.

He tossed the paper towel in the trash and exited the bathroom, but before he reached the gym, the sound of muffled voices reached his ears. He turned the corner to see a beefy, muscular kid poking a boy in a wheelchair. The boy in the wheelchair, Benji, was a regular, but he didn't recognize the other boy. He strained to hear the conversation, but the words were too soft to hear. However, the body language was easy to read.

"Hey, what are you two doing out here? You're supposed to be in the main gym."

The beefy kid turned to face him. An insincere expression of apology masked his face, and Tucker knew he was about to get fed a story. "Sorry, we got lost looking for his book, right, Benji?" He looked back at Benji as if daring him to contradict the story.

Benji's eyes dropped to his lap, and his shoulders stooped as if weighed down with defeat. He was probably used to getting bullied. "Yeah, I think I dropped it somewhere and Colson here was helping me look for it."

Tucker had no doubt that was the furthest thing from the truth, but it was clear from Benji's reaction that he didn't want to disobey Colson. Tucker had seen enough bullies in action to know that's what was going on here, and he was not going to let it continue. Benji was a great kid, one of his favorites, but he needed to know the details before he took any further action.

"Okay, well I'll help Benji find his book. You go on and head back to the gym, Colson. You can tell them I'll be right there."

Colson opened his mouth as if to object. His eyes shifted from Tucker to Benji, clearly trying to decide if Benji would rat him out once he was gone.

"Don't worry, I'll be sure to tell everyone how helpful you were," Tucker said.

Colson closed his mouth, and after another long stare at Benji, he headed back toward the gym.

Tucker waited until he was sure Colson was out of earshot before approaching Benji. "You want to tell me what that was about?"

Benji rubbed his hand across his neck before folding it in his lap again. "Just what we said. I lost my book. Colson was helping me look for it."

Tucker knelt down in front of the boy. "Benji, I know that isn't the truth. I couldn't hear what was said, but I could tell from his posture and your reaction that he was being aggressive. Now, I want to help you, but I can't do that unless I know what's going on."

Benji's bottom lip folded under, and unshed tears glistened in his eyes. "He told me that my father left because I was a cripple, that no father wants half a son."

Tucker clenched his jaw to keep the anger boiling within him from spilling over. He would save it for Colson and chew the kid's ear off, but this boy needed compassion. After taking a deep breath to calm his words, Tucker touched Benji's arm. "First of all, Colson was wrong. I don't know why your father left, but I'm sure it had nothing to do with you."

Benji shrugged and sniffed back the tears Tucker was sure were pressing against his eyes.

"Look, do you think I'm the type of son a father would want, at least according to Colson?"

"Of course." Benji's lips split into a wide smile. "You're a pro-football player, and I'll never be that. What kind of dad wouldn't want a pro-football player as a son?"

"Mine." As soon as Tucker uttered the word, he realized how profoundly his father's lack of engagement had affected him. "See, my mom died when I was about your age, and my dad disconnected. Threw himself into work. Do you know he's never even seen one of my games in person? I don't even know if he watches them on TV."

Benji's mouth fell open. "Seriously? But...but you're Tucker Jackson."

Tucker chuckled. "Yeah, but that doesn't matter to my dad. Sometimes dads just mess up. They aren't perfect either." He paused as he realized how true that was and how misplaced his anger at his father had been. Shelby was right. "I think I thought my father's avoidance was because he no longer loved me, but talking with you, I realize that he is just human. He's been dealing with his own pain, and my pain was just an unfortunate consequence of that."

"So, my dad might have left even if I wasn't different?"

The raw hope in Benji's voice tugged at Tucker's heart, and he nodded. "I'm certain that your father left because of his own issues and not because of you." Tucker felt that was the truth. Even if Benji's father had left because of his handicap, that action showed that he had some deeper issue he was dealing with or perhaps unable to deal with.

"Thank you, Mr. Jackson. I think I can go back now."

"You're welcome, and you can call me Tucker, Benji. All my friends do."

Benji smiled so brightly that even the corners of the room appeared to light up, and warmth flooded Tucker's heart. This was almost better than winning football games and hearing the crowd going wild. Maybe he could see why Shelby worked a job like this, even with the noise. Shelby. He would need to tell her she was right and talk to her about how to handle Colson, but he had to finish this clinic first.

"Okay, guys," he said, stepping back into the crowd. "Did you guys all have fun?" The answer was a resounding roar of voices and clapping of hands. "Great, I'm so glad. I have some time to sign autographs before we wrap up for the night. If you'll form a single line, I'll sign whatever you brought."

He wasn't sure the kids would be able to handle the directions, but thankfully Kenzi helped herd them into something resembling a line while he took his place at the table. One at a time, he signed footballs, shirts, books, stickers — whatever was passed across the table to him — until all the kids were taken care of. With the last item signed and the kids packing up and leaving, he shook out his cramping hand and looked around for Shelby.

There was still no sign of her, but he saw Kenzi speaking to a woman at the front door. Perhaps this would be a good time to find Shelby and tell her about the incident with Colson and Benji. He saw neither boy in the few who remained.

Tucker wandered over to the reception area and was about to

rap lightly on the doorframe when he heard Shelby's voice from inside.

"Please, Mr. Renfrow, if you could just tell me why. Maybe it's something we can remedy."

Renfrow? Why did that name sound familiar?

He waited a moment longer for her to finish the call. It felt like eavesdropping though that wasn't his intent. When he heard Shelby sigh, he figured she had hung up with whomever had been on the other end, and he poked his head in the doorway. "Hey, you got a minute?"

"What is it?" There was a note of defeat in her voice that he hadn't heard before, and he wondered if it was due to the phone call.

He leaned against the doorframe, keeping a professional distance between them even though he wanted to touch her. "I just wanted to tell you the boy's bathroom is out of paper towels and get some feedback on how to deal with a bullying situation. If you're busy though, we can discuss it tomorrow."

She let out another sigh which sounded as if it carried the weight of the world on its shoulders. "No, it's fine. I need a break from calling donors anyway."

"Sorry, I didn't mean to eavesdrop, but was that a donor on the phone just now?"

"Yeah. Jude Renfrow. He's a local investor who donated for the Christmas party last year. I thought he was on board this year, but now he says some recent event has changed his mind."

Jude Renfrow. Suddenly, Tucker knew why that name sounded familiar, but he forced his face to remain impassive. The last thing he needed was Shelby knowing that Jude's sudden change of heart was his fault.

"Anyway, that's not your burden," Shelby said with a wave of her hand. "Tell me about this bullying incident."

Tucker relayed the incident to her and watched as her face shifted from concern to anger and then back to its professional demeanor. He could tell that she tried not to dislike any of the kids in the center, but she definitely did not like bullying behavior.

"I think I made Benji feel better," Tucker continued, "but I'm not sure what to do next."

Shelby crossed to the file cabinet and pulled out Colson's file. She flipped it open. "There isn't much on him; he's never been a regular, just drops in once in a while. To be honest, he's probably only here now because of you, but we need to document it. If it continues," she opened a different drawer and pulled out a documentation form, "I'll have to reach out to his parents. If he shows up tomorrow, let's try to keep them separated and definitely make sure Benji is never alone with him. I'll tell Kenzi to keep an eye out too." She handed him the form.

He took it and began filling out the report. "The event went well. Do you think you earned enough money?"

"I don't know. I hope so, but I'm afraid we still won't have enough for the party. I hate not being able to do that for the kids."

"How about you let me take care of that?" Tucker asked as he finished filling out the form and passed it back to her. "I'll come in early tomorrow and we can discuss what you need, and I'll take care of the funding."

Shelby's brow furrowed with questions. "Why would you do that? I thought this was just community service for you."

"It was when I started, but these kids have grown on me." He grabbed her hand and pulled her close to him. "You have grown on me."

Her eyes widened as she gazed up at him.

"You were right, Shelby. I was angry because of my mother's death, and I was angry that I thought my father didn't love me either, but Benji helped me see that's not the case. I've been praying when I feel the anger rise, and God's been helping me. You've helped me. I didn't want to say anything while I was still serving hours in case you didn't feel the same, but I'd really like to take you out. Maybe tomorrow night after we close?"

He could almost feel the pounding of her heart in the air, and a soft electric buzz seemed to surround them. "I'd like that," she finally whispered.

"Good." His eyes traced the soft curve of her lips, and his breath caught. Every ounce of his body wanted to kiss her, but it didn't seem to be the right time or place. Besides, Kenzi or a parent could walk in on them at any moment. "Now, should I replace those paper towels before I leave?"

She blinked at him, clearly startled by the change in subject. "Of course," She grabbed a key off the rack on the wall and handed it to him. "Here's the key to the supply closet. You should find some there and you can replace them."

"Thanks, I'll take care of this."

SHELBY STARED AT THE DOORWAY LONG AFTER TUCKER HAD GONE. What had happened there? He'd asked her out on a date, she'd thought he was going to kiss her, and then he'd veered back to the paper towels. Perhaps, he just wanted to remain professional at work? She could understand and respect that. At least logically. It was a lot harder to tell her heart that.

"You all right?" Kenzi asked from the doorway.

"Yeah, just thinking." Should she tell Kenzi about the date? She knew her friend would be happy for her, but there was still a part of Shelby that didn't believe it was real. Maybe she could wait until tomorrow night to tell her, just to be sure.

"How'd we do?" Kenzi asked.

"Good. Enough to pay for January's rent and a little extra. I couldn't get any of the donors, but Tucker said he'd fund the party."

"He did, huh?" Kenzi's voice held that teasing lilt again. She fell into step as Shelby walked to the front door. "You know, he's pretty good with the kids too."

"Yeah, he seems to be. It's too bad he's only here for another week though because we are still behind on money."

Kenzi offered a crooked smile as she pushed open the door. "Don't worry so much. God will provide a way."

Shelby knew that. In her heart, she knew it, but it was often a lot harder to let go of the worries of tomorrow than it sounded. Were it just her, it would be one thing, but she also carried the worry for the families who needed the center.

She walked across the darkened parking lot and tried not to think about what she would do if the center closed. It had been her job for the last several years — first as a volunteer, then as the manager's assistant, and now as the manager. She couldn't imagine doing anything else.

Tucker slapped the alarm next to him to shut off the annoying beeping, but it didn't stop. His eyes snapped open, and he realized it was not his alarm going off but his phone. Darkness still lay on the other side of his windows. What time was it? And who would be calling him this early?

He grabbed the phone and dread flooded him as he recognized the number. Why was his sister calling him? Was she in trouble again? When their mother had died, Whitley had rebelled, acted out, but he'd thought she had outgrown most of that behavior.

"Hey, Whitley, what's going on?"

"Tucker, it's Dad. He had a heart attack. You need to come home." A thread of fear colored her voice. Tucker wasn't sure he had ever heard her scared, so he knew it must be serious.

"Is he in the hospital?"

"He is. They aren't sure what they are going to do next. They have to run some tests, but they're discussing a quadruple bypass."

A quadruple bypass? Tucker wasn't even sure what that all involved. "How? He eats fairly healthy, doesn't he?"

"They think the stress of work finally got to him. Please tell me you can come home."

Tucker bit the corner of his lip. He was supposed to be at the center in an hour, and he had practice after that. Blaine had told him not to miss any days, but if his dad were really sick that would be an okay reason to, right?

But then he had another shift at the center after practice and dinner with Shelby which he didn't want to miss. "I'll see what I can do, Whitley, but I've got practice and an obligation this evening."

Anger flooded her voice. "What could possibly be more important than seeing your father before he dies?"

"Wait, Dad's dying?" Even though he and his father hadn't always had the best relationship, Tucker knew that should his father die without Tucker getting to see him that he would regret it for the rest of his life.

"Well, no, but what if he has to have the surgery and dies on the table?" Whitley asked adding a sniffle for good measure.

"You're being dramatic, Whitley, but I'll do my best." He would have to call Coach and clear it with him first. Then he'd have to get ahold of Shelby and make sure she would allow him to make up the work next week. He didn't think it would be an issue, but he had learned that assuming something wasn't the best option.

He dialed Coach's number first. No doubt the man wouldn't be happy, but Tucker hoped he would grant the time off.

"What's up, Tucker?"

"Hey, Coach, I just received a call from my sister. My dad had a heart attack, and she wants me to come home and see him in case..." He couldn't bring himself to utter the words, for fear it would make them come true. "I know it means I'll have to make up some time at the center next week, and it's terrible timing with practice, but is there any way I can take a few days? It's my dad."

Silence echoed from the other end. Coach was probably debating if he were telling the truth or not. "It is a bad time, but family is more important than any game. Go, and I'll tell the team what's happening. Do you think you'll be back for the game?"

The Christmas game was only four days away, but there was no way he was going to miss it. "I'll come back for the game, Coach. I promise."

"All right. Go be with your dad. I'll be praying for him."

The words caught Tucker off guard. For a moment, Coach sounded like his old teammate, Emmitt Brown, but Tucker hadn't known Coach was a believer as well. Again, Shelby's words paraded through his mind, reminding him about his own decision to give his anger God; but he pushed them away for the moment. "Thanks, I appreciate it."

"You're welcome. Don't forget to call the woman at the center. You don't want to just not show up for the community service."

"I will." Tucker ended the call and then pulled up a browser window. He didn't have Shelby's number or even the number of the center. Probably, he should have asked for it, but he hadn't thought he would actually have to call her.

The center information appeared on his screen and he clicked on the link to dial the number. Shelby probably wouldn't be there yet, but hopefully they would have voicemail so he could leave a message.

The phone rang four times in his ear. He was about to hang up and try again later when a click finally sounded in his ear. The recording was faint and not very clear, and he wondered if they were using an old answering machine instead of voicemail. He didn't think anyone used them anymore, but the center was so behind the times that it was possible they hadn't joined the rest of the world in that area either.

When he finally heard the beep signaling the end of the announcement, he rambled off his message. "Shelby, it's Tucker. My dad had a heart attack, and I have to return home. I don't know how long I'll be there, but I'll try to be back as soon as I can. I'll make up whatever hours I miss next week, and we'll do dinner when I get back. Thanks."

As Tucker hung up the phone, he hoped the message would get

to her. She would no doubt be livid if it didn't and she thought he was just ducking the responsibility or standing her up. He'd seen it on her face last night when he'd been late, but he'd done all he could. At least for now.

SHELBY GLANCED AT HER WATCH AND DECIDED SHE HAD TIME TO check the news before heading into work. It wasn't a daily habit, but she did like to know what was going on in the community in case the center needed to help out in any way.

"The Texas Tornadoes have issued a statement that Tucker Jackson will not play in Sunday's game."

Shelby's fork clattered to her plate as her jaw dropped. Not play? Why?

"The decision comes amid charges that Jackson was involved in a bar brawl after the last game. He has been serving community service at the Southlake Community Center, but evidently that wasn't retribution enough for victim, Jude Renfrow, who came forward last night with the allegations."

Jude Renfrow? So, was that why he had pulled his donation? Had Tucker known? She thought back to the day she'd spoken to Mr. Renfrow. Yes, Tucker had been there, and she'd definitely mentioned Renfrow's name. Yet, Tucker had said nothing. Had he not known the name of the man he fought with? That seemed unlikely. Even if he hadn't known Renfrow, his name would have appeared in the police report unless perhaps the police weren't called. Were police called to bar brawls? Shelby had no idea. She'd never witnessed a bar fight, and she didn't follow police activity on a regular basis.

Then her mind flew to last night. Was that why Tucker had offered to fund the party? Because he knew he'd been the reason her donor pulled? Why wouldn't he just tell her that? Was he ashamed? Or was he playing her? Maybe the dinner invitation had been to butter her up as well, but that made no sense. He couldn't have known Mr. Renfrow would come forward, could he?

Shelby flicked off the TV and grabbed her coat and purse. She had questions, and she wasn't going to let Tucker off easy. He'd mentioned he had anger issues, but he should have told her about the bar brawl. Especially with the center's reputation at stake.

The parking lot was empty when she arrived, but Tucker had said he'd be in at eight to discuss the Christmas party. It was ten till, giving her just enough time to open the center and rehearse what she was going to say to him.

"Whoa, that is a face that could kill," Kenzi said as she opened the front door. "You better fix that before the kids start showing up or you might scare them away."

Shelby had been expecting Tucker, but he was late. "Did you watch the news this morning?"

A look of incredulousness blanketed Kenzi's face. "You're kidding, right? I never watch the news. It's too depressing. They never talk about the good things, only about all the awful stuff happening in the world, and I don't need to fill my head with that. Why?"

"Turns out Tucker was serving community service for punching a guy in a bar," she said through clenched teeth.

Kenzi's eyes widened to the size of quarters. "What? That's bad, right?"

"Yeah, that's bad. If the parents see this story, they might pull the kids. Even worse? The guy he fought with is Jude Renfrow."

Kenzi's face blanked, and Shelby knew she was trying to place the name. When her eyes widened, Shelby knew she had figured it out. "Like our donor Jude Renfrow?"

Shelby crossed her arms and nodded. "The very one. No wonder Tucker was willing to fund the party. He has to know he's the reason Mr. Renfrow pulled his donation."

Kenzi's brow furrowed. "But, Tucker is still funding it, right? I mean, the party is still going to happen?"

Shelby shook her head. Kenzi was missing the point. "Well, he said he was going to fund it, but he's not here, and he was supposed to be here ten minutes ago. What if he saw the news and decided he didn't need to fund it anymore since he can't play on Sunday?"

"Wait, what?" Kenzi asked.

Shelby sighed in frustration, but as Kenzi hadn't seen the story, she explained the situation. "The team suspended him for Sunday's game because of Mr. Renfrow's allegation. What if they told him and he decided he didn't need to finish his service? What if he was playing us? Making us think he was having fun, but he was only here because of the requirement?" The thought sobered her. Mostly because she'd thought he'd been connecting with the kids and enjoying himself, but also because of his words last night. If he was pretending to enjoy volunteering, then perhaps he was only pretending to like her. But what could he possibly hope to get from that?

Kenzi rolled her eyes. "You're the sensible one, Shelby, but you're acting crazy right now."

She was, and she knew she was, but what other explanation was there? He hadn't shown up, and he hadn't called. "There's something else I haven't told you, Kenzi. Last night, he asked me to go to dinner with him tonight."

"But that's great. Why do you look like that's not great?"

"Because he's not here." Shelby threw her hands up in frustration. "What if he was playing me too?"

Kenzi crossed the room to Shelby and picked up her hand. "I think you know that isn't true. Now, I don't know why Tucker hasn't called, but maybe he's stuck in traffic. Or maybe he overslept. He was probably tired after last night. Have you tried calling him?"

"Of course I tried calling him, but I just got his voicemail."

"Then you keep trying. I don't know what happened in the bar fight, but you should hear his side of the story before you jump to any conclusions. You owe him that much."

Kenzi was right. Shelby knew that what was on TV was usually only half of the story, and Tucker hadn't given her a reason to doubt him. Other than his not being here right now. The phone rang beside her, and Shelby picked it up. "Southlake Community Center, how can I help you?"

"Is this Shelby Doll?"

"Yes, may I ask who this is?"

"This is Melissa Utting. I'm Colson's mother."

Shelby's heart sank. Had Colson said something about Tucker's intervention last night? "Yes, Mrs. Utting, how can I help you?"

"I'm calling about the story I saw on the news this morning." Shelby forced herself to remain calm and collected, but this was exactly what she'd been afraid of. "Why on earth do you have someone who was charged with assault working with the kids there?"

Assault? The story she had watched had said nothing about assault charges. Had there been something more or had Melissa read more into the story than what was said? "I understand your concern, Melissa. However, I am unaware of any assault charge."

Melissa cut her off, and the anger in her voice could have started a fire. "Did you watch the news this morning?"

"I did. I saw that Tucker has been suspended due to allegations, but there was no mention of an assault charge. Besides, we are a center that allows people to serve community service here. I am not sure of the circumstances behind the allegations, but I can tell you that Tucker has been great with the kids."

"Well, Colson will not be returning. Any center that would allow an athlete to work there who probably bought his way out of an assault charge is not some place I want my son."

Shelby was about to respond when the loud click followed by

the dial tone told her that Melissa was no longer on the other end. While she didn't feel Melissa pulling Colson was that big of a loss, especially after the bullying incident, she feared that this phone call was going to be the first of many.

❧ 33 ❧

Tucker stared at the looming hospital in front of him and swallowed his discomfort. Even though his mother had died at home and not in a hospital, he still equated the sterile buildings with her death. Maybe it was the smell of antiseptic that coated the halls, the same smell that masked his mother's scent after she was gone. Or maybe the pale cream walls themselves were to blame. They were the same pale cream color that reminded him of the sheet they had pulled over her face before taking her away. Whatever it was, he hated hospitals! Hated the sight, the sound, and the smell of them. Now, he was being forced to enter one again.

His foot took a step as if it remembered how to walk even while his brain didn't, but it was a slow and halting step. He probably looked as if he was the injured one in need of a hospital as he crossed the parking lot instead of his father. His father. The man who hadn't been there for Tucker or Whitley since his wife died, so why was Tucker here for him now? Because he felt obligated to? Because he was family? Or was it because of the frailty of life? Perhaps it was a combination of all three. It was one thing to be angry at his father and to allow that to keep him from coming home more often, but it was another thing entirely to not come see him knowing he could be on his deathbed.

Heart surgeries were more common now than they once were, and, after searching quadruple bypasses, he knew that most ended well. But it was the ones that didn't end well that had stayed with him. Any surgery had a risk of complication, but he imagined the risks were higher when your chest was cracked open, and someone messed around with your heart.

Somehow he made it across the parking lot and through the main doors. A stop at the reception desk earned him a visitor pass and directions to room 312. And then he was in the elevator. As the doors closed, he felt as if they were closing off his air supply as well. His hand pulled at his collar as if the few inches of give would allow him to breathe easier. Black spots darted across his vision, and his hand found the wall as a wave of dizziness swept over him. Then the elevator chimed, and the doors slid open.

The black dots receded, but the pressure did not. Still, Tucker managed to step over the line, allowing the doors to close behind him. The dim hum of conversations and computers floated on the air, sounding muted in his brain. His eyes found the small gray plaque indicating room 312 lay to the left, and he forced his feet that direction.

The door to room 312 stood ajar, and he paused to take one final deep breath before pushing the door open. His father appeared still and quiet in the bed, and Whitley sat in a chair nearby with a book on her lap. Her gaze lifted at the sound of Tucker's footsteps, and her eyes widened.

"Tucker, you made it," she said as she launched herself out of the chair and across the room.

She was thinner than he remembered, but her smile appeared the same. Bright and wide, it showed off her dimple and dispelled all the shadows that had been hanging over his head. "I told you I would try, Whit."

Her arms wound around his neck and squeezed as if she was

afraid he might be an apparition and disappear if she wasn't holding onto him. "I know, but I didn't think you'd actually show up."

Guilt pulled at his heart. It had been too long. He should have come home, even if it was just to see her.

"Tucker?" His father's voice was quiet and scratchy and it ended the brother-sister reunion.

Reluctantly, Tucker stepped toward the bed. "I'm here, Dad."

"I told her not to call you. I know how busy you are with football and the incident."

"It was dropped, Dad. The team gave me community service for it, but it's okay. Thank you." The words reminded him that his father had been too busy to show up and bail him out in the first place.

"I'm sorry I didn't come. Big case."

"There's always a big case, Dad." Tucker didn't mean for the words to be hurtful, but he saw the emotion flash in his father's eyes nonetheless. "I'm used to you not showing up by now."

"Tucker." Whitley hissed in a shocked voice, but their father held up his hand.

"No, he's right, Whitley. I haven't been there for him, for either of you. I've been so consumed with my own grief that I didn't realize you two must have been grieving as well."

The conversation with Benji played again in Tucker's head. He'd figured out that night that his father hadn't hated him, but he hadn't realized how much he needed to hear the words until now. Was this what Shelby had meant when she'd discussed forgiving his father? Was this God at work? Shelby. She still hadn't returned his call. He hoped she wasn't too angry with him.

Before he could say anything, his phone vibrated in his pocket. He pulled it out expecting it to be Shelby, but the number wasn't the one he had called previously. "I'll be right back." Tucker wasn't sure why he felt the need to explain his actions. He was a grown man, and he could take a phone call if he needed to.

"Hello?" he asked when he crossed the doorway and entered the hall.

"Tucker, it's Coach."

Dread filled Tucker, coursing like poison through every vein. Coach never called unless there was trouble, and he'd cleared the leave with him this morning. "Hey, Coach. What can I do for you?"

The man exhaled a large sigh. "It's about Sunday, Tucker. The man involved with the altercation called the league."

"What?" Anger and frustration erupted within Tucker, fighting for control. "Can he do that? I was never charged."

"I know, but you know how image is. It's everything; and so, even though the league knows you weren't at fault, they want to send a message. They're suspending you for Sunday's game."

"No, they can't do that. It's the playoffs, Coach. The next game is the wild card game. If we lose, we're out. I can't not play in the possible last game of the season." Frustration edged ahead of anger, and Tucker ran his hand across the back of his neck, massaging the muscles that now stood rigid with tension.

"I know it's the playoffs, Tucker, but I can't get you out of this one. It's just one game. If we win it, you'll still be able to play in the quarterfinals, the semifinals, and the championship game."

"Is there anything I can do?" Tucker asked. This was a nightmare. He'd worked so hard the last few days. And he'd changed. He could feel it.

"I doubt it, but you could try doing something to improve your image. Issue a public apology, help out a charity — something to show them that the bar fighter is not the real you."

Images of the center and it's used equipment flashed into Tucker's mind. He'd brought some footballs already, but what if he supplied a whole new collection of sports equipment? What if he did it at the Christmas party? In fact, what if he got some of the other guys to go with him to the party? It could be a big team event and maybe even boost morale before the big game.

"STILL NO WORD FROM HIM?" KENZI ASKED AS SHELBY MASSAGED her temples.

"None, and I just keep getting his voicemail. I don't know why he wouldn't at least call and explain. Now, it appears he might not be funding the party after all, and I have no one else to call and no money to buy gifts for the kids." She lifted her eyes to Kenzi's and sighed.

"Okay, that does stink," Kenzi said. True to her personality, Kenzi was still trying to find the silver lining in the dark clouds that filled Shelby's vision. "Maybe we can find some leftover things around here?"

"That's all we have is leftover things, Kenzi. Leftover things that nobody wants." The ringing of the phone interrupted her pity party, and Shelby forced a smile she didn't feel to her face as she picked up the phone. "Southlake Community Center, this is Shelby, how may I help you?"

"Shelby, thank goodness. Did you get my message?"

Tucker's voice both irritated her and sent her heart fluttering. Ugh, why did he affect her so much? "No, I saw no message, and I've been trying to call you for hours. Where are you Tucker? You're supposed to be here helping plan the Christmas party for tomorrow night."

"I know, but my dad had a heart attack. I had to fly to San Antonio to see him and I just got your messages, but I want you to still go ahead with the party for tomorrow."

"Tucker, are you sure? The news—"

"I don't care about the news, Shelby. I should have told you sooner about Jude Renfrow, and I'm sorry. But he's not important now. What's important is making sure those kids have a Christmas."

Was she dreaming? She pinched her arm to make sure she was really awake. Tucker Jackson didn't care about the suspension and he still wanted to fund the party? She could barely believe it, but though she appreciated his selflessness, it still didn't answer the bigger problem. "How? I have no money, no decorations, nothing."

"I'm going to wire you some money. Use it to get whatever decorations you need. Also, call the media and see if you can get Sylvie Sanders back out. I'll cover the gifts, and I promise I'll be back tomorrow for the party."

"But your dad?"

"I'll figure it out. You take care of things on your end, and I'll take care of things on mine. Seven o'clock tomorrow evening, we'll show those kids a party they won't soon forget."

"Okay, if you say so." She hung up the phone and turned to Kenzi, still dazed at what had just transpired.

"Was that Tucker?"

"It was. He said he left a message about today. Evidently his father had a heart attack."

Kenzi's hand flew to her mouth. "Oh my gosh, is he okay?"

"I don't know. I forgot to ask." Shelby couldn't believe she had forgotten that simple courtesy. She definitely had too much on her mind right now. "Anyway, he said he was wiring money and that I was to take care of the decorations and spreading the word. He said he'd take care of the gifts."

"Well, we better get started then. We've got a lot to do before tomorrow night."

34

"So, has a doctor told you anything?" Tucker asked when he returned to the room. He suddenly had a lot on his plate that he needed to do.

"The doctor was in this morning before you got here. They think they can insert a stent. Why? Are you in a hurry to run off somewhere?" Whitley crossed her arms and arched her left eyebrow as if she thought she could intimidate Tucker with her expression.

"That call was my coach. The guy who punched me contacted the league and they want to suspend me for Sunday's game."

"Can they do that?" his father asked. "I thought I got the charges dropped."

"You did, but evidently they want to make a lesson out of this. However, that's water under the bridge. The bigger issue is this center where I've been volunteering. I was supposed to be there today to help fund and plan a Christmas party for the kids, and these kids deserve a party. Some of them have very little. So, I need to make some calls; and I'll have to fly back tomorrow, but I want to be here for the surgery if I can."

His father's eyes glistened with unshed tears, and he blinked them away then coughed to clear his throat. "I think that's a great idea, Tucker, and even if it means you have to miss my surgery, it's okay with me."

Whitley stood and placed her hand on his forehead. "Are you sure you're feeling okay? You're willing to spend money to throw a party for other people even though it might not help you out? Who are you and what have you done with my big brother?"

"Hey, I help people," Tucker said, but as the words left his mouth, he realized Whitley was right. He had been selfish. He'd been thinking about how the losses affected him and not about the rest of the men on the team. He'd been wallowing in his sorrows which had caused him to be in the wrong place at the wrong time. And he'd dismissed community service at first because it would take up his time.

"Okay, maybe you're right. I haven't been the best example of helping people, but working at the center has made me see things differently."

"Well, I'm proud of you," Whitley said squeezing his shoulder.

"Me too," his father said from the bed. "What can we do to help?"

"I want to purchase new equipment for the center and then I need someone to go shopping for toys for the kids."

Whitley tossed her hair over her shoulders and placed her hands on her hips. "I'm a great shopper. I could run and get the toys."

"Awesome." He pulled his wallet out of his pocket and handed her a credit card. "Take this and buy at least fifty gifts."

Her eyes widened. "Fifty? Do I have a limit?"

Tucker chuckled. "Well, try not to break the bank but no, no limit."

"This is going to be so much fun." As the light glistened in her eyes, he wondered if he had just made a terrible mistake.

"Dad, do you think you feel up to shopping online for some

equipment for the center? I need basketballs, softballs, jump ropes, the like."

"I can do that," his father said. "Scrolling and clicking is my specialty."

"Great." Tucker handed the laptop to his father. "No work, just shopping."

His father rolled his eyes but promised. Tucker took out his phone and sat down in one of the nearby chairs. He had a lot of phone calls to make, but before he dialed the first number, his eyes wandered to his father. Could this be the start of a better relationship for them? If so, he knew he had two people he needed to thank — Shelby and God.

"Yes, that's right. Tomorrow night at seven p.m. It's going to be an amazing community event and Tucker Jackson asked specifically for Sylvie Sanders. Can she make it?" Shelby swallowed the seed of jealousy that had sprouted in her stomach when Tucker requested Sylvie. She knew it was probably just because the woman had already covered one story and would be the natural choice to do the next one as well; but as she still wasn't sure where she stood with Tucker, she couldn't help the jealous feelings swimming through her body. He hadn't mentioned rescheduling their date when he'd called.

"I think we can make that work. I'll put the story on Sylvie's docket."

"Thank you so much." Shelby hung up the phone and shook her head. She'd spent the last week worrying that this event would never happen, but now it appeared unstoppable. She and Kenzi had picked up the money from Tucker and purchased Christmas decorations and food. Then Kenzi had started decorating while Shelby had called to get the media coverage in place. The newspaper and the local news and radio stations had agreed to send someone out, and Shelby had a feeling this would be their best Christmas party ever.

A giant smile parted Shelby's lips as she exited the reception area to see the kids helping Kenzi decorate. Jingle Bells played softly on an old boombox, but the kids didn't seem to care. They were laughing and smiling in a way that Shelby hadn't seen in a long time. Darby was standing on a chair helping Kenzi hang streamers while Benji sorted out the strings of Christmas lights. Quinn and Kayla were setting up the artificial tree while still others were pulling the freshly purchased ornaments out of the box.

"How can I help?" Shelby asked as she neared the group. "We have to get this place ready for tomorrow night."

"Is Mr. Tucker coming to help too?" Benji asked.

"He had to go see his dad, but he's helping from down there. However, he promised he'll be back tomorrow for the party," Shelby said.

"We should do something special for him for hosting the thing last night," Darby said as she pushed her glasses up her nose. "That was really nice of him to show us how to play even though I don't really like football."

Shelby smiled at the girl. "You're right. It was. We should do something nice for him. Do you guys have any ideas?"

"We could make him a card," Darby said. "Something colorful and pretty and maybe with unicorns on it."

Shelby mashed her lips together to keep from laughing. Somehow she doubted Tucker was the unicorn kind. "I think that would be lovely, but maybe something else as well since he's a boy and probably more of a sports fan than a unicorn fan."

"We could give him a football," Quinn said, "though I'm not sure he would want any of ours."

"Do we have enough to purchase a new football, Ms. Shelby?" Benji asked, pausing his untangling to shoot her a very serious look.

"I think we might. What are you thinking?"

"What if we got him a new football and we all signed it? You know like people do with a cast. Only he wouldn't have to cut it off, and he could keep it forever."

Shelby swallowed the emotion rising in her throat and forced her hand to stay at her side and not dab at her eyes. She knew if she did, the flood gate would drop, and she would end up crying in front of the kids which would probably scare them more than anything. "That's a great idea, Benji."

"Yeah, great idea, man," Quinn said as he clapped a hand on Benji's shoulder.

The other kids echoed their agreement, and Shelby watched Benji sit just a little taller in his chair. Yes. This. This was exactly what had been missing before Tucker came into their lives. "Well, I guess I better run to the store and grab a football then so you guys have a chance to sign it tonight. Can you hold down the fort for a bit, Kenzi?"

"Are you kidding? I'm totally in my element here."

It was true. Kenzi looked like a natural as she hung the streamers. As Shelby looked around, she realized the gym had already been transformed into something magical. Perhaps Kenzi had found her calling after all.

35

"Where is he?" Shelby asked, wringing her hands for the fifth time in fewer than five minutes as she checked the front door again. It was six-thirty, and they would be opening the doors soon, but Tucker was nowhere to be seen.

Kenzi placed a hand on her arm. "Relax. He'll be here."

"What if he doesn't show up? He hasn't even called today. What if he got in a wreck or something happened to his dad? We have no presents if he doesn't show up."

Kenzi grabbed both of Shelby's shoulders and shook her. "Stop it. You'll drive yourself crazy with what ifs. What is it you always say about worry?"

Shelby sighed as she pictured the pastor at her church sharing the wisdom that had stuck with her for so many years. "Worrying accomplishes nothing except taking time away from today." She knew the pastor was right, and the Bible instructed God's children not to worry or fear but to cast those worries and fears on Jesus instead, but it was a lot easier said than done.

"Right. This is going to be a magical evening, Shelby. Don't tarnish it by worrying about what you can't control."

Shelby took a deep breath and nodded. The place was magical. Kenzi had hung twinkly lights around the room along with wreaths and streamers in red, green, and white. The artificial tree, while small, twinkled merrily and boasted the many ornaments the kids had hung on it. It even had a few uneven strands of popcorn though none long enough to wrap all the way around as the kids had eaten it before it reached that point. A long table held the cookies and treats Shelby had picked up on the way here. She had also set out punch and cups, plates, and napkins. All that was missing were the kids, who were on their way, and the presents.

Shelby glanced out the window again and ran a hand down her red party dress. She almost never wore red, but Kenzi had been adamant that she wear something bright and festive tonight. Kenzi had also done her makeup even though Shelby had protested the red lip color that matched her dress but seemed too bright for her. Without a conscious thought, her hand found the tendril that never stayed up with the rest of her hair and tugged on it.

"Will you stop?" Kenzi scolded, slapping her hand down.

Shelby flushed. She hated getting caught twirling her hair, but she supposed she could have worse habits. In high school, she had known a girl who pulled out her eyebrows and eyelashes. Often times, she would come to school with entire patches missing. There was also a boy who had scratched at his arm so often that it would bleed. The teacher would stop the bleeding, the wound would scab over, and then he would scratch the scab off and make it bleed again. Yes, in comparison, her hair twirling was a minor, albeit obnoxious, habit.

Headlights flashed, blinding her, as a car pulled into the parking lot. *Please be him*, she thought. *Please be Tucker.*

But it wasn't. She recognized Benji's mother's car as soon as it grew closer. "Do we go ahead and let them in?" she asked Kenzi in a quiet voice.

"Of course we do," Kenzi said. "It's freezing out there, and I promise everything will be okay."

Shelby nodded, but as another car pulled in, she couldn't help but wonder what they would do if Tucker didn't show.

"THANKS FOR AGREEING TO DO THIS, GUYS." TUCKER LOOKED around at the assembled group of football players. Not only had most of the guys from his team agreed to come; but Emmitt, his old teammate from the Rebels, had arrived as well. The Rebels were already out of the playoffs for the year, and as his wife's family lived close to Southlake, he had decided that he would help out and then drive out to meet them.

"What exactly are we doing, Tucker?" Emmitt asked.

"We are playing Santa to some kids who deserve it," Tucker said with a smile. He had spent entirely too much money on the toys and new equipment, but he knew in his heart it would be worth it. "Everyone grab a gift and let's load up."

He glanced at his watch as the guys began grabbing packages. They were a little behind schedule, but he didn't think Shelby would mind when she saw what he had in store. He grabbed a few packages and carried them out to his truck. The back was already loaded up with presents, but there was room for two more. He slid them in and then turned to see how the other guys were doing. They had decided to ride three in a truck, but even with that, they still needed four trucks to carry all the packages.

When the last box was loaded and the men were situated in the trucks, Tucker climbed behind the wheel of his own. Emmitt and Blaine were riding with him, something he never thought he'd see.

"This is a nice gesture," Emmitt said as Tucker turned the key.

"Thanks, Rev. I guess you rubbed off on me more than you or I knew."

Blaine, surprisingly, stayed quiet. Tucker didn't mind though. He enjoyed catching up with Emmitt as they drove to the center.

His eyes widened as he pulled into the center's parking lot

though. There were more cars than he could ever remember seeing parked in the parking lot. So many that he was forced to park in the fire lane because there were no open spots.

"Are all these cars here for the party?" Blaine asked.

"I think so," Tucker said.

"I hope we brought enough gifts," Emmitt said as if reading Tucker's mind.

"Well, if we didn't, then I'll just have to go shopping again tomorrow."

As he turned the engine off, he spied a figure clad in red speeding in his direction. Was that Shelby? He blinked, not believing his eyes. He'd assumed from the color of the dress that it had to be Kenzi, but Kenzi's hair was dark; and the hair on this woman was definitely blonde. His heart skipped a beat as he stepped out to meet her.

"What took you so long?" she asked when she was within earshot. "The kids are waiting inside, and I'm running out of ways to entertain them."

He could hear the frustration in her voice, and it matched the expression on her face. But he couldn't concentrate on her words. His focus was drawn to her mouth. Her beautiful lips were painted cherry red, and they screamed that they wanted to be kissed. There was makeup around her eyes that brought out their color as well, and something about the red against her skin made it appear creamier than he remembered. Every bone in his body ached to take her in his arms, but he couldn't do that right now. Right now, it was all about the kids.

"I'm sorry." He took her hands, unable to keep himself from touching a small part of her. "We took a little longer loading up than I thought we would, but I promise it will be worth it."

She glanced briefly down at their hands before meeting his gaze. "We?"

At that moment, the passenger door opened behind him and Blaine and Emmitt stepped out. Then, as if in sync, the door of the other three trucks opened and their players tumbled out as well.

"Yeah. We. I brought a few friends." He squeezed her hands, enjoying the expression of shock painted across her face. "Now go tell those kids that it's time to open presents."

With a final incredulous glance, she turned around and dashed back into the center. Tucker turned to his friends and motioned them with his hands. "Let's go, boys."

Tucker could scarcely believe it was the same center as he walked in. The feel of Christmas was everywhere — from the decorative wreaths hung about the room to the sounds of "White Christmas" playing softly over the speakers to the artificial Christmas tree near the far end. It sparkled with every color of light and probably every ornament the center had from the looks of it. The only thing it was missing was presents.

The room had been filled with a dull chatter, but as he and the other football players walked in, a hush fell across the room. Kids and parents alike stared at them as if the men were mirages in a desert, and everyone appeared afraid to make the first move or say a word for fear they might disappear.

"It's Tucker." Benji's voice echoed across the room, and Tucker smiled. He was glad Benji was here. He had a special present for the boy. "I knew he'd make it."

And then the dam broke. The kids raced across the floor shouting "Merry Christmas" and asking about the presents. "Are those for us?"

"One at a time," Tucker said with a smile. "Let my friends set the gifts down first." The children quieted, but Tucker could see their barely-contained energy with each bounce of a foot or bob of a head. They were calm now, but it wouldn't last long. "First, let me introduce my friends. This is my friend Emmitt Brown. I played with him on the San Antonio Rebels where he still plays. He drove down here just to meet you guys."

Eyes widened and jaws dropped as the kids looked at Emmitt.

"Next to him is Blaine Hollis. I'm sure you guys recognize him as the quarterback for the Tornadoes." He continued the process until every player had been introduced. "Now, my friends have some gifts for you guys. Who wants presents?"

The screams of the children rocked Tucker back, and he chuckled. They were certainly excited. "All right, let's open some presents. If you like dolls and dress-up clothes, I want you to find a player holding a pink gift, and if you like sports and cars, find a player with a blue gift."

As they hadn't known who all would be in attendance or what they might like, Tucker had figured wrapping all of the presents in pink and blue would be the easiest way to get the right type of gift to the right child. This would allow the kids to choose the type of gift they might enjoy more. The children scrambled around deciding on which gift they wanted, and when every child had one, Tucker gave the announcement they could open them.

Chaos ensued. Paper was ripped and thrown into the air. Squeals of laughter and shouts of joy echoed throughout the room, and, as soon as their gift was open, the kids were off showing it to their parents, their friends, or just playing with it in the middle of the floor.

Tucker touched the gifts still in his pocket as he made his way over to Benji and his mother. Benji had ended up with a microscope, something Tucker was sure the boy would enjoy with his love of science. "Hey Benji, do you like your gift?"

The smile on the boy's face said more than words ever could. "I love it, Mr. Tucker. Thanks for doing this for us."

His mother — a pale, slender woman with mousy brown hair who looked as if life had been harder on her than necessary — sniffed and wiped a tear from her eye. "Yes, thank you. This is more than we could have hoped for."

Emotion choked Tucker's throat, and he coughed to clear it. "I actually have one more gift for Benji if that's okay?"

Questions filled her eyes, but she nodded.

"Benji, I probably won't be playing in the game, but I have two tickets with your name on them. Would you like to come see the Tornadoes play in person? You and your mother would be my guests in the luxury box."

Benji's eyes grew to the size of half dollars. "Really? Me?"

"Yes, you." Tucker knelt in front of the boy and placed a hand on his knee. "I don't have any kids yet, but when I do, I hope I have a son just like you, so it would be amazing if you could come to the game."

Benji turned his face to his mother. "Mom, can we?"

"It's too much." Emotion filled the woman's voice and another tear escaped from her eye.

"No, it's not. Please, come." He placed the two tickets in her hand. "I insist. Merry Christmas."

She nodded and though she could say no more, he could read the thanks in her teary gaze.

"That was very kind of you, Tucker."

Tucker turned to see Sylvie Sanders and her cameraman behind him. "Thank you. I'm glad you could make it. Have you had a chance to get some footage of the party?"

"I have, but I am curious as to why you called me out here. Does this have anything to do with your suspension for Sunday's game?"

So, she'd heard about that. He opened his mouth to tell her it did. To tell her that Jude Renfrow had been the donor last year and pulled his donation because of the skirmish with Tucker, but then he realized his motives for donating to this party would come into question. Yes, he wanted to play Sunday, more than anything; but he didn't want to ruin this moment for the kids.

"No, it actually isn't, Sylvie. I called you out here because I wanted the people of Southlake to see what an amazing center this is, what fantastic kids these are, and what an outstanding job Director Shelby Doll is doing here. This party almost didn't happen because they couldn't find a donor to fund it. I couldn't let that happen. After volunteering here for the last week, I have seen firsthand how important this center is to the families who use it. I know that not everyone can donate the way I did, but everyone can do something even if it's volunteering their time."

"So, you don't care about the game Sunday?"

Tucker smiled and shook his head. "Of course I care about the game Sunday. It's the wild card game. If we win, we continue on in the playoffs, but if we lose it will be the last game of the season. Do I wish I was playing? Absolutely. But I learned an important lesson. I was suspended because I got into an altercation with someone after our last game. Even though I didn't throw the first punch and was just defending myself, I was in the bar because I was angry. I was angry at our loss, angry at being traded, angry at my father. Working here has let me see how misplaced that anger was. It has showed me how lucky I am to play on a great team with these other amazing players who came out tonight to help me bring some Christmas cheer to these kids."

"Well, that is certainly a feel-good story that our viewers will enjoy," Sylvie said as she motioned for the cameraman to stop rolling. "Off the record though, do you know why the previous donor chose not to donate this year?"

Tucker flashed her a tight-lipped smile. He knew what she was trying to do, but he wasn't going to bite. He'd given her enough information that if she really wanted to run with that story, she could look it up herself. Instead, he pointed over her shoulder at the refreshment table. "I need to see Shelby about something. If you'll excuse me."

36

"This is amazing, Tucker. I can't believe you pulled all this together in just a day," Shelby said as he approached her. She held out a glass of punch to him and then filled a second cup for herself.

"You did all the hard work, Shelby. I just got the toys here." He took a sip of the punch, but his eyes never left her face.

Shelby's heart quickened in her chest. The way he was looking at her felt like a caress. She could almost feel his hand against her cheek, and the thought of it sent her blood pulsing through her body. "You did a lot more than that, Tucker Jackson. Don't think I don't know it."

"Well, I have two more things for you. Will you follow me?"

Follow him? With the way he was looking at her right now? She'd probably follow him off a cliff right now if he asked. "Sure." The word barely made it past her throat and came out more like a whisper than an answer, but he seemed to understand it anyway.

He took her cup and placed it on the table along with his own. Then he reached for her hand. Warm tingles shot up her arm as their skin touched, and Shelby fought to compose her breathing. He led her toward the door. "Wait, my coat."

"Don't worry about it. You can use my jacket. We won't be long." He paused long enough to shrug out of his suit jacket and place it on her shoulders.

She knew the chill was biting outside, but even when they stepped out of the warmth of the center, she didn't feel it. It was as if their connection was heating them both.

"I got a few more things for the center," he said as he steered them toward the back of his truck.

Her eyes widened as she saw the new sports equipment in the bed of the truck. "Tucker, you didn't have to do this."

"Yes, I did. Have you tried playing basketball with those balls?"

She chuckled at the seriousness in his voice and shook her head. "I know how awful they are. I don't play, but I've watched the kids try to use them. Still, this is too much. You've done so much already."

"If I plan to keep volunteering, I'd like to have better equipment."

Her lips parted and she stared up at him. "Do you mean it? You want to keep volunteering?" She had hoped he would want to stay, but she hadn't wanted to ask him for fear of his answer.

He took her other hand and pulled her close to his chest. "If you'll let me."

Suddenly, it was hard to breathe. It was as if a hand was squeezing her lungs closed. "Of course I'll let you."

The corners of his lips twitched, showing off the dimple in his cheek. "Good, there's just one more thing then."

"What's that?" Shelby could hardly get the words out. She felt locked in his gaze. The smell of him intoxicated her — this manly scent that reminded her of campfires and woods. It made her want to close her eyes and breathe in deeply.

"We need to get you to relax a little." He let go of one of her hands, and she watched in slow motion as his hand touched her hair. With deft fingers, he pulled the first pin out, and she felt a chunk of hair fall and bounce by her face. Then another pin and finally the clip holding it all in place.

She wanted to say something, to do something, though she had no idea what. But she couldn't. Her feet were frozen in place. Her eyes were locked with his. It was taking all her effort just to remember to breathe. And then his hand was in her hair, and the feel of it sent the tiny hairs on the back of her neck up. Goosebumps broke out on her arms, and she closed her eyes, relishing the sensation.

"That's much better." His hand moved from her hair to the back of her neck, and Shelby's eyes snapped open. Was he going to kiss her? She could see the desire in his eyes and hear it in the thudding of his heart. Or was that hers? It appeared she could no longer tell the difference.

"I have one more question for you, Shelby Doll." His voice was husky and constricted with emotion.

"Yes?" The word was airy, far off, as if she had answered from another plane.

"Would it be breaking any rules if I kissed the director of the center?" The twinkling in his eye told her he didn't really care if it did. He was going to kiss her unless she protested, and she had no plans to do that.

She managed a small shake of her head, and then warmth flooded her body as his lips touched hers. Having always been the shy, quiet one, Shelby hadn't kissed that many men; but she didn't think she would ever forget this kiss with Tucker. Electricity buzzed through her, racing down her legs and curling her toes in her shoes.

"Oh, I do have one more gift for you," Tucker said when they pulled back.

Shelby couldn't imagine what else he might have for her. He'd already given her more than she had ever expected. "What is it?"

"I probably won't get to play because of this suspension, but will you be my guest at the game on Christmas?" He pulled out two tickets from his pocket. "There's one for Kenzi too."

"Of course, I'd be happy to, but there has to be something we can do so you can play." She couldn't stand the thought of him not getting to do the thing he loved the most. He had changed so much. The man who stood before her today was no longer the angry man who had entered her center a week ago.

He brushed her hair behind her ear and shook his head. "No, but it's fine. It's just a game. Working with you and with these kids the last week has shown me that."

Shelby could tell it was still more than a game to him, but he was trying to accept it. She had to try and help him.

TUCKER COULD TELL FROM THE GLINT IN HER EYE THAT SHELBY wasn't going to just let it go, but at least she didn't push him for more information.

"Okay, if you're sure."

"I am." She shivered in his arms, and the reality of the cold air around them landed on his shoulders. "We should get back inside. You're freezing."

"I'm fine," she said through chattering teeth. "How's your dad?"

"He's good. They put the stent in yesterday afternoon. He has to stay another day for observation, but then he should be able to return home. I — uh — took your advice too, on the way back here. I opened my heart to God. He's helping me forgive my father and myself."

Tears clouded Shelby's eyes, and she blinked them back. "That's wonderful, Tucker. Oh, and I almost forgot. The kids have something for you too."

"For me?" He couldn't imagine what the kids might have for him, but he followed Shelby back into the center.

"There you two are," Kenzi said, hurrying up to them. "The kids have been asking for you. They want to give Tucker his gift."

"Let's not make them wait any longer," Shelby said with a smile. She led Tucker to the middle of the room and held up her hands to get the attention of the crowd. "Thank you all for coming out. I especially want to thank Tucker Jackson and the rest of the Texas Tornadoes for helping out. I know the kids have enjoyed having you here the last week, Tucker; and as a way of saying thank you, they have a gift for you."

Tucker watched as Benji rolled his direction with a colorfully wrapped package on his lap. "I hope you like it, Mr. Tucker."

"I'm sure I'll love it," Tucker said as he took the box. He shot the crowd a teasing grin. "Should I open it now?"

"Open it," the kids hollered back at him.

"Okay, okay." He tore the paper and lifted the lid to see a football inside. "Ah, you guys, this is great."

"It's not just a football, Mr. Tucker," Benji said with a shake of his head. "Take it out."

Tucker did as instructed, and his throat swelled with emotion as he pulled out the football covered in kids' scribbles. They had all signed the football and some had even left him a note or encouraging word. "This is perfect, guys. Thank you."

And it was. Tucker knew that even if they made it to the championship game that this would be the highlight of his season.

37

T he ringing of his phone woke Tucker on Christmas
morning. Was it his father? Whitley? She'd promised to
call when his father got released. His hand grabbed the
phone, and he hit the answer call button without looking at the
caller ID.

"Hello?"

"Tucker? It's Coach. You ready to suit up today?"

"Suit up? But I thought I was suspended."

"You were, but your teammates called the league last night and
said they weren't playing without you. Then the league received a
second call informing them of Mr. Renfrow's decision to pull his
donation to the community center. In light of those two things, they
have lifted your suspension."

His teammates refused to play without him? Tucker could
barely believe it. Here he'd thought he wasn't fitting in on this
team, yet they had shown up to help him out last night and then
stood up to the league for him. He couldn't have asked for better
team members. "Thanks, Coach. I'll be there." Tucker couldn't
help smiling as he hung up the phone and headed into the shower.

This Christmas was already shaping up to be his best since his mother passed away, and getting to play was icing on the cake.

Two hours later, he pulled into the stadium parking lot. He'd told Shelby and Benji's mother where to go, but he hoped he would get to see them before the game started. Tucker saw his favorite guard Dennis on duty; and he made his way over to him.

"Merry Christmas, Dennis. How's the family?"

"A little irritated that I'm here on Christmas Day," Dennis said, "but they're good."

Tucker had never considered all the people who also had to give up Christmas with their families to be here. "I'm sorry you have to be away from your family on Christmas. I'll tell you what, next year I'll save Christmas Day tickets for you. That way your family can watch from the luxury box. They still won't get to spend the day with you directly, but at least you'll be in the same place."

Dennis's eyes widened. "You would do that?"

"Of course I would. I'd give you some for today, but I already gave them out which reminds me of why I came over here. If a boy in a wheelchair and a beautiful blonde come through here with my luxury box tickets, will you tell them I'll come see them before the game starts if I can?"

"You bet, Mr. Jackson. I'll keep my eyes open for them."

"Thanks, Dennis. Again, Merry Christmas."

"Merry Christmas to you, Mr. Jackson, and good luck today."

Tucker flashed another warm smile before he continued into the dressing room. Somehow, he didn't think they would need good luck today. Everything about it just felt right.

"Oh my goodness," Kenzi said as she entered the luxury box behind Shelby. "This is amazing."

"This is insane!" Shelby said as she took in the luxurious gold and blue interior. "Who needs this much?"

Kenzi shook her head and rolled her eyes. "Nobody needs it. That's why it's called a luxury, but isn't it fantastic?" She held her arms wide and fell onto a plush leather couch.

Shelby didn't know if fantastic was the word she would use. She felt like an imposter in the exorbitant room, and she couldn't help thinking about all the kids she could help if she had this kind of money.

"I know what you're thinking, Shelby, but can't you just relax for one day? Can't you just take a step back and enjoy this for what it is? A treat. An inside look into how the other half lives."

"You're right," Shelby said with a sigh. "It's Christmas, and I should enjoy this. I'll probably never do this again."

Kenzi snorted and sat up. "Who are you kidding? I saw the way Tucker was looking at you last night. I have a feeling you'll be attending a lot of these in the future."

Heat flamed up Shelby's face. Kenzi didn't even know about the kiss. Shelby normally told her everything, but she hadn't told her about the kiss with Tucker. It had just been too mind blowing.

"Whoa, look at this place!" Benji's voice gave Shelby a reprieve from answering Kenzi, one she was very grateful for.

"Hey Benji. Pretty cool, right?" Shelby had been thrilled when Tucker had told her he had given a ticket to Benji and his mother, but seeing the awed expression on the kid's face was even more heartwarming. Maybe if she did continue dating Tucker, they could bring a different kid each week. That might be the only way she wouldn't feel so bad about watching the game from this box.

"Oh good, you all made it."

Shelby turned at the sound of Tucker's voice. She'd never seen him up close in his football gear, and it took her breath away. He'd always been just Tucker to her, but in his tight pants and jersey, he looked like the football player that he was. "Thank you for inviting us."

"Thank you for coming."

Tucker didn't cross the room and take her in his arms as she'd hoped he would, but his gaze said it all. It was as if time slowed around them, and every sound was muted. She could read the desire in his gaze, and the heat returned when she realized everyone else probably could too.

"Mr. Tucker, this is so cool." Once again, Benji came to her aid even though he had no idea he was doing it.

"I'm glad you're enjoying it," Tucker said with a chuckle. "I have to get down to the field for the warmup, but I wanted to say hi before I did." His eyes shifted back to Shelby. "Will you wait for me after?"

"Of course." There was no way Shelby would leave without seeing him. It was Christmas Day and though she didn't get to spend the day close to him, she had hopes they would spend at least a little of the evening together. She watched him wave and exit the room before going to sit on the couch next to Kenzi.

"See, I told you," Kenzi whispered as Shelby sat down.

"Yes, you're very smart. Now hush so I can focus on the game." Shelby knew nothing about the game of football, but it gave her a good excuse to avoid Kenzi's prying gaze. If she continued dating Tucker though, she'd have to get him to teach her the rules.

As she watched him run out on the field, she realized she was practically his date. Her. Shelby Doll. The woman who had always blended into the background was here as Tucker Jackson's guest, and hopefully, they'd be going on their first official date soon.

"What are you smirking about?" Kenzi asked, dispelling Shelby's daydream.

"Nothing. Just enjoying the game." And she did enjoy it. At least as much as she understood it. She might not have known what each play was or exactly how the points were scored, but she knew to cheer every time the Tornadoes put points on the board. When the final whistle blew, they had secured a win by a mere three points. But a win was a win, right?

EPILOGUE

Seven Months Later

Tucker touched the box in his pocket to make sure it was still there. He'd spent a week shopping for the perfect ring, but had found nothing he liked. Thankfully, when he'd mentioned it to his father, whom he was now talking to on a regular basis, he'd suggested Tucker's mother's ring. The ring was simple and elegant — just like Shelby, and he couldn't wait to see the look on her face when he slid it on her finger. What better time than the re-opening of the center?

"You ready?" his father whispered in his ear.

Tucker still couldn't get over the change in his father. After the heart attack, his father had cut back on his case load. He'd begun spending more time with Whitley, and he'd even started attending church again where he'd met a wonderful woman, Meredith.

"Yeah, thanks again, Dad." Tucker smiled at his father, glad for their mended relationship.

"Good luck, big brother," Whitley said as she tossed him a wink before continuing into the center with his father and Meredith.

"What was that about?" Shelby asked as she rejoined him.

She'd been conversing with her own family who was now following his family into the center.

"Nothing, just wishing us luck." He searched her face for any clue she might have guessed his intentions for tonight.

"Are you okay?" Her brow furrowed as she touched his arm.

"What?" He realized he was staring and shook his head. "Yes, I'm fine. Just excited to see what Kenzi's done with the place." After the Christmas party, Kenzi had realized she had a knack for decorating and had returned to college to work on her interior design degree. The Texas Tornadoes team, after seeing the center at the Christmas party, had agreed to donate a sizable amount of money to help renovate the center and hired Kenzi to head it. It had been a rush renovation because they couldn't close the center too long, but a local church had offered to let them use its building until the work was completed. Tonight would be the first time Shelby and Tucker would get to see the results.

"I'm sure she did an amazing job, but don't you think we're a little overdressed?" Her hand slid down the side of her dark blue evening gown as if she could smooth out the nerves she was feeling. Kenzi had planned a formal reveal. She'd gotten several wealthy families and business owners to attend by connecting the reveal to a donation dinner.

Tucker turned to her and took her hands. "We're not overdressed, Shelby. This is a huge deal, and there are going to be a lot of eyes on you. You just need to remind yourself how amazing you are."

A soft pink glow raced across her cheeks, making her even more beautiful. "Thank you, Tucker. I just... I feel very out of my element."

"Hah, well now you know how I felt working at the center when I first started." Tucker had been completely out of his element, but he wouldn't change it for the world now. Not only had he met Shelby and the amazing kids, but he had learned to value the important things in life. Things like family and love.

His hand touched his pocket again. He couldn't wait to propose to her.

Her shoulders rose and fell with her deep breath. Then she tossed him a smile and lifted her chin. "Okay, I'm ready."

Shelby could never have imagined the center looking as it did now. The floor had been waxed and the walls redone. Instead of the sad faded cream walls, they were now filled with kids' artwork and exploded with color. The carpet in the office and hallways had been replaced as had the computer in the reception area. It almost looked like a brand-new building.

Tables covered in white tablecloths filled the gym area, and decorative candles and flower arrangements added pops of color. As Shelby and Tucker entered, those already seated stood and began clapping. Shelby couldn't believe how many people Kenzi had persuaded to come. Of course, she shouldn't have been surprised. Kenzi had a charming and persuasive personality.

"Here she is, the lady of the hour," Kenzi said from the front of the gym where a makeshift microphone had been set up. "Shelby, get up here and tell us about the new plans for the center."

Tucker squeezed her hand and planted a quick kiss on her lips before motioning her to the front. As she walked through the crowd, butterflies woke and took flight in her stomach. Speaking to large crowds of donors had always been nerve wracking for her.

Shelby took the mic and cleared her throat. "First, I just want to say thank you to everyone who came out tonight. Didn't Kenzi do an amazing job on the interior of this place?" Cheers and applause answered her question, giving Shelby the courage to continue.

"Well, thanks to a wonderful donation from the Texas Torna-does, not only were we able to redecorate, but we've also created a collaborative program. Once a month, a football player will host a day here at the center to teach kids about exercise, teamwork, and of course football. This day will be free for all who are regular attenders at the center, and I'm pleased to announce that this program has brought in over fifty new children." Another round of clapping ensued.

"We'll be hiring a few full-time staff members to help accommodate our new numbers as well as several part-time members, allowing us not only to serve the kids but also to bring jobs to the community. This couldn't have been possible without our very first volunteer from the Texas Tornadoes, so would you please give a round of applause to Tucker Jackson?"

Shelby smiled as the cheers grew louder for Tucker as he approached the stage. She handed him the mic and moved to step back, but he caught her hand, holding her in place.

"Thank you, Shelby. I didn't know what to expect when I was first told I had to volunteer here, but I quickly learned that these kids had more to teach me than I could ever teach them. As did Shelby here. Many of you know that we've been dating for the last seven months. I would have been a fool not to pursue this amazing woman, but tonight you guys get to join in on what I hope will be our next step." He motioned to Kenzi who Shelby hadn't even noticed had been waiting off to the side. Then he handed her the mic.

Shelby's face clouded with confusion and then surprise as he reached into his pocket. He lowered to one knee and held out the box to her. As unobtrusively as possible, Kenzi held the mic so his words would carry as well. "Shelby, you changed my life the day I met you, and I can't imagine a day without you in it. Would you do me the honor of becoming my wife?"

He flicked open the box, and Shelby gasped and covered her mouth with her hands. Inside was the most beautiful ring she had ever seen. Tears blurred her eyes, and she was afraid no sound would come out of her mouth so she nodded. Cheers took over the place as he slipped the ring on her finger.

Though Shelby had prayed for a man, she had never expected

God to send her one like Tucker Jackson. She supposed that just confirmed what she'd always known in her heart. God was an amazing, loving Father, and life worked out better when you let Him be in control.

The End!

If you enjoyed this story, Please leave a review. Just a few words really helps

IT'S NOT QUITE THE END!

Thank you so much for reading *Run With My Heart*. This book was inspired by my love of football and the amazing feedback I received on Her Second Chance Forever Groom.

I hope you enjoyed the story as I really enjoyed writing it. If you did, would you do me a favor? If you did, Please leave a review. It really helps. It doesn't have to be long — just a few words to help other readers know what they're getting.

I'd love to hear from you, not only about this story, but about the characters or stories you'd like read in the future. I'm always looking for new ideas and if I use one of your characters or stories, I'll send you a free ebook and paperback of the book with a special dedication. Write to me at loranahoopes@gmail.com. And if you'd like to see what's coming next, be sure to stop by authorloranahoopes.com

I also have a weekly newsletter that contains many wonderful things like pictures of my adorable children, chances to win awesome prizes, new releases and sales I might be holding, great books from other authors, and anything else that strikes my fancy and that I think you would enjoy. I'll even send you the first chapter of my newest (maybe not even released yet) book if you'd like to sign up.

Even better, I solemnly swear to only send out one newsletter a week (usually on Tuesday unless life gets in the way which with three kids it usually does). I will not spam you, sell your email address to solicitors or anyone else, or any of those other terrible things.

God Bless,
   Lorana

III

LOVE ON THE LINE

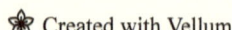

To my wonderful readers who inspire me to write every day.
To my father who got me into watching football when I was young.
To Emmitt Smith who was my favorite ball player of all time. He
had so much class, and I loved how he finished his degree as well.
Such an inspiration!

❧ 38 ❧

BLAINE

laine watched as his friend and teammate Tucker Jackson dropped to one knee, but his eyes weren't on the happy couple. Instead, they were drawn to the stunning brunette who stood behind them holding the mic out for the proposal to be heard while trying her best to blend into the background so as not to be a distraction. As if that was possible for her. With her dark velvet locks pulled up on top of her head, the slender curve of her neck was even more pronounced. Her skin glowed like fresh cream, and his eyes followed the lines of her neck to her slim shoulders before he shook his head to clear it.

He wondered how her skin might feel under his fingertips, but he had no business thinking about Kenzi like that. Not with Heidi, or was it Jennifer, he was seeing this week? It didn't matter. While Kenzi wasn't like the women he usually dated, she was too good for him. Besides, she deserved a man who could give her a future like Tucker was doing for Shelby, and that certainly wasn't him. He shouldn't even be thinking about settling down. Not with his past.

Still, since the day he'd met Kenzi, she'd made appearances in his mind. Not every day but often enough that he'd memorized the slight tilt of her upper lip, the way her eyes sparkled when she smiled. Enough to know that he thought of her more often than he should.

Cheering erupted around him, and he realized Shelby had said yes. She held her hand up for the crowd to see, and a tightness seized his heart. He wanted that - what Tucker had. He wanted a beautiful woman who would smile at him the way Shelby was smiling at Tucker now. Someone who would look at him with pride and admiration. A woman he could pamper and love and protect - but there was the rub. He wasn't good at protecting. He was great at pretending he was. Sometimes he even convinced himself he could do it. He was, after all, older now and wiser.

Maybe. But what if he failed again?

He knew he shouldn't - it was wrong, it was dangerous, it would never work - but as if they had a mind of their own, his feet pushed into the floor and he stood, clapping with those around him. Then he moved. Not towards the door where he should have been moving. Of course not to where he should be going. Fresh air. That's what he really needed. That would clear his head and push this stupid idea away, but then why were his feet moving away from the door? Away from the door and toward Kenzi. *Turn back*, he thought. But his feet did not seem to be getting the same message his brain was sending. Before he knew it, he stood before her.

"Hey, Blaine, I'm so glad you could come tonight." Her eyes sparkled like emeralds held under a light, and the sincerity of her smile only deepened her beauty. Oh man, was he in trouble.

"Thanks. You did an amazing job with the place." He'd volunteered a few times since the Christmas party last year, but he was still in awe of how many improvements Kenzi had managed to do to the bland building in such a short time.

Her gaze scanned around the room, and he could see the pride on her face. "Thanks. There was more that I wanted to do, but we couldn't keep using the church forever. The kids need this space."

Her eyes came back to his, and the corners or her mouth lifted in another smile - one that made his heart do funny things inside his chest. "I hear you'll be volunteering around here more often."

"I will. Each of us will be hosting a day a month, but I figured I would set an example and do more than that. My hope is that more of the players will follow. You and Shelby have certainly done something amazing here."

She shook her head, sending the dark tendrils that framed her face bouncing. How he wanted to touch those tendrils, to see if they felt as soft as they looked. "Shelby is the one who has done amazing work. I simply did what she needed. Working at the center was never my dream, but I'm glad I was able to help her fulfill hers."

"And decorating? Is that your dream?" Blaine had been following the scuttlebutt he could gather from Shelby and Tucker, and he knew that Kenzi was finishing her certificate in interior design.

Her lips pursed in an adorable position as her head tilted slightly. "I think so. I'm really enjoying school and doing this was so much fun."

"Do you think you'd be open to doing a cabin?" He broke out in a sweat. He could feel it along his hairline. What was he doing? Inviting her into that house - even though it didn't feel like his house - was dangerous, but he couldn't seem to stop himself. There was something about Kenzi that made him want to put his guard down and figure himself out so he could have nice things. One side of him knew it was impossible to ever not feel this heavy burden of guilt; that was the cold sweat part. The other half wanted more than anything to try and be better; that was the mouth part.

Her head cocked a little farther to the right as her eyes narrowed at him. "Are you looking for a designer, Blaine Hollis?"

His name sounded like honey from her lips, and he forced himself to remain aloof even though the way she looked into his eyes like that terrified him. Could she see his demons? "Maybe. If you're up to it, but it's probably a lost cause, I don't know." He stumbled, trying to backtrack and maneuver away from his betraying mouth. "I've inherited a lakeside cabin, but I don't know what to do with it. I'm probably just going to sell it." He should have sold it already with all the ghosts it held, all the memories, but some of them were good memories. "I've looked at a few designers but haven't found any I liked and trusted. Until now."

As if gauging his sincerity, her eyes searched his face. "I'd be happy to come take a look, but it would be my first real job. I mean this was a job, but," she shrugged, "it's not the same as redecorating a house or cabin. I'd love to take a look and see if it's something I could do. I've been looking for things to add to my portfolio. Are you sure you want me?"

Was he sure he wanted her? If she only knew how loaded her words were. He wanted her more than he'd wanted a woman in a long time. "Yeah," he paused, feeling a lightness he hadn't felt since the last good day at the lake house. "I think I'm sure."

She walked over to a small table and picked up a handbag before returning to him. His eyes followed her brightly painted nails as she flicked the clasp open and reached inside. A moment later, they reappeared with a pink business card and tilted towards him. "Here. Shelby got me some business cards as a graduation present. I don't know how she did pink, but I love it. It's so me. Anyway, my number's on here. Call me tomorrow and we'll set up a time to check it out, so I can see what I can do."

He took the pink business card from her and bit the inside of his lip. She couldn't do just a normal white business card like everyone else. Nope, she had to be different. The pink with gold sparkly letters fit her completely.

Blaine watched her walk away and then slipped the card into his pocket. He'd either just made the smartest move of his life or the dumbest. He just wasn't sure which.

KENZI

"Ooh, let me see." Kenzi squealed as she lifted Shelby's hand to critique the ring. She'd seen it earlier, of course, when Tucker had showed it to her before the proposal in order to make sure Shelby would like it, but diamonds always looked better on hands than in boxes - no matter how beautiful the velvet wrapping was. "It's perfect, Shelby. It's so you."

Shelby's eyes dropped to the ring and pure rays of happiness shone from her gaze. "I know, right? It's just what I would have picked if I'd been asked. Did you help him pick it?"

Kenzi chuckled and shook her head. "Nope. He showed it to me after he had it just for reassurance you would love it, but picking it was all him."

Shelby's gaze wandered to her fiancé who was currently chatting and laughing with several other members of the team including Blaine Hollis and Mason Dixon. "I never thought I would find someone who knew me so well, and I certainly never expected him to be a football player."

"Yeah, I would never have believed it if someone had told me that either." Kenzi laughed and sat down in the chair next to her. Shelby had barely even known what football was before she met Tucker Jackson, much less how to play it, so it was completely ironic she was now engaged to a football player.

Shelby turned her gaze to Kenzi, a mischievous smile on her lips. "Now, we just need to find someone for you."

Kenzi held up her hands. "No, thanks, I'm good right now. Though Blaine Hollis did just offer me a job. I think. And he's a cutie. A little mysterious and intense, but a cutie."

Shelby's eyes lit up, and the mischievous smile was joined with a twinkling light. "A job, huh? Are you sure that wasn't code for a date?"

Kenzi shook her head. Her friend had jumped off the deep end. Shelby had always been a romantic, but put a ring on her finger and she was a regular Cupid shooting love arrows at anything that moved. "No, he wants me to redecorate some cabin he inherited." It definitely wasn't a date, because he would have actually asked her on a date if it was a date, right?

"Sure he does."

Shelby was on a roll tonight, but she might be able to give Kenzi some insight on Blaine, seeing as how she had spent more time with the team members. There were definitely some things Kenzi was curious about. "Do you know anything about the members of the Tornadoes? Blaine's been on the team for years and no one has ever seen him with the same girl more than once. Not once. Doesn't that seem odd to you?"

It certainly did to Kenzi. When she'd begun gaining interest in football about six years ago in order to impress a college quarterback, Blaine Hollis had been the first member of the Texas Tornadoes to catch her eye. With his blond hair and warm brown eyes, he exuded this odd mix of masculinity and sensitivity that Kenzi found attractive. She had figured she couldn't be the only one and had dug into his personal life, surprised when she found no mention of a steady girlfriend. Nor did they ever mention one on TV or show a woman in the stands. Occasionally he was spotted with a woman, but never the same woman twice. Six years and still no relationship. He was either celibate or…

Shelby's voice interrupted her rabbit train of thought. "Maybe he just hasn't found the right woman yet."

"Maybe." Kenzi agreed because she knew there was no use arguing with Shelby when she was like this. She was sweet and loyal and stubborn as a mule when she wanted to be. Besides, it was possible she was right. Maybe Blaine was just waiting for the perfect woman, but Kenzi didn't think so.

❧ 39 ❧

B laine Hollis paused, the weighted bar just inches from his chest, as the smart watch on his wrist vibrated, letting him know he was receiving a call. It was his workout time. Who in the world would be calling him right now? Everyone he was close friends with should be working out now too, and his family... well that was a whole other story. Surely nothing was wrong with them. He pushed the bar up and placed it back in the rack before glancing at his wrist. The unknown number only served to stir up the apprehension bubbling in his stomach.

He pulled his phone out of the arm band pouch, where it stayed nestled and sweat-free during his workout, and paused the Toby Mac song pumping through his ears before answering. "Hello?" The word came out labored due to the adrenaline coursing through his body.

"Blaine? It's Tucker. I need your help."

Tucker Jackson. Of course. If he'd checked his phone instead of his watch, he would have seen Tucker's name, but his watch only flashed numbers, and he had long ago stopped memorizing them. He should have guessed it was Tucker though. He was the only Texas Tornado team member not at workout practice right now because he'd been given emergency leave to return home due to his father's heart attack.

"Tucker? Aren't you supposed to be with your dad?" Blaine grabbed a towel from his bag and wiped it across his forehead.

"I am, and he's doing okay. I actually need help for the Christmas party tomorrow."

Blaine's hand froze. Had he missed a memo? He didn't remember hearing anything about a Christmas party. "What party, Tucker?"

"At the community center. I promised Shelby that I would bring presents for the kids."

"But aren't you in San Antonio?" Was Tucker asking him to bring presents to the center? He didn't have presents nor did he feel like going out and getting any, and somehow, he doubted Tucker had purchased any before leaving town.

He didn't mind kids, really, at least as long as they belonged to someone else and he only had to be around them for small windows of time. Anything longer than that dredged up memories that he wanted to keep hidden.

"I'm driving back tomorrow, so I can keep my word. Look, my sister Whitley is purchasing a ton of items and asking that they be available for collection at the stores in Southlake. Do you think you could round up a few guys to help you pick up the toys and help me deliver them tomorrow night?"

Blaine rolled his eyes, even though he knew Tucker couldn't see the gesture over the phone. Picking up toys was not how he had intended to spend his Christmas Eve, but it wasn't like he had much else planned. He certainly wasn't going home to a family. They hadn't spent a Christmas together in years, and bringing gifts to the kids at the center seemed like a worthy use of his time. "How many toys are we talking about?" He thought about his red Mustang - he wouldn't be putting many gifts in there.

"Fifty, at least."

"Fifty?" Blaine spat the word out in surprise. "I can't carry fifty toys in my car."

Tucker sighed on the other end. "Which is why I asked you to see if some of the guys could help out. Doesn't Mason have a large truck?"

Mason Dixon (his parents had an odd sense of humor) was one of the wide receivers on the team, and he did, indeed, drive a large, souped-up truck. But Blaine didn't know if it would even hold fifty toys.

"Please, Blaine." The silence must have made Tucker think Blaine was refusing his request. "Those kids really deserve Christmas."

"Yeah, I get it. I was thinking of who else to ask." Though Blaine was not a fan of Christmas - not anymore anyway - he couldn't deny that the kids Tucker had been working with could probably use a little Christmas cheer. At least if the stories Tucker had told him were true. "Okay, I'll get it done. Where do you want to meet?"

"How about at the stadium? Can you gather a bunch of the guys?"

"I'll do my best, Tucker, but it is Christmas Eve we're talking about here. Some of the guys have little kids."

"Whatever you can manage, Blaine. Thanks. You're a lifesaver."

The phone went dead in his ear, and Blaine sighed. Not only had he lost a good five minutes of his workout, but he'd have to pause it a little longer to ask the guys about helping before they left for the day. It was a good thing no one would be waiting on him tonight because he had a late night ahead of him.

He found Mason and Rodney soaking in the hot tubs. They were a hot commodity after a hard workout. The two men must have already finished their workouts, and a small seed of jealousy stirred within him. A hot tub sounded so relaxing right about now. Well, at least Rodney drove a rather large truck as well. Maybe they would both agree and he could get back to his workout quickly.

"Hey guys, I have a favor to ask. Well, actually Tucker does."

Mason opened one eye and looked at Blaine. "Where is Tucker anyway?"

"Family emergency, but he's coming back tomorrow night. Evidently the center he's been volunteering at is having a Christmas party. He's asked that we collect the toys he ordered and bring them to the stadium tomorrow night. Can you guys help out?"

Rodney shrugged and nodded. "Sure. My family is local, so I can always visit them afterwards. What about you Mason?"

Mason's eyes shifted to the side. "Yeah, I'm free. I wasn't planning on catching up with my family until after the game tomorrow, so I can be there."

Blaine found Mason's reaction curious. He almost seemed as if he were hiding something, but he had no time to pry. "Thanks guys. I'm going to see who else I can round up. Think you can be ready in half an hour?"

The two men nodded and Blaine headed out of the room to see who else might still be around and willing to help out.

KENZI

Kenzi watched Shelby's face as she ended the call. Her friend had been so wound up today - first with the news about Tucker being involved in a bar brawl and then him not showing up to help plan the party he'd said he would pay for. For his sake, Kenzi hoped he had been the one on the line because if he didn't apologize soon, Shelby would tear him a new one when she saw him again.

Her best friend was not normally an angry person, but the kids at this center meant everything to her. And if she had to disappoint them, someone was going to pay.

"Was that Tucker?" Kenzi kept her voice light as she posed the question. She certainly didn't want to earn a spot on Shelby's bad side if the news wasn't good.

"It was. He said he left a message about today." Shelby's eyes roamed over the desk, and she lifted papers as if she expected to see a handwritten note somewhere. "Evidently his father had a heart attack."

Kenzi's hand flew to her mouth. She knew firsthand how serious heart attacks could be - her grandfather had died of one at the age of sixty-eight. "Oh my gosh, is he okay?"

Shelby paused her search and lifted her eyes to meet Kenzi's in a blank stare. "I don't know. I forgot to ask."

She'd forgotten to ask? How was that possible? Shelby was the poster child for courtesy and decorum. She always said "bless you" when somebody sneezed, sent thank you cards for every gift she received, and kept a stack of "get well" notes in her drawer for whenever the occasion might arise. Kenzi knew Shelby had been distracted lately, or perhaps consumed was a better word, with the center's rent and the Christmas party, but she couldn't believe she hadn't asked Tucker how his father was. She definitely had too much on her mind right now.

"Anyway," Shelby continued with a shake of her head, "he said he was sending me money through PayPal and that I was to take care of the decorations and to spread the word. He said he'd take care of the gifts."

Decorations? Money? The words were like manna to Kenzi's ears. "Well, we better get started then. We've got a lot to do before tomorrow night."

"Right. Why don't I transfer the money to you and you pick up the decorations while I start calling?"

Disappointment flooded Kenzi. She'd been hoping to spend a few hours with her friend like they used to - before Shelby took over managing the center and trying to carry the weight of the world on her shoulders. "Can't you come too? Just for an hour or so? It will be like old times."

"Kenzi, there's so much to do," Shelby began. The pinched look covered her face again.

"And it's not going anywhere," Kenzi said, interrupting her. "It will still be here when we get back, and I promise we'll be quick. I'd just like to spend some time with my best friend. Please?" Kenzi put on her best puppy dog eyes. Shelby swore she was immune to Kenzi's charms, and maybe she was, but more often than not, Kenzi could convince her to say yes with a few eye bats and a well-timed pout.

Shelby's face eased into a smile, and a small chuckle escaped her lips. "Okay, you win. One hour and then I have to get back to work."

It wasn't as much as she'd hoped for, but Kenzi would take it. Any time with Shelby outside the center felt like a gift and one she planned to make the most of.

"Okay, so I'll transfer the money to my account. That shouldn't take too long. It will probably take us about fifteen minutes to get to the store which leaves us approximately thirty minutes to shop. That is, of course, if we can keep our travel time under fifteen minutes because we'll need time to get back as well." Kenzi wasn't sure whether Shelby was talking to her or herself since her head was down and her gaze was focused on her wristwatch. "We need to make sure we're back in time to set up for the kids this afternoon."

Kenzi rolled her eyes good-naturedly. Shelby was nothing if not efficient, and Kenzi had never known her to mess up a schedule. Ever. "Don't worry. We'll have plenty of time. I've already got an idea of what I'd like to do."

Shelby glanced up with a look of surprise as if she'd forgotten Kenzi was even with her. "Right. That's good because you know me and decorating." Kenzi smiled as she opened the driver's side door. She did know Shelby's idea of decorating, and it was atrocious.

Shelby's mother had let her decorate her room when she turned sixteen, and as Shelby couldn't decide whether she preferred purple or red that year, she'd used both - on the walls, on the curtains, on the bed. When she'd finished, it looked like someone had massacred Barney the Purple Dinosaur in there. So, when Shelby had finally moved into her own apartment, she had called Kenzi to help her decorate it. They'd left the walls white, as most landlords didn't let you paint walls anyway, and used accents to bring color into the room. The effect was a much more subdued, cohesive atmosphere. Of course, it also helped that Shelby had finally decided on lavender as her favorite color. Kenzi shivered at the memory and turned the key in the ignition. "Yep, no decorating for you."

"Hey!" Shelby slugged her on the shoulder, but it was light and a smile graced her lips, so Kenzi knew she wasn't really mad. Besides, she'd been the one who brought it up. Not Kenzi.

"Simply Having a Wonderful Christmas Time" came on as Kenzi drove to the store. She loved Christmas, and this was her favorite Christmas song. Something about the beat stuck with her long after the song ended, and she would find herself humming or whistling the tune hours later, but she didn't mind.

Since the age of three, she had loved all things Christmas - Santa, presents, the tree, but most of all the lights. There was something magical about Christmas lights, both on the tree and on houses at night. It transformed them, brought out magic and made them appear brighter, warmer, cheerier. No matter how cold, Kenzi loved to walk around the neighborhood after dark and stare up at the lights. Her imagination would create stories of the people inside - mothers in aprons baking gingerbread cookies, fathers in Santa hats reading stories to the kids, and the children bundled in footie pajamas drinking hot chocolate as they listened to their fathers read. Of course, her own childhood had been nothing like that, so she wasn't sure why that was the picture she created, but maybe it was *because* her own family had been nothing like that.

No, her family had been the other kind. The kind that paid people to come hang their Christmas lights because they didn't have time to do it. Or didn't want to make the time. And forget colorful lights or icicle lights - those were too impractical. Solid white lights were the only way to go. In a single solitary row, like good little soldiers. The tree was an enormous twelve-foot artificial tree that had been purchased before Kenzi was born, but her father never set it up. No, hired help did that too. And while Kenzi was allowed to hang ornaments, the maid was told to come in after and rearrange them all so that they were spaced evenly and uniformly apart. There were never stories or gingerbread men or hot cocoa, but still Kenzi loved it.

When she'd been old enough to earn an allowance, she had saved up until she could purchase a small artificial tree for her room. No one complained how she decorated that one. Every year, she would pull out her little two-foot tree the day after Thanksgiving, and after she decorated it, she would add her cheer to the rest of the house. Then, she would record all the Christmas movies and marathon watch them when she had time. She was determined that one day not only would she have a Christmas like they did in the movies, but that her parents would join her and enjoy it too.

Kenzi parked the car in the Wal-Mart lot, and they headed inside and toward the Christmas section. Several rows had been dedicated to the holiday and were overflowing with ornaments, wrapping paper, and lawn displays. Kenzi knew exactly what she wanted though, and with the five hundred dollars Tucker had wired over, it would be more than enough.

❧ 40 ❧

BLAINE

Blaine could not believe all the toys Tucker had purchased. In addition to the five men he'd gotten to help him last night, another four had agreed to help out tonight. Tucker had returned with his former teammate, Emmitt Brown, so including Blaine there were twelve guys. Still it took them almost an hour to get all the gifts loaded up. Almost an hour and four trucks.

"Blaine, you wanna ride with us?" Tucker asked as the men began choosing their rides.

Blaine glanced around and nodded. Most of the other guys had already teamed up. Besides, he was curious about Emmitt. He held the door open and let Emmitt climb in first. Then he entered beside him and shut the door. A moment later, Tucker's door closed as well.

"This is a nice gesture," Emmitt said as Tucker turned the key.

"Thanks, Rev. I guess you rubbed off on me more than you or I knew."

Rev? Blaine wondered how the man had gotten that nickname. He would have to ask Tucker later. As they drove, he realized there was a lot about Tucker he didn't know. All he had seen before now was the confident running back with a chip on his shoulder, but here was a man going out of his way to bring gifts to kids he barely knew. Had it been the center that changed him so profoundly or something else?

"So, how's married life treating you?" Tucker asked.

A wide smile broke out on Emmitt's face. "It's the best, man. I can't believe I was so stupid and prideful at first not to see how amazing Mia was from the beginning. I still kick myself that I let so many years go by, that I missed Carter's birth." He shook his head and sighed. "Anyway, I hope one day you find what I have. Both of you. God said it was not good for man to be alone, and He was right. The two of them complete me in so many ways I never even thought possible."

Blaine wondered what the story was with Emmitt. Not only was he married, but he had a kid as well? He wanted to ask him if it was hard to balance a family with the requirements of pro-foot-ball - not that he was looking to start a family anytime soon, or ever with his past, but it was still good information to know. He kept his mouth shut though. It didn't feel right to interrupt their reunion.

As Tucker pulled into the parking lot of the center, Blaine's eyes widened. He wasn't sure he'd ever been to the center, but it had been a long time since he'd seen this many cars anywhere besides the stadium on game day. There were so many that Tucker was forced to pull the truck into the fire lane.

"Are all these cars here for the party?" Blaine asked.

Tucker nodded and turned off the ignition. "I think so."

Emmitt chuckled softly. "I hope we brought enough gifts."

"Well, if we didn't, then I'll just have to go shopping again tomorrow."

Before anyone could say another word, a woman in red came barreling their direction. Tucker opened the door and climbed out.

"Who's that?" Emmitt asked, leaning forward to see around Blaine.

"I'm not positive, but my guess is that is the director. Shelby something or other."

"Is there something going on between them?"

"What?" Blaine looked again at the scene unfolding outside the window. Could it be? Was that the reason for Tucker's recent change? "I have no idea."

"I rather hope it is. He deserves to find someone."

Blaine glanced at Emmitt, wondering what he knew about Tucker that Blaine didn't. Perhaps Blaine should have tried harder to get past Tucker's rough exterior. He would do better in the future. Being captain of the team meant responsibilities, and part of those responsibilities was knowing his teammates. "Shall we?" He nodded toward the window.

Emmitt nodded, and Blaine opened the door. To his right, he heard the sound of the other men opening their doors and climbing down as well. Tucker exchanged a few words with the woman in red and then she turned and strode into the center. A large smile adorned Tucker's face as he pivoted to face the players. "Let's go, boys," he said and motioned with his hand for them to begin unloading the gifts.

Blaine loaded one under each arm and followed Emmitt into the center. Christmas had lost its excitement for him years ago, but a tiny twinge of something still tugged on his heart as he entered the center. White twinkle lights hung in low loops from the ceiling along with red, green, and white streamers. Cheery wreaths of green and gold hung around the room like pictures frozen in time, and a small artificial tree completed the scene. The children had obviously decorated it as the ornaments were uneven - clumped in places and sparse in others - but somehow that only added to the magic. A table with food and drinks sat off to one side almost like an afterthought. Certainly no one was paying any attention to it at the moment. No, the attention was very clearly on the players as they entered with their brightly wrapped boxes.

A silence hung in the air for just a moment, and then one child spoke up. "It's Tucker. I knew he'd make it." That was all the encouragement the other kids needed. Like a giant wave, their energy washed over Blaine as little feet and eager faces scurried towards him. Memories of previous Christmases flooded him, and he forced them from his mind. He couldn't think about them now or he would lose it, and tonight wasn't about him. It was about these kids. Their voices spoke over each other as if a prize existed for whoever could be the loudest.

"One at a time," Tucker said with a smile, and he held up his hands to calm the children. "Let my friends set the gifts down first."

Like magic, the children quieted, but their energy did not dissipate. Instead, it zinged around inside each one like a pinball. Blaine could see it in the bouncing of their feet or the shifting of their eyes as they looked from one player to the next. He hoped Tucker didn't speak long because he felt like the invisible dam holding the kids back might break any second.

"First, let me introduce my friends."

Inwardly, Blaine groaned. This was exactly what he'd been afraid of. While he didn't mind introductions, there were twelve of them. He didn't think the kids would last that long. A movement to the side caught his attention, and the world around him seemed to freeze as he caught sight of a beautiful woman in a dark green dress.

Blaine was not normally one to fawn over a pretty face. He knew he was damaged, and he had no intention of dragging a woman into his mess. At least not long term, which was why football had become his wife and women had been a nice way to spend a Friday evening, but there was something about this woman that held his interest. Something that drew his eyes to her, and he didn't think it was just her looks. She was gorgeous, no doubt, with her dark hair and creamy white skin, but he felt there was something else. Felt? What was he doing? He was not supposed to feel anything when it came to women. Not only did he have nothing to offer a woman, but he would never be able to give a woman a family, so feelings were not allowed. He was supposed to ignore these feelings - swallow them and lock them away deep inside. It was fine to take a woman out once, for companionship, but feelings were not allowed. Ever! Not after the accident.

KENZI

Kenzi felt his eyes on her before she actually caught him staring. Tucker had managed to bring eleven teammates with him, and they stood in a line facing the children, wrapped boxes placed at their feet. Most were smiling though she could tell a few felt completely out of their element. They were easy to spot by their rocking motion or restless eyes. Her gaze traveled up the line, but it stopped when she realized one pair of eyes was staring back at her.

Deep and brown, they looked warm and inviting but also as if they contained secrets. Blaine Hollis. Of course. She'd found him attractive when the team roster had been first announced, but she'd been sure he had a girlfriend like most of the other players did. However, as time went on, she realized the one thing about Blaine that stood out was that he never had a woman on his arm. Or at least never the same woman. The television crews must have even caught on because they never panned to one in the crowd cheering him on, and there was never mention of one on news stories or in the tabloids. For some reason, he seemed intent on not dating seriously. Yet here he was staring at her.

Before she could react, his gaze slipped away and returned to Tucker who was explaining the rules of picking a present. The children rocked back and forth as if an invisible field kept them in place until he gave them the word, and then pandemonium struck. Kids raced to grab a gift and then began tearing into them. Cheers and gales of laughter filled the room, and Kenzi turned when a hand touched her arm.

Shelby smiled at her and then nodded toward the kids. "We did good, didn't we?"

"Yeah, you did." There was no way she was taking credit for this party. All of this work had been Shelby's doing.

"What are you talking about? This place is gorgeous, and it wouldn't have looked so amazing if you hadn't decorated it. I know you left college because you weren't sure what you wanted to do, but I think you might have found your niche."

Kenzi let the words sink in and gazed around the room. Maybe Shelby was right. She *had* enjoyed decorating the space, and it *did* look amazing. Could it be that she'd finally found her calling? "But, if I go back to school, how will you keep the center running?"

Shelby grinned and shook her head. "I don't think that's going to be a problem. I have a feeling this event will bring kids into the center, and once enrollment is up, I can hire more help if I need to."

"I'll think about it," Kenzi said, but her mind was already walking through the possibility. She'd enjoyed college when she'd attended until she'd realized she was taking classes she might never need. After changing her major twice and watching her graduation date move from four to five and then to six years, she'd decided she should save her parents some money and figure out what she wanted to do before taking any more classes. Kenzi had no idea what kind of degree an interior designer might require nor how many hours it would be, but it might be worth looking into.

When the commotion of opening presents began to die down, Kenzi moved to the refreshment table to help serve food and drinks. Her stomach rumbled as her eyes took in the delectable desserts, but she was not going to partake. Not only because the food was for the kids, but because she didn't need the sugar. People never understood when she told them that. "But you're so thin," they always said. "Surely a little sugar wouldn't hurt a little thing like you." But they didn't know about her past. They didn't know about the merciless teasing she'd endured in middle school and junior high or the rigorous diet she followed now to keep the weight off. Not even Shelby knew about that.

"Looks good."

Kenzi glanced up to see Blaine Hollis standing across from her. "Excuse me?" Surely, he had been referring to the food and not her.

A light pink color tinged his cheeks, and he shook his head. "The food, I mean. It looks good. Not that you don't, but-"

She should stop him, tell him she understood what he'd meant, but she was rather enjoying watching him try to recover. He always looked so cool and collected on the field. It was nice to know there was another side to him.

He took a deep breath. "Let me start over. The food looks amazing. What would you recommend?"

Recommend? She could recommend nothing because she had tried nothing, but she didn't want to explain that to him because when she admitted the truth, questions always followed. "Well, if you like chocolate, the brownies are always a good bet, or if you prefer fruit, the apple pie has been a big hit."

"Which would you choose?" His gaze held hers, and a tingle ran down her neck at his boldness.

"Um." She licked her lips as she looked from the brownies to the apple pie. "Well, chocolate has always been my poison, so I guess I'd do the brownies." A part of her wanted to see him take a brownie, to know they had at least that in common. It wasn't much to build a relationship on, but it was a start, right? Relationship? What? She was getting *way* ahead of herself. The man was here for dessert, not to ask her out. But if they ever did go out, it would be nice to know they had a love of chocolate in common. Except - if he loved chocolate and ever offered her any, she knew she would take it because there was no way she was explaining to him why she avoided it now. And then where would she be? Maybe she wanted him to take the fruit after all.

"I guess it is a little like poison," he said with a chuckle, "but then that's why I work out so much. What's your name?"

"Kenzi. Kenzi Lanham." Her words felt tight in her chest. She couldn't believe she was talking to Blaine Hollis. She didn't have a poster of him on her wall or anything - she was too old for that - but she did have a jersey with his name on it. Folded up and in her bottom drawer, but there. He was her celebrity crush, one of them anyway, and here she was having a conversation with him.

He nodded and reached for a brownie. His eyes stayed locked on hers as he took a bite. Kenzi held her breath, hoping she had made the right recommendation.

The corners of his mouth pulled into a smile. "This is delicious, Kenzi. You have good tastes. Speaking of, do you know who did the decorating around here?"

Kenzi's heart fluttered in her chest. He liked the decorating? Did that mean she really did have talent? "Actually, I did. It's not much, but it was rather last minute."

His eyes widened. "You did this? Are you a designer?"

Kenzi chuckled even as her teenage self screamed and swooned inside her. "No, not yet anyway, but," she looked again at the room, "I think I might be going back to school to get my degree."

"I think you should definitely consider it." He flashed her another smile though it didn't quite reach his eyes. "Well, Kenzi Lanham, it was nice meeting you. Perhaps I'll see you around?"

"Definitely." Kenzi held on to the lip of the tabletop to keep herself from folding to the ground as he flashed her a smile and then disappeared back into the crowd.

❄ 41 ❄
BLAINE

Blaine walked out of the Christmas party uplifted and also weighed down. It had been amazing to see the kids receive their gifts. Seeing them so excited had brought a smile to his face and reminded him of how much he used to love Christmas. It was obvious many of those kids had little money and didn't receive gifts often. That realization had convicted him, making him even more sure that volunteering and helping these kids out was important even if it pained him. As long as he never had to be solely in charge of them, he would be fine.

Then there was Kenzi. While he knew that would never amount to anything, it had been fun watching her and imagining, and that moment when she had licked her lips while studying the desserts had almost done him in. In fact, it had been a pretty perfect night until the text from Coach. "The league is suspending Tucker for tomorrow's game."

Suspending. Blaine couldn't believe it. True, Tucker's anger had gotten him in trouble a week ago. After their last loss, he'd stopped at a bar to let off some steam and gotten into a brawl with a patron who antagonized him, but the bartender had said it hadn't been Tucker's fault. Tucker had even tried to leave, but the man wouldn't let him. No charges had even been filed. The Texas Tornadoes had decided that serving community service would be payment enough for Tucker, and he had served it diligently at the center, but evidently the other man hadn't felt that was enough.

He had complained to the league, and, wanting to make an example of Tucker, the league had suspended him for tomorrow's game - the biggest game of the season so far. If they won this game, they would move into the quarter finals, but if they lost, their season was over. Tucker hadn't been Blaine's favorite player to work with, but he was their best running back. And they needed him. Besides, it was obvious from tonight that Tucker was no longer the angry man he'd been a week ago. Something had changed him, and he deserved a fresh start.

"What's going on with you, man?"

Blaine glanced up at Mason who had offered him, Jefferson, and Rodney a ride back to their vehicles. "Just got a text from Coach that Tucker is suspended for tomorrow's game."

Shock and disbelief registered on the other men's faces. "What? How can they do that?"

Blaine bit the inside of his lip as he thought about whether he should share Tucker's secret. After the altercation, he and Coach had decided it would be best if they were the only ones who knew about it. Plus, it wasn't really his story to tell, but it had been on the news the night before. The guys might have heard about it already and perhaps if one man complaining could get him suspended, then maybe fifty men complaining could get him re-instated.

"Tucker had a recent run-in with the law. No charges were filed, but the guy he got in the fight with wasn't happy with that. I guess he complained to the league and they decided to make an example of him."

"We can't let them do that," Mason said. "I know Tucker has had his anger issues, but look at what he did tonight for these kids. He's not the same guy he was even a week ago."

"That was my thought too," Blaine said with a nod. "Maybe if we all call the league and tell them what he's been doing, we can get him re-instated."

Jefferson ran a hand across his smooth face. He was the baby of the offensive line, but his maturity often matched the older players. "I think I know of someone else who might be able to help. I overheard that reporter, Sylvie Sanders, talking to Tucker. She was asking him why the previous donor decided not to help out this year, but Tucker wouldn't say anything. I'm pretty sure he knows though, so maybe we can get her to do a story on it."

Blaine's mood perked up at that tidbit of information. "That's a great idea. Why don't you see if you can get her number while Rodney and I start calling the rest of the team. It looks like we're going to need a Christmas miracle."

KENZI

"Okay, that was a pretty amazing night," Kenzi said as she took down the last of the decorations still left on the wall. They'd been careful enough they would be able to reuse them again next year.

"Yeah, it was good," Shelby said, but her voice did not hold the excitement Kenzi would have expected. The woman had worked tirelessly to make sure this party happened, so why wasn't she happier?

"But?" Kenzi could tell something was up with Shelby, but like always, she was going to have to pry it out of her friend. Getting Shelby to open up sometimes was like trying to get a ship out of a bottle without breaking it.

Shelby set down the trash bag she had been filling with discarded wrapping paper. "But I feel bad for Tucker. He did all of this-" she waved her arm around the now empty gym that had been teeming with delighted children earlier- "but because of Jude Renfrow, he's not going to get to play tomorrow."

"What?" Kenzi set the decorations down on the table and turned her full attention to Shelby. "What does Jude Renfrow have to do with this?" Jude Renfrow was a local businessman who had donated to the center last year, but Kenzi had always assumed he did it for the tax break and the recognition and not for the children. This year, he had decided to withhold his donation.

"Well, you know how I told you Jude Renfrow was the guy he got in the fight with?" Shelby folded her arms across her chest.

Kenzi nodded. This part she had heard before. She wanted to know why Tucker wouldn't be playing in the biggest game of the season so far.

"So, not only did Jude decide not to donate to the center this year because of Tucker, but when he found out Tucker had been working here, he called the league and got Tucker suspended."

"Can he even do that?" Kenzi followed football and knew suspensions happened, but they were usually for crimes or using athletic-enhancing drugs. "I didn't think one man could have that much sway."

"I guess one man with the amount of money he has can."

The words were filled with disdain as they left Shelby's mouth, but Kenzi couldn't blame her. Not only had Shelby grown up relatively poor, but she managed this center which existed to help the less affluent families in town. Money, and the right that some people thought it gave them, had always been a bone of contention for Shelby.

"Wait, wasn't Sylvie Sanders here tonight?" A wicked idea was forming in Kenzi's head.

"Yeah, why?" Shelby had no love for the reporter who'd made a pass at Tucker.

"Well, I happened to see her talking to Tucker earlier. Wonder what she could do if she knew the donor who left all these kids high and dry was the same man causing Tucker's suspension?"

The dots connected in Shelby's head, and her eyes lit up. "You're suggesting I tell Sylvie about Jude Renfrow?"

Kenzi shrugged. That was exactly what she was suggesting, but sometimes Shelby needed to think the idea was hers in order to execute it. "I'm just saying that if the league had that information, they'd have to decide if they wanted to please a business man or the whole community of Southlake kids who were treated to a wonderful night tonight by Tucker Jackson."

Shelby threw her arms around Kenzi and squeezed. "Kenzi, you are a genius. I'm going to call her right now."

Kenzi smiled as Shelby scurried away in her high heels, the hem of her red dress held high so as not to trip. Though Kenzi was normally the more persuasive one, she had no doubt that Shelby and Sylvie would accomplish lifting the suspension. Sylvie Sanders might be obnoxious, but she was doggedly determined. And she loved a good story.

Kenzi picked up the trash bag that Shelby had left and walked it to the large container in the kitchen. On her way back, she grabbed her bag from the refreshment table where she had left it earlier and opened it to stare at the ticket Shelby had given her earlier. Tucker had given Shelby two tickets to the player's box, and she had invited Kenzi. It was her own Christmas gift. Not only would she get to watch a live game - get to watch Blaine play - but she was going to get to do it from the fantasy suite.

❧ 42 ❧
PRESENT DAY - KENZI

The night of the Christmas party kept playing in Kenzi's mind as she followed her GPS to the address Blaine had given her for his cabin. That had been the night she met him, and though she'd only seen him a few times since, he'd played a starring role in her mind. There was just something about him that made her so curious. There was this hidden depth to him, something holding him back. She was both excited and worried about her mental health in taking this job. What if he hated what she did? What if she found out some horrible secret about him? There must be some reason he was a serial dater and had never ventured into a meaningful relationship. What if she found out the reason and it changed her view of him?

She gripped the steering wheel tighter. No, she could do this. He might be the quarterback for the Champion Texas Tornado football team, but he was still human. He still put his pants on one leg at a time just like she did. At least she assumed he did. Unless he had a butler who did that for him, but did people have butlers these days? And if they did, did they really allow someone else to dress them? Good grief, her thoughts had the attention span of a gnat today.

The voice of her GPS brought her back to reality. "Turn right on Lost Lake Road."

Lost Lake Road. That was kind of ominous. She was getting close, though, and the thought sent her heart thudding in her chest. It was a beautiful road with gorgeous views. Blaine's cabin appeared to be rather secluded, so it would just be the two of them. Alone. Out in the middle of beautiful nature. Romantic, beautiful nature.

"Ugh!" Kenzi gripped the steering wheel as the car jostled her around again. Perhaps cruel, unpaved nature was a little more accurate. Lost Lake Road was hardly a road. Bumpy and unpaved, it wound through the middle of a growth of trees so thick that the sun above was obscured. She might even have to turn on her headlights to be able to see even though it was the middle of the day.

The contents of her lunch shifted in her stomach with the bumps, but finally she saw Blaine's red Mustang parked in front of a quaint cabin. It reminded her of the kind she used to build with Lincoln Logs when she was younger, only this one had flower pots sitting in the window sills and a chimney that she could imagine smoke drifting lazily out of on a cold winter night. A cold, romantic winter night.

The clump of trees nestled around it like they were guarding the cabin, protecting it, but Kenzi didn't get a scary vibe from it. More a feeling of tranquility.

She parked the car and checked her hair in the mirror. She'd spent an hour on it this morning trying to get it perfect, though the ride had undone some of her perfections. She didn't even know why she'd spent so much time on it. Was it because she was trying to get the job or trying to get Blaine? Maybe the two went hand in hand. After giving her cheeks a quick pinch to add a little more color, she grabbed her keys and her laptop and headed for the door.

Her spike heels immediately sank into the dirt. The sinking of her heels was not only coating her shoes and therefore her feet in dirt, but it was also offsetting her balance, giving her a stilted kilter of a walk up the path. She moved forward, putting most of the weight on her toes the way her mother taught her, the rest of the way.

The air was warm, but as she raised her hand to knock, she wondered if she should have paired a jacket with her dress. Did she look unprofessional without one? She was not used to second guessing herself so much. Her self-confidence wasn't high in every area, though she liked to pretend it was, but it hadn't been low in the area of fashion for quite some time. She'd found that love in high school and had often been the sought-after trendsetter. However, something about Blaine brought back the insecurities and fashion faux pas of middle school.

She ran her hand down her dress one more time to smooth any wrinkles before rapping on the heavy door. The sound of footsteps reached her ears a moment before the door swung open, and Blaine - looking comfy in a t-shirt and cargo shorts - smiled at her.

"You made it," he said with an easy going smile that lit up his eyes.

A girl could swoon looking into those big brown eyes.

He leaned forward as if to hug her, but as Kenzi leaned in to meet him, he shifted his posture and the result was an awkward sort of shuffle that left her cheeks pink with embarrassment.

She shifted her eyes to her laptop as she tried to regain her composure. "I did. The directions were pretty clear, and my map app helped too."

"Great. Well, come on in." He stepped back to allow her entrance, and the masculine scent of him flooded her nose as she passed by. Dark and woodsy, she was unsure if it was his deodorant, cologne, or his natural scent, but what she did know was that it sent her heart thudding in her chest.

She wasn't used to a man having this sort of effect on her. Normally, it went the other way. She would go out with a man she thought she was attracted to only to find out he didn't fit her ideal image after all, and she would end up breaking it off even though they seemed to really be interested in her. Was this what those men had felt like? This mix of nausea and elation? A feeling of regret flooded her; she certainly hadn't meant to make them feel this way. Though she was unsure if Blaine knew the effect he was having on her, she doubted it. He might avoid relationships, but he seemed like a decent guy.

The door closed behind her and then Blaine was beside her again. "Would you like something to drink? I'm afraid I only have water."

"Water would be fine," she answered as she looked around, following him to the kitchen. He must not use this cabin much if he didn't even have it stocked with drinks. The coating of dust on the bookshelves she passed bolstered that conclusion.

The kitchen was a small room with barely enough space for two people to maneuver. Cozy, but slightly claustrophobic, Kenzi chose to stay near the table. Made from wood, the table appeared sturdy enough to withstand decades, and the scratches and worn areas in the top led her to believe it had been around awhile. "So, have you had this place long?"

Blaine shrugged as he opened a cabinet door and pulled down two glasses. "It's been in my family for years, but I don't spend much time here." He looked around the room like he was looking for memories, that deep, dark look in his eyes.

There was more to that story, wasn't there? But he wasn't ready to tell her yet. He handed her a glass but didn't sit as he sipped from his own. He seemed uneasy. Was it her or the house?

"Would you like the tour?" he asked suddenly.

"Sure." Yes, he was definitely nervous. "Do you mind if I leave this here?" She motioned to the laptop she had set on the table. It wasn't heavy, but there was no reason to lug it around either.

"Of course." He set his glass down on the table and then held out his hand to help her to her feet.

She smiled at the gesture and placed her hand in his, but she was not expecting the heat that filled her palm. Her gaze caught his, and his wide eyes, before he dropped her hands, told her he had felt something unexpected as well.

"This way," he said as he shifted away from her.

The cabin wasn't fancy, but it was fairly spacious. He led the way first to the large master bedroom that lay to the right of the kitchen. A rustic looking bed and dresser were the only pieces of furniture in the room, but both appeared to be hand-crafted, adding to the charm. The carpet was worn but not threadbare, and while she would like to replace it if the budget allowed, she could work with it if it had to stay. Kenzi could envision a rustic retreat, somewhere to escape to. Calming and serene colors and cozy bedspreads. It could be gorgeous.

"What do you want to do here?" she asked as she walked around the room. She would take exact measurements later, but walking the perimeter always gave her an idea of the size she was working with. Plus, she would take pictures with her phone before leaving, in case she forgot anything.

"Honestly, I don't know. I'm probably going to sell the cabin when you're done renovating it anyway." Blaine leaned against the doorframe with his arms crossed.

"Sell it? But it's so beautiful and what an ideal place to come to get away from the hurry of city life." She couldn't imagine selling her family's lake house if she ever inherited it.

He shrugged. "I don't have much time to get out here with my football schedule, so there's no real reason to keep it."

"But what about your parents or other family members? Won't someone want to keep it in the family?"

"My parents never come here anymore, and there's no one else in the family who would want it." He bit his lip and frowned like he might want to tell her something, and she waited expecting him to put his thoughts together.

Instead he said nothing more, and his brusque tone and manner caught her off guard; she'd only ever seen him happy and smiling. This was a whole new side. "I get that."

He nodded and shook himself out of his funk. "So, what do you think?"

She looked at the room, her heart thumping. "Well, I was thinking of making it a place you could relax in, a nice little getaway. I have some ideas. Are you opposed to landscape paintings?"

"No." He offered a tender smile as if realizing he'd been too abrupt before. "Whatever you think is fine. Really. I didn't have anything in mind; I just know it needs something."

"Great. After I see all the rooms, we can work out a budget."

He nodded and pushed himself off the doorframe. "Across the hall is the main bathroom. It's small, but it works."

Kenzi poked her head in and bit her lip. Small was an understatement. There was a tub with a shower attached, a toilet, and a sink. However, it was an old fashioned one, so there wasn't even a vanity with storage, and the pieces were so close together that someone standing in the middle of the room could touch all three. There wasn't much she could do with this space unless he was open to tearing down some walls.

"Over here is a small laundry room. It has an exit to the back porch as well, so there's a place to take shoes off if they're muddy."

There was no washer and dryer in the laundry room. Only a basin and sink along with a shelf she assumed was used to fold clothes or hold detergent. She saw no other cabinets in the room. Okay, so running water but no washer and dryer. That might be a challenge, but then again, people probably came out here to get away, so maybe they wouldn't mind having to wash their clothes by hand. Or maybe they would pack enough for however long they planned to stay.

"I'm not sure I'll be able to do much with this room or the bathroom, but I'll put my thinking cap on."

He nodded. "I'll show you the outside in a minute, but let's finish the rest of the inside." He headed back into the main area where a terrifying staircase led the way to the loft upstairs. The steps were narrow and spaced too far apart. This might have to be replaced, especially if they wanted to appeal to families.

Upstairs, there were another two bedrooms and a small bathroom, each decorated as simply as the master bedroom downstairs. At least it was a pretty blank palette to work with. In addition to the bedrooms, there was an open area that looked down on the main living room of the cabin. Kenzi could see it being a small playroom for kids or a comfy reading nook. She'd have to find out which direction he wanted to go.

The main room was easily the largest part of the cabin, but it had no soul. There was no color tying it together, no pattern, no preference of any kind, but she could see how it could be an amazing space. It was large enough to hold two couches and a chair as well as a coffee table in the middle. An ornate stone fireplace completed the look, and Kenzi could imagine curling up on one of the couches and watching the crackling fire for hours. If he were open to renting the cabin, she just might have to rent it a few nights herself. Maybe he would consider a night as part of her compensation.

"Ready to see out back?" he asked, breaking into her daydream.

"Absolutely." She felt warmth spread on her cheeks as she followed him back to the utility room. Had he caught her mind wandering?

"Well, out back," he said opening the door, "is the lake."

Kenzi stared in awe at the breathtaking view. She'd had no idea his cabin was on the lake. This would definitely offset the lack of a washer and dryer. Crystal blue water shimmered a mere twenty feet or so from the porch they stood on and stretched as far as the eye could see. Tall trees shielded every side of it, but the sun shone down in the middle, sending sparks of color across the surface. "Wow, this is amazing."

He only nodded, not able to bring himself to look at it. His eyes stayed focused on her or the railing of the porch, never drifting out to the expansive blue beyond. Something must have happened here, but he was clearly not willing to discuss it right now. It killed her to think he would never enjoy this view, that this wondrous sight would be forever tarnished in his mind. "Well, it certainly is the cabin's best feature. It's gorgeous."

His answer was another shrug. He had shut down.

"Okay, well, I've got some ideas. Should we discuss the budget?"

Blaine stared at the cabin in front of him and sighed. He didn't want to be here - he'd never wanted to come back - but the cabin had been left to him. He still didn't understand why his uncle willed it to him instead of his parents, and while he could have refused it, he felt that would be a slap to his family. This was his responsibility now, and he could figure out what to do. And even though it was painful, maybe it was time too.

He sucked in a deep breath and inserted the key in the lock. He'd never been entrusted with the key before. The last time they had been here, he'd been only ten, and his parents hadn't trusted him with the key. Odd, how they'd trusted him to look after his brother but not with the small metal object.

The door creaked open, and the musty smell of unopened rooms wafted out. Had anyone used this cabin since that winter? His family certainly hadn't been back, but his uncle had kids. Had they avoided it as well?

He stepped into the living room and tried not to get sucked into the memories. The blue checkered couch was exactly as he remembered it if not a little more worn and faded. That had been his favorite place to curl up when the fire was burning brightly in the large brick fireplace. The other couch - "his" place - also looked the same, and he could imagine him there, asking questions, hanging upside down, eating popsicles and getting messy and sticky like always.

Blaine crossed to the windows and lifted them open. He didn't plan to stay long, but the musty smell was overpowering, and the fresh air would help alleviate it. As he opened the window, a memory of it breaking filled his mind. He and Kevin had been playing baseball out front, and a wild tip had sent the ball careening into the window, shattering it completely. Not only had they gotten in trouble, but they'd had to pick up all the pieces of glass and replace it with their own money. That had been the last summer they played ball near the cabin. Ironically, it had been the last summer they'd visited the cabin.

The memories had been locked away so deep down for so long, only coming out in self-loathing and bad decisions. But being here - in this place where his presence was strongest - was bringing them all back. And it was rough. He'd even been dreaming about it again.

Blaine continued through the house, opening windows and checking for mice. Luckily, the cabin had remained almost preserved, like a mausoleum, and he found no traces of rodents. It did have a copious amount of dust covering almost every surface, and much of it was old and outdated. He would probably have to hire a designer to update it before he could sell it. He didn't really have time to be hunting for a designer, not with summer practice starting soon, but at least once the deed was done, he could get rid of the cabin. Maybe then the memories would disappear with it.

KENZI

At the buzzing in her pocket, Kenzi set down her lunch and pulled out her phone. She tapped the app and stared in disbelief at her email. The top one was from the Texas Tornadoes, but why would they be emailing her? Shelby was the center manager. She bit her lip and opened the email. Her eyes scanned the words, skimming over them and barely registering their significance until she got to the end. "Oh, my gosh!"

"What?" Her voice must have startled Shelby as the hand holding her drink jumped and liquid flew out of her cup, spilling the contents down her hand and onto the floor. "Darn it."

She set her cup down and stood to grab paper towels from the dispenser, but Kenzi barely looked up as Shelby began mopping up her mess. "I just got an email from the Texas Tornadoes. They want to hire me to redecorate the center and update it." She could not believe it; she was still finishing her degree at the college and hadn't even thought of putting out feelers for jobs yet. "They said they loved what I did for the Christmas party and want to do something special for the kids. They want me to do the whole center, and they're going to pay for it all and pay me on top of it."

Shelby tossed the paper towels in the nearby trash can and returned to her seat. "I knew it. I told you decorating was your thing. Now you have a job, and I'm sure more will come. In fact, I think we need to get you business cards so you can start handing them out."

Kenzi shook her head as she packed up her food. Lunch had felt too short, but that didn't dim her excitement. "Business cards would be silly right now. I don't even have my degree yet."

"But you will, and you want to be prepared when you do. Besides, it's my gift to you, and I refuse to take no for an answer." Shelby wadded up the rest of her trash and carried it to the dispenser.

Kenzi laughed at her best friend's insistence. She wasn't sure who was more excited at this point, her or Shelby. "Okay, but can I have something fun and not just boring white?"

"Of course. I was thinking something pink and glittery."

Kenzi chuckled as she followed Shelby out of the small break room. "Do they even make pink and glittery business cards?"

Shelby glanced down at her watch. "I don't know, but we have a few minutes. We could jump online and check."

"Let's do it." Kenzi had no idea what this might mean for her future, but it definitely felt like a sign.

❧ 44 ❧

PRESENT DAY - BLAINE

Blaine groaned as the alarm blared in his ear. He loved playing football, but the early morning wakeups of training camp were definitely the worst part. The darkness felt thick in front of his face; the sun wouldn't be up for hours. He breathed deeply a few times to try and draw enough oxygen in to wake his weary body and then shut off the alarm. At least he had time for a hot shower before he had to head out. He knew people who could set the alarm and hit the snooze button two or three times, but he'd never been one of those people. When it went off, he was awake for better or worse.

Pushing back the covers, he swung his feet over the side and shuffled to the bathroom. Why did he feel so tired today? As he glanced in the mirror, he cringed at his face. Dark circles surrounded his eyes. He had clearly not slept well, but why? As if summoned by his thoughts, snippets of a dream flashed through his mind. Or perhaps nightmare was a more appropriate word. He saw himself laughing on the frozen lake, then the sound of the ice cracking changed his smile into a look of terror.

Blaine shook his head. He didn't have time to travel that road again. Nor did he want to. Thinking about the lake house had definitely dredged up some suppressed memories and emotions. He knew it had been a bad idea to go back there - he'd known it would bring up memories he didn't want - but it had to be done. Still, he had no time for this today. He needed to shower and get focused for practice.

An hour and a half later, Blaine pulled into the parking lot of the training center. The sun was just sending the first rays of gold and orange across the sky as he turned off the engine. Ten minutes until six. Perfect timing. He grabbed his bag and locked his Mustang before heading toward the door.

"Hollis, how's your summer going, man?"

The deep voice of Mason Dixon called out from behind him, and Blaine paused long enough to let his wide receiver catch up.

His summer. That was certainly a loaded question. His summer had been going great until he'd received the phone call informing him of his uncle's death. He hadn't seen the man in years, but he had been like a father to Blaine when his own father had grown distant. That had been distressing enough but then he'd gotten the call from the lawyer about the family cabin. Finally, he'd made the mistake of visiting the cabin, first alone and then with Kenzi.

And then there was Kenzi. He still didn't understand what was going on there, only that she lingered in his mind like no woman had. When she'd showed up at the cabin, it had taken all of his composure not to pull her in for a hug. He wanted to feel her in his arms - to see if she was the perfect fit he believed she was. He wanted to sniff her hair and find out if the sweet fruity scent that tickled his nose was real or just his imagination, but Mason didn't need to hear about any of that. Blaine had always tried to keep his personal life out of his professional life. It was better that way, so he swallowed these thoughts as well and shrugged. "It's a typical summer, I guess. How about yours?"

Mason nodded and shifted his bag higher on his shoulder. "Can't complain too much. Got to go home and see my family for a bit. Small towns though," he shook his head, "I'm ready to get back to work. You know what I mean?"

Blaine did. Training was exhausting, but it kept his mind from wandering to other things. Things from his past that haunted him if he dwelled on them. Mistakes he'd made, before and after the accident. "I hear you. I start to go stir crazy with too many days off, but I sure hope Glenn has added more to the menu this year than just oatmeal and eggs."

Glenn was the team's cook during training camps. He was a large muscular man who believed in only eating natural foods, but at least he was decent at seasoning the food so it had flavor.

"You and me both, man. I've been eating like a king, and I have a feeling it's going to come back to bite me." Mason pulled open the front door to let Blaine enter first.

Even if they hadn't known where the cafeteria was, they would have found it easily by following the noise. Having arrived close to the beginning of breakfast, many of the other team members were already inside and grabbing food.

Blaine dropped his bag by the door with the others and joined the line. It had been a while since he'd been in this training facility, but he was pretty sure there had been some major changes made. The serving line looked essentially the same, but off to his right was a smoothie bar area complete with blenders, protein powder, greens, and fruit. Past the serving line, he could make out a wood-fired oven. Did that mean pizza was possible this year?

"Is it just me or did they make some changes here?" he asked Mason.

Mason's eyes widened as if he was really looking at the space for the first time. "I think you might be right. I certainly don't remember a smoothie bar, and weren't the chairs red last year?"

Blaine looked to the seating area and smiled. The red chairs had either been replaced or recovered in a dark blue that matched their team colors. "Yeah, they were. Perhaps this bodes well for the food this year as well."

He was not disappointed. His heart lifted as he reached the serving line and spied the myriad of options. There were eggs and oatmeal but also omelets, steak, and even a fish dish. Evidently Glenn had stepped up his game, and Blaine wasted no time grabbing the steak and eggs. He hadn't thought he would be able to stomach eggs again, but paired with a steak, he could make it happen.

After filling his tray, he found an empty spot at a table and sat down. Mason sat down beside him, and a moment later, Tucker slid in across from him.

"How's engaged life treating you?" Mason asked when Tucker finished praying and raised his head.

"It's good, but, man, there is a lot to do for a wedding. No wonder women plan these things their whole lives. I had no idea the number of things that needed to be done." He shoveled a mouthful of oatmeal into his mouth, made a face, and then swallowed. "I have not missed this food. In fact, I'm pretty sure I haven't eaten oatmeal since the championship game until today."

Blaine took a bite of his steak and smiled. "Why did you grab oatmeal with all the choices up there? This steak is amazing. Glenn must have been inspired or something."

Tucker raised an eyebrow. "You didn't hear?"

"Hear what?"

"Glenn left. He eloped with his girlfriend a few months ago, and they moved to California to open up some healthy bistro. There's a new cook now - some classically trained person - and I heard they hired like five other chefs to help out."

"Wow." How had Tucker heard about this before Blaine had? As captain of the team, it was his job to be informed. Of course, a few months ago was about the time he got the news of his uncle and the cabin, so it was possible he had heard and just forgotten or that the news had gotten lost in the shuffle. "Well, I hope they keep whoever this cook is around. I don't think I've eaten this well in a long time, and if there are this many options for breakfast, I can only imagine how good lunch will taste."

"I'll second that." Mason lifted his glass of orange juice into the air as if making a toast. A silence fell between the three men for a moment before Mason steered the conversation back to Tucker's upcoming wedding. "So, what are all the things you have to plan for that you didn't know about?"

"Why? You getting hitched soon?" Tucker asked with a teasing grin.

Mason snorted and rolled his eyes. "Doubtful. I just want to be fully prepared, just in case." His words were blasé, but Blaine noticed a shift in his eyes. Sadness? Regret? It appeared Mason might have a story he would need to flesh out one of these days as well.

Tucker took a drink of his orange juice and shook his head. "Man, it's crazy. There are invitations to pick out, and you can't just pick any invitation, it has to match the color palette. I didn't even know what a color palette was until a few weeks ago. Then there's the venue, flowers, cake..."

As Tucker continued to rattle off all the steps for planning the wedding, Blaine's mind wandered. He'd given up the idea of marriage a long time ago when he'd realized he couldn't be the protector a woman would need, but that didn't mean he never thought about it. He still had memories of when his parents were happy. When smiles and hugs were the normal behaviors instead of the angry voices and bitterness. Before the divorce. Before the accident.

No, he would not let his mind dwell on that. It was in the past, and it needed to stay there, and he needed to stay sharp. Focused. Training camp was hard enough already. He didn't need to be fighting demons along the way. And he didn't need to be obsessing over a woman. A very sweet, beautiful woman. A woman that made him feel like all his history and all his problems were fixable. He didn't need to be thinking about her, and yet, his mind kept going back to her.

He was a mess. A certified mess. And he still had to earn a paycheck, so he had to get his head in the game and keep it there.

KENZI

"Tell me again why you are picking out a dress so early. Isn't the wedding still a few months away?" Kenzi enjoyed shopping with her friend, especially since Shelby had taken a rare afternoon off from the center to do it, but she had just gotten engaged. Why was she already shopping for her wedding dress?

Shelby stared at her as if she'd just sprouted a third eye or something. "There's generally a minimum of six months to get a gown. I'm already pushing it with five and some change. Besides, Tucker and I want to be completely ready. January isn't that far away, and if we are going to pull this wedding off with a shortened time frame, we have to get everything in order now." She held up a lacy, cap-sleeved dress. "What about this one?"

Kenzi tilted her head as she tried to picture the dress on her friend. "I'd have to see it on, but I think a sweetheart neckline would look better on you." She shifted through a few dresses on the rack before finding what she felt might be the perfect one. "Try this one on for sure."

Shelby smiled as she added it to the rack of ones to try. "So, are you going to tell me about the meeting with Blaine?"

Kenzi bit the inside of her lip. What could she say? The meeting had been... nope, there wasn't just one word for it. It had started off good when he'd opened the door with a smile, then it had turned weird as he gave her the tour of the house and refused to look at the lake. Finally, it had turned interesting as they went over her ideas and their hands touched. Yes, that's what she would go with. Interesting. "It was... interesting."

The squeak of hanger sliding against the metallic rack ceased as Shelby stared at her. "Interesting? What does that mean?"

Kenzi blew out a breath of air and shook her head. "I wish I knew. He was nice and friendly when I first got there. In fact, I thought he was going to hug me, but then he didn't and it turned kind of awkward. Then he showed me the cabin, but it was weird. He acted like he'd rather be anywhere else. This cabin sits right on the lake, but he wouldn't even look at it. And when I mentioned the amazing view, he just shrugged it off. Blaine definitely has some layers, and I'm never quite sure which one I'm getting."

"Okay, that is a little strange, but he hired you, right?"

"Yeah, he did. He said he liked my ideas, and we're getting together tomorrow to go over designs, but there was something off about him, Shelby. Something different than I've seen from when he's at the center." Her hand landed on the dress of her dreams. A picture of Blaine in a tux waiting for her at the end of the aisle as she wore this dress and walked to him filled her mind. What was she doing? She barely knew if the man liked her ideas, much less liked her.

Shelby's attention returned to the dresses, and the metallic creaking began again. "Well, maybe he was uncomfortable with it just being the two of you. Maybe he has feelings for you, but he doesn't know how to tell you and that's why he acted so odd."

Kenzi chuckled and smiled at her friend. Leave it to Shelby to jump to some romantic conclusion. Of course, she was doing the same thing. If only that were the case. She certainly wouldn't mind if Blaine showed a romantic interest in her, but if that was his idea of flirting, she had a lot to teach him. In fact, if that was his idea of flirting then maybe she could see why women only went out with him a few times. She'd always thought the reason was his choice, but maybe it was just him.

"What do you think of this one?" Shelby held up a beautiful white dress with a sweetheart neckline and iridescent pearls across the bodice. The dress picked up the light and reflected soft arcs of pinks and yellows. It was stunning.

Kenzi's smile spread slowly across her face. "That might just be the one. You ready to start trying them on?"

Shelby ran her hand down the white satin again and nodded. "I think I'll start with this one."

Kenzi sat on the pink, heart-shaped chair near the changing area and waited as Shelby changed. She had said she was going to model the last dress they had seen first, but she must have changed her mind because it was not the dress she stepped out in when the door finally opened.

This dress was pretty, but the neckline was far too high for Kenzi's tastes. Shelby was more reserved than she was, but this dress reminded her of eighteenth-century wedding dresses instead of today's current fashions.

"You're right," Shelby agreed as she looked in the full-length three-sided mirror. "This is a little stuffy."

The next dress she modeled was better, though still not her. Something in the cut just didn't flatter her waist the way it should have. The third dress got closer, but it wasn't until Shelby walked out in the last dress - the one they had liked even on the rack - that Kenzi perked up.

"Yes, I knew that was the one. Why'd you have to save it for last?"

Shelby smiled and turned a slow circle like Cinderella admiring herself before the ball. "I just wanted to be sure. I was afraid if I had tried it on first, I wouldn't have wanted to try on the other ones and then I would wonder if I really had the best dress. Now I know."

Kenzi rolled her eyes and shook her head, but she knew her friend was right. Shelby wasn't always decisive about clothes anyway, and her wedding dress was not something she wanted to waffle on. "Well, I'm glad you found it. Tucker will be swept off his feet."

"As will Blaine when he sees your ideas." Shelby's lips pulled into a teasing smile. "Now, when are you seeing him again?"

"Tomorrow after his practice. I'll finish up the designs tonight, and if he likes them, we'll start shopping and get to work next week."

"He'll like them because you're an amazing designer." Shelby stepped off the raised platform and linked her arm through Kenzi's. "Now, how about we find you your dress?"

45

BLAINE

Blaine sighed blissfully in the Epsom salt bath. After a long day of meetings, video review, weights, and finally practice, his muscles were tired and Epsom salts always made him feel better. He was no longer sure if the effect was physical or purely psychological from having done it so long, but he didn't care as long as the tension left his shoulders.

The alarm he'd set blared beside him, earning a groan from his lips. He'd promised to meet up with Kenzi to look over ideas tonight, and while he didn't mind seeing Kenzi again, he didn't really care what she did with the cabin. Once that cabin had held fond memories of summers at the lake, weeks when his parents weren't working and they relaxed as well, but that had been before. Before the accident. Before his world turned upside down. Now, he hated the place. He wished his uncle had sold it long ago, so he didn't have to walk down memory lane to do it himself.

He released a frustrated breath and pulled the plug. Another half hour would have been so nice, but maybe he could take another one after Kenzi left. He toweled off and pulled on his faded college t-shirt. It was too old and ratty to be seen in public, but he loved the comfort of it. It fit like a... well, not really like a glove. He knew that was the saying, but gloves had never fit his hands perfectly. His fingers had always been too long for most gloves. No, his shirt fit more like a perfectly worn-in pair of shoes - the kind that supported your foot in all the right areas, the kind that felt like you weren't wearing shoes at all.

The doorbell rang as he zipped up his jeans, and he ran a hand through his wet hair as he walked to the entrance to let her in.

Her eyes widened as he opened the door and she took in his still damp appearance. "Oh, was this a bad time? I thought we said seven, but I can come back." Her face turned pink with her flustering, and Blaine bit back a smile. He'd never seen her look so uncomfortable. Normally Kenzi appeared polished and sure of herself.

"No, you're fine. I just got out of a soak and I'm ready to see what you came up with." He hoped his words didn't sound as forced as they felt in his head. Honestly, if he could get paid to demolish the cabin, he would just do that. He stepped back to let her in.

"Okay, if you're sure." Her eyes scanned the large room. He'd purchased the house when he first signed with the Tornadoes, but he hadn't done much with it since then, and he was sure her designer eyes were cringing at the lack of style.

The room had matching furniture, but he hadn't gotten around to hanging anything on the walls yet - he wasn't even sure what he would want on them. Nor had he painted any of them; they still had the bright white that houses tended to come with so people could add their own style. His teammates all seemed to use designers or had wives or girlfriends that took on their houses. He just hadn't gotten around to it. Way too much going on all the time for him to set aside brain space for it.

"Wow, this is…" she paused as if searching for the right word, "big."

Blaine couldn't help the chuckle that escaped his lips. "Yeah, I guess it is and blank. One of these days I should do something with it."

He saw the spark in her eyes, and he wished he could see the images that were clearly flashing through her head. "Shall we set up here in the living room or the dining room?"

She looked toward the couch and her lips twisted in an adorable tilt. "Let's do the dining room if you have a table there. It might make it easier to see." Some sort of portfolio book filled her arms and a laptop bag hung off her shoulder.

He led the way through the living room and into the slightly smaller but no better decorated dining room. A large table that could seat ten took up most of the room. Blaine wasn't even sure why he had a table so large; he never had that many people over. Perhaps he should invite his teammates over more often; he certainly had the room to entertain them.

Kenzi set her laptop down on the table and opened the portfolio book, revealing paint chips and drawings and samples of fabrics. "Now keep in mind, you and this place are my guinea pig projects, so I need your feedback, okay? I don't have computer programs for everything yet, so I did a lot of the drawings by hand, but I brought my laptop so I could show you pictures of furniture and rugs if my drawings weren't enough."

The first sketch was of the master bedroom, and it was perfect. "Kenzi, this is amazing." She had found a way to bring life into the room without changing everything about it.

"I haven't even shown you everything yet. If you think this is gorgeous, wait until you see the other rooms."

She laid out the next board, and his jaw dropped. "Here's the living room currently," she said pointing at a picture she had taken of it, "and here's what I'd like to do."

Blaine stared at the images. The worn couches were replaced with new brown leather ones. A masculine but romantic theme ran through the room with horns on the walls but candles placed on the mantle and the tables. Reds, blues, and browns were brought to life from the run in the center of the room and throw pillows on the couches. It looked comfortable but sophisticated, like it was meant to be lived in and enjoyed. He could almost see himself there, with family and friends, teammates and kids. It gave him a sinking feeling. No. No kids. And while he was at it, maybe no one else either. Just a good-looking place for someone to enjoy because he certainly couldn't. Not after what happened there.

He was overwhelmed. She ran him through the design. He touched the fabric swatches and took in the feelings that came with the changes she suggested. She was amazing. Even the way she talked was so soothing.

"Wow, that's pretty amazing." He knew it was the same room, the one where he'd played card games with his brother, where the two of them used to sit and read comic books, but it looked so different with Kenzi's touch. So different in fact that he wondered if perhaps he could spend time there again.

When she turned to him, he was surprised to see insecurity in her eyes. "You like it? Really?"

She looked so worried that he placed his hand on her arm out of reflex. He knew he shouldn't; he'd felt the jolt the last time he'd touched her hand, but he wanted to reassure her. He didn't want to be the cause of her doubt. "Really, it's great." The jolt was there again, humming beneath his fingers on her skin. What was it about Kenzi that affected him so? Normally he was able to turn off any feelings he might have for the women he dated, but something about her kept his defenses down, but could he really take a chance with her? No. He shouldn't. He shouldn't pull her into his messy life. It wasn't fair to her.

Her eyes held his for a moment. "Good, well, let me show you the rest." She dragged her eyes back to the portfolio and flipped another board. The two smaller bedrooms appeared and were similar in color and style to the master bedroom. His heart seized at the sight of the rooms he used to spend so much time in. Could he really sell the cabin?

"And finally, the kitchen." She turned the board over and he marveled at how she'd even managed to work the colors into the small kitchen. "I think we should replace the countertops along with the fridge and the stove, but the original cabinets are beautiful, so I just want to sand and refinish them."

He could barely believe it was the same kitchen. The yellowish countertop had been replaced with a beige and brown flecked marble that looked clean and somehow made the room appear bigger. "I always hated that countertop," he said with a slight chuckle.

"Can't say I was a big fan either."

She joined in with a smile and then caught his eyes again. Their laughter faded as the connection between them pulsed invisibly in the air. He wanted to kiss her, to see if her lips felt as soft as he thought they must, but that was madness. He opened his mouth to commend her, but instead he bit down on his lip, looking too long at her mouth before she fidgeted in her seat and he looked at her eyes, feeling the heat. Too hot. Too close. "Would you like to have dinner with me tomorrow night?"

Shock registered on her face, followed by surprise, and then indecision. She probably knew of his aversion to dating and didn't want to get involved with that. Or perhaps she thought him a womanizer who went through women like socks - he knew there had been a few rumors floating around of that variety. Or maybe she just didn't date clients. Whatever the reason, he wished more than anything he could take the words back, but they hung in the air suspended by tiny threads as they waited for her to answer.

"I'd like that."

They were only three words. Three little words that could mean anything on a normal day, but coming from her mouth in answer to his question - he knew that they were going to change his life. Possibly forever.

KENZI

She'd like that? What had she been thinking? Yes, she found him attractive, but getting all flustered and distracted by his pretty eyes wasn't smart. Being attracted to him after accepting the job wasn't smart either. Plus, what about his reputation? Did she really want to be just one of the women he went out with a few times before moving on to something else? No, she didn't. She craved commitment, and she didn't feel he was ready for that, but it was too late now. Backing out now would be rude, and as she'd just secured payment for the job, it would be too uncomfortable.

With a sigh, Kenzi set her portfolio and laptop down on the passenger side and slid into the driver's seat of her car. She meant to go home, but she wasn't really surprised when her car pulled into Shelby's apartment complex instead.

Kenzi parked and bit the inside of her lip. Darkness had fallen while she'd been in Blaine's house, but it wasn't that late. Surely, Shelby would still be awake. Just to be safe though, Kenzi shot her a text as she walked up the walkway that led to her apartment.

The reply that she was always welcome came just as Kenzi reached the door. She knocked, expecting the look of surprise that covered Shelby's face when she opened the door.

"I was in the neighborhood," Kenzi said with a shrug.

Shelby smiled and pulled her inside. "So, what's going on?" she asked as they sat on the couch.

Kenzi sighed and dropped her head into her hands. "It's Blaine. I went over there tonight to show him the plans."

"And?" Excitement filled Shelby's voice.

"And he loved it."

"That's great. Why are you acting like that's not great?"

Kenzi lifted her head to stare at her friend. "It is great. I mean he actually relaxed, which was amazing, and he looked like he enjoyed my work...."

"As he should," Shelby said, interrupting her.

"Yeah, but then we had this weird moment."

Shelby's smile didn't fade as Kenzi had expected it would. Instead, one of her eyebrows lifted as she asked, "What kind of a weird moment?"

"Like a moment where he touched my arm like this." She demonstrated the motion, trying to have the same intense expression on her face that Blaine had, the one that made her squirm.

"Oh! That is something," Shelby said, fanning herself.

"I know!" Kenzi threw herself back on the cushions of the couch and covered her face with her hands. "And then he asked me out." She moved her fingers slightly to view her friend's reaction.

Shelby's eyes widened. "What?" A mischievous smile tugged at her lips.

Kenzi squeezed her eyes shut behind her hands and grimaced. "And I said yes." She lowered her hands and opened her eyes, expecting to see shock or dismay on Shelby's face, but she was grinning like a loon and staring expectedly at her.

"Okay, so what's the big deal?"

"The big deal is now he's my boss! What if it goes badly? What if it gets awkward? What if he forgets about me like he does all the other women he's seen? How am I supposed to keep working for him if that happens?" How could Shelby not see what a huge mistake this was?

Shelby placed a calming hand on Kenzi's arm and tilted her head down in the motherly gesture she had perfected. "Okay, first of all, you don't know why he doesn't see those women again. Maybe he goes out with them and realizes they aren't compatible. Second, what if it doesn't?"

"What?"

"What if it doesn't go badly? What if it doesn't get awkward? What if it actually works out? What if he didn't date those other women more than once or twice because they weren't the woman for him? What if it turns out God sent him into your life for a reason and you realize the two of you are perfect for each other?"

Kenzi both loved and hated this trait of Shelby's. On one hand, she'd wanted her friend to commiserate with her, to tell her how awful this was going to be. After all, misery loves company, but on the other hand, Shelby was right. Maybe Blaine offering her this job had been at God's prompting though she didn't know if he were a believer or not. And maybe him asking her out had been the same. He'd certainly looked shocked when the words left his mouth, as if he hadn't planned them, but they had burst forth spontaneously. If that was the case, then maybe he could be attracted to her.

"Okay, maybe you're right."

Shelby rolled her eyes. "Of course I'm right. Besides, it's my turn to be the calming influence, especially after you helped me so much last year."

Kenzi chuckled. Shelby was usually the calming influence but the stress of finances and the lack of a donor during the Christmas season last year had sent Shelby spinning much the same way Kenzi was now, and Kenzi had been the voice of reason then.

"So, when are you going out with him?"

"Tomorrow night after he finishes practice." Kenzi tried not to let the excitement she felt flood her voice. It was one thing to feel it inside, but if she let it out then it might take control of her and she couldn't let that happen.

❦ 46 ❧

BLAINE

"**Y**ou in a hurry tonight, Hollis?"

Blaine looked up to see Tucker just a few feet away. His hair was still wet from the shower, but he'd already gotten dressed.

"Yeah, I have a meeting with Kenzi Lanham." His eyes slid from Tucker's as he said Kenzi's name.

"A meeting or a date?"

Though he wasn't looking at Tucker, Blaine could hear the teasing tone in his voice. "Sort of both, I guess. She's redecorating this cabin I inherited earlier this summer, and I offered to take her to dinner." Actually, he'd asked her to dinner, but really the two were similar, right?

"Uh huh, and which does she think it is?"

Blaine swallowed and lifted his eyes to Tucker. "A date, probably."

Tucker laughed and shook his head. "Blaine Hollis and Kenzi Lanham. I can't decide whether that's a match made in heaven or a train wreck waiting to happen."

"What do you mean?" Blaine shut the locker and zipped up his bag.

"Look, I've spent more time with Kenzi than you have. I like the girl, but she's always seemed a little flighty. Sure, she's settled down more now that she knows what she wants to do, but only in her job. I haven't heard of her having a relationship since I met her. And then there's you. The man who's never brought the same woman to an event twice. You two are either going to be perfect together or set a record for who can run away fastest."

Though Blaine knew Tucker was right, hearing it didn't sit well with him. "You better watch it, Jackson. I can make practice extra hard for you next week."

Tucker Jackson held up his hands in surrender. "Hey, I'm just stating what I see. Really, though I hope you guys hit it off. Kenzi is a nice girl, and you both deserve a little happiness." With that he turned and exited the locker room before Blaine could say anything else.

He deserved a little happiness. The words ran through his mind like a broken record as he drove to pick up Kenzi. Was he giving off a vibe that he wasn't happy or was Tucker just issuing platitudes? And did he deserve happiness? After what he'd done? True, it had been years, but that didn't make the guilt any less real. Nor did it change the past.

The thoughts flew from his mind when Kenzi opened her front door. She was stunning. Her dark hair was pulled to one side and lay in curls down her neck and shoulder. The skirt she was wearing showed off her toned legs, and the smile she flashed at him seemed to brighten even the darkest places in his soul. "Wow," was all he could utter.

Pink sprouted on her cheeks, and her gaze dropped to the ground for just a moment. "Thank you. I'll take that as a compliment. So, where are we going?"

"There's a really great barbecue place I've been wanting to try out. How does that sound?"

She flashed a dazzling smile at him as she locked her apartment door behind her. "Blaine, I'm a Texas girl. Barbecue is what we do best."

He chuckled as he led her to his car, and he wondered just how much of a Texas girl she was. He'd never seen her in cowboy boots, but he could imagine she would make them look good.

"Are you really a native Texan?" he asked when she was settled in the car. Nothing about her, save a tiny hint of an accent, screamed Texan.

"Through and through," she said as he started the car. "I was Miss Southlake in high school."

Now that he could believe. Kenzi had the look of a home-coming queen.

"What about you?" she asked. "Are you native or an implant? I don't hear much of a drawl when you speak."

He chuckled as he pulled to a stop at the red light. "Native as well, and I used to have a thick accent, but when I began doing interviews, the coaches told me I needed to get rid of the accent so people could understand me. Took a few lessons and a lot of speaking with a pencil in my mouth, but I finally broke it."

Kenzi's forehead wrinkled as she stared at him. "A pencil in your mouth?"

"It's supposed to help you enunciate," he said with a laugh as he remembered his drama teacher making them all read their lines with pencils in their mouths. He hadn't really wanted to take drama, but it satisfied a fine art requirement and he had actually enjoyed it.

Kenzi joined in with his laughter. "I guess I'll have to try that sometime."

He shot her a quick glance before turning his focus back to the road. "Don't you dare. You have a beautiful voice just the way it is."

She smiled, and he enjoyed the soft pink that graced her cheeks again as silence fell between them again.

The restaurant wasn't overly crowded for which he was glad. He wanted to spend some time getting to know Kenzi. The hostess led them to a table in the back, and Blaine held out the chair for Kenzi as she sat.

"Thank you."

After he sat, the hostess left them with menus promising the waitress would be back soon to take their order.

"So, you said I would be your first real client after the center? Do you have any other jobs lined up?" The light from above cast a soft glow on her face which made her eyes seem to sparkle and shimmer, and he was having a hard time making his brain process even simple statements.

Her teeth chewed lightly on her bottom lip. "I had a few interviews last week, but I haven't heard back from any of them." Her eyes darted to his. "I hope that doesn't make you reconsider hiring me."

Blaine wondered where this lack of confidence was coming from. From what he'd seen, she was amazing, and he had no doubt he would be pleased with her work. "Not at all. I have no doubt that your business will take off, especially after seeing your designs. I'll help in whatever way I can."

"Thank you. I appreciate that." She paused and took a sip of her water glass, but he could sense that she wanted to say something more.

"What is it?"

"It's probably none of my business, but I am curious."

Curious. Now there was a dangerous word. What exactly was she curious about and was he willing to answer her question? Normally, now would be the time that he would shut down and deflect the question away, but he found himself opening up instead. "What do you want to know? I'm an open book." Well, mostly open. He wouldn't discuss his brother, but he doubted she would know about him anyway.

She considered him another moment before tilting her head and asking, "How is it that you're still single? You have this amazing job and this great personality, but I've never heard of you being in a relationship." Her eyes held his gaze for another moment before slipping to the side.

He should have known this question would come up, and while it wasn't an easy one to answer, it was definitely better than discussing his family. He shrugged, his eyes flitting around the room while he tried to come up with as much of the truth as he was willing to share. "Well, I guess I just haven't found a woman I wanted to spend a lot of time with." That wasn't a total lie. "You know I could ask the same question of you."

A knowing smile crossed her face. His change of subject hadn't gotten past her. "Yes, I guess you could, and I suppose my answer would be very similar to yours. I've been told I'm a little picky."

"Well, I hope you're not so picky that you can't find something you enjoy on the menu."

"I don't think that will be a problem at all."

It was odd how comfortable he was around her, how he could laugh and joke with her. He couldn't remember ever feeling like this around a woman. And it scared him to death. Eating with her was nice. Spending time with her was refreshing. He could see himself falling for her, but what if he couldn't protect her when she needed it? He wasn't sure he could live through the past again. Nor could he imagine spending another lonely night at home knowing he could have a night like this.

KENZI

Kenzi could see the invisible wall Blaine kept up lowering as the night went on. She wasn't sure what he kept the wall up for, but she was certainly enjoying getting to know this side of him. He was funny and caring and she could feel herself falling for him even though she kept reminding herself that she couldn't. Her brain knew there were a million reasons she couldn't, but her heart just didn't seem to agree.

It was her heart that spoke as she set her glass down. "If you have time tomorrow, would you like to come with me to pick appliances?" The words flew past her lips before they registered in her brain, and she hoped they didn't dampen the mood. She didn't want him to think she only cared about business, but she did want to see him again. This would be a perfect opportunity. She clamped her lips shut as she waited for him to answer. The need to explain her reasoning thudded in her brain, but she figured it would be safer to hear his answer first.

His eyes twinkled as he regarded her. Darn her face and its inability to mask her emotions. "What would that entail?"

His teasing response caught her off guard. She had expected him to make an excuse as to why he couldn't, not flirt with her across the table. "Um, well, I like to save money on appliances because I usually need it for other areas, so I generally buy them at Home Depot. So, I guess that would entail meeting me there and helping me decide on which appliances."

"And is that all it would entail?"

All? What was he asking? Did he expect to get a massage after it or something? "I don't know what you mean."

He smiled at her obvious discomfort, and a tiny dimple appeared in his cheek. Was he razzing her?

"How about this? I'll help you pick out appliances if we can have dinner again afterwards."

Dinner again? Kenzi's head was spinning. Blaine, the guy who never saw the same woman twice, wanted to have dinner with her two nights in a row? She should say no. Her mind knew that much. This was too weird, too unlike him.

What if this was like fifth grade when Brian Harding asked her out in a note at lunch and sent her little heart thumping in her chest? Brian had been her first crush, and the thought that he - one of the most popular boys - would like her when she wasn't the thinnest or the cutest or the most popular girl had been more than she could bear. She'd floated through the next few classes until they had social studies together, but when she'd entered that room and told him her answer was yes, he laughed it off and told her it had all been a joke. It hadn't been funny to her, and the next day he was seen flirting with Wendy Wiseman - the thinnest, cutest, most popular girl in the fifth grade. A part of her had died that day, and she never wanted to feel that way again. So, what if she said yes and then Blaine never showed?

She knew there was danger here, but that didn't keep her mouth from saying, "Okay, dinner sounds good."

"Good. You ready to get out of here?"

He stood and held out his hand to her. Had he already paid? How had she missed the check coming? Was this a date then since he'd paid? Even more importantly, was tomorrow a date? Kenzi prided herself on being in control, but right now, she felt like a kid on roller skates for the first time. The only thing she was sure of was that she was enjoying spending time with Blaine and she didn't want it to end.

Placing her hand in his, she let him pull her up. She expected he would drop her hand as soon as she was on her feet, but he didn't. Instead, he gripped her hand tighter as he led her out of the restaurant.

"You feel like a walk?" he asked when they exited the restaurant and the cool evening air hit them. It was almost eight and the sun was setting in the sky, sending brilliant oranges, reds, and pinks across the sky. She'd visited a few other states, but there was nothing like a Texas sunset, and she couldn't imagine seeing it a better way.

"Sure."

He led the way away from the restaurant and down a lighted path. Kenzi's gaze dropped to their entwined hands every few minutes. She still couldn't believe she was on a date with Blaine Hollis. Nor could she believe he was holding her hand. It was too bad Brian Harding couldn't see her now.

The silence between them wasn't strained, but Kenzi had so many questions. "When did you start playing football?"

"Young. I used to play…" he paused and his jaw tightened, "with my dad in the yard. Then I began playing for school in the seventh grade, and it just went from there."

She wondered what that pause had been about. Did he not have a good relationship with his father? Had it soured for some reason? She realized she knew nothing about his family. Even when he was interviewed, Blaine always shifted the focus away from his family and to the game. She was no detective, but something was definitely going on there. "So, did you always want to play professionally?" Kenzi knew it was a common desire for young boys. Many at the center had listed that as their dream occupation when asked.

The vein in his neck bulged and his eyes slid away from her. "Yeah, pretty much."

A follow-up question burned in her throat, but before she could ask it, the sound of children's voices came their way.

"Kevin, wait up."

"No, you're being a bully, and I don't want to play with you anymore."

Blaine tensed beside her, and his hand turned clammy against hers. The two boys rounded a corner and hurried past them with barely a second glance, but even after they were gone, Blaine remained rooted to the spot.

"Are you okay?"

He was silent a moment and then shook his head as if clearing away some memory. "I'm fine. Let's just go."

His gruff demeanor had returned, and as he turned around, he dropped her hand as well. Kenzi missed the warmth it had provided, but more than that she wondered. Why had the two boys affected him so badly? Had he known them? They had been having such a wonderful time, and then all of a sudden, it was over. She missed the feeling of his hand in hers.

47
BLAINE

Blaine took a deep breath as he parked in front of the Home Depot. He should never have suggested this; he'd let himself get caught up in the moment with Kenzi last night. He'd held her hand and let himself think about the way she smelled and how soft her skin was. He'd let himself believe that maybe he could have a relationship, and then that dream had been shattered when he'd heard the name. Kevin. The sound of his brother's name from the young boy's lips had drawn him back to the past faster than a bullet train.

The two boys had come around the bend, and Blaine knew they had to be brothers; they looked so much like he and his own brother had at that age. As he'd watched them, he'd seen, for just a moment, a similar time from his past. A time when he'd wanted to run through the forest and his brother had been afraid and hung back. He'd goaded his brother in much the same way as those boys last night, and that memory had reminded him again of his failure as a protector. He hadn't protected his brother then, and he couldn't protect Kenzi or anyone else now.

He took another deep breath, dreading this meeting, dreading seeing the worry and confusion on her face like he had last night. Unfortunately, he had already issued the invitation before the painful reminder came, and now he had to follow through. Bailing on her would be rude, and he couldn't bring himself to do it. He would just have to keep his distance and remain strictly professional with her, but that was easier said than done. He really liked her.

It had felt good holding her hand last night. So good that for a time he had forgotten he couldn't have that for real. He could pretend for a night, maybe even two - heck, he was used to that - but she deserved more. She deserved someone who could always be there for her, and that just wasn't him.

He locked the Mustang and headed toward the front entrance. Kenzi was there already, her long dark locks piled on her head. Her top hung crooked, baring one shoulder completely, and her tight jeans showed off her toned legs. This was going to be harder than he thought.

Her lips split in a wide smile when she recognized him. "You made it."

He nodded, wondering if he could feign illness to get out of having dinner with her. It wasn't that he didn't want to have dinner with her, he just didn't trust himself to have dinner with her again. She had a way of getting him to lower his walls, and he needed to keep them firmly in place.

Her smile faltered a little as if she'd expected a different greeting, but she kept her composure. "Shall we then?"

He followed her inside and tried not to think about the disappointment that had flashed across her face momentarily. It was better this way, and if he could just keep himself from flirting with her, then maybe they could go back to the way it was before he asked her out, before he held her hand, before he felt his heart thaw in his chest.

"So, where do we start?" He was careful to keep his eyes

focused on anything except her face as he spoke. If he looked in those eyes for too long, his resolve would fade, and he couldn't let that happen.

She flipped open the notebook she'd been carrying under her arm. "Well, I thought we'd start with the oven and the fridge. They're the biggest purchases by far. Then, we can look at vanities and paint."

"Okay, lead the way." Blaine was careful to let her stay just a bit ahead of him to minimize the chance of them locking gazes. Still, he couldn't help but think about what it would be like to shop with her like a real couple. Would she take charge like she was now or would she defer to him and let him help make decisions?

"Based on your space, I've already narrowed down the options. I tend to think Stainless Steel will look the best, but I believe they also carry ones in cream or black that would fit your space."

Black? He couldn't imagine a black fridge and cream sounded like it would show dirt easily. He didn't know who might be buying the cabin, but if they had kids anything like him and his brother when they were younger, they would probably appreciate the Stainless Steel. He smiled slightly as the memory of peanut butter handprints on the fridge and cabinet doors flew to his mind.

"Blaine! Kevin! What is going on here?" Their mother stood in the kitchen doorway, hands on her hips and fire flying from her eyes.

"We wanted to make peanut butter toast," Blaine said.

"On the cabinets?" She threw her hands up in exasperation. "Did you have to touch every surface?" She reached on top of the fridge for a tub of wipes. "I'll be cleaning this for hours."

"Sorry, Mom," Kevin said. His big brown eyes filled with tears and Blaine knew they were going to rocket down his cheeks any minute. Kevin was definitely the more emotional of the two of them.

Their mother sighed. "It's okay, Kevin. Why don't you boys go out and play while I clean this up and get dinner started?"

"Sure, Mom." Blaine, having finished his toast, wrapped his arm around his little brother and headed for the back door.

"But stay away from the lake," she called after them as they exited the cabin.

Blaine squeezed his eyes shut to push away the painful memory. That had been one of their last summers spent at the cabin. "I think I agree with you on the Stainless Steel."

She turned his direction faster than he could shift his gaze, and her eyes caught his. Darn it; he was trapped now. "Great, Stainless Steel it is. Do you think the same for the oven?"

He wanted to look away, but there was something in her stare that held him like a tractor beam. What was it? As he looked into her eyes, he suddenly knew. Questions and self-doubt swam in there beneath her confident bravado, and he found his wall lowering again. He wondered what had happened to her to make her second guess herself so much. "Yeah, I think whatever you think will be amazing."

Her lips pulled into a tight line and tiny lines erupted on her forehead as her brows pulled together. "What's going on with you, Blaine?"

"What do you mean?"

"I mean last night you were all smiles and laughter and hand holding. You agreed to come only if we could have another dinner afterward, but now you're acting as if you'd rather be anywhere else. If you've changed your mind about having me decorate the cabin..."

"No." He grabbed her arm to stop her derailment; he couldn't let her doubt herself. The touch of his fingers stopped her voice, but it also sent pulsing waves up his arm. "It's not that at all, Kenzi. You know how you asked me why I've never had a relationship?"

She nodded but said nothing, waiting for him to continue.

"Well, the reason I haven't is because I can't."

Her face furrowed in confusion. "What do you mean you can't?"

"I mean physically I can, I guess, but..." He sighed. This wasn't coming out right at all. "Something happened in my past that keeps me from connecting emotionally. Does that make sense?" He hoped she wouldn't ask what because he wouldn't go into details. Couldn't go into details. They were too painful, and they needed to stay locked away in his mind.

"A little, I guess. Something happened that made you think you don't deserve a relationship?"

Yes. She understood. Relief flooded him and he grabbed her other arm. "Exactly."

Her eyes softened and compassion filled her face. "Blaine, you deserve happiness. I don't know what's in your past, but it's the past. It doesn't have to define your future. There are things in my past as well, but God forgave me of all of them when I gave my heart to Him. He will do the same for you."

Her mention of God caught him slightly off guard. He supposed he should have guessed she was a believer. After all, Shelby and Tucker were, but he still wasn't used to people speaking so frankly about God. No one in his family had mentioned God since the accident, and he wasn't sure God would forgive him for what he'd done. "You might be right. I do feel differently around you, but I don't know if I'm ready."

"Okay, let's just get to work then." She slipped her arms out of his hold and turned toward the ovens.

"Wait, Kenzi." She stopped and turned to him. "I'd like to try though."

She frowned softly. "You'd like to try what?"

All the feelings of guilt and outrage at himself flooded him. He probably couldn't do it. He would have to acknowledge and own up to his mistakes first, and he didn't know if he was strong enough to do that. It was easy enough to pretend he was a relatively good person with a past, but opening himself up to let people see how truly horrible he was-- that took courage he didn't have. Not now. Not yet. "I'd like to try to be honest, and forgive myself. To give it to God and let go." He looked into her eyes as she stood there frowning. He picked up her hand. "If you can be patient with me, then I'd like to try. And if I can't, then you're better off without me anyway. I like you. I like being around you."

Her eyes searched his, and he willed her to say something, anything. Finally, her mouth opened, "I like you too, Blaine. If you can be honest with me, then I'd love to try too."

KENZI

Kenzi smiled as Blaine laced his hand through hers. She had thought he was going to break things off before they even really got started, but then he'd said he wanted to try a relationship. With her. On one hand, she was delighted and astonished. She'd had a crush on Blaine for years and he was willing to take a chance with her, but on the other hand, she was terrified. He hadn't had a real relationship ever from the sounds of it, and she wasn't sure she wanted to be the guinea pig. Of course her track record wasn't much better. After her last serious boyfriend wasn't there when she needed him, she hadn't dated anyone seriously either. It hit her then that his situation might be similar, and she should give him the benefit of the doubt.

"So, ovens?"

"Huh?" She looked over to see him grinning at her, and that's when she realized she had been standing in the middle of the aisle holding his hand but not moving. Probably looking like a dazed and confused moron. "Yes, ovens. Every kitchen needs an oven." She turned that direction and tried to focus on the task at hand, but the warmth of his skin against hers kept pulling her mind off track.

"Or a barbecue grill. This is Texas after all."

Kenzi shook her head and nudged him with her shoulder. "You can't have a barbecue grill in a house. Especially not that cabin. The whole thing would go up in smoke."

His lips split in a wide smile. A natural smile. The first natural smile she'd seen on him. "I didn't mean in the house. Just on the property. If I have a grill, I don't really need a stove."

"Ew, what about breakfast?" Kenzi loved barbecue as much as the next Texan, but there was a time to grill and there was a time to bake. A grill couldn't make all of the foods in her dietary rotation.

"Steak and eggs."

"Eggs on a grill?" That not only sounded disgusting, but how in the world did he keep them from falling through the cracks?

"Yep, a little tin foil and you're good to go."

Tin foil? She shuddered at the thought of the flavor of eggs cooked in tin foil. "Remind me not to let you make breakfast." The words died in her throat as she realized the innuendo she had just thrown down without meaning to. Great, now what did she say? She glanced at him, but he seemed unsure of how to respond as well.

"Anyway, your cabin needs a stove. We're pretty tight on space, so really I just need to know if you want a flat top or the traditional kind?"

"I'm not sure I have a preference, so I'll let you decide."

Kenzi nodded and picked out the oven she had been eyeing online. "I think this one will go well with the plans I have for the kitchen. Okay, fridge and oven down. Now, we just need a vanity and paint."

"For the bathroom?"

Confusion threaded his voice, but she couldn't blame him. The bathroom was tiny and fitting a vanity in there would be a squeeze. "Yes, the vanity is for the bathroom. A woman is going to want some counter space and a drawer or two underneath to store necessities. We just need something thin enough to fit the small area."

His eyes betrayed his doubt, but he motioned for her to lead the way.

The bathroom vanities left a lot to be desired, and after measuring all of the ones that looked small enough, Kenzi sighed. "None of these will work. I may have to hire a carpenter."

"Maybe I could help with that."

She tilted her head as she regarded him. "Are you a carpenter too?"

"I am a jack of a lot of trades, but yes, carpentry is one of them."

Kenzi shook her head in surprise. There was definitely more to Blaine than he let on, but she supposed she could see him as a carpenter. He had the rugged build of someone who worked with their hands, and she had felt a rough patch or two when they were holding hands.

"Okay, I may take you up on that."

"Great. So, paint?"

"Yes, paint. I don't want to do much to the living room due to the exposed wood, but the bedrooms could use some paint."

"Paint it is then," he said, leading the way to the colorful aisle.

Kenzi perused the many colors, finally deciding on a dusty tan and a pale blue. The tan would be for the master bedroom, and she would bring in the blues with pillows and bedding. The upstairs' rooms would be opposites - blue walls and tan accessories.

"Okay, we have a fridge, an oven, and paint. What's the next step in the decorating process?"

She placed a finger to her lips as she thought. She did want to discuss the carpet with him, but was now the right time?

"What? I can tell something is on your mind."

"I was hoping maybe we could talk about ripping out the carpet and putting hardwood floors in? It would really add charm to the place. Not that it's not charming," she added quickly.

He smiled and shook his head. "Don't worry, I get it. The carpet is old and looks worn. In fact, in some places, it is worn."

She tilted her head at him and waited for him to elaborate.

"I happen to know there is a small burn in the carpet of one of the rooms upstairs from a reading lamp."

"A reading lamp? How does that cause a hole in the carpet?"

Blaine scratched at his chin and averted his eyes. "Well, if the lamp has an adjustable neck, and it's a little old so it doesn't always stay up. And if a boy fell asleep while reading, it might be possible for the lamp to fold and the light bulb to heat the carpet enough to burn a hole in it." He turned a sheepish gaze on her and shrugged his shoulders.

Kenzi bit the inside of her lip to keep from laughing at the visual. "I wouldn't have taken you for such an avid reader, Blaine Hollis."

"Well, when it's night time in a cabin with no TV or video games, books have their appeal."

She batted his arm playfully. "Books always have appeal. Okay, so hardwood floors are a go. I'm glad because they're so versatile. Plus we can get a few ornate rugs because I'm sure the floor gets cold in the winter."

The muscles in his face tensed slightly, but then his smile reappeared. "It certainly does. So, let's get some hardwood."

Kenzi was surprised that Blaine had agreed so easily. True, she was the designer, but she always thought clients would be opinionated about aspects and push back. Blaine seemed to be completely the opposite. Whether that was because he had the money and therefore wasn't worried about the price or because his desire to sell the cabin was so strong, she wasn't sure. However, the more she interacted with him, the more certain she became that something had happened at that cabin in his past.

With the hardwood picked and ordered, Kenzi led the way to the front of the store to check out. "Okay, so now we need to check out and set up a delivery time for what we have here, and then I'll need to get out there and remove the current appliances and furniture, so we can do the floors and then move the new appliances in. Then I'll work on the colors - pillows, bedding, and the like."

A grimace crossed his handsome features. "I'm not sure I'll be much help with colors. I'm color deficient."

"Color deficient? Like you can see some colors but not all of them?"

He nodded. "I wanted to join the Air Force and become a pilot when I graduated, but one day they did one of those color blindness tests in school. Turns out I can't distinguish between some shades of brown and green, so flying was out."

"But you can still play football?" If he had issues with browns and greens, she wondered if he ever had issues with the ball and the turf.

He chuckled and his eyes twinkled as he regarded her. "Notice that I only throw the ball though. I don't catch it."

Her eyes widened. "So, you would have issues if you had to catch it?"

His laugh deepened, and she didn't think she'd ever heard a sweeter sound. There was a low rumble to it that reminded her of s'mores and warm camp fires. "Not like you think. I can tell the difference between the ball and the ground, but if I were a wide receiver, I might have issues seeing the ball as it flew through the air."

"Oh." She felt stupid though it wasn't like she had any experience being color deficient or playing football. She was a sideline cheerleader only.

He placed a finger under her chin to lift it in order to get her attention again. "Don't worry. You aren't the first person to ask me what it's like. I think I've heard every question by now."

His eyes were like a magnet, drawing her to him and making it impossible to look away. They say eyes are the windows to the soul, but Kenzi couldn't decipher what she saw in his eyes. Desire, fear, joviality, anxiety. It was like for every positive emotion she saw, a negative one existed as well. What had happened to him in his past?

His lips parted, and for just a second, Kenzi thought he was going to kiss her right there in the middle of the store. Instead, he dropped his hand and leaned back. "Shall we check out and grab that dinner then?"

Kenzi swallowed the disappointment flooding her body and forced a smile across her lips. "That sounds nice."

❧ 48 ❧
BLAINE

Blaine pulled up to the center and took a deep breath. He could do this. He could be around these kids. They weren't his sole responsibility, and they deserved this. His issues weren't their fault. The words were easy enough to say, but they were a lot harder to believe, especially with his memories from the past flooding him more and more often.

Even though things seemed to be going better - he'd actually been out with Kenzi twice now which he was pretty sure was a record for him - he knew that one familiar word, one specific memory could send him spiraling back down again. He'd felt it when he looked at the one picture he still had, a picture of them together at the lake.

"I'm going to try and make it work," he'd told the boy in the picture next to him. "I don't want to end up alone." The boy had said nothing, but Blaine was certain he'd felt the boy's scorn. He could almost hear the words the boy might say - the words that had played over and over in his head for the last eighteen years. "I ended up alone. You couldn't protect me, and you won't be able to protect her. You'll fail her too."

But he was determined not to. He wasn't sure what it was

about Kenzi, but something about her made him want to break free, made him want to try again. Perhaps it was the simple way she seemed to accept him just the way he was. Perhaps it was her faith in God. Perhaps it was just the brilliant smile that warmed his soul when she flashed it his direction. Whatever it was, she was the first woman to pierce his wall in years, and he wasn't ready to give up. Not yet.

With a final sigh, he stepped out of his Mustang and headed toward the front door of the center. A small jingling sound announced his arrival, and Shelby glanced up with a smile.

"Hey, Blaine, Kenzi's not here if you were looking for her."

He wondered if Kenzi had told Shelby about their dates. Probably. Though his experience with women was limited, he'd heard the other guys talk enough to know that women loved to share those kind of experiences. Besides, Shelby was looking at him differently, with a mischievous twinkle in her eye.

He shoved his hands in his jean pockets and rocked back on his heels. "I'm actually not here for Kenzi. I'm here because it's my day to hang out with the kids."

Shelby's eyes widened, and her mouth formed a silent "o". "Right, of course. I knew that." But the pink color spreading across her cheeks told him she had forgotten. Her head dropped to the counter in front of her as her hands sifted through the papers. "I just need to find your original form. Aha, here it is."

She brandished a piece of paper as if it were some lost treasure and then slid it across to him. "I just need you to check the information and make sure it's still accurate, so that we have it on file. Then you can add today to the bottom."

Blaine scanned the form, but everything appeared in order. He took the pen she handed him and began filling out the requested information.

"I'm actually really glad you came in today," Shelby continued, "I was going to ask Tucker if he could set up a time for me to come talk to the team or at least you anyway."

"What for?" he asked without looking up.

"I thought it would be a great idea if we started a Big Brother type thing here."

Blaine's grip on the pen increased, and a hole formed in the paper from the pressure he was applying. A Big Brother program was out of the question. At least for him. It would involve taking the child out of the center and being responsible for them, and there was no way he was doing that. No way.

"The guys on the team could each adopt one of the kids here as a younger brother or sister. Take them out, hang out with them, with parental permission of course."

"No." The word came out more forcefully than he intended and cut off Shelby's explanation.

Her mouth hung open as she stared at him. "No? Why not? The kids would love it."

Great. Now, he'd done it. How did he convince her not to do this without telling her his real reason? "I just... We're going to be too busy with the season starting soon. Maybe that's an idea we can save for after the season ends."

She stared at him, and he knew she was trying to decide if he was telling the truth. No doubt she would ask Tucker to confirm Blaine's excuse. Should he try to convince Tucker to agree with him? He had a feeling that Tucker wouldn't lie for him. He'd changed since becoming a believer. Would the man agree on his own? It was possible. The schedule was challenging, especially at the beginning of the season, but Tucker might think helping the kids was more important than their challenging season.

"Okay, I'll table the idea for now," her voice held a note of sadness, "I still think it's a good one."

Blaine breathed a sigh of relief. It wasn't a perfect solution, but it was better than nothing, and maybe by then he would be able to take it on. "So, what would you like me to do today?"

"The kids really love when you guys teach them drills or whatever it is you do for football. Do you have some you could share?"

Blaine smiled at Shelby's clear lack of knowledge about the sport. He'd have to remember to tease Tucker about it later. If he was planning to marry this woman, she needed to at least have a working idea of the game. "I can probably figure something out."

"Great. Two of our high schoolers are with them now, but I'm sure they'd love a break."

Blaine nodded and continued into the main gym area. The kids were playing some form of tag with two teenagers, but the game came to a screeching halt when they saw him. Almost like a tidal wave, they discarded their game and came barreling toward him.

He recognized many of the faces from the Christmas party and the last few times he had volunteered, but there were several new ones as well. Word must be spreading and the thought made him smile. Kids needed a place like this.

"You're Blaine Hollis, aren't you?" The question came from one of the newer faces, a stocky boy who had all the classic markings of a bully - the fierce eyes, the crossed arms, the tight line of his lips.

"I am. How would you guys like to learn how to throw a football today?" Blaine quickly scanned the room. He knew the center had used some of the money they'd received to buy new footballs, but he wasn't sure if they would have enough for all the kids. They'd have to take turns.

"I want to learn how to throw a football," a young girl with braids piped up.

The bully turned on her. "Girls don't play football. They can't throw and they definitely can't take a hit."

The girl's face fell, and her head dropped to her chest. Blaine knew he should do something, say something, but was he allowed?

"That's not true. Girls can play football if they want to." He saw the girl look up at him. "There are a lot of people in this world who will try to tell you what you can't do, but the only one who really knows that is you." He shot a pointed stare at the bully before turning back to the girl. 'What's your name?"

"Belinda." Her voice was quiet as if she wasn't sure she believed him, and he noticed her eyes shift to gage the other boy's reaction.

"Well, Belinda, how would you like to be my helper today? I'll show you first and when you have it down, you can help me show the other kids. Would you like that?"

The light returned to her eyes and her shoulders lifted a little higher. "I'd like that."

He held out his hand to her and let her lead the way to the sports closet.

KENZI

Kenzi smiled as she responded to the text from Blaine. He was off tomorrow and willing to meet her at the cabin to remove the old furniture if it worked for her schedule. She had nothing pressing taking priority over his job, so she'd readily agreed. Besides, she couldn't wait to see him again.

He hadn't kissed her the other night, even after dinner, but she'd seen the want in his eyes more than once, and the want was definitely in her eyes. She'd been thinking about his lips a lot lately. A lot. Perhaps tomorrow at the cabin would be the perfect opportunity, but before she let her mind skip too far down that trail, she needed to let Shelby know the good news.

The venue she had wanted for the wedding, an old church with an elaborate reception area, had just responded to Kenzi's message that they were available. Even though the wedding was still months away, Kenzi knew she would need to devote a lot of her time to making it the perfect space for Shelby, especially after she finished Blaine's cabin. Hopefully, by then she would have some more jobs lined up, but currently her phone was still silent. Though daunting, she was trying hard not to be discouraged. She knew that if worse came to worse, she could always return to the center and work with Shelby, but that wasn't what she wanted.

"God, I think decorating is my call, but I want to make sure I'm following Your will. Please show me if I'm wrong and open doors if I'm right." The short prayer was one she'd been repeating often, but she knew that God worked in His time and not in hers. "Oh, and please give me a sign about Blaine. I know something is going on with him, but I don't know how much I should invest. Can you help me guard my heart if he's not the guy for me?" Though she heard no audible reply, she knew He had heard her and would answer. As hard as it was, she would be patient.

Grabbing her laptop and purse from the passenger seat, Kenzi stepped out of the car and headed for the center. Shelby would probably just be closing, so it was a perfect time to meet her.

The front door was already locked, but thankfully Kenzi still had her key. She unlocked the door and called out, "I've got good news," before locking the door behind her again.

Shelby's head popped up in the reception window. She'd probably been running the reports for the night. "Oh yeah? I've got some news too, but you go first."

Kenzi continued around the small reception area to the open door and set her computer and purse on the table. "I got a call from the church you wanted. They can fit you in, so we need to decide how you want it to look."

"That is fantastic," Shelby said as she sat next to Kenzi, "but I'm not sure I have that all figured out yet. I know I want pink and white flowers and tulle and ribbons, but you are way better at what it will look like than I am."

"Okay, well that at least gives me some ideas to work with." Kenzi opened her laptop and pulled up a blank document to begin typing the notes in. "Do you care what kind of flowers?"

"Ranunculus. I've always loved how they looked, and maybe a few orchids. Only a few though for some color. I know they're expensive."

Kenzi noted the choices and tried to picture the flowers. If she was right, ranunculus looked similar to white roses only fuller. "Peonies might be pretty too, but they're also kind of pricey. Oh, and once I saw this bouquet that had flowers that trailed down like ribbons."

"Stephanotis," Shelby said with a nod. "Yeah, those are pretty and inexpensive."

Kenzi narrowed her eyes at her friend. "When did you get so informed on flowers' names?"

Pink spread across Shelby's cheeks along with a look of chagrin as if she'd been caught stealing cookies from the jar. "Since I got engaged. I've been spending my free time in the evenings going over pictures and finding what I liked. I figured I might as well learn their names too."

Kenzi wondered if she would be like that if she ever got engaged, and then she realized she'd probably be worse. The designer in her wouldn't allow anything mismatched or out of place. Her poor future husband. "Okay, well that sounds good. I can start working up some ideas based on this, and if you think of anything else you can always reach out to me. Now, what was your news?"

Shelby's smile faded and concern flooded her eyes. "Are you still working with Blaine?"

Uh oh. Shelby looked as if bad news was coming next. "Yeah, why?"

Shelby bit her bottom lip and stared at the table a moment before speaking again. "He came in today, for his day here. You know how they're doing one day a month?"

Kenzi nodded. She was aware of the plan. "Was he awful or something? I thought he did fine the last few times he was here." She knew she was falling for him, but if he wasn't good around children, would that change her opinion? She did want to be a mother one day.

"No, he was great with the kids. He stood up to one of our

newer kids who's a bit of a bully and really made this little girl's day."

"But?" Kenzi didn't know why Shelby looked apprehensive. That was good news. She wished she'd had someone like Blaine to stand up for her in middle school when the bullying and teasing was the worst. She thought back to her last day of eighth grade.

Kenzi's stomach clenched as she watched Tyson James take the white board marker. The teacher had allowed the students to play Win, Lose, or Draw on the board, and Tyson had nearly bounded out of his seat to be the first. She wasn't sure what to make of Tyson. He always seemed to have a cruel word to throw her way as they passed in the hall, but he would always end it with a wink. Her mother had assured her that he was only picking on her because he liked her, but Kenzi wasn't so sure.

He began drawing across the white board, and her heart sank as she saw a stick figure come to life. Around her, the other kids began guessing, but Tyson just laughed and kept drawing. As soon as he added the pants, rounding around the waist, she knew he was drawing her. She'd put on a few pounds this year, but her mother had refused to purchase any more, claiming that Kenzi should just lose weight or take responsibility and buy her own clothes if she wanted more after the initial beginning of year purchase. Tyson hadn't let her too tight pants go unnoticed and often asked her if maybe she should consider skipping a few lunches.

As soon as he stepped back, one of his friends piped up. "It's Kenzi, getting ready for feeding time." Laughter broke out across the room, and Kenzi grabbed her bag and fled.

She'd spent the rest of the day in the nurse's office, hiding out. That event had been the straw that broke the camel's back and sent her on her strict journey of eating better and staying in shape. Even though she had entered high school looking completely different, that memory of eighth grade had stayed with her and affected her self-confidence. How different it might have been if one of her classmates had stood up for her.

"But... I floated an idea by him about the players being Big Brothers to the kids, and he was dead set against it."

"Did he say why?" Kenzi was still getting to know Blaine, but she couldn't see him not wanting to help out the kids, especially after the story Shelby had just shared.

"He said it was because the players would be too busy at the start of the season, but I don't think that was the real reason. I'm only saying something because I want you to be careful. I know you've had a crush on him for ages, and I was pushing you toward him at the dinner."

Kenzi placed a hand on Shelby's arm to stop her friend's rambling. "Don't worry. I am being careful. Something in his past is affecting him, but I don't know what yet. He told me something kept him from connecting emotionally but that he wanted to try with me."

An expression of deeper concern etched in Shelby's face, and she squeezed Kenzi's arm. "Just be careful. I don't want to see you get your heart broken."

Neither did Kenzi.

❦ 49 ❦
BLAINE

Blaine steeled himself for the onslaught of memories as he pulled up to the cabin. Though he still wasn't sure God would forgive him, he had been spending some time the last few days praying for the ability to get beyond his past. The blowup at Shelby had been a setback, but he was hopeful he would get through today without anything triggering him.

He turned off the engine and walked up the quiet path to the cabin. It was too bad it held such terrible memories for him because it really was a great space. A space to relax and unwind. Southlake wasn't a huge city, but it *was* still a city with noise and traffic and too many people. Sometimes, Blaine just wanted to get away.

He unlocked the front door and forced his feet over the threshold. When he'd been younger, he'd dreamed of the day the cabin would be his, when he could bring his wife and family here, but that had been before the accident. Now, just getting it sold and hoping some other family would find happiness here was enough for him.

Blaine shut the door behind him, and in the quiet, he could almost hear the sound of two boys running through the small floor plan. "We don't run in the cabin," their mother would say, and the echo of those words lingered in the air. But the boys would race up the stairs to the loft and grab their comic books and flashlights, or badger their parents to take them down to the lake. Those were always the best days, when their parents would take time off and let them swim in the lake.

The lake. The thought of it sent a shudder down his spine. He would not think about the lake now. Kenzi would be here soon and he needed to make sure he was in the right frame of mind to interact with her.

As if summoned by his thoughts, he heard the sound of a car pulling up to the cabin. He took a deep breath, pulled back his shoulders, and forced the unhappy memories from his mind.

"Sorry, I'm late," she said as she stepped out of her car. "Traffic was a bear leaving Southlake. You'd think there was a game going on or something." Her lips pulled into a small smile at her slight joke.

She looked different today, more relaxed. Her dark hair was pulled back into a ponytail, and her skirt had been traded in for a pair of comfy looking jeans. A short sleeve top was tied at the top of her jeans, displaying the tiniest line of skin, and his heart started in his chest. He liked her even more this way. Images of her wearing one of his jerseys and sitting in his box seat flashed through his mind, and he could see her fitting in with the other players' wives and girlfriends.

"No worries," he said, pushing that thought away. This was only their third date. He was a long way from proposals and wedding bells. "I just got here myself. Shall we get to work?"

She glanced around before shooting him a questioning look. "Where do you want to put everything? Just out here in the open?"

"Put everything?" And then it hit him. "I should have gotten a storage unit or something, right?"

Her lips mashed together, but he could tell she was holding back a smile. "Yeah, a storage container would have helped, but I brought some sanding supplies. We can start with the cabinets, and I'll see if I can get a storage unit out ASAP." She leaned back into the car and removed a box before shutting the door with her hip and continuing up the path. "I also have a plumber coming later to help remove the oven and the fridge, but I figured you and I could handle removing the cabinet doors and sanding and painting them. You don't mind getting a little dirty, do you?"

He laughed as he thought of how filthy he got in every game. He couldn't remember the last time a shower he'd taken after a game hadn't run brown for the first few minutes. "Until you've been tackled to the muddy ground by a three-hundred-pound line-backer, I don't think you even understand the meaning of dirty."

Her lips pulled into a wry smile as she eased past him and into the living room. "Touché, but I might be able to top that with cleaning vomit from the bathroom floor without a mop."

His face wrinkled in disgust. "Yuck, what did you clean it with?"

Kenzi rolled her eyes and laughed as she set the box down on the couch. "With a rag that I had to rinse in the sink repeatedly. It's a long story, but things have a tendency to get misplaced at the center if the kids get their hands on them. Let me tell you, that was not the day to lose the mop."

"Okay, yours might be grosser than mine." He couldn't believe they were actually comparing who had gotten dirtier. Kenzi was definitely different from any woman he'd gone out with lately.

"We'll see who takes the prize this afternoon." She held a screwdriver out to him and lifted her left eyebrow. "You know how to use this, right?"

He chuckled and nodded as he took it. Their fingertips brushed slightly, and he looked down at the heat burning up his hand. He was in so much trouble if just touching her fingertips did this to him.

Kenzi made a quick call on her phone for a storage unit, then grabbed a screwdriver from the box for herself before heading into the kitchen. He wouldn't have pegged her for being good with tools, but she kept up with his pace as they unscrewed all the cabinet doors and laid them on the table.

Half an hour later, his shoulders burned, but the adrenaline of hard work pumped through him. He enjoyed using his muscles, feeling them stretch and constrict. It was probably one reason he enjoyed football. It was a physical sport, and he was always exhausted when the game ended.

"Need a break?" Kenzi teased as he collapsed into one of the kitchen chairs.

The grueling work had caused a few strands of her hair to escape the ponytail's hold, and sweat now glued them to her forehead, but somehow it worked on her. He wondered if she had any idea how beautiful she was with her messed up hair and bright eyes.

"I'm fine," he said, answering her question. "Just a little thirsty."

"Allow me," she said, grabbing two cups out of the now-open cupboard and filling them with water. She handed one to him and took a long swig of hers. When it was empty, she set it on the counter and turned to him. "Ready to sand?"

He wasn't sure he was, but there was no way he was going to let her best him. "Bring it on," he said, setting his own cup down and picking up one of the doors. She walked into the living room and returned with a sander in each hand.

"Pick your poison."

The sanders looked exactly the same to him, but he took a second longer just to make sure before grabbing the one in her left hand. "Let's do this."

"Outside though," Kenzi said with a laugh. "I know we plan to redo the floors, but there's no reason to dirty it all up before then."

Blaine glanced out the back door. "Outside? You mean on the porch?" He'd been doing so well - ignoring the memories and pretending they didn't bother him - but could he really sit on the porch that close to the lake without his past overtaking him?

"Unless that's a problem." She raised an eyebrow at him as she waited for his answer.

He swallowed the lump that was threatening to choke off his air and pulled his shoulders back. He could do this. If he didn't look at the lake, if he sat with his back to it, then surely, he could do this. "No, it's fine."

KENZI

Kenzi tried to keep her focus on the task at hand, but Blaine and his muscular arms kept dragging her attention away from her door. He looked at home sanding doors, but then he had said he had some carpentry skills, so she shouldn't be surprised. Really, she was just glad to see him smiling. The last time they'd been at this cabin, he'd been different. Sullen. Like an invisible weight lay around his shoulders. But today, he seemed lighter. He had still hesitated about going outside, and he was sitting with his back to the lake, but it was an improvement from last time, and she was definitely enjoying the banter they were trading back and forth.

"Done," he said, laying his last door down. He looked at her stack, still three to go, and shook his head. "I thought you said you were good at this."

Some noise that was a cross between a snicker and a snort escaped her mouth. "I never said that. I just asked if you were ready." Ugh, why couldn't she scoff like a normal person?

He chuckled - probably at her - and leaned back in his chair. "I suppose I should have made sure you were ready then. Shall I help you out?"

"If you want." She could finish her doors without a problem, but allowing him to help her would give her the opportunity to watch him a little longer.

"Well, I can't just sit here and watch you work. That hardly seems fair." He leaned across and grabbed the next door off her stack. "I don't know if I ever asked you, and I know this is only your second job, but have you always been into design?"

Kenzi pursed her lips as she thought. "I guess in a way. I remember always wanting to change my room around. It drove my mother nuts. I would move my bed from one side of the room to the other." She chuckled at the memory of her frazzled mother banging her toe against something in Kenzi's room that hadn't been in that spot the day before. "She finally said I was only able to rearrange the furniture once a month and paint once a year. It was high school when I got into fashion. I suppose the two kind of work together, but it's not what I originally went to college for."

"No?" His eyebrow lifted on his head, but his focus remained on the door he was sanding.

"No. I thought I wanted to be an actress and then a lawyer and then a journalist." Kenzi couldn't believe how flighty she had been. "After a few years, I decided I didn't know what I wanted to do, but I should probably stop wasting my parent's money. So, I worked with Shelby for a while. Decorating for the Christmas party was my first gig, I guess you could say, though I didn't get paid for it. Still, I think I knew then that was where my passion lay."

"It's good to find your passion," he said with a nod. "It certainly makes a job seem less like work."

"Do you think carpentry is your passion? I mean when you retire from football?" She knew he still had a few good years left, but few football players were still playing in their mid-thirties and even fewer quarterbacks. Shoulder injuries or concussions from all the hits tended to put them into retirement sooner.

His sanding paused for a moment as if he was contemplating her question. His jaw tightened, and his shoulders rose with a deep breath. Then the sanding resumed. "I don't know."

He'd paused for so long, she'd begun to wonder if he was

going to answer the question, and she certainly hadn't expected what he had said. He seemed like someone who knew what he was doing with his life, but this, apparently, was one area he hadn't figured out completely. Nor did he appear to want to talk more about it. She wondered if it had anything to do with whatever had happened in his past. "Well, I'm sure whatever you decide to do, you'll be great at it. I haven't seen you be bad at anything yet."

She looked over to see him flash a half smile, but before either of them could say more, the sound of a large truck pulling up to the cabin carried on the air.

"Ooh, I think our storage container might be here."

❧ 50 ❧

BLAINE

Blaine couldn't believe the hideousness of the monstrosity the truck dropped off. The container was huge and grey and ugly. "This won't stay long, right?"

Kenzi rolled her eyes and shook her head. "No, just long enough for us to load up all the furniture and get the floors redone. Then, we'll move the stuff we're keeping back in, and this bad boy," she banged on the side sending a hollow metallic sound through the air, "will go away."

"Good. Let's get started." He wasn't sure what was bothering him so much about the storage container, but something about the sight of it just rubbed a nerve.

Kenzi nodded and led the way back into the cabin. "Let's load the furniture first, and then we can look at packing up some of the smaller items."

Hefting the two couches was not an easy feat, but Blaine was impressed that Kenzi held her own, and though beads of sweat broke out on her forehead and trickled down the side of her face, she did not give up.

He was able to grab the chair by himself, leaving her the coffee table. It wasn't extremely large, so he figured she could muscle it out herself. As he placed the chair in the container though, he realized Kenzi wasn't behind him. Had she had trouble with the table after all? Or had she tripped and injured herself? The thought spurred him into action, and he burst out of the container to scoop her up. But she was not on the ground. Nor was she injured inside the cabin.

Instead he found her rooted to the spot in the center of the room. The table was on its side as if she had lifted it and then had to set it back down, but that wasn't what held his attention. The faded piece of newspaper she held in her hand was what held his attention and hers too as she didn't even look up when he entered.

In fact, it wasn't until he was only a few feet from her that she seemed to realize he was there. Her eyes lifted to his, and they were filled with sadness. And he knew. He knew what the paper in her hand said. He knew she had read it, and he knew that she would never look at him the same way again. He'd seen the same sadness in everyone's eyes after the accident. It had been in his father's eyes when he told Blaine about the divorce and in his mother's eyes when she moved them from their house. He had never wanted to see it in Kenzi's eyes, and now it would always be there.

"Blaine..." It was all she could seem to manage. Emotion strangled her voice and pity flowed from her gaze.

"Don't," he said, snapping the paper from her. "Don't say you're sorry. Don't say it wasn't my fault." He could feel the anger boiling inside him. The red-hot anger he had buried for years and successfully kept down was now clawing up his throat and demanding to be let out.

"Is this why you've never had a relationship? Why you think you can't connect?"

She was probably asking out of curiosity and concern, but that didn't matter to Blaine. "I said don't. I don't want to talk about it. In fact, I don't think this was a good idea." His voice came out in a growl, much harsher than he meant it to be, but he seemed unable to tame the fire burning through him.

"This?" Confusion contorted her pretty features, and then her face shifted, hardened. "Do you mean me decorating the cabin? Or do you mean us?"

Blaine could hear the hurt in her voice, see it written all over her face, but he couldn't take back his words. He had known coming back here was a mistake. He should have forfeited the inheritance and let the lawyer deal with it or left the cabin the way it was and put it up for sale himself. Bringing Kenzi here had been a mistake and getting involved with her... His thought trailed off as his fists balled at his side. He had known better. "Maybe both."

He regretted the words as soon as he said them. They cut her in a way a knife never could. He saw her flinch, saw her jaw clench and her eyes tear up, and then he saw her grab her bag and walk out of the door and out of his life.

Blaine sank to the floor and stared at the faded newspaper story. Would he ever get past this?

KENZI

Tears blurred Kenzi's vision as she drove. She should have known better. No, she did know better. There was a reason her father always said to keep work and play separated, but how could she have known Blaine would blow up at her like that?

She'd had no idea what the paper was when it fluttered out of the table, and her heart had broken for Blaine as she read the story. No wonder he had trouble connecting emotionally. No wonder he hid behind so many walls, but why push her away now that she knew? That was what hurt the most. She'd thought they were building something, something they could share, but he'd only been pretending. Just like Brian. Just like Jeff. Why did she always seem to fall for guys who weren't able to commit?

Even worse, what was she going to do now? She'd have to give back the rest of the money Blaine had paid her. She couldn't keep it. And she had no other jobs lined up. The other jobs she had applied for still hadn't called. Maybe she didn't have what it took to be a designer. Maybe the job redoing the center had been offered out of pity from the team. They'd seen her as this pretty girl in her mid-twenties who hadn't known what she wanted out of life and they'd thrown her a bone. Maybe she was destined to go through life without a real talent, with only a pretty face. All the memories of middle school, junior high, and later of Jeff flooded her mind.

"Stop it," she said the words aloud as she banged on the steering wheel. "This is Blaine's issue. Not yours." The words were easy to say but a lot harder to believe. Ever since the incident with Brian and the teasing in junior high, her confidence had been shot.

Then, she'd reached high school and changed her image. She'd lost weight, discovered fashion, and met Jeff. And she'd thought Jeff really cared for her, but then he'd dumped her after home-coming and told her he'd only been seeing her to be assured the crown. Kenzi had told no one, not even Shelby. It had been too embarrassing, so instead, she'd put on a good front and claimed they had a fight. It had worked- on the outside - but inside, she was still that pre-teen girl looking for acceptance, for love, and not finding it.

She didn't even bother to warn Shelby she was coming. Kenzi knew she would be at home working on wedding plans. Her tears waited until she knocked on Shelby's door, but when the door opened and she saw the look of concern on her friend's face, she could hold them back no longer.

"What's wrong?" Shelby led her inside and to the couch.

Kenzi shook her head as the tears flowed down her face. She couldn't form words just yet. Emotions clenched her throat, blocking any sound other than sobs. Shelby placed her arm around

Kenzi and let her cry. She seemed to know that's what she needed most.

When the tears finally slowed and her throat loosened up, Kenzi lifted her head to look at Shelby. "I think I just got fired."

Shelby's eyes widened. "What? You must be mistaken. Surely he didn't fire you."

Kenzi shook her head. "He told me he didn't think it was a good idea. I asked him if he meant hiring me or dating me and he said both."

Confusion covered Shelby's face. "That makes no sense. I thought things were going well."

"They were and then I found something I don't think I was supposed to see. We were moving furniture out in order to take out the old flooring, and when I picked up a table, a newspaper clipping fell out. I didn't know what it was or I never would have read it."

"I don't understand. What was in the newspaper clipping?"

Kenzi took a deep, shuddering breath. "The death of his brother."

❧ 51 ❧

BLAINE

Anger still floated around Blaine as he pulled into the training facility Monday morning. After he'd sent Kenzi away, he'd not only had to finish taking out the furniture by himself, but he'd had to deal with the plumber and the flooring guy. Neither of them would be singing his praises to anyone soon. In addition, guilt over how he'd treated Kenzi had plagued him the rest of the weekend. He knew she didn't deserve the way he'd yelled at her, and now he had no idea how to make it right.

Even though breakfast was the first thing on the agenda, Blaine walked to the locker room before heading to the cafeteria. He hoped a few minutes of silence and solitude would calm him enough that he could face his teammates without displaying his anger. He'd certainly told them often enough not to bring emotions into the practices. Unfortunately, his hope for solitude was whisked away at the sight of Tucker in the room.

Tucker glanced up, and his stance stiffened when he saw Blaine. "You told Shelby we couldn't do the big brother thing? Why?"

Blaine sighed as he set his bag down. He'd been hoping Shelby wouldn't mention the issue to Tucker, but he should have known better. "I have my reasons, but mainly because the season starts next week. We need our focus to be on the game. Teams are going to be gunning for us this year after our championship win last year, and we can't get distracted by outside influences."

Tucker folded his arms across his chest and raised his eyebrows. "Outside influences like Kenzi?"

Okay, Tucker had him there. He should have chosen his words better. "Kenzi is helping me redecorate a cabin I inherited so I can sell it." Was she still helping him? He was no longer sure.

"That's not the entire truth, and you know it." Tucker shook his head. "You may have hired her, but you were also dating her. You can't lie to me, man. Not when I'm engaged to her best friend."

"We went on three dates," Blaine said as he shoved his bag into his locker. "I'd hardly call that dating."

"Don't do that to her."

"Do what?" Blaine asked, but he knew the answer.

"Don't treat her like the other women that you go out with once or twice and then dump. I know something happened between the two of you the other day. Shelby told me Kenzi showed up at her place and was a mess. Now, I know you're the captain, but something is going on with you, Blaine, and it's not good. You told me once that I needed to change my perspective. Well, I don't know what your deal is, but maybe it's time you change your perspective. Those kids need us. They look up to us, and all Shelby is asking is that we take some time and hang out with them. I don't think that's too much to ask, even during our season."

"I can't be a big brother." The words exploded out of Blaine's mouth and reverberated in the locker room, but he was almost glad. This secret had been tearing him up for years, and saying the words out loud brought a small sense of relief.

Tucker threw his hands out in exasperation. "Why not? It's just spending some time with someone younger. Take them out to movies, the park. What's so hard about that?"

"Because I was a big brother once, and I let my little brother drown." Blaine collapsed onto the bench and hung his head. "I couldn't protect him, and I can't be responsible for another kid."

Tucker sat down next to him and placed a hand on his shoulder. "Blaine, I'm sure whatever happened wasn't your fault."

"No, it was my fault. We were supposed to be reading in the cabin, but I got bored. I suggested we go out on the lake even though my parents said we weren't to go outside. He trusted me, so he went with me." Blaine rubbed a hand across the back of his neck as the memories rushed in.

"At first it was great. The lake had frozen over and we were sliding all over the place. Then I heard the crack and Kevin's scream. I saw him go down, but I couldn't swim and neither could he." He closed his eyes and shuddered as the hardest memory of all surfaced in his mind's eye. "I could see him under the ice, but I couldn't get to him. I watched him drown."

There was a moment of silence before Tucker let out a long sigh. "Okay, that's definitely a heavy weight to bear, but you were just a kid, Blaine. You should never have been put in that situation, but I think you've carried this long enough."

Blaine's head shot up. "How can you say that? He was my brother!"

"I know, but what happened was an accident. You remember how angry I was last year?"

Blaine nodded, wondering what this had to do with his story.

"Well, my mother died when I was young. Then, my father grew distant and threw himself into his work. I thought he blamed me for my mother's death somehow, but really he was just grieving."

"I'm sorry for your loss, Tucker, but what does that have to do with me?"

Tucker's lips pulled into small smile. "I'm telling you because you saw what the misconception did to me. I turned to anger and drinking. You've distanced yourself from people, but you deserve love, Blaine. You deserve a relationship, and I don't know if Kenzi is that girl for you, but don't you think you owe it a chance?"

Blaine looked at his friend and wondered if he was right. Maybe it was time he changed his perspective.

KENZI

The knock on the door startled Kenzi out of her daydream. Or nightmare more like it. The bills were coming due, and now she had no money and no job on the horizon. She couldn't believe how things had turned bad so quickly.

She closed her laptop as she pushed back from the table. A hand-me-down from her mother, it was still in pristine condition as was everything her parents owned. Even though it belonged to Kenzi now, she still had trouble putting a glass down without a coaster or doing any design work at it in case her pen slipped and marred the tabletop. Her mother believed that people judged you by your house, and that had been drilled into Kenzi.

She glanced at her watch as she crossed to the front door. It was nearly eight. Other than Shelby, she knew of no one who would show up at her door so late. Her parents certainly wouldn't, and she didn't have many other close friends. She hoped Tucker and Shelby hadn't had a fight. There was no doubt they would one day, but so far, they'd been like two people sharing one mind.

Her heart tightened as she peeked through the spy hole to see Blaine Hollis standing on her doorstep. His hands were shoved in his jean pockets, but his face was impossible to read. She bit her lip as she unlocked the door. If he was here to demand his money back, she didn't know what she would do. She'd used most of it to purchase the floors and hire the plumber.

When the door opened and she saw his face up close, that thought flew from her head. His shoulders were rolled forward, and a look of contrition covered his face. "Hey, Kenzi, can I come in?"

She stepped back, allowing him entrance. She had no idea why he was here, but something was definitely weighing on him. "Would you like to sit down?" Her hand pointed to the couch, but it was more out of habit than an actual request.

His eyes darted around the room before he shook his head. "No, I'll be quick. I came to say I'm sorry."

She waited to see if he would expound. What exactly was he sorry for? Hiring her? Asking her to dinner? Yelling at her?

"I don't know if you read the whole story on that newspaper clipping, but I lost my little brother when I was ten. He was my best friend. My parents trusted me to watch him inside, but I got bored and convinced him to go out on the lake with me." He lifted one hand from his pocket and ran it across the back of his neck.

"It had been cold that winter, and the lake had frozen. I didn't know the ice wasn't thick enough to hold us. When Kevin went under, I tried to save him, but neither of us could swim, and I couldn't get him back to the part where he'd fallen in."

Kenzi gasped and covered her gaping mouth with her hand. The newspaper certainly hadn't shared that bit of information in its story.

"My life fell apart after that. My parents got divorced. My dad turned to drinking, and my mom worked two jobs just to keep us in a tiny apartment. I lost my brother and my family that winter, and I don't have relationships because I don't want to fail anyone else. Nor am I sure I could handle the pain of losing anyone else, but I shouldn't have taken it out on you." He shook his head and took a few steps away from her.

"I felt different with you, but then you found the story, and I knew you would look at me differently. Everyone looks at me differently when they find out." He paused as if waiting for her to say something. Then he shrugged. "Anyway, I'm sorry."

Kenzi felt the weight of his guilt, and she placed a hand on his arm. "Blaine, you were just a kid. I'm sorry about your brother, but you've beat yourself up long enough. It's time to forgive yourself."

"How am I supposed to do that?"

"With God's help."

Blaine lifted his arm to run his hand across the back of his neck. "I don't think God wants anything to do with me."

"That's where you're wrong, Blaine. God loves you. He sent His son to die for you. For all of us. It sounds awful, but the death of your brother was not a surprise to Him. Nor is what you're feeling now, but that doesn't mean He loves you any less."

Blaine's hand shifted to his chin. "Do you really believe that?"

Kenzi crossed to him and placed a hand on his arm. "I do, and if you'll let me, I'd love to help you know Him like I do."

He held her gaze, and she could feel the emotions flowing between them. They crackled like electricity in the air.

"I'd like that." His voice was husky, and his eyes shifted from hers down to her lips and back again. He wanted to kiss her, and she wanted that too, more than anything.

Her hand found his chest, and she could feel his heartbeat pounding beneath her palm. She lifted her face to his, and before she could move another inch, his mouth was on hers. Tentative at first, his lips barely brushed against hers, soft as a whisper. Was he afraid she would say no?

She moved her hands to behind his neck and stood on her tiptoes in order to deepen the kiss. And boy did it work. Her knees trembled and grew weak, and though she knew there was nothing there, she could have sworn she heard the sound of explosions. She had never experienced a kiss like that in her life, and he responded as if she were a lifeline in the ocean. His lips explored hers as if they held the answer to relieve his pain.

"Does this mean I'm not fired," she asked when they finally pulled back.

Blaine laughed and responded with another kiss. "You're definitely re-hired, and I may just owe you a bonus for putting up with me."

Kenzi knew there was a serious truth to his lighthearted words, but she had already fallen for Blaine. She just hoped he wouldn't break her heart.

52

BLAINE

Blaine took a deep breath before entering the center. After his conversation with Kenzi last night, he knew he needed to apologize to Shelby. He was still terrified to be alone with a kid, but he hoped with her help that he could move past that.

"Blaine, what are you doing here?" Shelby looked at him and then down to a clipboard. "I didn't know you were on the schedule today."

"I'm not. I came to apologize to you for my behavior the other day."

A look of confusion crossed her face for a moment, and then her eyes widened. "About the Big Brother thing."

"Yeah, I wasn't completely honest with you. Our schedule *is* about to get busy, but I said no because I was afraid. My brother died when I was supposed to be watching him, and I was afraid the same thing might happen to one of these kids if they were left in my care. To be honest, I still am afraid. However, Kenzi and Tucker have promised to help me, and these kids do deserve it. It's a great idea, Shelby."

Shelby's eyes were an ocean of compassion. "Blaine, I'm so sorry to hear about your brother, but thank you for telling me.

We'll set it up so that you feel comfortable, whether that means having your time here or making sure someone else is always with you, we'll make it work."

"Thank you."

As Blaine left the center, he felt a little lighter. He'd been carrying around this weight by himself for so long that it felt good to share it with others, even if all they could do was lend a listening ear.

Climbing into his Mustang, he pointed the car toward the lake house. Since it was his day off from training, he and Kenzi had made plans to meet up and put the doors back on in the kitchen.

The large storage container was still outside the cabin when he pulled up as was Kenzi's car. She had said she wanted to get an early start to check the floor installation. Blaine had left the cabin unlocked for the flooring guy before he left for the weekend because the man had said it would take a few days to finish the job.

His mouth dropped open in surprise when he opened the front door moments later. The room not only looked different without the old furniture, but now a beautiful hardwood floor covered the floor. He'd agreed to let Kenzi change the floor because he figured it would raise the value of the cabin, but now he could see what she had seen in her head. It made all the difference in the world. The grain in the floor complemented the exposed wood in the living room, and even without furniture, the place felt warm and inviting.

Kenzi appeared in the doorway that led to the kitchen. "It's nice, right?"

"It's more than nice. It's amazing. You have a real knack for this, Kenzi."

A soft blush colored her cheeks, and her teeth chewed at her bottom lip. "Thank you, but I still haven't lined up another job after this one. It doesn't matter how great I am if I can't get people to take a chance on me."

He entered the rest of the way and closed the door behind him.

"You let me worry about that. I've got an idea that should have your phone ringing off the walls soon."

She raised her eyebrow in silent question, but he wasn't prepared to share that secret yet. "Trust me. It will be great. Now, how about we finish those doors?"

"I thought you'd never ask." She held a screwdriver out to him, and he laughed as he joined her in the kitchen.

She turned some music on with her phone and Blaine chuckled as she bopped to the beat while screwing the doors back on. When the song shifted and slowed, he dropped his screwdriver and grabbed her hand, pulling her to his chest for an impromptu dance.

"I know it's short notice, Kenzi, but our first game is Sunday, and I'd love to have you in the box seat cheering me on. Do you think you can make it?" His heart paused as he waited for her answer. Asking her was a huge step for him. He'd never asked a woman to use his tickets before; he'd never wanted the media to associate him with any of them, but he didn't mind being seen with Kenzi.

She tilted her head and stared thoughtfully at him as her hand caressed the back of his neck. "I will; on one condition."

"Condition?" His throat constricted at the word. Was she going to ask him to face his fear? Or talk about his brother? He was glad that she knew, but he wasn't sure he was ready to share any more just yet.

"Don't worry. It's nothing too bad." She smiled up at him. "I want you to come to church with me tomorrow night. I know you can't do Sunday due to the game, but we have a great sermon on Wednesday night too, and I think you really need God back in your life to heal completely."

His jaw tightened as he swallowed. She was probably right, and he'd seen the change God had made in Tucker's life. But was he really ready for that? Was he ready to forgive God for taking his brother? Was he ready to trust that God would forgive him? He took a deep breath and nodded. "Okay. I will."

The happiness that radiated from Kenzi told him he'd made the right choice even though his stomach still clenched at the thought.

KENZI

Kenzi walked to her car on cloud nine that evening. Not only had she spent an amazing afternoon with Blaine, but he'd said yes. He'd asked her to come to his game on Sunday which was exciting, but more importantly he'd said he would go to church with her. She couldn't remember the last time a man had come to church with her. For that matter, she couldn't remember the last time she *wanted* a man to come to church with her. She had to tell Shelby.

Fishing her phone from her pocket, she set it up for hands free and then punched in her friend's number as she started the car. Shelby picked up on the third ring.

"He said yes," Kenzi said before her friend even had a chance to say hello.

Shelby laughed on the other end. "Well, hello to you too, Kenzi. Now please explain. Who said yes?"

"Blaine. He said he'd come to church with me tomorrow." She craned her head both directions as she exited Lost Lake Road. It hardly saw any traffic, but the street it connected with was a busy two-lane highway.

"That's great, Kenzi. I'm so glad."

"It was great. He loved the floors, and we got the cabinets up. He even danced with me in the kitchen. The cabin is actually coming along nicely, and he asked me to Sunday's game. Please tell me you're going too." She would go regardless, but she knew she would have much more fun with Shelby by her side.

"Yes, I'm going," Shelby said with a chuckle. "I think it's kind of expected now that we're engaged."

"Good. I can't believe this is happening, and I can't believe he said he'd come to church." Kenzi felt like a giddy school girl, like the way she had when Jeff Carpenter asked her to homecoming. Jeff Carpenter. The image of the broad-shouldered jock forced its way into her mind.

"Kenzi Lanham, how are you?"

Kenzi nearly dropped her books. Jeff Carpenter, starting quarterback for the football team, leaned against the locker next to hers. Even though he'd said her name, she still looked around as if unsure he meant to address her. "Me? You're talking to me?"

Her popularity had been increasing the last few years, ever since her fashion style began trending, but while she was enjoying attending parties and being greeted in the halls, Jeff Carpenter had never spoken to her until now. Was it because she'd finally made it on the cheerleading squad?

"Of course I'm talking to you. Homecoming is just around the corner, and I need to ask the prettiest girl in the school to be my date."

Kenzi blinked. She couldn't be the prettiest girl. She was still the chunky middle schooler in her head.

Jeff reached out and tucked a strand of hair behind her ear. "Say you'll go with me. I'd really like to get to know you better."

A horn blared, and Kenzi shook her head to clear the image from the past. She raised her hand in apology as the driver behind her sped past.

"Kenzi, you okay?" Concern filled Shelby's voice.

"Yeah, sorry, I spaced out for a second and a car honked at me. Shelby, what if he's like Jeff?"

"Jeff? Jeff who?"

"Jeff Carpenter from high school. You know the quarterback I dated for a few months. The one who…" She stopped herself from finishing the sentence.

"The one who broke your heart? Kenzi, why would you think he's like Jeff? Jeff was a jerk."

Kenzi bit her lip. She'd never told Shelby the whole story

behind Jeff, but maybe it was time to now. Perhaps Blaine wasn't the only one who needed God's healing. She took a deep breath and let the story flow from her lips. "Shelby, Jeff and I didn't just break up. He dumped me after we were crowned and told me he'd only dated me to guarantee he would get the crown."

The sharp intake of breath belayed Shelby's shock. "I knew he was awful, but I had no idea. I'm so sorry, Kenzi."

Kenzi bit the inside of her lip. "Jeff's dumping me is part of the reason I've avoided relationships. I know Blaine isn't Jeff, but there are some similarities. I don't know if I could take it if he is playing with my emotions."

"Kenzi, Blaine has his own issues, but the nice part about them is that he knows better than to play with someone's emotions. If he asked you to the game and agreed to go to church, I think he meant it."

"You're right." Kenzi let out a shaky breath. "I've been guarding my heart, well trying to, since I knew his relationship with God was rather rocky, but maybe this is a sign of good things to come."

"Oh, Kenzi, I hope so. I've been praying for you guys, and I know Tucker has too."

"Thanks, Shelby. I'll see you tomorrow." As she hung up the phone, Kenzi knew she had some work to do on herself as well.

❧ 53 ❧

BLAINE

Blaine tugged at his collar as they approached the door of the large building. He hadn't been in a church in years, and while he didn't think he would be struck down by lightning or anything, he still worried that God might not want him back.

"Relax," Kenzi said, taking his hand. "I'm right here with you, and Shelby and Tucker will be here too."

The thought eased his anxiety slightly, and he forced his lips into a tight smile. He could do this. It wasn't a game, it wasn't taking care of a kid, it was just sitting through a sermon. An hour of his life, and maybe he could find the healing Kenzi hoped for.

Tucker and Shelby were already inside, and they greeted the two of them with wide smiles.

"Glad to see you could make it man," Tucker said, extending his hand as the two women hugged.

"Yeah, me too." Blaine shook Tucker's hand and hoped his teammate couldn't see how nervous he was.

"Don't worry. It'll be great. Coming back is hard, but life looks so much better when you do."

Blaine wasn't sure about that. Tucker's past had been hard but not as hard as Blaine's. Still, he was willing to enter with an open mind. Kenzi took his hand once again, and the four of them entered the large sanctuary.

Blaine wasn't sure he'd ever attended a Wednesday night service, and he was not prepared for the upbeat contemporary feel. Church had always been boring and a chore when he'd attended in his youth, but right now, with a full band on stage, it almost felt more like a concert. He found himself clapping to the beat and sharing a smile with Kenzi even though he didn't know the words to many of the songs.

When the music ended, a young man took the stage. He didn't appear to be much older than Blaine - no more than thirty for sure. Could pastors be that young?

"Good evening, everyone. I hope you are all having a blessed week. I feel like God has asked me to remind you of the story of Paul, and how it's never too late to come home."

Blaine's ears perked up as the man continued.

"I've had a lot of people tell me that they think God won't accept them because they've done bad things, but we all know Paul was a disciple. Jesus picked him. What we forget sometimes is that Paul, before he found God, was one of the worst. Here was a man who condemned and killed Christians. He murdered the very people God loved, yet God still loved him and used him. Paul is an example for all of us. No matter what we've done or maybe haven't done, God still has a plan for us. He still loves us and seeks after us. All we have to do is open our hearts to Him and let Him work."

The pastor spoke longer, but Blaine didn't hear the rest. He was focused on the last few words. *All we have to do is open our hearts and let Him work.* His heart had certainly been closed for a long time. Was it really that easy?

Before he even knew what he was doing, he found himself whispering, "Please open my heart, Lord. Let me see You again."

Kenzi placed a hand on his knee and squeezed, and he

wondered if she had heard his words. He decided it didn't matter. She was the reason his heart had thawed enough to be here, to hear this message. It was still too early to be certain, but he felt that Kenzi would be in his life for the foreseeable future.

KENZI

Kenzi replayed the night in her head as she brushed her teeth and got ready for bed. She was sure another piece of Blaine's emotional wall had fallen tonight. Near the end, she'd heard him whisper something though she couldn't make it out. She'd squeezed his knee to let him know she was there for him though.

The story had touched her too. While she hadn't been like Paul in the way the pastor spoke of, she knew her self-confidence issue was just as upsetting to God. He'd made her perfect, yet she couldn't see it. She'd felt that God grieved for her just as much as he did for Blaine. Just as much as he had for Paul, and as she'd listened to the sermon, she was reminded that she shouldn't care how others saw her because God saw her differently.

It was one thing to know it, but it sure was much harder to believe it. Especially when she'd checked her email upon arriving home to find that all the jobs she had applied for had turned her down. What was she going to do when she was done with Blaine's cabin? She had no second job lined up. Nor did she know how to go about drumming up business. She'd thought God was leading her into design, but maybe she'd been wrong again.

She turned out her bathroom light and padded to her bed. Perhaps if she spent some time alone with God, He might make the answer clear to her.

After situating herself on her bed with her legs crossed beneath her, she grabbed her Bible and opened it to the last book she'd been reading. Philippians was a pretty hopeful book anyway, but as she began reading chapter four, she marveled at how God could put the exact verse she needed in front of her. Worry about nothing, pray for everything, and thank Him for all He has done. Then peace will transcend. She definitely needed to do a little more of that.

She finished the chapter and then set her Bible aside. "God, thank you for the opportunity to work with Blaine. Thank you for bringing him into my life and for helping him open up about his past. Lord, if it's Your will, help us to grow stronger in You, and help me not to worry but know that You will provide the work I need. Amen."

The words didn't ease all of her anxiety, but she did feel a little better as she turned out the light and pulled the covers up over her shoulder.

❧ 54 ❧
BLAINE

Blaine couldn't keep his gaze from traveling up to the boxed seats as he threw the ball to Mason. Kenzi was up there with Shelby though he couldn't see her face, and it was the first time he'd had a woman in there cheering for him.

"What's the distraction, man?" Mason called out as he tossed the ball back. "That's the second pass you've thrown over my head."

Blaine pulled his attention from the glass windows just in time to catch the ball. "I'm sorry, Mason."

"It's a girl, isn't it?"

Blaine glanced quickly over at Tucker who was running sprints. "Did Tucker tell you?"

Mason laughed and caught the next pass easily. "He didn't have to. You've been happier than normal, and your gaze keeps traveling up to the box. I know what having a woman does to you."

His jaw tightened as he said the last words and Blaine could tell some woman had done a number on Mason in the past. Was that what his behavior at Christmas had been all about? He'd have to remind himself to check in with Mason later, when the first game of the season wasn't looming over their heads.

"You're right. It's a woman. I've never invited one before and I just keep wondering what she's thinking." He caught the ball, spun it in his fingers, and sent it sailing back.

"She's probably taking in the sights and enjoying the free food and being hounded by the other women," Mason said with a smile. "But if you keep getting distracted, then she's going to be worrying about you and your health when you keep getting sacked, so get your head in the game."

Blaine knew Mason was right. He spared one more glance at the box and then focused his attention on the warm-up. It was less than an hour to kickoff, and he needed to be prepared.

KENZI

Kenzi was glad Shelby was with her as they entered the box. It wasn't her first time - she'd come to their Christmas game with Shelby last year - but it was her first time being here as Blaine's girlfriend. She wondered if the other women knew, if they would welcome her like they had Shelby.

"Don't worry," Shelby whispered in her ear as they made their way to the front chairs. "You've got this. Miss Southlake, remember?"

Kenzi managed a tight smile. Yes, she could put up a fake facade with the best of them - smile, wave, and pretend to be happy - but she wanted to be genuine with these women. If things worked out with Blaine, she'd be spending more time with them, and she wanted them to know the real her. Even if it meant sharing her faults.

"Shelby, so good to see you again."

Kenzi turned to the woman with the velvety voice and froze. It was Margaret, the owner's wife. She was a frightening woman. Not only did she ooze money on the outside, but she had a nasty habit of talking about the other women behind their backs. Kenzi had only heard a few of her comments at the Christmas game, but it was enough to let her know she wanted to avoid this woman as much as possible.

"Hello, Margaret. So good to see you again." Shelby's voice sounded just as bright as always, but Kenzi could see the stiffness in her posture. Evidently Shelby felt the same way toward Margaret as Kenzi did.

Margaret's icy blue eyes turned to Kenzi. "And who is your friend? I'm not sure we've met." The woman's gaze traveled up and down Kenzi, making her feel as if she were an item at an auction.

"This is Kenzi, my best friend and Blaine's girlfriend."

Margaret's eyes widened. "Girlfriend? I wasn't aware he had one."

Kenzi felt as if Margaret was examining her under a microscope. "I don't know if I'd say girlfriend, but he did invite me."

That was the wrong thing to say. Margaret's brow arched almost to her hairline. "So, you're not his girlfriend? Are you the flavor of the month then?"

The woman's harsh words and disdainful tone transported Kenzi back to middle school. Embarrassment clawed at her face, and she stuttered as she tried to remedy her words. "I mean I don't know what we are yet. We've been on a few dates, but we haven't labeled our relationship yet."

"I see. Well, we'll see how long you last."

With that the woman spun away from them and toward her next victim. Kenzi sank down into the nearest chair and sighed. "That was awful."

"She's awful," Shelby said, sitting beside her and placing a hand on her arm. "Don't worry about her. Blaine wouldn't have asked you here if he didn't want you here. Plus, he did come to church. I think things are going well for you guys."

Kenzi took a deep, shaky breath. "Yeah, you're right. I'm trying to work on not caring what people think, but it's hard, especially with a woman like her." She chanced a glance over her shoulder, but Margaret was engaged in a conversation with another woman.

"Maybe the game will take your mind off it," Shelby said softly.

The game. Right. Kenzi turned her attention back to the field and tried to enjoy the game.

K enzi looked down at the frame in her hands. She hoped Blaine would like it. It was the final piece to place in the cabin before she called it done and showed it to him.

The last few weeks had flown by for Kenzi. She'd spent nearly every day working at the cabin to finish it. The new appliances had arrived and been installed as had the beautiful new kitchen counter. Pillows and bedding and other accents had been purchased and placed artfully around the rooms. Even the bathroom vanity had made it in, though she'd worried about that one with Blaine's work schedule. Now that games had started, he was definitely busier than he had been before. When he wasn't at work, he was usually at home sleeping the exhaustion away. Still, he'd managed to find time to finish it as well as attend church with her when he was free.

She wasn't sure if he'd forgiven himself yet or come back to God completely, but he did appear to be improving. He could talk about Kevin without shutting down which was why she hoped he would appreciate the gift. She'd found an old picture of the two of them in the nightstand that had been upstairs and she'd had it blown up and framed. Kenzi hoped it might allow him to find peace and keep the cabin, but if not, then at least it would be something he could hang in his place.

"Knock, knock," he called as he stepped inside.

Kenzi tucked the frame she'd been holding behind her back and smiled as his eyes took in the place.

"Wow, this is amazing, Kenzi."

"Do you like it?" She knew it looked beautiful, but a part of her still needed to hear it from him.

"I do. It's," he paused and shook his head, "more than I ever thought it would be."

"Good." Her word came out in a sigh of relief. "I'll give you the tour in a minute, but I have one final touch that I wanted to add."

He tilted his head in question, and she smiled at him before walking over to the mantle and placing the framed picture on the top. She bit her lip and turned to face him, hoping she hadn't overstepped.

His jaw was tight - she could see it in the bulging vein of his neck - but he didn't look angry. "Kenzi, this is…" His voice broke and he coughed to try and clear it. "Where did you find that?"

She stepped toward him. She ached to touch him, to make sure the shimmer she saw in his eyes was from happiness and not sadness, but she wanted to give him time to process. "I found the picture in the nightstand upstairs. I'm assuming that was where you and Kevin stayed when you were here."

He brought a fist to his mouth and nodded.

"I know this place has awful memories for you, Blaine, but I was hoping that maybe this would allow you to remember the good times too." She took another step and touched his arm.

His eyes found hers, and they were a hurricane of emotions. Had she made things worse? Then he pulled her into his arms and crushed her to his chest. "Thank you," he whispered into her hair. "Thank you."

BLAINE

Blaine took a deep breath and squeezed Kenzi's hand before pulling the door open. Today was the day he would meet his "little brother" or "little sister" and while he was feeling braver, especially with her by his side, his heart was still beating faster than normal.

"Hey guys," Shelby said as they approached the front desk.

"Hey, Shelby." He was glad to hear only a slight tremble in his voice. Kenzi flashed him a reassuring smile, and he soaked up the strength she sent his way.

"You ready to find out who your "little sister" is?"

A little sister. A sliver of relief coursed through him. It was still a small human being he was responsible for, but at least it wasn't a boy. Plus, Kenzi was here to help him. "Yes, I suppose I am." He smiled back at Kenzi.

"Great, because I have paired you with Darby. Her father was killed last year in the line of duty. She could really use a strong male presence in her life, and I thought you would be perfect."

Kenzi hugged his arm closer. "Darby is perfect. You'll love her."

He nodded as he tried to remember who Darby was. Generally, he was decent with names, but the added anxiety of working with kids had made it harder for him. He thought she was the cute girl with the big glasses, but he wasn't sure.

He and Kenzi continued into the gym and found Darby sitting with her mother at one of the makeshift tables that had been set up.

"Hello, Darby, I'm Blaine Hollis. Remember me?"

Darby looked up at him with her big brown eyes and nodded. "You're one of the football players, right?"

"That's right, I am, and if it's okay with you and your mom, I'm also going to be like your big brother."

"And big sister," Kenzi added. "You'll be our special sibling. Would you like that?"

Darby looked to her mother who smiled and nodded. Blaine could see the emotion building in her eyes.

"Will you do things with me like my dad did before he died?"

"We can do anything you want," Blaine said, squatting down so he was face to face with her. He was surprised at how easily the words came out of his mouth.

"My dad used to take me fishing. Will you take me fishing?"

Blaine paused as his heart stilled in his chest. Fishing meant water and water meant memories of Kevin sinking away from him forever. He couldn't do this. Shelby had made a terrible mistake; she'd have to find him another kid. He was about to say as much when he felt Kenzi's hand on his shoulder.

"You can do this." Her words were soft, barely more than a whisper, but the surety of them pushed a strength through him.

"I don't know much about fishing, but I can sure try. I don't have poles right now, but I'll get some." Darby's face fell in disappointment, so Blaine continued, "But it is a nice day out. Would you like to go to the lake and feed the ducks?"

Sunshine returned to Darby's face and a hopeful smile followed. She turned to her mother. "Can I?"

Her mother nodded and mouthed "thank you" to Blaine and Kenzi.

The look in the woman's eyes bolstered Blaine's courage even more. He could do this. She needed him to do this. Single motherhood was obviously wearing her down, and he could do this small piece to help her. Even if it meant being around water.

He took one of Darby's hands and Kenzi took the other. Together, they walked out of the center. As Darby swung their hands back and forth, he wondered seriously for the first time if he could have this someday. A wife. A kid. God was working on his heart, and he was falling for Kenzi, but he was still broken. Would she want a broken man?

After a quick stop at the store for some bread, he pulled into the parking lot of Southlake, the body of water for which the town was named. It wasn't a huge lake, but it was large enough that a path around the outside of it measured three miles from start to finish. It was nearly always bustling with activity from joggers, moms pushing strollers, and more. Today was no exception. Though it was nearing the end of October, the sun still shone brightly and it was warm enough to get by without a jacket.

After turning off the engine, he helped Darby out of the seat, smiling as she bounced up and down on her feet. "Can I go feed them now?"

"Hold on, honey, we'll all go together," Kenzi said, as if she could sense Blaine's unease both with approaching the water and letting Darby go running off by herself.

His feet didn't start slowing until they were about ten feet from the water. Suddenly, it felt like he was walking in quicksand. His heart pounded in his ears and his throat dried up. He felt like a noose was slowly encircling his neck.

"Darby, honey, let's slow down for Blaine. Approaching the water is a hard thing for him."

Darby turned wide eyes up at him. "Why?" There was no condescension in her voice, just the curiosity of a child.

Blaine swallowed, knowing he had to answer her but unsure of how much to share. "I lost my brother when I was younger. He drowned."

Darby nodded as if this was the most natural thing in the world to hear. "I lost my dad recently so I know about being scared. But Miss Kenzi and Miss Shelby told me that God was always holding my hand even when my daddy couldn't. Whenever I get scared, I just remember that." She squeezed his hand tighter. "I'll hold your hand like God does, so you'll understand, okay?"

Emotion overwhelmed Blaine, and he heard Kenzi sniffle beside him. How did this young girl have it all figured out when it had been years for him and he still struggled?

God, give me the faith of this child, he thought as he followed Darby closer to the lake's edge. A sense of peace covered him, and his heartbeat returned to normal. He opened the bag they had brought with them and handed a slice to Darby and one to Kenzi.

Darby smiled as she tore the bread and threw it out to the ducks who honked and fought for the pieces. Beside him, Kenzi nudged his shoulder and flashed him a smile. She was so amazing. He would have to do something in return for her. And he knew just what he could do.

✻ 56 ✻
BLAINE

Blaine opened the door to the cabin and smiled at the woman on the other side. "Diane, thanks for coming." Diane was a photographer for Novel Home magazine. She'd done a spread on their owner's house when he'd bought it, and after Blaine explained his situation, Ron had called in a favor. Blaine just hoped this cabin would be enough.

"Thanks for inviting me. You said you'd make it worth my while." Diane's no-nonsense attitude oozed with every fiber of her being. From her pulled back hair to the pressed suit she wore, to the three-inch heels gracing her feet that looked like they could double as a weapon in a pinch. Suddenly he wasn't sure she would find this so impressive.

"I hope you'll find this worth a spread in your magazine." He stepped back and allowed her entrance to the cabin. "This cabin has been in my family for years. I inherited it this summer but had no idea what to do with it. I have some before pictures I can show you."

"I've seen them," she said with a wave of her hand as she stepped in, her eyes combing over the living room. She nodded as she walked the floor. "It's definitely nice. Who's the designer?"

Blaine felt his lips twitching. He'd known Kenzi was talented. "A new designer, and one who could really use the exposure. Is it good enough?"

Diane pinched her tight lips together and paused in front of the fireplace. "What's this?" She pointed at the picture of him and Kevin.

Blaine paused, but he didn't feel the suffocating pressure he usually felt. "That's a picture of my brother and me. We used to come here every summer as a family. I hired Kenzi to redo the cabin because I was planning to sell it."

"Why?" Diane turned to him with a quizzical expression. "It's such a beautiful space and location."

"Because Kevin died here. In the lake out back."

Her eyes widened, and her mouth fell open in shock.

"But Kenzi showed me there was still life here. She added that picture to remind me of the good times we had. To help me forget about the bad. She's not just a designer. She's a healer as well." He hadn't meant to tell the story of his brother, and he hadn't planned to talk about Kenzi, but even as the words spilled out, he knew they were the truth. Kenzi had healed him in more ways than one.

Diane turned back to the picture and stared at it again. "I think this is a piece our readers will love." When she faced him again, her stern features were gone, replaced by a sincere smile. "And whoever this Kenzi is, I hope you've scooped her up before some other man does."

Blaine returned the grin. "I'm working on it, and this will definitely help."

"Good. I'll be back with my camera."

KENZI

Kenzi stared at the woman's name on the slip of paper and bit her nail. She wanted to reach out, to do something for Blaine, but what if this was overstepping? He'd made such strides since the first outing with Darby. She could see his heart opening up every time she was around him, but now Christmas was quickly approaching, and she had yet to hear him discuss plans of seeing his family. She knew he was slowly healing the part of his heart that had died with Kevin, but could she help him heal his family as well?

Taking a deep breath, she picked up her cell phone and dialed the number. She'd managed to get his mother's name from him during their conversations and then she'd spent an hour scouring the internet for the woman's number. Lisa Hollis had turned out to be a fairly common name, but after calling the first nine numbers on the list, she was sure this one would be his mother.

"Hello? This is Lisa."

The woman's voice was nothing like she had expected. Though she'd never met the woman, she'd created a picture in her head from Blaine's description. Haggard was the best word that came to mind. A woman beaten down from losing her youngest son and her husband in one year then being forced to work two jobs to provide for the oldest son she rarely saw, but the voice on the other end of the phone was light, sweet.

"Um, hello, my name is Kenzi Lanham. You don't know me, but I was wondering if you are Blaine Hollis's mother." Kenzi bit her lip as she waited for the woman's response. She'd practiced what she was going to say over and over before she'd called, but she still wondered if it was too forceful, too bold.

The silence stretched so long that Kenzi feared the woman had hung up, but finally she spoke. "Yes, my son's name is Blaine. What is this about?"

Kenzi sighed with relief and sent a prayer up both thanking God and asking for the right words. "I'm his girlfriend, and I was hoping that maybe you could help me bring a little Christmas magic to him this year."

"What did you have in mind?" the woman asked. There was

still a hint of hesitation in her voice, but Kenzi could make out the curiosity as well.

"Well, I'm not sure if you know but Blaine volunteers occasionally at a local center here in Southlake. Every year we have a Christmas party for the children. This year we're hosting it a little before Christmas since the Tornadoes play on Christmas Eve. Blaine will be there reading to the children, and I was hoping you could come by."

Another long bout of silence followed before the woman spoke. "Blaine is working with kids?"

Kenzi couldn't help but smile on the other end. It had obviously been awhile since Blaine and his mother had connected. "He is. In fact, he even took on a "little sister" with the program and plans to take her fishing next summer. I think you'll find Blaine a slightly different person from the last time you saw him. So, will you come?"

"I wouldn't miss it for the world," the woman said.

"Great." Kenzi rattled off the details and ended the call. One down and one to go.

57

BLAINE

"Oh, thank goodness, Blaine, can you help me hang the tinsel?" Kenzi greeted him with a quick kiss on the cheek before grabbing his hand and pulling him across the gym floor.

"Uh, sure." He tightened his hold on the package in his arms as he followed her. He supposed it would have to wait until he could steal her attention for a minute.

She stopped at the far end of the wall where a chair, doubling as a ladder, sat. "Can you hand the tinsel up to me, so I can hang it?" She had a tape dispenser on her wrist and was already pulling out a piece.

Grabbing the tinsel from the floor, he handed it up to her. "Are you sure you don't want me to do that? I am a little taller."

She smiled down at him. "No thanks, I've got it." She stretched up on her tiptoes and just managed to attach the tinsel to the wall before losing her footing and tumbling off the chair.

Blaine dropped the package in his hands, thankful it wasn't breakable, and caught her just before she hit the floor.

She splayed her hands across his chest as she tried to regain her footing. A soft pink blush of embarrassment covered her cheeks. "Okay, maybe I didn't have it, but at least I had you to catch me."

His heartbeat increased in his chest as she gazed up at him adoringly. He had definitely fallen for this woman; he could feel it in every fiber of his body. "You'll always have me to catch you, Kenzi. I love you," he whispered before lowering his mouth to hers.

He opened his eyes and blinked at her in surprise when he felt her fingers on his lips instead of her mouth.

"You cannot just tell a girl you love her without giving her time to say it back," she said with a smile. Her hands moved up his chest and to the back of his neck. "I love you too, Blaine Hollis."

He chuckled as he resumed his position and met her lips. Their bodies pressed closer together, and he marveled at how well she fit him.

"Um, not to interrupt, but the kids will be here soon." Shelby's voice interrupted their intimate moment, and they jumped apart.

Blaine ran a hand across his chin as he swallowed first his disappointment and then his chagrin. "Sorry, you're right. What else do you need help with, Kenzi?"

She placed her hands on her hips as she turned and surveyed the room. "Actually, I think we're good."

"Then, can I steal you for a moment?" Blaine asked as he retrieved the package from the floor. He turned his attention to Shelby. "Is there enough time for that?"

She didn't know what was in the package; he hadn't told anyone, but she nodded and smiled. "I think there's enough time for that." She flashed a wink at Kenzi before returning to the office.

"What is this?" Kenzi asked when they were alone again.

"An early Christmas present. I just got it this morning, and it couldn't wait for Christmas Day." He held the thin present out to her.

She took it, her brow furrowing in curiosity. "It feels like a book," she said as her fingers explored the package, "but a very bendy one."

Was she always this slow and meticulous with gifts? He had always been the type to rip it open in eagerness. "Just open it."

She pulled back the paper and stared down at the magazine in confusion. "Novel home? I don't understand. I'm not looking for a new home, nor could I probably afford any in here."

"Will you open it to page seven please?" The excitement bubbling inside of him threatened to spill out and open the magazine for her.

She flipped to the page, eyes widening as she realized what the pictures were. "Is this?"

"My cabin? Yes, and the story is about you and how you not only managed to bring it to life but to convince me to keep it."

Her eyes glistened as they met his. "You're going to keep it?"

"I am. There are some bad memories there, but I had always hoped to make memories with my own family there one day, and the only way to do that is to keep it."

"Blaine, I'm so glad. I think you would have regretted selling it." She looked as if she were going to say more, but the ringing of her phone interrupted her. "Hold on," she said, holding a finger up to Blaine. "This is Kenzi Lanham."

He watched as she listened to the caller on the other end. She blinked as a look of shock covered her face.

"Yes, I'm the designer who did Mr. Hollis's cabin."

He bit back his smile as she paused to listen some more.

"Of course, I would be delighted to take a look at your project. Tomorrow? Yes, I can meet you at four. Thank you."

She ended the call and stared up at him. "I just got a potential job offer."

His smile broke free as he squeezed her arm. "I have a feeling you'll have many more in the future."

"I… I don't know what to say. Thank you."

"No, Kenzi. It's me who owes you thanks. You brought me back to life and helped me heal. I can never repay you for that."

KENZI

Kenzi smiled as she watched Blaine read to the kids. He appeared so relaxed and natural; it was hard to believe he had once been afraid to spend time alone with them. Though they hadn't discussed their future, she could imagine being married to him and watching him read like this to their own kids.

"How did you manage this?"

Kenzi turned to smile at the man and woman next to her. Life had been hard on them both as evidenced by her graying hair and crow's feet and his lack of hair and wrinkles, but her eyes were the same color as Blaine's and his smile was just as bright.

"It wasn't all me. God had a big hand in helping him come around."

Blaine finished his story and set the book down. He began making his way toward Kenzi, his eyes widening as he spied the woman next to her. "Mom? Dad?"

"Hi, Blaine." Lisa's voice had taken on a more reserved tone, and Kenzi saw her posture tense as she waited to see if Blaine would accept her or not. Joe, his father, stood still as well.

He glanced at Kenzi as he pulled his mother in for a hug before turning to his father and embracing him as well. She saw the silent question in his eyes and smiled. They could share the details later. For now, she was just glad to be sharing this scene with him.

At the buzzing of her phone in her pocket, she excused herself.

"This is Kenzi Lanham," she said when she was far enough out of earshot not to bother anyone with her conversation.

"Kenzi Lanham. This is Mayor Shelley. I have a beach house that I would love to update. I saw your work in Novel Homes today, and I'd like to schedule a meeting with you."

Kenzi's knees nearly buckled beneath her. This was the second call she'd received from the spread in the magazine, and while these interest calls didn't guarantee she would land the job, it was certainly more than she'd had going for her a week ago. She couldn't believe Blaine had done this for her. He had made not only her Christmas wish but all her dreams come true.

EPILOGUE
KENZI

Kenzi stepped into her soft pink satin gown and turned so Whitley could zip it up. Then she returned the favor. Shelby had opted for a smaller wedding, so she and Whitley, Tucker's sister, were the only bridesmaids, but that was fine with Kenzi. She'd had her hands full decorating for the wedding, and she was glad the room now was quiet and comfortable and not buzzing with conversation.

She couldn't believe Shelby's wedding day was finally here. Ever since the Christmas party, her life had been a whirlwind of activity. She'd had meetings with potential clients, Shelby's wedding to help plan and decorate, and football games to attend with Blaine. It barely left any time for her and Blaine to just hang out, but she knew that after this wedding was over, at least some of her burden would be lifted.

"That dress is beautiful on you," Shelby said as she adjusted her veil in the mirror. "Both of you."

"Thank you, but I think all eyes will be on the bride. As they should be." Kenzi stepped behind Shelby and leaned down to hug her. She knew she wasn't losing her best friend, but she also knew that marriage changed things. Showing up on her doorstep would be more of an inconvenience and girl's nights out might be harder to come by. Still, she wouldn't change a thing. Shelby was happier than she had ever seen her, and marrying Tucker would only increase that happiness. "You ready?"

"I think so. I'm still trying to adjust to the fact that in an hour my new last name will be Jackson. Shelby Jackson. It still sounds foreign in my mouth."

Whitley laughed and helped Shelby to her feet. "You'll get used to it. Besides, it will make us real sisters."

The two girls hugged, and Kenzi couldn't help feeling just a little jealous. Shelby had two sisters now through marriage, but Kenzi would never have that. Blaine was now an only child, just as she was. There would be no sisters in her future if she married him. Married him? She was getting ahead of herself. They'd been dating for a few months, but he'd offered no hints that a proposal was near.

She grabbed Shelby's bridal bouquet from the table a few feet away and handed it to her. "I think the new name sounds perfect, and you will get used to it." Then she picked up the two smaller bouquets of pink and white flowers and handed one to Whitley, keeping the other for herself. "Now, let's go get you married."

BLAINE

Blaine couldn't help the smile that spread across his face as he watched Kenzi walk down the aisle. Her eyes stayed locked on his with every step, and he forced himself not to pull out the box that was in his pocket and propose to her right then and there. This was Tucker's day, and he wouldn't ruin that, but he couldn't wait to ask her to be his forever.

She took her place on the other side of the stage. The distance seemed so far. Farther than he wanted to be from her. The music changed, and it took all his effort to turn and face the entrance of the church.

Shelby was a vision in her white dress, and Blaine was elated for his friend, but all he could think about was what Kenzi would look like when it was their turn. Would she want a big wedding? Or something smaller like this?

He thought back to the first day of training camp when Tucker had rattled off all the monotonous details of wedding planning, and he realized as much as he would have hated it then, he would cherish every moment of it now.

The pastor began speaking, but Blaine heard few of the words until he was asked to produce the rings. He'd been floored and honored when Tucker asked him to be his best man, but he'd accepted knowing he might be returning the favor before too much longer.

Tucker and Shelby exchanged their vows, kissed, and then the wedding was over. He held out his arm for Kenzi and followed the bride and groom out of the sanctuary and toward the reception area. The box burned in his pocket, but the time wasn't right yet. Just a little longer.

He tried to focus on the food and the toast during the reception, but it was no use.

"What is going on with you?" Kenzi asked as he led her to the dance floor when it was time.

"Nothing. I'm just enjoying the moment and how beautiful you look."

Kenzi furrowed her brow at him but stepped into his arms. "You look pretty dapper yourself."

"Good, I would hate to look scruffy on the day I ask you to be my wife." He twirled her around and waited for the words to sink in.

"The day you do what?" she asked when she was facing him again.

He stopped moving and dropped to his knee. Around them, the

crowd stilled and every eye in the place turned to them. He hoped Tucker wouldn't mind the minor interruption as he reached into his pocket and pulled out the black box.

"Kenzi Lanham, you have changed my life and made it worth living again. I would be a fool to ever let you go. I love you, and while I know I'm not the man you deserve yet, I promise to get better every day. Will you marry me?"

A single tear escaped out of the corner of Kenzi's eye before she nodded and held out her hand. The crowd around them cheered as he placed the diamond ring on her finger and rose to kiss her.

"Just so you know," she whispered as she pulled back. "You are the perfect man, and I'm the one who would be a fool to let you go. I love you Blaine."

As he picked her up and twirled her around, he knew this was just the beginning, and though he couldn't see him, somehow, he knew Kevin was smiling down on him.

THE END!

IF YOU LOVED BLAINE AND KENZI'S STORY, THEN YOU WON'T want to miss Mason's story. Be sure to preorder your copy of Touchdown on Love today!

AND IF YOU ENJOYED THIS STORY, PLEASE LEAVE A REVIEW. Reviews help other readers find books they will enjoy.

58

NOT READY TO SAY GOODBYE YET?

Love on the Line is the second book in the Texas Tornado series. Continue the journey with Touchdown on Love — Mason's story

Touchdown on Love

He's the wide receiver who had his heart broken.

She's the new team doctor.

When the present throws them back together, will they find their way back to their past

TURN THE PAGE FOR A SPECIAL SNEAK PEEK.

59

SNEAK PEEK AT TOUCHDOWN
ON LOVE

Chapter 1: Clara
Clara stared at the letter in disbelief. Yes, she had applied, but she hadn't really expected to get an interview. After all, the Tornadoes were National Champions, and she was just one of the athletic trainers for a local university. True, it was one of the larger, more well-known universities and she had helped rehabilitate several up and coming athletes, but there had to have been hundreds of qualified applicants.

"Is that what I think it is?" Her friend and fellow trainer, Stacy, said as she leaned over her shoulder to read the paper. It had been Stacy's idea for Clara to apply. The girl was always pushing her to do more, challenge herself. Well, she'd certainly done it this time.

"It is. They want to interview me."

Stacy's arms wrapped around her and squeezed her like a vice. "I knew it. I don't want to say I told you so, but I told you so."

Clara chuckled at those words. Stacy enjoyed being right, so being able to say "I told you so" was definitely something she wanted to say. The only problem was, she didn't know about Clara's past. She didn't know that her ex-boyfriend was a wide receiver for the Texas Tornadoes. Could she really work on his team knowing that she would have to see him? And what if he got injured? Could she work that closely with him? Would he even let her?

Stacy stepped back from Clara and crossed her arms. "Okay, what's going on? You should be ecstatic about this interview yet pensive and hesitant are more the vibes I'm getting from you."

Clara bit her lip. Did she want to share this story with Stacy? Yes, they had been friends for the last few years, having gone through the same program at college and then ending up on the same college team, but this was not something she was proud of. "I used to date one of the players on the Tornadoes."

Stacy's eyes grew larger than quarters. "You did? Which one?"

"Mason Dixon."

A confused expression clouded Stacy's face. "Like the boundary line that separates Pennsylvania and Maryland?"

Clara chuckled. "No, like the wide receiver for the Tornadoes, but yes, like the line. His parents have an odd sense of humor."

"So, who broke it off?" Stacy's eyebrow lifted as she leaned back and crossed her arms.

Boy if that wasn't a long story, but not one that Clara was going to go into right now. "I guess I did, sort of."

A knowing look covered Stacy's face, and she nodded. "And you're worried... what? That you'll fall for him again?"

That was exactly what she was worried about, among other things. "No, not really. It's been a few years."

"So, you're worried that he's found someone else?"

Well, now she was. She hadn't even thought of that possibility until it crossed Stacy's lips. Could she watch him with another woman? "I don't know exactly what I'm worried about. I guess that it might be weird, that he might not want to work with me."

That no-nonsense look took over Stacy's face. It was the same one she used whenever guys tried to say women couldn't work with football players, and Clara loved it. Normally. "Honey, I'm sure he's a professional. It's his job to work with whoever the team hires, and if that's you, then I'm sure he'll be fine.

Clara hoped Stacy was right. Of course, she didn't have the job yet, but this would be a huge stepping stone for her if she got it. She'd be crazy not to go to the interview, but then why did she feel like her life was about to get turned upside down?

CLICK HERE TO PREORDER TOUCHDOWN ON LOVE. RELEASING soon!

❧ 60 ❧

A FREE STORY FOR YOU

E njoyed this story? Not ready to quit reading yet? If you sign up for my newsletter, you will receive The Billionaire's Impromptu Bet right away as my thank you gift for choosing to hang out with me.

The Billionaire's Impromptu Bet

A SWAT officer. A bored billionaire heiress. A bet that could change everything....
Read on for a taste of The Billionaire's Impromptu Bet....

THE BILLIONAIRE'S IMPROMPTU
BET PREVIEW

B rie Carter fell back spread eagle on her queen-sized canopy bed sending her blonde hair fanning out behind her. With a large sigh, she uttered, "I'm bored."

"How can you be bored? You have like millions of dollars." Her friend, Ariel, plopped down in a seated position on the bed beside her and flicked her raven hair off her shoulder. "You want to go shopping? I hear Tiffany's is having a special right now."

Brie rolled her eyes. Shopping? Where was the excitement in that? With her three platinum cards, she could go shopping whenever she wanted. "No, I'm bored with shopping too. I have everything. I want to do something exciting. Something we don't normally do."

Brie enjoyed being rich. She loved the unlimited credit cards at her disposal, the constant apparel of new clothes, and of course the penthouse apartment her father paid for, but lately, she longed for something more fulfilling.

Ariel's hazel eyes widened. "I know. There's a new bar down on Franklin Street. Why don't we go play a little game?"

Brie sat up, intrigued at the secrecy and the twinkle in Ariel's eyes. "What kind of game?"

"A betting game. You let me pick out any man in the place. Then you try to get him to propose to you."

Brie wrinkled her nose. "But I don't want to get married." She loved her freedom and didn't want to share her penthouse with anyone, especially some man.

"You don't marry him, silly. You just get him to propose."

Brie bit her lip as she thought. It had been awhile since her last relationship and having a man dote on her for a month might be interesting, but.... "I don't know. It doesn't seem very nice."

"How about I sweeten the pot? If you win, I'll set you up on a date with my brother."

Brie cocked her head. Was she serious? The only thing Brie couldn't seem to buy in the world was the affection of Ariel's very handsome, very wealthy, brother. He was a movie star, just the kind of person Brie could consider marrying in the future. She'd had a crush on him as long as she and Ariel had been friends, but he'd always seen her as just that, his little sister's friend. "I thought you didn't want me dating your brother."

"I don't." Ariel shrugged. "But he's between girlfriends right now, and I know you've wanted it for ages. If you win this bet, I'll set you up. I can't guarantee any more than one date though. The rest will be up to you."

Brie wasn't worried about that. Charm she possessed in abundance. She simply needed some alone time with him, and she was certain she'd be able to convince him they were meant to be together. "All right. You've got a deal."

Ariel smiled. "Perfect. Let's get you changed then and see who the lucky man will be.

A tiny tug pulled on Brie's heart that this still wasn't right, but she dismissed it. This was simply a means to an end, and he'd never have to know.

Jesse Calhoun relaxed as the rhythmic thudding of the speed bag reached his ears. Though he loved his job, it was stressful being the SWAT sniper. He hated having to take human lives and today had been especially rough. The team had been called out to a drug bust, and Jesse was forced to return fire at three hostiles. He didn't care that they fired at his team and himself first. Taking a life was always hard, and every one of them haunted his dreams.

"You gonna bust that one too?" His co-worker Brendan appeared by his side. Brendan was the opposite of Jesse in nearly every way. Where Jesse's hair was a dark copper, Brendan's was nearly black. Jesse sported paler skin and a dusting of freckles across his nose, but Brendan's skin was naturally dark and freckle free.

Jesse flashed a crooked grin, but kept his eyes on the small, swinging black bag. The speed bag was his way to release, but a few times he had started hitting while still too keyed up and he had ruptured the bag. Okay, five times, but who was counting really? Besides, it was a better way to calm his nerves than other things he could choose. Drinking, fights, gambling, women.

"Nah, I think this one will last a little longer." His shoulders began to burn, and he gave the bag another few punches for good measure before dropping his arms and letting it swing to a stop. "See? It lives to be hit at least another day." Every once in a while, Jesse missed training the way he used to. Before he joined the force, he had been an amateur boxer, on his way to being a pro, but a shoulder injury had delayed his training and forced him to consider something else. It had eventually healed, but by then he had lost his edge.

"Hey, why don't you come drink with us?" Brendan clapped a hand on Jesse's shoulder as they headed into the locker room.

"You know I don't drink." Jesse often felt like the outsider of the team. While half of the six-man team was married, the other half found solace in empty bottles and meaningless relationships.

Jesse understood that — their job was such that they never knew if they would come home night after night — but he still couldn't partake.

Brendan opened his locker and pulled out a clean shirt. He peeled off his current one and added deodorant before tugging on the new one. "You don't have to drink. Look, I won't drink either. Just come and hang out with us. You have no one waiting for you at home."

That wasn't entirely true. Jesse had Bugsy, his Boston Terrier, but he understood Brendan's point. Most days, Jesse went home, fed Bugsy, made dinner, and fell asleep watching TV on the couch. It wasn't much of a life. "All right, I'll go, but I'm not drinking."

Brendan's lips pulled back to reveal his perfectly white teeth. He bragged about them, but Jesse knew they were veneers. "That's the spirit. Hurry up and change. We don't want to leave the rest of the team waiting."

"Is everyone coming?" Jesse pulled out his shower necessities. Brendan might feel comfortable going out with just a new application of deodorant, but Jesse needed to wash more than just dirt and sweat off. He needed to wash the sound of the bullets and the sight of lifeless bodies from his mind.

"Yeah, Pat's wife is pregnant again and demanding some crazy food concoctions. Pat agreed to pick them up if she let him have an hour. Cam and Jared's wives are having a girls' night, so the whole gang can be together. It will be nice to hang out when we aren't worried about being shot at."

"Fine. Give me ten minutes. Unlike you, I like to clean up before I go out."

Brendan smirked. "I've never had any complaints. Besides, do you know how long it takes me to get my hair like this?"

Jesse shook his head as he walked into the shower, but he knew it was true. Brendan had rugged good looks and muscles to match. He rarely had a hard time finding a woman. Jesse on the other hand hadn't dated anyone in the last few months. It wasn't that he hadn't been looking, but he was quieter than his teammates. And he wasn't looking for right now. He was looking for forever. He just hadn't found it yet.

Click here to continue reading The Billionaire's Impromptu Bet.

THE STORY DOESN'T END!

You've met a few people and fallen in love….

I bet you're wondering how you can meet everyone else.

Star Lake Series:

Sealed with a Kiss: Meet the quirky cast of Star Lake and find out if Max and Layla will ever find love.

When Love Returns: Return to Star Lake to hear Presley's story and find out if she gets the second chance with her first love.

Once Upon a Star: Continue the journey when aspiring actress Audrey returns home with a baby. Will Blake finally get the nerve to share his feelings with her?

Love Conquers All: Meet Lanie Perkins Hall who never imagined being divorced at thirty or falling for an old friend, but will his secrets keep them apart?

The Star Lake Collection: Get the latter three stories in one place. Series will include book 1 when it releases around November 2020.

The Heartbeats Series:

Where It All Began: Sandra Baker finds forgiveness and healing even after making a horrible choice.

The Power of Prayer: Will Callie Green find true love or be defined by her mistake?

When Hearts Collide: When Amanda Adams goes to college, she finds a world she was not ready for. But will she also find true love?

A Past Forgiven: Jess Peterson has lived a life of abuse and lost her self worth, but when she finds herself pregnant, will she find new hope?

The Heartbeats Collection: Grab all four Heartbeats novels in one collection

Sweet Billionaires Series:

The Billionaire's Impromptu Bet: Can a spoiled rich girl change when a bet turns to love?

The Billionaire's Secret: Can a playboy settle down when he finds out he has a daughter who needs him?

A Brush with a Billionaire: What happens when a stuck up actor lands in a small town and needs help from a female mechanic?

The Billionaire's Christmas Miracle: A twist on a Cinderella story when a billionaire meets a woman who doesn't belong at the ball.

The Billionaire's Cowboy Groom: Will one night six years ago keep Carrie from finding true love?

The Cowboy Billionaire: Coming Soon!

The Billionaire's Bliss: This collection contains The Billionaire's Secret, The Billionaire's Christmas Miracle, and The Billionaire's Cowboy Groom

The Lawkeeper Series:

Lawfully Matched: When the man she agreed to marry turns out to have a dark past, will Kate have to return home or will she find love with her rescuer in this historical fiction?

Lawfully Justified: Can a bounty hunter and a widow find love together in this historical fiction?

The Scarlet Wedding: William and Emma are planning their wedding, but an outbreak and a return from his past force them to change their plans. Is a happily ever after still in their future in this historical fiction?

Lawfully Redeemed: What happens when a K9 cop falls for the brother of her suspect? Contemporary romance.

The Lawkeeper Collection: Get all four books in one collection

The Are You Listening Series:

The Still Small Voice: Will Jordan listen to God's prompting in this speculative fiction?

A Spark in the Darkness Will Jordan be able to help Raven before the rapture occurs?

Blushing Brides Series:

The Cowboy's Reality Bride: He's agreed to be the bachelor on a reality dating show, but what happens when he falls for a woman who's not one of the contestants?

The Reality Bride's Baby: Laney wants nothing more than a baby, but when she starts feeling dizzy is it pregnancy or something more serious?

The Producer's Unlikely Bride: What happens when a producer and an author agree to a fake relationship?

Ava's Blessing in Disguise: Five years after marriage, Ava faces a mysterious illness that threatens to ruin her career. Will she find out what it is?

The Soldier's Steadfast Bride: coming soon

The Men of Fire Beach

Fire Games: Cassidy returns home from Who Wants to Marry a Cowboy to find obsessive letters from a fan. The cop assigned to help her wants to get back to his case, but what she sees at a fire may just be the key he's looking for.

Lost Memories and New Beginnings: A doctor, a patient with no memory, the men out to get her. Can he keep her safe when he doesn't know who he's looking for?

When Questions Abound: A Companion story to Lost Memories. Told from Detective Graves' point of view.

Never Forget the Past: Fireman Bubba must confront his past in order to clear his name and save lives.

Love on the Run: Graham is forced into lockdown with one of his employees. Will he be able to save her from her ex and will she steal his heart?

Secrets and Suspense: Cara Hunter is hiding something about her military past. When she's suspected of murder, will she be able to convince Cole she's the victim?

Rescue My Heart: Al's sister has gone missing. Can she save her? And who is the man she meets? Friend or foe?

The Men of Fire Beach Collection: Books 1-3

Texas Tornadoes

Defending My Heart: Forced to confront his past, Emmitt finds news that will change his life.

Run With My Heart: Sentenced to community service, Tucker finds himself falling for the manager.

Love on the Line: Blaine has hired Kenzi to redo his cabin, but what happens when she finds his darkest secret?

Touchdown on Love: When Mason's injury throws him together with ex-girlfriend, will sparks fly again?

Second Chance Reception: Jefferson is hiding something. When he falls for the team cook, will he let her in?

Small Town Short Stories

Small Town Dreams

Small Town Second Chances

Small Town Rivals

Small Town Life

Life in a Small Town: All four stories in one collection

Stand Alones:

Love Renewed: This books is part of the multi author second chance series. When fate reunites high school sweethearts separated by life's choices, can they find a second chance at love at a snowy lodge amid a little mystery?

Her children's early reader chapter book series:
    The Wishing Stone #1: Dangerous Dinosaur
    The Wishing Stone #2: Dragon Dilemma
    The Wishing Stone #3: Mesmerizing Mermaids
    The Wishing Stone #4: Pyramid Puzzle
    The Wishing Stone: Mary's Miracle
    The Wishing Stone Collection
    To see a list of all her books

authorloranahoopes.com
loranahoopes@gmail.com

ABOUT THE AUTHOR

Lorana Hoopes is an inspirational author originally from Texas but now living in the PNW with her husband and three children. When not writing, she can be seen kickboxing at the gym, singing, or acting on stage. One day, she hopes to retire from teaching and write full time.

www.ingramcontent.com/pod-product-compliance
Lightning Source LLC
Chambersburg PA
CBHW031957060726
47497CB00015B/221